F REIGN AFFAIRS

Swept ...

Seduce ...

The world's most eligible men.

Dreaming of a foreign affair? Then, look no further!
We've brought together the best and sexiest men the
world has to offer, the most exciting, exotic locations
and the most powerful, passionate stories.

This month, in *Desert Desires*, we bring back two best-
selling novels – by talented Tender Romance™
authors Sophie Weston and Barbara McMahon. Be
swept up into a world of desire under the desert
stars… And from now on, every month in **Foreign
Affairs** you can be swept away to a new location –
and indulge in a little passion in the sun!

Meet two hot-blooded Latin men in
LATIN LIAISONS
by Emma Darcy & Lynne Graham
Out next month!

SOPHIE WESTON

Born in London, Sophie Weston is a traveller by nature who started writing when she was five. She wrote her first romance recovering from illness, thinking her travelling was over. She was wrong, but she enjoyed it so much that she has carried on. These days she lives in the heart of the city with two demanding cats and a cherry tree — and travels the world looking for settings for her stories.

The Prince's Proposal is Sophie Weston's compelling new book, available in Tender Romance™ next month!

BARBARA McMAHON

Barbara McMahon was born and raised in the south but settled in California after spending a year flying around the world for an international airline. Settling down to raise a family and work for a computer firm, she began writing when her children started school. Now, feeling fortunate in being able to realise a long-held dream of quitting her 'day job' and writing full-time, she and her husband recently moved to the Sierra Nevada mountains of California, where she finds her desire to write is stronger than ever. With the beauty of the mountains visible from her windows, and the pace of life slower than the hectic San Francisco Bay Area where they previously resided, she finds more time than ever to think up stories and characters and share them with others through writing. Barbara loves to hear from readers. You can reach her at PO Box 977, Pioneer, California, USA.

Coming end of 2002, Barbara has a new sheikh story, *The Sheikh's Proposal*. Don't miss it!

desert desires

SOPHIE WESTON & BARBARA MCMAHON

FANTASY IN THE SAND...

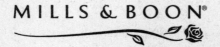

MILLS & BOON®

*All the characters in this book have no existence outside the imagination
of the author, and have no relation whatsoever to anyone bearing the
same name or names. They are not even distantly inspired by any
individual known or unknown to the author, and all the incidents are
pure invention.*

*Harlequin Mills & Boon Limited,
Eton House, 18-24 Paradise Road, Richmond, Surrey, TW9 1SR*

Desert Desires © Harlequin Enterprises II B.V., 2002

The Sheikh's Bride and *Sheik Daddy*
were first published in Great Britain by
Harlequin Mills & Boon Limited in separate, single volumes.

The Sheikh's Bride © Sophie Weston 2000
Sheik Daddy © Barbara McMahon 1996

ISBN 0 263 83187 6

126-0502

*Printed and bound in Spain
by Litografia Rosés S.A., Barcelona*

desert desires

THE SHEIKH'S BRIDE

SHEIKH DADDY

THE SHEIKH'S BRIDE

SOPHIE WESTON

PROLOGUE

'WHAT are we waiting for?' asked the co-pilot.

The pilot looked down from his cockpit at the Cairo tarmac. In the early morning, the dust was tinged with diamond light and the roofs of the distant airport building gleamed. A couple of men in dark suits were doing an efficient sweep of the apron on which their plane had come to a halt.

'Security,' he said briefly.

The co-pilot was new to flying the Sheikh of Dalmun's private fleet. 'Do they always go through this?'

The other man shrugged. 'He's an influential guy.'

'Is he a target, then?'

'He's megarich and he's heir apparent to Dalmun,' said the pilot cynically. 'Of course he's a target.'

His companion grinned. His girl-friend regularly brought home royalty watching magazines.

'Chick magnet, huh? Lucky devil.'

The security men had finished their surveillance. One of them raised a hand and a white stretch limousine came slowly round the plane. The pilot, his cap under his arm, stood up and went to shake hands with the departing passenger.

An early-morning breeze whipped the Sheikh's white robes as he strode towards the limousine. In spite of the entourage that followed, he looked a lonely figure.

The pilot came back into the cockpit.

'We're on stand-by,' he said briefly.

Other cars arrived. The security team swung into them then the limousine drew away, flanked by its guardians.

The pilots sat back, waiting for an escort to the plane's final parking place.

'What's he doing here?' asked the co-pilot idly. 'Business or pleasure?'

'Both, I guess. He hasn't been out of Dalmun for months,' said the older man unguardedly.

'Why?'

The pilot didn't answer.

'I heard there was a bust up. His old man wanted him to marry again?'

'Maybe.' A second monosyllabic answer.

'So what do you think? Has he been let out to find himself a bride?'

The pilot was betrayed into indiscretion. 'Amer el-Barbary? A *bride*? When hell freezes over.'

CHAPTER ONE

LEONORA pushed a grubby hand through her hair and breathed hard. The lobby of the Nile Hilton was full to bursting. She had lost three of the museum party she was supposed to be escorting; she had not managed to spend time with her mother who was consequently furious; and now this week's problem client had come up with another of her challenging questions.

'What?' she said distractedly.

'Just coming in now.' Mrs Silverstein nodded at the swing doors. 'Who *is* he?'

A stretched white limousine, its windows discreetly darkened, had pulled up in the forecourt, flanked by two dark Mercedes. Men in dark grey suits emerged and took up strategic stances while a froth of porters converged on the party. The doors of the limousine remained resolutely closed. Leo knew the signs.

'Probably royal.' She was not very interested. Her father's recently acquired travel agency did not have royal clients yet. 'Nothing to do with me, thank God. Have you seen the Harris family?'

'*Royal,*' said Mrs Silverstein, oblivious.

Leo grinned. She liked Mrs Silverstein.

'A lord of the desert,' the older woman said.

'Quite possibly.'

Leo decided not to spoil it by telling her the man was probably also Harvard educated, multilingual and rode through the desert in an air-conditioned four-wheel drive instead of on a camel. Mrs Silverstein was a romantic. Leo, as she was all too aware, was not.

'I wonder who he is…'

7

Leo knew that note in her voice. 'I haven't the faintest idea,' she said firmly.

Mrs Silverstein sent her a naughty look. 'You could ask.'

Leo laughed aloud. It was what her client had been saying to her for three weeks.

'Listen,' she said, 'I'm your courier. I'll do a lot for you. I'll ask women how old they are and men how much it costs to feed a donkey. But I won't ask a lot of armed goons who it is they're guarding. They'd probably arrest me.'

Mrs Silverstein chuckled. In three weeks they had come to understand each other. 'Chicken.'

'Anyway, I've got to find the Harris family.'

Leo slid through the crowd to a marble-topped table where a house phone lurked behind a formal flower arrangement. She dialled the Harris' room, casting a harassed eye round, just in case they had come down without her catching them.

The limousine party were on the move, she saw. Men, their mobile phones pressed to their ears, parted bodies. Behind them walked a tall figure, his robes flowing from broad shoulders. Mrs Silverstein was right, she thought ruefully. He was magnificent.

And then he turned his head and looked at her. And, to her own astonishment, Leo found herself transfixed.

'Hello?' said Mary Harris on the other end of the phone. 'Hello?'

She had never seen him before. Leo knew she had not. But there was something about the man that hit her like a high wind. As if he was important to her. As if she *knew* him.

'Hello? Hello?'

He wore the pristine white robe and headdress of a desert Arab. In that glittering lobby the severe plainness was a shock. It made him look even more commanding than he already did given his height and the busy vigilance of his entourage. His eyes were hidden by dark glasses but his expression was weary as his indifferent glance slid over her and on across the crowd.

'Hello? Who is this?'

Leo read arrogance in every line of him. She did not like it. But still she could not stop staring. It was like being under a spell.

Mrs Silverstein slid up beside her and took the phone out of her hand. Leo hardly noticed. All she could do was look—and wait for his eyes to find her again.

I'm not like this, said a small voice in her head. *I don't stare blatantly at sexy strangers.* Leo ignored it. She did not seem as if she could help herself. She stood as still as a statue, *waiting*...

A man Leo recognised as the hotel's duty manager was escorting the party. He was bowing, oblivious to anyone else. As he did so, he brushed so close to her that she had to step back sharply. She hit her hip on the table and grabbed a pillar to save herself. Normally a gentle and courteous man, the duty manager did not even notice.

But the object of all this attention did.

The white-robed figure stopped dead. Masked eyes turned in Leo's direction.

It was what she had been waiting for. It was like walking into an earthquake. Leo's breath caught and she hung onto the pillar as if she would be swallowed up without its support.

'Oh my,' said Mrs Silverstein, fluttering.

Leo clutched even tighter. She felt cold—then searingly hot—then insubstantial as smoke. Her fingers on the pillar were white but she felt as if the strength had all been slammed out of her.

Then he turned his head away. She was released.

Leo sagged. She found she had been holding her breath and her muscles felt as weak as water. She put a shaky hand to her throat.

'Oh *my*,' said Mrs Silverstein a second time. She gave Leo a shrewd look and restored the phone to its place.

Across the lobby, there was an imperious gesture. One of the suited men stepped respectfully close. The tall head inclined. The assistant looked across at Mrs Silverstein and Leo. He seemed surprised.

Leo knew that surprise. The knowledge chilled her, just as it had in every party she had ever been to. She was not the sort of woman that men noticed in crowded lobbies. She and the man in the grey suit both knew it.

She was too tall, too pale, too stiff. She had her father's thick eye brows. They always made her look fierce unless she was very careful. Just now, too, her soft dark hair was full of Cairo dust and her drab business suit was creased.

Not very enticing, Leo thought, trying to laugh at herself. She had got used to being plain. She would have said that she did not let it bother her any more. But the look of surprise on the man's face hurt surprisingly.

The white-robed figure said something sharply. His assistant's face went blank. Then he nodded. And came over to them.

'Excuse me,' he said in accentless English. 'His Excellency asks if you are hurt.'

Leo shook her head, dumbly. She was too shaken to speak—though she could not have said why. After all, with his eyes hidden by smoked glass, she had no evidence that the man in the white robes was even looking at her. But she knew he was.

Mrs Silverstein was made of sterner stuff.

'Why how kind of—of His Excellency to ask,' she said, beaming at the messenger. She turned to Leo, 'That man didn't hurt you, did he dear?'

'*Hurt* me?' echoed Leo. She was bewildered. Did he have laser-powered eyes behind those dark glasses?

Mrs Silverstein was patient. 'When he bumped into you.'

Leo remembered the small collision with the under manager.

'Oh. Mr Ahmed.'

She pulled herself together but it was an effort. The sheikh was no longer looking at her. Leo knew that without looking at him. She was as conscious of him as if her whole body had somehow been tuned to resonate to his personal vibration.

No one had ever done that to her before. *No one;* let alone a regal stranger whose eyes she could not read. It shocked her.

She swallowed and said as steadily as she could manage, 'No, of course not. It was nothing.'

Mrs Silverstein peered up at her. 'Are you sure? You look awful pale.'

The security man did not offer any view on Leo's pallor or otherwise. She had the distinct impression that this was not the first time he had carried a message to an unknown lady. But that the messages were normally more amusing and the ladies more sophisticated; and about a hundred times more glamorous.

'Can I offer you assistance of any kind, madam?'

Leo moistened her lips. But she pulled herself together and said more collectedly, 'No, thank you. It was nothing. I don't need any assistance.' She remembered her manners. 'Please thank His Excellency for his concern. But there was no need.'

She turned away. But Mrs Silverstein was not going to pass up the chance of a new experience so easily. Not when royalty was involved. She tapped the security man on the arm.

'Which Excellency is that?'

The security man was so taken aback that he answered her.

'Sheikh Amer el-Barbary.'

Mrs Silverstein was enchanted. 'Sheikh,' she echoed dreamily.

Just a few steps away the dark glasses turned in their direction again. Leo felt herself flush. She did not look at him but she could feel his sardonic regard as if someone had turned a jet of cold water on her.

She shivered. How does he do that? she thought, aware of the beginnings of indignation.

Uncharacteristically her chin came up. Leo was a peacemaker, not a fighter. But this time was different. She glared across the lobby straight at him, as if she knew she was meeting his eyes.

Was it her imagination, or did the robed figure still for a moment? Leo had the feeling that suddenly she had his full attention. And that he was not best pleased

Help, she thought. *He's coming over.* The hairs on the back of her neck rose.

And then rescue came from an unexpected quarter.

'Darling!' called a voice.

Leo jumped and looked wildly round. The lobby seethed with noisy groups talking in numerous languages. They were no competition for her mother. Years of ladies' luncheons had given Deborah Groom a vocal pitch that could cut steel.

'Darling,' she called again. 'Over here.'

A heavily ringed hand waved imperiously. Leo located it and counted to ten. She had tried to persuade her mother not to come to Cairo in the busiest week of the agency's year. Deborah, predictably, had taken no notice.

Now Leo pulled herself together and said briskly to the hovering security man, 'Thank you but I am quite all right. Please—' she allowed herself just a touch of irony which she was sure the man would miss '—reassure His Excellency.' Then, more gently to Mrs Silverstein, 'Give me ten minutes. I have to clear up a couple of things. Then, if you still want to go, I'll take you to the pyramids at Giza.'

'You go right ahead,' said Mrs Silverstein, still entranced by her brush with royalty. 'I'll go sit in the café and have a cappuccino. Come and find me when you're done.'

Leo gave her a grateful smile. Then she tucked her clipboard under her arm and swarmed professionally through the crowd.

'Hello, Mother,' she said, bending her tall head. Leo received the scented breath on the cheek which Deborah favoured with a kiss and straightened thankfully. 'Having a good time?'

Deborah Groom was known for going straight to the point. 'It would be better if I saw something of my only daughter.'

Leo kept her smile in place with an effort. 'I warned you I'd have to work.'

'Not all the time.'

'There's a lot on.' If she sounded absent it was because in the distance she could see Andy Francis trying to herd a group towards their waiting bus. He was not having much success but then he should not have been doing it alone. Roy Ormerod, the head of Adventures in Time, was scheduled to be with the party too.

Deborah frowned. 'Does your chief know who you are?'

Leo gave a crack of laughter. 'You mean does he know that I'm the boss's daughter? Of course not. That would defeat the whole object. I'm called Leo Roberts here.'

Deborah snorted. 'I just don't understand your father sometimes.'

That was nothing new. She had walked out on Gordon Groom fourteen years ago, saying exactly that and leaving him to care for the ten-year-old Leo.

'He thinks it's a good idea for me to learn to stand on my own feet like he did,' she said patiently. 'Look, Mother—'

'You mean he thinks if he turns you out in the world to cope on your own you'll turn into a boy,' Deborah snapped.

Leo's eyes flashed. But there was enough truth in the accusation to make her curb her instinct to retort in kind. She and her mother both knew that Gordon had always wanted a son. Training Leo to succeed him in the business was just second best. He did not even try to disguise that any more.

Deborah bit her lip. 'Oh, I'm sorry darling, I promised myself I wouldn't start that again,' she said remorsefully. 'But when I see you looking like death and running yourself ragged like this, I just can't help myself.'

'Forget it,' said Leo.

She cast a surreptitious look at her clipboard. Where was Roy? He should have paid the bus driver for the Japanese party. If he didn't turn up she would have to deal with it.

And what about the Harris family? She had forgotten all about them and the museum tour was leaving.

Her mother sighed. 'I suppose there's no hope of seeing you at all today?'

Leo's conscience smote her. 'Not a chance unless—'

Mary Harris panted up to her.

'Oh, Leo, I'm so sorry. Timothy got locked in the bathroom. I didn't know what to do. The room attendant got him out. Have we missed the tour?'

Leo reassured them and plugged them rapidly onto the departing group. She came back to Deborah, mentally reviewing her schedule.

'Look, Mother, there's one more group I've got to see on its way. And then I'm supposed to take someone to the pyramids. But it will be hot and she's quite elderly. I doubt if she'll want to stay too long. Tea this afternoon?'

Deborah perked up. 'Or could I give you dinner?'

Leo hesitated.

'You think your father wouldn't like it,' Deborah diagnosed. Her mouth drooped.

Leo almost patted her hand. But Deborah would have jumped a foot. They were not a touchy-feely family.

So she said gently, 'It's not that. There's a conference dinner. We've arranged it at an historic merchant's house and there's going to be a lot of bigwigs present. I really ought to be there.'

'If the wigs are that big, why can't your boss do it?' Deborah said shrewdly.

Leo gave a choke of laughter. 'Roy? He doesn't—'

But then she thought about it. The guest list included some of the most illustrious charitable foundations in the world, including a high royalty quotient. Roy liked mingling at parties where he had a good chance of being photographed with the rich and famous. He called it networking.

'Mother, you're a genius. It's just the thing for Roy,' she said. She pulled out her mobile phone.

All she got was his answering machine. Leo left a crisp message and rang off.

'Right, that's sorted. I'll see you tonight. Now I've got to take a seventy-year-old from New Jersey to Giza.'

Deborah muttered discontentedly.

Leo looked down at her.

'What?'

'Surely someone junior could take this woman to the pyramids?'

Leo grinned. Deborah had been a rich man's daughter when she married rising tycoon Gordon Groom. There had been someone junior to take care of tedious duties all her life. It was one of the reasons Gordon had fought so hard for the custody of his only child.

'As long as I'm a member of the team, I do my share of the chores,' she said equably.

'Sometimes you are so like your father,' Deborah grumbled.

Leo laughed. 'Thank you.'

Deborah ignored that. 'I don't know why he had to buy Adventures in Time, anyway. Why couldn't he stick to hotels? And civilised places? What does he want with a travel agency?'

'Diversify or die,' Leo said cheerfully. 'You know Pops—' She broke off. 'Whoops.'

In the Viennese café Mrs Silverstein was chatting to an alarmed-looking man in a grey suit. Leo was almost certain he was a member of Sheikh el-Barbary's entourage.

'It looks as if my client is getting bored. I'll pick you up at eight this evening, Mother.'

She darted into the crowd. It was a relief.

Deborah's divorce from Gordon Groom had been relatively amicable and her settlement kept her luxuriously provided for, but she could still be waspish about her workaholic ex-husband. It was the one subject that she and Leo were guaranteed to argue about every time they got together.

Tonight, Leo promised herself, she was not going to let

Deborah mention Gordon once. Leo was beginning to have her own misgivings about her father's plans for her. But she was going to keep that from Deborah until she was absolutely certain herself. So they would talk about clothes and make-up and boyfriends and all the things that Deborah complained that Leo wasn't interested in.

One fun evening, thought Leo wryly, after another wonderful day. She went to rescue the security man.

The Sheikh's party swept into the suite like an invading army. One security man went straight to the balcony. The other disappeared into the bedroom. The manager, bowing, started to demonstrate the room's luxurious facilities. He found the Sheikh was not listening.

An assistant, still clutching his brief-case and laptop computer, nodded gravely and backed the manager towards the door.

'Thank you,' said the Sheikh's assistant. 'And now the other rooms?'

The manager bowed again and led the way. The security men followed.

The Sheikh was left alone. He went out to the balcony and stood looking across the Nile. The river was sinuous and glittering as a lazy snake in the morning sun. There was a dhow in midstream, he saw. Its triangular sail was curved like scimitar. It looked like a small dark toy.

He closed his eyes briefly. It was against more than the glare reflected off the water. Why did everything look like toys, these days?

Even the people. Moustafa, his chief bodyguard, looked like a prototype security robot. And the woman he was seeing tonight. He intended quitting the boring conference dinner with an excuse he did not care if they believed or not in order to see her. But for an uncomfortable moment, he allowed himself to realise that she reminded him of nothing so much as a designer-dressed doll. In fact, all the women he had seen recently looked like that.

Except—he had a fleeting image of the girl who had tumbled against the pillar in the hotel lobby. She was too tall, of course. And badly turned out, with her hair full of dust and a dark suit that was half-way to a uniform. But uniform or not, she had not looked like a doll. Not with those wide, startled eyes. The sudden shock in them had been intense—and unmistakeably real.

The Sheikh's brows twitched together in a quick frown. Why had she looked so shocked? He suddenly, passionately, wanted to know. But of course he never would, now. He grunted bad temperedly.

His personal assistant came back into the suite. He hesitated in the doorway.

The Sheikh straightened his shoulders. 'Out here, Hari,' he called. There was resignation in his tone.

The assistant cautiously joined him on the balcony.

'Everything appears to be in order,' he reported.

The Sheikh took off his dark glasses. His eyes were amused but terribly weary.

'Sure? Have the guys checked thoroughly? No bugs in the telephone? No poison in the honey cakes?'

The assistant smiled. 'Moustafa can take his job too seriously,' he admitted. 'But better safe than sorry.'

His employer's expression was scathing. 'This is nonsense and we both know it.'

'The kidnappings have increased,' Hari pointed out in a neutral tone.

'At home,' said the Sheikh impatiently. 'They haven't got the money to track me round the world, poor devils. Anyway, they take prosperous foreign visitors who will pay ransom. Not a local like me. My father would not pay a penny to have me back.' He thought about it. 'Probably pay them to keep me.'

Hari bit back a smile. He had not been present at the interview between father and son before Amer left Dalmun this time. But the reverberations had shaken the city.

A terminal fight, said the palace. The father would never

speak to the son again. An ultimatum, said Amer's household; the son had told his father he would tolerate no more
interference and was not coming back to Dalmun until the
old Sheikh accepted it.

Amer eyed him. 'And you can stop looking like a stuffed
camel. I know you know all about it.'

Hari disclaimed gracefully. 'I just hear the gossip in the
bazaars, like everyone else,' he murmured.

Amer was sardonic. 'Good for business, is it?'

'Gossip brings a lot of traders into town, I'm told,' Hari
agreed.

'Buy a kilo of rice and get the latest palace dirt thrown
in.' Amer gave a short laugh. 'What are they saying?'

Hari ticked the rumours off on his fingers. 'Your father
wants to kill you. You want to kill your father. You have
refused to marry again. You are insisting on marrying again.'
He stopped, his face solemn but his lively eyes dancing. 'You
want to go to Hollywood and make a movie.'

'Good God.' Amer was genuinely startled. He let out a
peal of delighted laughter. 'Where did that one come from?'

Hari was not only his personal assistant. He was also a
genuine friend. He told him the truth. 'Cannes last year, I
should think.'

'Ah,' said Amer, understanding at once. 'We are speaking
of the delicious Catherine.'

'Or,' said Hari judiciously, 'the delicious Julie, Kim or
Michelle.'

Amer laughed. 'I like Cannes.'

'That shows in the photographs,' Hari agreed.

'Disapproval, Hari?'

'Not up to me to approve or disapprove,' Hari said hastily.
'I just wonder—'

'I like women.'

Hari thought about Amer's adamant refusal to marry again
after his wife was killed in that horse riding accident. He
kept his inevitable reflections to himself.

'I like the crazy way their minds work,' Amer went on.

'It makes me laugh. I like the way they try to pretend they don't know when you're looking at them. I like the way they smell.'

Hari was surprised into pointing out, 'Not all women smell of silk and French perfume like your Julies and your Catherines.'

'Dolls,' said Amer obscurely.

'What?'

'Has it occurred to you how many animated dummies I know? Oh they *look* like people. They walk and talk and even sound like people. But when you talk to them they just say the things they've been programmed to say.'

Hari was unmoved. 'Presumably they're the things you want them to say. So who did the programming?'

Amer shifted his shoulders impatiently. 'Not me. I don't want—'

'To date a woman who has not been programmed to say you are wonderful?' Hari pursued ruthlessly. He regarded his friend with faint scorn. 'Why don't you try it, some time?'

Amer was not offended. But he was not impressed, either.

'Get real,' he said wearily.

Hari warmed to his idea. 'No, I mean it. Take that girl down stairs in the lobby just now.'

Amer was startled. 'Have you started mind reading, Hari?'

'I saw you looking her way,' Hari explained simply. 'I admit I was surprised. She's hardly your type.'

Amer gave a mock shudder. 'No French perfume there, you mean. I know. More like dust and cheap sun-tan lotion.' A reminiscent smile curved his handsome mouth suddenly. 'But even so, she has all the feminine tricks. Did you see her trying to pretend she didn't know I was looking at her?'

Hari was intrigued. 'So why were you?'

Amer hesitated, his eyes unreadable for an instant. Then he shrugged. 'Three months in Dalmun, I expect,' he said in his hardest voice. 'Show a starving man stale bread and he forgets he ever knew the taste of caviar.'

'Stale bread? Poor lady.'

'I'll remember caviar as soon as I have some to jog my memory,' Amer murmured mischievously.

Hari knew his boss. 'I'll book the hotel in Cannes.'

It was not a successful visit to the pyramids. As Leo expected, Mrs Silverstein insisted on walking round every pyramid and could not be persuaded to pass on the burial chamber of Cheops. Since that involved a steep climb, a good third of which had to be done in a crouching position, the older woman was in considerable pain by the end of the trip. Not that she would admit it.

Ever since Mrs Silverstein arrived in Egypt on her Adventures in Time tour, she had wanted to see everything and, in spite of her age and rheumatic joints, made a spirited attempt to do so. When other members of the group took to shaded rooms in the heat of the afternoon, Mrs Silverstein was out there looking at desert plants or rooting affronted Arabs out of their afternoon snooze to bargain over carpets or papyrus.

'The woman never *stops,*' Roy Ormerod complained, looking at the couriers' reports. 'She'll collapse and then we'll be responsible. For Heaven's sake get her to slow down.'

But Leo, joining one of the party's trips, found she had a sneaking sympathy for Mrs Silverstein. She was a lively and cultivated woman with a hunger for new experience that a lifetime of bringing up a family had denied her. She also, as Leo found late one night when the local courier thankfully surrendered her problem client and retired to bed, had a startling courage.

'Well, it's a bit more than rheumatism,' Mrs Silverstein admitted under the influence of honey cakes and mint tea. 'And it's going to get worse. I thought, I've got to do as much as I can while I can. So I'll have some things to remember.'

Leo was impressed. She said so.

'You see I always wanted to travel,' Mrs Silverstein confided. 'But Sidney was such a homebody. And then there were the children. When they all got married I thought *now*.

But then Sidney got sick. And first Alice was divorced and then Richard and the grandchildren would come and stay...' She sighed. 'When Dr Burnham told me what was wrong I thought—it's now or never, Pat.'

Leo could only admire her. So, instead of following Roy's instructions, she did her best to make sure that Mrs Silverstein visited every single thing she wanted to see in Egypt, just taking a little extra care of her. It was not easy.

By the time Leo got her back to the hotel she was breathing hard and had turned an alarming colour. Leo took her up to her room and stayed while Mrs Silverstein lay on the well-sprung bed, fighting for breath. Leo called room service and ordered a refreshing drink while she applied cool damp towels to Mrs Silverstein's pink forehead.

'I think I should call a doctor,' she said worriedly.

Mrs Silverstein shook her head. 'Pills,' she said. 'In my bag.'

Leo got them. Mrs Silverstein swallowed three and then lay back with her eyes closed. Her colour slowly returned to normal.

The phone rang. Leo picked it up.

'Mrs Silverstein?' said a harsh voice she knew all too well. Even when Roy Ormerod was trying to be conciliating he sounded angry. 'I wonder if you can tell me where Miss Roberts went when she left you?'

Leo braced herself. 'This is me, Roy. Mrs Silverstein wasn't feeling well, so I—'

He did not give her the chance to finish.

'What the hell do you think you're doing? I told you to stop that old bat going on excursions, not give her personal guided tours. You should be back at the office. And what do you mean, leaving me a message that you won't be at the dinner, tonight? You've got to be there. It's part of your job....'

He ranted for several more minutes. Mrs Silverstein opened her eyes and began to look alarmed.

Leo interrupted him. 'We'll talk about this at the office,'

she said firmly. She looked at her watch. 'I'll come over now. See you in half an hour.'

'No you won't. I'm already—'

But she had cut him off.

'Trouble?' said Mrs Silverstein.

'None I can't handle.'

'Is it my fault?'

'No,' said Leo.

Because it was not. Roy had been spoiling for a fight ever since she first arrived from London.

Forgetting professional discretion, Leo said as much. Mrs Silverstein looked thoughtful. She had met Roy.

'And he doesn't like it that you're not attracted to him,' she said wisely.

Leo stared. 'What? Oh, surely not.'

Mrs Silverstein shrugged. 'Good at your job. Independent. Clients like you. All sounds too much like competition to me, honey.' She struggled up among the pillows. 'The only way you could put yourself right with the man is by falling at his feet.'

Leo stared, equally fascinated and repelled.

'I hope you're wrong,' she said with feeling.

There was a knock at the door. Leo got off the side of the bed.

'That must be your lemon sherbet.'

But it was not. It was Roy. His eyes were bulging with fury.

'Oh, you were calling from the desk,' said Leo, enlightened.

He brushed that aside. 'Look here—' he began loudly.

Leo barred his way, giving thanks for the carved screen behind the tiny entrance area. It masked the doorway from Mrs Silverstein's view.

'You can't make a scene here,' she hissed. 'She's not well.'

But Roy was beyond rationality. He took Leo by the wrist

and pulled her out into the corridor. He was shouting. He even took her by the shoulders and shook her.

An authoritative voice said, 'That is enough.'

They both turned, Leo blindly, Roy with blundering aggression.

The speaker was a man with a haughty profile and an air of effortless command. A business man, Leo thought. Someone who had paid for expensive quiet on this executive floor and was going to see that he got what he paid for. The dark eyes resting on Roy were coldly contemptuous.

Roy did not like his intervention. 'Who are you? The floor manager?' he sneered.

Leo winced for him. On the face of it, the stranger's impeccable dark suit was indistinguishable from any of the other business suits in the hotel. But Leo's upbringing had taught her to distinguish at a glance between the prosperous and the seriously rich. The suit was hand tailored and, for all its conservative lines, individually designed as well. Add to that the air of being in charge of the world, and you clearly had someone to reckon with.

But Roy had never been able to read nonverbal signs.

He said pugnaciously, 'This is a private conversation.'

'Then you should conduct it in private,' the man said. His courtesy bit deeper than any invective would have done. 'You have a room here?'

'No,' said Leo, alarmed at the thought of being alone with Roy in this mood.

For the first time the man took his eyes off the belligerent Roy. He sent her a quick, cool look. And did a double take.

'Mademoiselle?' he said blankly.

Leo did not recognise him. She tried to pull herself together and search her memory. But Roy's shaking of her seemed to have scrambled her brains.

Meanwhile, the fact that the stranger seemed to recognise her had sent Roy into a frenzy.

'You want to be careful with that one, friend,' he said. 'She'll stab you in the back as soon as look at you.'

Leo's head spun as if she had been shot. All she could think of was that Roy must have found out who her father was.

'What?' she said hoarsely.

The stranger sent her a narrow-eyed look. 'It is perhaps that I intrude unnecessarily,' he said, his accent pronounced. 'Mademoiselle?'

Leo shook her confused head.

Roy snarled, 'You're fired.'

Leo paled. She could just imagine what her father would say to this news.

'Oh Lord,' she said with foreboding.

This time the stranger did not bother to look at her.

'Your discussion would benefit from a more constructive approach,' he told Roy austerely.

Roy snorted. 'Discussion over,' he snapped. He sent Leo one last flaming look. 'You don't want to come to the dinner tonight? Fine. Don't. And don't come near the office again, either. Or any of my staff.'

Leo began to be alarmed. She shared an apartment with two of his staff.

'Roy—'

But he was on a roll. 'And don't ask me for a reference.'

Leo was not as alarmed about that as he clearly thought she should have been. When she said, 'Look, let's talk about this,' in a soothing voice, two bright spots of colour appeared on Roy's cheeks.

He took a hasty step forward. Leo thought in a flash of recognition: He is going to hit me. It was so crazy she did not even duck. Instead she froze, panicking.

Fortunately their companion did not panic so easily. He stepped swiftly in front of her.

'No,' he said.

It was quiet enough but it had the force of a blow.

Leo winced. It stopped Roy dead in his tracks. For a moment he and her rescuer stood face-to-face, eyes locked. Roy was a big man and the red glare in his eyes was alarming.

The other was tall and his shoulders were broad enough but, under the exquisite tailoring, he was slim and graceful. No match for a bull like Roy, you would have said. Yet there was no doubt who was the master in this encounter.

There was a moment of tense silence. Roy breathed hard. Then, without another word, he turned and blundered off, sending a chair flying.

Leo sagged against the wall. Her heart was racing. Now that it was over she was horrified at the ugly little scene.

Out of sight, she heard the lift doors open...several people get out...voices. Her rescuer flicked a look down the corridor. The voices got louder, laughing. He slipped a hand under her arm.

'Come with me.'

And before the new arrivals caught sight of them, he had whisked her to the end of the corridor and through impressive double doors. Before she knew what was happening, Leo found herself sitting in a high-backed chair in what she recognised as the Presidential Suite. The man stood over her, silent. He looked half impatient; half—what? Leo felt her heart give a wholly unfamiliar lurch.

'Are you all right?' he said at last.

Leo thought: I want him to put his arms round me. She could not believe it.

'What?' she said distractedly.

He frowned. As if people usually paid closer attention when he spoke, Leo thought. Now she came to look at him closely she saw there was more to him than grace and good tailoring. The harsh face might be proud and distant but it was spectacularly handsome. And surely there was a look in those eyes that was not proud or distant at all?

I must be hallucinating, Leo thought feverishly. This is not my scene at all. I don't fancy chance-met strangers and they don't fancy me. This is the second time today I've started to behave like someone I don't know. Am I going mad?

'I said, are you all right?'

'Oh.' She tried to pull herself together. 'I—suppose so.'
She added almost to herself, 'I just don't know what to do.'

He sighed heavily. 'In what way?' His distaste was obvious.

If he dislikes this situation so much, why doesn't he just
leave me alone, Leo thought irritated.

'He said I wasn't to go back. But everything I have is at
the flat...'

Unexpectedly her voice faltered. To her horror, Leo felt
tears start. She dashed them away angrily. But the little gesture gave her away more completely than if she had started
to bawl aloud.

The man's face became masklike.

'You live with this man?'

But Leo's brain was racing, proposing and discarding
courses of action at the rate of ten a minute. She hardly noticed his question.

'I'll have to call London.' She looked at her watch. 'And
then book a room somewhere. If I can get one in the height
of the tourist season.'

The man sighed. 'Then it will be my pleasure to offer you
my assistance,' he said in a long-suffering tone. He picked
up the phone.

Leo's brows twitched together. There was something oddly
familiar about the formal phrase.

'Have we met?'

He was talking into the phone in quick, clicking Arabic.
But at that he looked down at her.

'We have not, Miss Roberts.'

He had the strangest eyes. She had thought they would be
brown in that dark face but they were not. They were a
strange metallic colour, somewhere between cold steel and
the depths of the sea; and dark, dark. Leo felt herself caught
by their icy intensity; caught and drawn in, under, drowned...

She pulled herself up short. Was the man a mesmerist?

'You know my name,' she pointed out breathlessly.

He smiled then. For the first time. It made him devastating.

'I can read.'

She stared at him, uncomprehending. He reached out a hand and brushed her shoulder. Even through the poplin jacket of her suit, his touch was electric. Leo shot to her feet with a gasp.

'What—?'

'Your label,' he said gently.

He had removed the large lettered name tag that she had worn to the airport this morning. He dropped it into her hand, not touching her fingers.

Leo's face heated. She felt a fool. That was not like her, either. *What is it about this man that makes me lose my rationality? And feel like I've never felt before?*

The phone rang. He picked it up, listened without expression and only the briefest word of acknowledgement before ringing off.

'The hotel has a room for you. Pick the key up at the desk.'

Leo was startled into protesting. 'A room? *Here?* You're joking. They're booked solid for weeks. I know because I was trying to get a room for a late attender at the conference.'

He shrugged, bored. 'One must have become available in the meantime.'

Leo did not believe that for a moment. Her eyes narrowed.

But before she could demand an explanation, the door banged back on its hinges and two large men in tight suits appeared at it. One of them was carrying a revolver. Leo gaped.

Her rescuer spun round and he said something succinct. The gun stopped pointing at her. The two men looked uncomfortable. Leo turned her attention from the new arrivals to her rescuer.

'Who *are* you?'

He hesitated infinitesimally. Then, 'My name is Amer,' he said smoothly.

Leo's suspicions increased. But before she could demand further information, one of the men spoke agitatedly. Her rescuer looked at his watch.

'I have to go,' he said to her. 'Moustafa will take you down to the lobby and ensure that there are no problems.'

He gave her a nod. It was sharp and final. He was already walking away before Leo pulled herself together enough to thank him. Which was just as well. Because she was not feeling grateful at all.

CHAPTER TWO

LEO was not really surprised when the room proved to be not only available but also quietly luxurious. When a discreetly noncommittal porter ushered her in she found there were gifts waiting on the brass coffee table: a bowl of fruit, a dish of Arabic sweetmeats and a huge basket of flowers.

Leo blinked. 'That's—very beautiful.'

The porter nodded without expression. He surrendered the plastic wafer that served as a key to her room and backed out. Neither he nor the hotel receptionist had expressed the slightest surprise about her lack of luggage.

It was unnerving. Leo felt as if the unknown stranger had cast some sort of magic cloak over her. Oh, it was protective all right. But it made her feel as if he had somehow made her invisible as well.

Still, at least it had got her a roof over her head tonight. Be grateful for small mercies, she told herself. He's given you the opportunity to get your life back on track. She checked her watch and started making phone calls.

Her mother was fourth on the list. She expected to have to leave a message but Deborah was there.

'Sorry, Mother, you're going to have to take a rain check for tonight,' she said. 'I've got problems. They'll take a bit of time to sort out.'

'Tell me,' said Deborah.

Leo did.

Her mother was indignant. She might not approve of her only daughter toiling as a menial courier but that did not mean that she thought anyone had the right to sack her. She urged various strategies on Leo, most of which would have ended with both Roy and Leo being deported. Used to her

29

mother's fiery temperament, Leo murmured soothing noises down the phone until her mother's fury abated.

'Well,' said Deborah pugnaciously, 'Mr Ormerod is certainly not interrupting my dinner plans. You have to eat and I want your company. See you at eight o' clock.'

'But I haven't got anything to *wear*,' wailed Leo.

'You've got a credit card.' She could hear the glee in her mother's voice. Deborah was always complaining about Leo's lack of interest in clothes. 'And you ought to know this town well enough to know where the class boutiques are. I'll see you downstairs *now*.'

Leo knew when she was beaten. She negotiated a fifteen-minute delay to allow her to make the rest of her calls. But that was as much of a concession as Deborah was willing to make.

Deborah was waiting in the lobby.

'I've got a car,' she said briskly. 'And I know where to go, too, so don't try to fob me off with any old shopping mall.'

She led the way purposefully. Leo grinned and followed.

Installed in the back of the hired limousine, Leo tipped her head back and looked at her mother appreciatively. Deborah fluffed up the organza collar to her stunning navy-and-white designer dress. The discreet elegance of her earrings did not disguise the fact that they were platinum or that the navy stones which echoed her ensemble were rather fine sapphires.

'You look very expensive,' Leo said lazily.

She did not mean it as a criticism. But Deborah flushed. She swung round on the seat to inspect her weary daughter.

'And you look like a tramp,' she retorted. 'Do you dress like that to make a point?'

Leo was unoffended. She had been taller than her exquisite mother when she was eleven. By the time she entered her teens she had resigned herself to towering over other girls. She had even started to stoop until an enlightened teacher had persuaded her to stand up straight, mitigating her height by simple, well-cut clothes. Deborah had never resigned herself to Leo's chosen style.

Now Leo said tolerantly, 'I dress like this to stay cool and look reasonably professional during a long working day, Mother. Besides,' she said as Deborah opened her mouth to remonstrate, 'I like my clothes.'

Deborah gave her shoulders a little annoyed shake.

'Well, you won't need to look professional tonight. So you can buy something pretty for once. It's not as if you can't afford it.'

Leo flung up her hands in a gesture of surrender.

The car delivered them to a small shop. The window was filled with a large urn holding six-foot grasses. Leo knew the famous international name. And the prices that went with it. Her heart sank.

'It's lucky I paid off my credit card bill just last week, isn't it?' she said.

Deborah ignored this poor spirited remark. 'We're going to buy you something special,' she said firmly, urging her reluctant daughter out of the car.

'Here comes the frill patrol,' groaned Leo.

But she did her mother an injustice. Deborah clearly hankered after a cocktail suit in flowered brocade. But she gave in gracefully when Leo said, 'It makes me look like a newly upholstered sofa.' Instead they came away with georgette harem pants, the colour of bark, and a soft jacket in a golden apricot. Deborah gave her a long silk scarf in bronze and amber to go with it.

'Thank you mother,' said Leo, touched.

Deborah blinked rapidly. 'I wish you were wearing it to go out to dinner with someone more exciting than me.'

For a shockingly irrational moment, Leo's thoughts flew to her mystery rescuer. She felt her colour rise. Inwardly she cursed her revealing porcelain skin and the shadowy Amer with equal fury. To say nothing of her mother's sharp eyes.

'Ah,' said Deborah. 'Anyone I know?'

'There's no one,' said Leo curtly.

She stamped out to the limousine. Deborah said a more graceful farewell to the sales staff before she followed.

'Darling,' she began as soon as the driver had closed the door on her, 'I think we need to have a little talk.'

Leo stared in disbelief. 'I'm twenty-four, Mother. I know about the birds and the bees.'

Deborah pursed her lips. 'I'm glad to hear it. Not that anyone would think it from the way you go on.'

'Mother—' said Leo warningly.

'It's all right. I don't want to know about your boy-friends. I want to talk about marriage.'

Leo blinked. 'You're getting married again?'

Deborah enjoyed the attentions of a number of escorts but she had never shown any sign of wanting to have her pretty Holland Park house invaded by a male in residence.

Now Deborah clicked her tongue in irritation. 'Of course not. I mean *your* marriage.'

Leo was blank. 'But I'm not getting married.'

'Ah,' said Deborah again. She started to play with an earring. 'Then the rumours about you and Simon Hartley aren't true?'

Leo stared at her in genuine bewilderment. 'Simon Hartley? Dad's new Chief Accountant? I hardly know him.'

Deborah twiddled the earring harder. 'I thought he was the brother of a school friend of yours.'

Leo made a surprised face. 'Claire Hartley, yes. But he's quite a bit older than us.'

'So you've never met him?'

Leo shrugged. 'Dad brought him out here a couple of months ago. Some sort of familiarisation trip. All the Adventures in Time staff met him.'

'And did you like him?'

Leo gave a snort of exasperation. 'Come off it, Mother. The strain is showing. Believe me, there's no point in trying to make matches for me. I'm not like you. I honestly don't think I'm cut out for marriage.'

Slightly to her surprise, Deborah did not take issue with

that. Instead she looked thoughtful. 'Why not? Because you've got too much to do being Gordon Groom's heir?'

Leo tensed. Here it comes, she thought. This is where she starts to attack Pops.

She said stiffly, 'I chose to go into the company.'

Deborah did not take issue with that, either. She said abruptly, 'Leo, have you ever been in love?'

Leo could not have been more taken aback if her mother had asked her if she had ever flown to the moon.

'Excuse me?'

The moment she said it, she could have kicked herself. Deborah would take her astonishment as an admission of failure with the opposite sex. Just what she had always warned her daughter would happen if she did not lighten up, in fact.

'I thought not.'

But Deborah did not sound triumphant. She sounded worried. And for what must have been the first time in her life she did not push the subject any further.

It made Leo feel oddly uneasy. She was used to maternal lectures. She could deal with them. A silent, preoccupied Deborah was something new in her experience. She did not like it.

Amer had given Hari a number of instructions which had caused his friend's eyebrows to climb higher and higher. He took dutiful notes, however. But at the final instruction he put down his monogrammed pen and looked at Amer with burning reproach.

'What am I going to tell your father?'

'Don't tell him anything,' said Amer fluently. 'You report back to my uncle the Minister of Health. My uncle will tell him that I made the speech I was sent here to make. *Et voilà.*'

'But they will expect you to say something at the dinner.'

Amer gave him a wry smile. 'You say it. You wrote it, after all. You'll be more convincing than I will.'

Hari bit back an answering smile. 'They'll find out,' he said gloomily. 'What will they say?'

'I don't care what a bunch of dentists say,' Amer told him with breezy arrogance.

'I wasn't thinking of the dentists,' Hari said ironically, 'I was thinking of your uncle the Health Minister, your uncle the Finance Minister, your uncle the Oil Minister...'

Amer's laugh had a harsh ring. 'I don't care what they think, either.'

'But your father—'

'If my father isn't very careful,' Amer said edgily, 'I shall go back to university and turn myself into the archaeologist I was always meant to be.'

Hari was alarmed. 'It's my fault, isn't it? I shouldn't have said that the women you know were programmed to think you are wonderful. You've taken it as a challenge, haven't you?'

Amer chuckled. 'Let us say you outlined a hypothesis which I would be interested to test.'

'But why Miss Roberts?'

Amer hesitated for the briefest moment. Then he gave a small shrug. 'Why not?'

'You said she was like stale bread,' Hari reminded him.

Amer's well-marked brows twitched together in a frown.

'I hope you weren't thinking of telling her that,' he warned.

'I'm not telling her anything,' said Hari hastily. 'I'm not going anywhere near her.'

Amer frowned even more blackly. 'Don't be ridiculous. That's not the way to stop me seeing her.'

'I'm not being ridiculous,' said Hari. A thought occurred to him. He was beginning to enjoy himself. 'If you want to play at being an ordinary guy, the first thing you'll have to do is fix up a date in person like the rest of us.'

There was a startled pause. Then Amer began to laugh softly.

'But of course. I never intended anything else. That's part of the fun.'

'Fun!'

'Of course. New experiments are always fun.'

'So she's a new experiment. Are you going to tell her that?' Hari asked politely.

'I don't know what I'm going to tell her yet,' Amer said with disarming frankness. 'I suppose it partly depends on what she tells me.' He looked intrigued at the thought.

'The first thing she'll tell you is your name, title and annual income,' snapped Hari, goaded.

But Amer was not to be shaken out of his good humour.

'I've been thinking about that. If she hasn't recognised me so far, she isn't going to unless someone tells her. So you'd better make the arrangements in your name.'

'Oh? And what about when you turn up instead of me? Even if you can convince the maître d' to be discreet what about the other people at the restaurant?'

'I've thought of that, too.' Amer was as complacent as a cat. 'Now here's what I want you to do—'

Back at the hotel Leo found her father had tried to return her call twice. He had left a series of numbers where he could be contacted. Immediately, according to the message. So he was serious about it.

Leo tapped the message against her teeth. She did not look forward to it. But years of dealing with her father had taught her that it was better to face up to his displeasure sooner rather than later. She squared her shoulders and dialled.

'What's happened?' Gordon Groom said, cutting through her enquiries after his health and well-being.

Leo sighed and told him.

She kept it short. Her father liked his reports succinct. He had been known to fire an executive for going on longer than Gordon wanted.

When she finished, slightly to her surprise, his first thought was for Mrs Silverstein. 'How is she?'

'Sleeping, I think.'

'Check on her,' Gordon ordered. 'And again before you go to bed.'

'Of course,' said Leo, touched.

'There's a real up side opportunity here. The retired American market has a lot of growth potential for us,' Gordon went on, oblivious.

That was more like the father Leo knew. She suppressed a grin. 'I'll check.'

'And what about Ormerod? Has he lost it?'

Leo shifted uncomfortably. She had been very firm with her father that she was not going to Cairo to spy on the existing management.

'Some of the local customer care is a bit archaic,' she said carefully.

'Sounds like they need an operational audit.' Gordon dismissed the Cairo office from his mind and turned his attention to his daughter. 'Now what about you? Not much point in making Ormerod take you back, is there?'

Leo shuddered. 'No.'

Her father took one of his lightning executive decisions. 'Then you'd better come back to London. Our sponsorship program needs an overhaul. You can do that until—' He stopped. 'You can take charge of that.'

Leo was intrigued. But she knew her father too well to press him. The last thing he was going to do was tell her the job he had in mind for her until he had made sure that she was up to it.

'Okay. I'll clear up things here and come home.'

Other fathers, Leo thought, would have been glad. Other fathers would have said, 'It'll be great to have you home, darling.' Or even, 'Let me know the flight, I'll come to the airport and meet you.'

Gordon just said, 'You've still got your keys?'

They shared a large house in Wimbledon. But Leo had her own self-contained flat. She and her father did not interfere with each other.

'I've still got my keys,' she agreed.

'See you when you get back.' Clearly about to ring off, a thought struck Gordon. 'You haven't heard from your mother, by the way?'

'As a matter of fact she's here. I'm having dinner with her tonight.'

Gordon did not bad mouth Deborah the way she did him but you could tell that he was not enthusiastic about the news, Leo thought.

'Oh? Well, don't let her fill your head with any of her silly ideas,' he advised. 'See you.'

He rang off.

Leo told herself she was not hurt. He was a good and conscientious father. But he had no truck with sentimentality; especially not if it showed signs of interfering with business.

It was silly to think that she would have liked him to be a bit more indignant on her behalf, Leo thought. When Deborah had ranted about Roy Ormerod, Leo had calmed her down. Yet when her father didn't, she felt unloved.

'The trouble with me is, I don't know what I want,' Leo told herself. 'Forget it.'

But she could not help remembering how the dark-eyed stranger had stood up to Ormerod for her. It had made her feel—what? Protected? Cared for? She grimaced at the thought.

'No regression to frills,' she warned herself. 'You're a Groom executive. You can't afford to turn to mush.'

Anyway she would not see the mysterious stranger again. Just as well if he had this sort of effect on her usual robust independence.

She made a dinner reservation for herself and her mother. Then she stripped off the day's dusty clothes and ran a bath. The hotel provided everything you needed, she saw wryly, even a toothbrush and a luxurious monogrammed bathrobe.

She sank into scented foam and let her mind go into free fall. When the phone rang on the bathroom wall, she ignored it, lifting a long foot to turn on the tap and top up the warm water. For the first time in months, it seemed, she did not have to worry about a tour or a function or timetable inconsistencies. She tipped her head back and gave herself up to the pleasures of irresponsibility.

There was a knock at the door.

Mother come to make sure I've plucked my eyebrows, diagnosed Leo. She won't go away. Oh well, time to get going, I suppose.

She raised the plug and got out of the bath. She knotted the bathrobe round her and opened the door, trying to assume a welcoming expression. When she saw who it was, she stopped trying in pure astonishment.

'You! What do you want?'

'Very welcoming,' said the mysterious stranger, amused. 'How about a date?'

'A *date?*'

'Dinner,' he explained fluently. 'Music, dancing, cultural conversation. Whatever you feel like.'

Leo shook her head to clear it.

'But—a date? With me?'

A faint hint of annoyance crossed the handsome face. 'Why not?'

Because men don't ask me on dates. Not out of the blue. Not without an introduction and several low-key meetings at the houses of mutual friends. Not without knowing who my father is.

Leo crushed the unworthy thought.

'When?' she said, playing for time while she got her head round this new experience.

'Tonight or never,' he said firmly.

'Oh well, that settles it.' Leo was not sure whether she was disappointed or relieved. But at least the decision was taken for her. 'I'm already going out to dinner tonight.'

She made to close the door. It did not work.

He did not exactly put his foot in the door, but he leaned against the doorjamb as if he was prepared to stay there all night.

'Cancel.' His tone said it was a suggestion rather than an order. His eyes said it was a challenge.

Leo found herself reknotting the sash of her borrowed robe in an agitated manner and saying, 'No,' in a voice like the primmest teacher she had ever had at her polite girls' school.

He bit back a smile. 'I dare you.'

She looked at him with dislike. 'I suppose you think that makes it irresistible?'

'Well, interesting, anyway.'

If Leo was honest, his smile was more than intriguing. She felt her heart give an odd little jump, as if it had been pushed out of a nice, safe burrow and wanted to climb back in again. She knew that feeling. She hated taking chances and always had.

She looked at the man and thought: I don't know where going out with this man would take me. Thank God I'm spending the evening with Mother.

And then, as if some particularly mischievous gods were listening, along the corridor came Deborah Groom. Leo groaned.

'Is that a yes, no or maybe?' said Amer, entertained.

'None of the above. Hello, Mother.'

He turned quickly. Deborah did not hesitate. Assuming that the man at Leo's door was Roy Ormerod, she stormed straight into battle.

'How dare you come here and harass my daughter? Haven't you done enough? I shall make sure your employer knows all about this.'

Amer blinked. A look of unholy appreciation came into his eyes.

'I didn't mean to harass her,' he said meekly.

Leo writhed inwardly. 'Mother, please. This is Mr—' thankfully she remembered his name just in time '—Mr Amer. He was the one who persuaded the hotel to find me a room.'

'Oh.'

Deborah took a moment to assimilate the information.

Then another to assess Amer. The quality of his tailoring was not lost on her, any more than it had been on her daughter.

'Oh,' she said again in quite a different voice. She held out a gracious hand. 'How kind of you, Mr Amer. I'm Deborah, er, Roberts, Leo's mother.'

'Leo?' he murmured, bowing over her hand.

'Ridiculous, isn't it? Especially with a pretty name like Leonora. After my grandmother, you know. But her father always called her Leo. And it just stuck.'

'Mother,' protested Leo.

Neither of them paid any attention to her.

'Leonora,' he said as if he were savouring it.

Deborah beamed at him. 'And how kind of you to check on Leo.'

He was rueful. 'I was hoping to persuade her to have dinner with me. But she is already engaged.' He sighed but the dark grey eyes were sharp.

Deborah put her pretty head on one side.

'Well, now, isn't that odd? I was just coming to tell Leo that I really didn't feel like going out this evening.' She allowed her shoulders to droop theatrically. 'This heat is so tiring.'

Leo could not believe this treachery.

'What heat, Mother? Every single place you've been today is air conditioned within an inch of its life.'

Deborah looked annoyed. Amer's lips twitched. But, strategist that he was, he did not say anything.

Deborah recovered fast. 'Well, that's exactly the problem.' She turned to Amer appealingly. 'We English aren't used to real air-conditioning. I think I must have caught a chill.' She managed a ladylike cough.

Leo felt murderous. She was almost sure the beastly man was laughing at both of them.

'Then you'd better stay in your room,' she said firmly. 'We'll order room service.'

Deborah gave her a faint, brave smile. 'Oh no, darling. I'll be better on my own. You go and enjoy yourself with Mr Amer.'

Amer took charge before Leo could scream with fury or announce that the last thing in the world she would enjoy was an evening with him.

'If you are sure, Mrs Roberts?' he said smoothly, as if that was all it took to decide the matter. He nodded to Leo, careful not to let his satisfaction show. 'Then I shall look forward to our excursion, Miss Roberts. Shall we say, half an hour?'

He walked off down the corridor before Leo could respond.

'*Mother,*' she said between her teeth.

Deborah was unrepentant. 'Just what you need,' she said briskly, ceasing to droop. 'An evening with a seriously sexy article like that. Should have happened years ago. Now what are you going to wear?'

Leo knew when she was beaten. She stood aside to let her mother come in.

'There's not a lot of choice,' she said drily. 'My work suit. Or the sun flower job you've just talked me into.'

Deborah flung open the wardrobe door and considered the ensemble with a professional eye. 'That will do. It's versatile enough. How smart do you think it will be?'

Leo sighed in exasperation. 'I haven't the slightest idea. I only met the man once before you thrust me into this evening's fiasco.'

If she thought that the information would make Deborah apologise, she mistook her mother. Deborah was intrigued.

'Determined, isn't he? Very flattering.'

'Oh please,' said Leo in disgust.

Deborah ignored that. 'We should have bought you some shoes,' she said in a dissatisfied voice.

Leo picked up her low-heeled black pumps and held them to her protectively. 'They're comfortable.'

Deborah sighed. 'Oh well, they'll have to do. At least, there's stuff in the bathroom to polish them up a bit. Now what about make-up?'

Leo gave up. In her element, Deborah took charge. She shook her head over the ragged ends of Leo's newly washed hair and took her nails scissors to it. After that, she gave her a brief but professional make-up which emphasised Leo's long silky lashes and made her eyes look enormous. She ended by pressing onto her a magnificent pair of topaz drop earrings.

'I'm not used to all this,' protested Leo, surrendering her neat pearl studs with misgiving. 'I'm going to make a terrible fool of myself.'

'You'll be fine,' said Deborah.

But she did not pretend to misunderstand Leo's doubts.

'Darling, you're so capable. You can handle anything, not like me. How have you got this hang up about men?'

'It's not a hang up,' said Leo drily. 'It's the sure and certain knowledge that any man who goes out with me has been turned down by everyone else in the netball team. Unless he thinks he's dating my father.'

Deborah shook her head. 'I don't understand you.'

'I do,' muttered Leo.

'So explain it to me.'

'Big feet and too much bosom,' said Leo baldly. 'Plus a tendency to break things.'

Deborah was shocked. 'Leo! You have a wonderful figure. Think of all those girls out there having to buy padded bras. Men just love curves like yours.'

'Oh sure. A demolition expert with feet like flippers is pretty irresistible, too.'

Deborah sighed but she was a realist. 'Look, darling, men can be very unkind but they're not difficult to deal with if you know how. Tonight, just listen to the man as if he's an oracle. And try not to bump into the furniture.'

Leo's laugh was hollow.

CHAPTER THREE

THERE was no furniture to bump into.

First, Amer arrived in designer jeans and a loose jacket that was the last word in careless chic and made Leo feel seriously overdressed. Then, he announced that they were going out of Cairo. To Leo's increasing trepidation, this involved a short trip in a private helicopter.

'Where are we?' she said, when the helicopter set down and its ailerons stopped turning.

The airstrip was abnormally deserted. In her experience Egyptian airports heaved like anthills.

But her horribly hip companion just smiled.

The briefest ride in an open Jeep took them to a dark landing stage. The stars, like a watchmaker's store of diamond chips, blinked at the water. Silent as a snake, the river gleamed back. There was a warm breeze off the water, like the breath of a huge, sleepy animal.

Leo was not cold; but she shivered.

'Where *are* we?'

'Seventy miles up river from Cairo,' Amer told her coolly.

'Seventy—' Leo broke off, in shock. 'Why?'

'I wanted to give you a picnic by moonlight,' Amer said in soulful tones. He added, more practically, 'You can't do proper moonlight in the middle of a city.'

Leo looked at him in the deepest suspicion. Standing as they were in the headlights of the Jeep it was difficult to tell but she was almost certain he was laughing at her.

The dark harem pants wafted in the breeze. Her gold jacket felt garish under the stars and ridiculously out of place. She felt as clumsily conspicuous as she used to do at agonizing teenage parties.

'Why would you want to take me on a moonlit picnic?' she muttered resentfully. 'You know I thought I was signing up for dinner in a restaurant. Look at me.'

Amer was supervising the removal of a large picnic basket from the jeep. He turned his head at that. He looked her up and down. In the jeep's headlights, Leo somehow felt as if she were on display. She huddled the jacket round her in pure instinct.

'Do you want to go back?' he asked.

It should have been a courteous enquiry. It was not. It was a challenge. On the point of demanding just that, Leo stopped, disconcerted.

After a day of shocks, was this one so terrible, after all? At least it promised a new experience. Who knows, she might actually enjoy it. And she did not have to bother about an early night, for once. She did not have to get up in the small hours to meet an incoming flight. She would never have to again.

'I suppose, now we're here...' she said at last.

Amer raised his eyebrows. It was hardly enthusiastic.

'Shall we call it an experiment then? For both of us.' He sounded rueful.

The driver took the picnic basket down the slope to a wooden jetty. Amer held out a hand to help Leo. The bank was steep. He went first.

She took his hand and scrambled down the dusty path unsteadily. His arm felt like rock, as she swayed and stumbled. It also felt electric, as if just by holding on to him, Leo plugged herself in to some powerhouse of energy. She held her breath and did her best to ignore the tingle that his touch sent through her.

Amer seemed unaware of it. Leo did not know whether that was more of a relief or an irritant. How could the man have this effect on her and not know it? But if he did know it what would he do about it?

'Blast,' she said, exasperated.

He looked back at her. 'What was that?'

'Hurriedly she disguised it. 'I turned my ankle over.'

She began limping heavily. Amer came back a couple of steps and put a supporting arm round her, hoisting her with her own petard. It felt like fire.

'Thank you,' said Leo between her teeth.

On the jetty Leo stopped dead.

'It's a dhow,' she exclaimed, half delighted, half alarmed. The little boat did not look stable. She swayed gently against her mooring rope. There was an oil lamp on the prow; no other light but the stars.

Leo edged forward gingerly. And mother warned me not to bump into the furniture, she thought. With my luck I could have the whole boat over.

A sailor greeted them politely before taking the picnic basket on board. Amer turned and gave a few crisp instructions in Arabic to the driver.

Leo peered at the dark interior of the boat. She thought she could see cushions. They seemed a long way down.

The driver vaulted into the Jeep and gunned the engine. Amer turned back and took in Leo's wariness.

'Are you going to tell me you're seasick?' he said, amused.

Leo cast him an harassed look. Nothing was going to serve her but the truth, she realised.

'I am not the best co-ordinated person in the world,' she announced defiantly. 'I was just trying to work out how to get into this thing.'

The jeep roared off. It left behind the starlit dark and the soft slap of the river against the jetty. And the man, now no more than a dark shadow against shadows. It was a warm night. But in the sudden quiet, Leo shivered.

'That's easy,' Amer said softly.

He picked her up.

'Careful,' gasped Leo, clutching him round the neck.

She could feel the ripple of private laughter under her hands. Amer held her high against his chest and stepped down into the boat.

She was right. There were cushions everywhere. Amer

sank gracefully into them. He seemed, thought Leo, to hold on to her for far longer that was necessary. She inhaled the new aroma of expensive laundry and man's skin, all mixed with some elusive cologne that was hardly there and yet which she knew she would never forget.

None of the semidetached men in her life had made her feel like this. Was it because he was, as her mother had called him, a seriously sexy article? Would any woman have felt her pulses race in this situation? Or was it only Leo? Had her cool temperament and shaky experience led her to over-react to an embrace that was not an embrace at all? Somewhere deep inside there was still a clumsy sixteen-year-old who had hung around at the edge of the room at parties, marooned in her own self-consciousness. Had someone found the route to reach her at last?

If so, Leo was far from grateful. She disentangled herself, not without difficulty, and sat up. She pulled her jacket straight and smoothed her hair.

'Thank you,' she said primly.

'My pleasure.'

She believed him. There was a note in his voice that said he was enjoying himself hugely. Leo was suddenly grateful to the darkness. It meant he could not see the colour in her hot cheeks.

She moved along the cushioned seat to leave a small but definite space between them. Amer glanced down, noting it. But he did not object. Instead he called out to the boatman and they pushed off from the side.

The light breeze took them quickly out to midstream. Amer leaned back among his cushions and looked at the stars.

'How is your astronomy?'

'Not very good.'

'Mine is excellent. Let me be your guide.'

Leo looked up reluctantly. It hurt her neck but she was determined not to lounge at her ease as he was doing. She was not going to pretend she felt comfortable when she did not.

Amer began to point out the stars by name. He knew a lot of them. The strain on her neck became intolerable. Almost without realising she was doing it, she eased the pain by sliding down until she, too, was reclining among the cushions. Out of the darkness she thought she caught a gleam of white teeth as he smiled. But he was too clever to offer any comment. Far less to touch her.

Oh boy, am I out of my depth here, thought Leo.

The lamp at the prow swung with the motion of the boat, sending waves of shadow over them as if they were under the river instead of on it. She could hear the soft lapping of the water and the unhurried rhythm of his breathing. Nothing else.

Leo did not take her eyes off the stars. But she knew that Amer was less than a hand's length away from her. She had only to turn her body a fraction and they would be touching. She thought: I have never felt so totally alone with anyone in my whole life.

She became aware of the sound of her own breathing. She shivered a little.

'You are cold,' said Amer, coming to halt in mid-discourse on the starscape.

He sat up and shrugged out of his jacket. Leo turned her head. At that angle she had to look up at him. She caught her breath. For a moment it was as if they lay in a bed, drowsing among habitually shared pillows.

At the thought, her whole body convulsed. She jackknifed upright so violently that the frail craft dipped.

The boatman turned his head with a surprised question. Amer answered him, laughing.

He slid the jacket round her shoulders.

'How jumpy you are.' It sounded like a caress.

To Leo, shaking badly now with reaction, it felt as if he had reached out and run his hand over her flesh, though not an inch of skin was exposed. She huddled his jacket round her. Then realised that it still held the warmth of his body and wished she hadn't.

She swallowed. Loudly.

He did not move any closer. But he reached out a lazy hand and brushed her hair outside his jacket's collar. Leo went very still. It felt as if he owned her.

'Your hair is like silk,' Amer murmured. 'But too short.'

Leo had an involuntary picture of the two of them lying in bed, Amer propped on one elbow, running his free hand through her yards of soft and shining hair. It was so vivid that she almost believed he could see it as well. Her whole body buzzed with shock and embarrassment.

'It used to be long,' she said, her voice too high and fast. 'All through school. I used to be able to sit on it. But when I got older and tried to pin it up, it was too fine. So it was always collapsing. And then my boy friend in college said he couldn't sleep with it, because it was always getting wound round him or getting in his mouth...' She wished she hadn't said that. She was gabbling and she knew it.

Amer held up a hand to stop the flow.

'Don't tell me about other men,' he said in a pained voice.

Leo gasped. The light on the prow swung as the boat tacked. It showed him lounging among the cushions, regarding her quizzically.

'You really don't know how to play this game, do you?'

'What game?' said Leo.

Though she knew. Her racing pulse had been telling her ever since he picked her up and put her in the boat. Now she was almost sure he was smiling in the darkness.

'That's an interesting question,' he said thoughtfully. 'Maybe somewhere between a contest and a carnival. What do you think?'

Leo swallowed. He was right. This was a completely new game for her. She had no idea how to riposte.

'I think I'm in over my head,' she said honestly.

There was a pause as if she had surprised him. Not entirely pleasantly.

Then, 'Hey. You're supposed to be enjoying yourself, you know.'

Amer moved. At once her muscles clenched. She was burningly conscious of his body. He was so close, she could sense the latent power of him. And it was not fear that kept her alert and trembling, she realised.

But he was only stretching, making himself more comfortable. He put his arms behind his head and looked up at her thoughtfully. As the light swung again, she saw that he had pushed up the sleeves of his shirt. The brief glimpse of muscular forearms did unwelcome things to her stomach.

The boat tacked again and the light swung in the other direction. Leo tried to gasp for air quietly. She had not realised she was holding her breath.

She cleared her throat. 'Where are we going? I mean, is this it?'

Amer gave a soft laugh.

'Hungry are you?'

Leo decided to assume he was talking about food.

'Well breakfast was at five o'clock this morning and I haven't eaten since,' she told him.

'Good grief.' He sounded genuinely horrified. 'We must do something about that at once.'

He said something in quick Arabic to the boatman. The boat turned.

'What happened?' Amer demanded. 'The revenge of the unreasonable boss?'

Leo shook her head, laughing. 'Nope. That's normal at this time of year.'

'It sounds like slavery. Why do you do it?'

Leo felt better now they were discussing an ordinary subject at last. She could do polite conversation, she thought ruefully. It was subtle sexual repartee that defeated her.

'It's my job,' she said.

'Why did you choose a job like that?'

Leo thought about her father's announcement of her two-year assignment.

'Well, the job sort of found me,' she said ruefully. 'My chief told me where I was going. I didn't get a vote.'

'Then you should have looked for a new job with a more modern chief.' He sounded impatient.

Leo bridled at his tone.

'It's easy to say that if you have an infinite range of choices open to you. Most of us don't.'

Amer gave a bark of laughter. 'No one has infinite choice. Most people have fewer than you think.'

'Are you telling me that you're a slave of circumstance, too?' Leo challenged him mockingly.

He did not like that. He said curtly, 'We are not talking about me.'

And that, she thought, sounded like an order.

The boat was skirting a small island. It came to rest against the bank. The boatman moored it fore and aft and lowered the sail. He unhooked the lamp from the prow and brought it down to them.

Amer motioned to him to set out the picnic basket. Then waved him away. The man leaped over the side of the boat and disappeared into the darkness. All Leo's returning confidence went with him.

She thought Amer would expect her to unpack the basket and serve the food. But he did not. Instead he filled warm ovals of pitta bread with a deliciously aromatic salad and gave one to her. Watching his deft movements, Leo thought: He thinks if he left it to me, I'd drop the food all over the cushions. The truth was she thought so, too. It added to her constraint.

'Thank you,' she said in a subdued voice.

She sat up, curling her legs under her, away from him.

'Drink?'

There was tea, sherbet, juices. Leo chose water and drank a whole glassful.

Amer raised an amused eyebrow. 'You've got a real desert thirst there.'

'Anxiety always makes me thirsty,' Leo said unwarily.

He grimaced. 'Ouch.'

'What? Oh.' She bit her lip. 'That sounded rude. I didn't mean—'

'I think we both know what you meant,' he said drily.

Now the soft light was at their end of the boat and hardly swaying at all, he would see her blush. Leo cursed her porcelain-pale skin. It was always giving her away.

She said stiffly, 'I'm sorry.'

Amer did not answer for a moment. Leo hesitated; then dared a look at him under her eyelashes. His expression was unreadable.

'You're an education,' he said at last. 'I'm very much afraid that Hari was right.'

Leo was confused. 'Who's Hari?'

He gave an unexpected laugh. 'But then, I was right, too,' he went on unheeding. 'You're nobody's toy, are you? You're your own person. Right through to the beautiful frankness.'

Leo knew she was being mocked and did not like it. 'I've said I'm sorry,' she muttered.

'Don't be sorry.' He was amused again. 'You should be proud to be a truth teller. There aren't so many of them around.'

Leo wished she had her glasses to hide behind. In their absence, she munched on the pitta.

It was odd. She should have been starving after the turbulent day. But the last thing she wanted was food. If Amer would only stop looking at her like that, as if he had never seen anything like her, she would have turned away from the food with relief.

But Amer continued to play the attentive host, offering her delicacies from the basket and keeping up a steady flow of informative conversation. The Nile, the desert sky, ancient temples, modern dams—he covered them all while Leo worked her way stolidly through more calories than she cared to count. Eventually he gave her a thimbleful of thin, sharp coffee and said, 'Your turn.'

It was the moment Leo had been dreading. 'My, er, turn?'

'Talk to me,' he commanded.

'What—' Her voice wavered. She took command of it and started again. 'What shall I talk about?'

He gave a soft laugh. 'It is usual to start with whatever you want the other party to know about you.'

'But I *don't* want you to know anything about me,' Leo said unguardedly. There was more truth in that than she would have been willing to admit, if she had thought about it.

Amer took it calmly. 'Then tell me what I want to know.'

'Like what?' said Leo warily.

'Like where you come from. How you ended up in Cairo. How the men in your life like it.'

Leo considered. Nothing too private there, she thought.

So she said readily enough, 'I come from London—well a suburb of London. My company is basically an international hotel chain. They diversified into other leisure areas, including this local travel agency, and sent me out here for two years. To get experience of work at the coal face, so to speak. I've been here just over a year. Eventually I'll go back to Head Office.' She sighed. 'After the row with Roy sooner rather than later.'

'And the men in your life?' he prompted.

'Ah.'

Well, it was not *private,* exactly but Leo was not sure she wanted to discuss her romantic failures with this unreadable man. On the other hand, her father had taught her that the truth was never damaging. And after tonight she would never see Mr Amer again.

She squared her shoulders and said cheerfully, 'No men.'

His eyes narrowed. She caught the flicker of long lashes against the dark.

'Not even—what did you call him?—Roy?' he asked. He did not sound very interested. His tone was almost idle.

She gave a snort of laughter at the thought.

Amer did not share her amusement. 'So how did he man-

age to throw you out of your flat?' he demanded, swift as a
striking snake.

It shocked her into silence.

'I asked you if you lived with him, if you remember. You
did not answer then, either.'

Leo had the sudden impression of fierce anger. She
searched the shadowed face. He did not say any more but
his silence was somehow relentless.

She said hurriedly, 'It was a company flat.'

Still he did not say anything.

Leo found her tone was placating, as if he had accused her
of something. 'We go out of Cairo so much with the tourist
parties that it's not worth having a flat each. We all share.
Roy, Vanessa, Kevin, anyone else that comes out. Truly. Roy
wasn't there most of the time.'

Amer digested this for a moment. 'Not much privacy then,'
he said at last.

To Leo's relief it seemed as if he was no longer angry.
Instead he sounded thoughtful. 'Is that the reason?'

'Reason?' Leo echoed, puzzled.

She caught the flash of white as he smiled. 'You said there
were no men in your life,' he reminded her.

'Oh that!'

She was oddly relieved that he had decided to believe her.
What could it matter whether a stranger trusted her word,
after all? She would never see him again after tonight. But
she was glad and she knew it.

'Yes *that*,' he mimicked her, teasing. 'If there are no men
in your life there has to be a reason.'

And he was going to persist until she told him. Leo sighed
and gave him the truth.

'I don't really *work* with men, if you know what I mean.
Never have. Not really. Drives my mother mad.'

She felt him considering it. She gave him a quick, bright
smile. But she could not sustain it. Her eyes slid away from
him before she could read his expression.

He said thoughtfully, 'Does that mean you are not attracted to men?'

Leo was startled. 'Oh *no*. Well, at least, I haven't thought about it much. I've had a couple of sort of relationships. Pretty low-grade stuff. The guys walked away after a bit and to be honest it was a relief. I don't think I'm designed to stroke the male ego. Well not for long.'

Amer stiffened. 'There is more to a relationship between a man and a woman than ego stroking.'

'Is there?' Leo said drily. 'Didn't seem that way to me.'

This time she managed to look at him for longer. There was no doubt she had annoyed him. He was still smiling but his displeasure was tangible.

Leo was surprised; and then amused. Amer must have thought she would turn to toffee under his stylish not-quite-seduction. It was pleasant to have knocked his assumptions off course, however slightly.

He said shortly, 'It sounds as if you have been unfortunate in your encounters.'

Leo shrugged. 'No, I'd say it was pretty standard.'

'On the basis of—what did you call them?—a couple of low-grade relationships?'

She looked at him ironically. 'I don't just know about my own mistakes. Girls talk you know.'

'In that case,' Amer said triumphantly, 'you must know that most girls these days would have more than a couple of unsatisfactory experiments to base their theories on.'

'Ah but most girls keep on trying. They've got to. They want to marry.'

Amer was taken aback.

'And you don't?'

Leo shifted her shoulders. In her head she could hear Deborah saying anxiously, 'Darling, how on earth do you think you're going to get married if you go on like this?' She managed not to wince.

'I'd say the odds are against it,' she said evenly.

Amer noticed the evasion. 'You mean you *do* want to but

you don't think it's going to happen.' He sounded a lot more content with that.

It made Leo furious. She sat bolt upright, rocking the small craft again with the violence of the movement.

'Look,' she said, 'I said I'd have dinner with you. I didn't agree to be dissected because you happen to have a nasty taste in dinner party conversation.'

'Is that what I've been doing?' He sounded startled and not very pleased.

There was a pause while he considered it. Then he said in amusement, 'All right. Take your revenge. I'll tell you anything you want to know.'

'No, thank you,' said Leo distantly. 'I don't want to dissect you, either.'

He shook his head, still deeply amused. 'Still telling the truth? Not great tactics—but very impressive.'

'Thank you,' said Leo, not meaning it.

He stretched. The fine cotton stretched, too, across taut muscles. Leo remembered how those muscles had felt under her fingers when he put her into the boat and her mouth was suddenly dry.

'Look at that moon,' Amer said, unheeding. He sounded as self-congratulatory as if he had arranged it personally, Leo thought.

She looked up. The moon was not quite full, a champagne sorbet among all the diamond chips. She thought she had never seen it so clear or the sky so close. It made her feel slightly dazed. She closed her eyes against the whirling sensation.

Amer said softly, 'Puts human nonsense in perspective, doesn't it?'

Leo opened her mouth to demand whether her views fell into the category of human nonsense. Only then she opened her eyes. And found herself looking straight into his. The whirling sensation increased.

Hardly knowing what she did, she subsided among the cushions. She could not take her eyes off him.

Amer did not touch her. He did not even lean over her, though his eyes scanned her face intently.

'Yes,' he said, as if he was answering something she said.

Leo thought: I want him. He knows I want him. I've never felt like this before in my life. I didn't know I could feel like this.

He lowered himself until he was leaning on his elbow among the cushions, looking down at her. Leo felt as if he could see straight through her. He saw the defences; went through them to her galloping confusion; smiled, and went through that, too, right into her soul.

She went very still. They were as close as lovers. But still he did not touch.

She had thought she was immune. It was other girls who waited sleepless by the phone. Other girls who held their breath when their man looked at them.

Leo thought: their man? *Their* man? I am laying claim to this man, now? When he hasn't even kissed me? I don't even want him to kiss me. Do I?

The boatman was coming back. She heard his friendly greeting. Felt the small movement in the boat as he came aboard.

Amer did not move. Nor did Leo. She could feel her eyes widening, widening...

The boatman was busying himself with the sail.

Amer said softly, 'Shall I tell him to go away again and leave us alone for a couple of hours?'

The studded sky wheeled behind his head.

'I don't know what you mean.' Leo spoke with difficulty.

He was so close she could feel his little puffed breath of frustration. She thought: Why doesn't he touch me? But still he did not.

Instead he murmured, 'That's the first lie you've ever told me.'

She felt a sort of agony at his words.

She thought: No matter what happens now, I'm never going to be the same after this.

She held her breath. But Amer rolled aside and sat up. He gave the boatman a few orders and did not sound annoyed. He did not sound as if he cared very much at all.

Leo let out her breath very carefully. The men talked rapidly. Then the boatman packed the debris of their meal back into the picnic basket. Leo swung her legs aside and sat up, setting the boat rocking wildly. Probably for the first time in her life, she did not apologise. She was too wound up.

She smoothed her hair with a shaking hand. Every tiny area of exposed skin at neck and wrists quivered where the soft breeze brushed against it. She had never been so intensely aware of sensation before; nor of her own sensuality. Never realised so totally that she was a physical creature. Never *wanted*…

Leo halted her thoughts abruptly at that point. Never wanted what? she asked herself fiercely. Amer? Nonsense. Crazy nonsense.

She straightened, folding her hands in her lap. She did not care if she looked prim. She did not care what Amer thought of her at all. She suddenly, desperately, wanted to get back to her room and take stock of what had happened to her.

At least she had not reached for him, Leo thought. She thanked Heaven for that.

Leo was monosyllabic on the return journey. Amer did not push her. He was very much at his ease, courteous but slightly distant. When they entered the hotel he thanked her formally for her company and wished her good-night.

Leo shook hands. 'Thank you,' she said as politely as if he were one of Adventures in Time's regular bus drivers.

Her tone clearly amused him.

'We will meet soon,' he assured her.

Leo had not told him that she was expecting to fly out imminently. She did not tell him now. She just gave him a meaningless smile and headed for the lifts.

Hari knew that the evening had not been a success the moment that Amer walked into the suite. One look at the

Sheikh's face and Hari decided to keep the conversation strictly professional.

'Report of various conversations I had before the dinner,' he said, handing over a slim folder. 'Extract of speeches.' That was a substantial ring binder. 'Oh and a message from His Majesty.' An envelope from the hotel's fax bureau.

'My father can wait,' said Amer, showing his teeth.

Hari did not comment, though he knew what the old Sheikh's views would be if anyone reported that back to him.

'The South of France,' Hari said, consulting his notes. 'I've booked flights for Paris on Thursday. I thought you'd want to stop over.'

Amer was frowning. 'Hold on that for the moment,' he said curtly.

'You want to stay for the reception at the end of the conference?' asked Hari, surprised.

Amer shrugged. 'Maybe.' He paused, his frown dissolving into a speculative look. 'I've got unfinished business in Cairo.'

Hari hid a smile. 'Didn't she like the picnic?' he asked innocently.

'She—' Amer bit it off. 'She is not entirely what I expected. Nor was the evening, for that matter.'

Hari chuckled. 'That's what comes of not telling her who you are.'

Amer shook his head slowly. 'I don't think so. She is unusual. I don't think that would have made any difference at all.'

'In that case, she's not unusual, she's unique,' said the cynical Hari.

Amer was surprised into a sudden laugh. 'You could be right,' he said. He clapped Hari on the shoulder. 'Intriguing, isn't it?'

Leo was not sure whether it was too late to check on Mrs Silverstein. She compromised by knocking very softly on the lady's door. There was no answer.

Oh well, thought Leo, she was probably asleep. She was turning away when one of the hotel staff came running out of the service door. The lady had called room service asking for ice, he said. Then when they tried to deliver it, she had not opened the door.

'When was this?' said Leo with foreboding.

Just ten minutes ago. They had knocked several times.

'Have you got a pass key?'

He nodded.

'Then let's go and see what's happened.'

He was clearly relieved at this decision. He opened the door for Leo.

Mrs Silverstein was lying on the carpet in the main body of the room. Her fall had overturned the coffee table and sent Arabic sweetmeats flying. Her forehead was clammy and she had the beginnings of an almighty bruise on her cheek. But, Leo established, she was breathing.

She summoned a doctor, warning him that the patient would need to be admitted to a clinic fast. He arrived with an ambulance and paramedics and put Mrs Silverstein on oxygen immediately. Leo went with the stretcher.

In the lobby light, Mrs Silverstein opened her eyes. She looked anxious. Leo took her hand.

'It's all right,' she said reassuringly. 'I'm here.'

The weak eyes blinked and focused.

'Looking good,' said Mrs Silverstein, rallying a bit. 'Hot date?'

Leo smiled down at her. 'I've been out to dinner,' she tempered.

'Anyone I know?'

'A guest in the hotel.' Well, it sounded better than pick up, Leo thought ruefully. 'A Mr Amer.'

A beatific smile curved Mrs Silverstein's cherubic lips.

'Sheikh.'

Leo stumbled. 'What?'

'Sheikh Amer el Barbary,' said Mrs Silverstein with satisfaction. 'I looked him up.'

Leo stopped dead and stared. Slow realisation dawned. It was followed by horror.

He had lied to her. Deliberately misled her. Invited her to ask him questions, knowing she wouldn't, when he had already withheld the most important piece of information. Oh what an idiot, he must think her. What an idiot she *was*.

Mrs Silverstein's stretcher was disappearing through the door. Leo broke into a run.

CHAPTER FOUR

SIX months later, Leo could still feel the shock of that real-isation. It could bring her awake in the middle of the night, cold with embarrassment. And, at the same time, hot with longing. Which, of course, made the embarrassment worse and did nothing at all for her self-respect.

God knows what she would have said to him, if she had come face-to-face with Amer again. But she did not. Mrs Silverstein needed to be accompanied back to the States. As Leo was leaving Egypt anyway, she jumped at the chance to leave at once.

So now she was in London, trying to restart her life. Without much success.

'What's wrong?' said her friend Claire Hartley, as Leo drove her down to spend the weekend with the Hartley family. 'Missing the pyramids?'

'Not missing one damn thing,' said Leo with rather more emphasis than the casual remark required.

Claire digested this in silence as Leo concentrated on getting through the one way system. Eventually they got onto the motorway and Claire said, 'You've been seeing a lot of brother Simon, haven't you?'

Leo cast her a quick look of surprise. 'Only at work.'

'You went to the Nightingale Ball with him,' Claire reminded her.

Leo grimaced. 'That's work.'

'Then he's got nothing to do with your being glad to be home?'

'I didn't say I was glad to be home,' Leo said patiently. 'I said I didn't miss Cairo. There's a difference.'

'Oh,' said Claire enlightened. 'What happened in Cairo?'

She thought about it. 'Or should I say who happened in Cairo?'

Leo winced. An Arab prince had amused himself for an evening by offering a humble courier a night of high romance and princely luxury. Because that was all it had been for him, an amusement. Leo saw it clearly. That refusal to touch her which had set all her senses aflame and still shot through her dreams, only showed how little he cared whether she responded to him or not.

'That just about covers it,' she said with harsh self-mockery.

Claire had not heard that note in her voice before. 'What happened?'

'One minute I was an independent woman with a small local career problem and no roof over my head. The next—the aliens invaded.'

Claire slewed round on the leather seat and stared at her friend.

'What sort of aliens?'

'Rich, royal and thoroughly irresponsible aliens,' Leo said bitterly. 'Well, one alien.' She ground her teeth, remembering.

Claire was amazed. 'He really hit the spot, didn't he? New experience for you, Mrs Cool.'

Leo's smile was wry. Her reputation for indifference to the opposite sex had started long ago. At her boarding school dances to be precise. Gawky as she was, taller than most of boys and painfully shy, Leo found the best way to deal with being teased was to pretend that she did not care. Neither Claire nor anyone else ever detected the truth. They just thought Leo was too level-headed to suffer the traumas of adolescence. If only they knew!

'Amer el-Barbary would be a new experience for anyone.'

'Sounds like fun,' Claire said enviously. 'Tell.'

Leo looked at the long road ahead of them. In the sun it looked like a stream of melting black toffee. She sighed. It was going to be a long journey.

She told.

Claire was astounded. When Leo finished she sat in stunned silence for a moment. She shook her head in disbelief.

'And you didn't even write to him?'

'What would I have said?' Leo snapped. 'Thank you for an illuminating evening? By the way, I hope this finds you as you didn't bother to give me your real name?'

'There could have been all sorts of reasons for that,' protested Claire.

Leo was more suspicious than her friend. 'Like what?'

'Well, maybe he thought you wouldn't go out with him if you knew he was terribly grand.'

Leo said something very rude. Claire grinned. 'No. All right. Well how about this one—he wanted you to go out with him as a man and not his position in the world.'

Leo snorted. 'I don't believe in fairy stories. He just thought it was amusing to hand me a smooth line. In fact—' for a moment her expression lightened '—he got very annoyed when I didn't respond as predicted.'

'Did he say so?'

'He said we would meet soon,' Leo admitted reluctantly.

Claire made an exasperated noise. 'So you ran away to America with an eighty-year-old widow. Honestly, Leo, I despair of you.' She added curiously, 'Hasn't he tried to get in touch with you?'

'It wouldn't do him any good if he did. All my records have gone from the Cairo office. Nobody there knew who I was. I used my grandmother's name.'

'The office could still forward mail, presumably.'

'I told you,' Leo said patiently, 'they don't know there's anyone to forward it to. None of the staff there know that Miss Roberts is the boss's daughter, Miss Groom.'

Claire shook her head, dissatisfied with this ending to the romance. 'If you saw him again—'

'I'd spit in his eye,' Leo said militantly.

Claire was a good friend but she was not noted for her

tact. 'But it sounds as if you were half-way to falling in love with the guy.'

'Love,' said Leo ferociously, 'is the biggest fairy story of the lot.'

'Most people expect to fall in love at some time or other.' Claire's tone was dry.

Unbidden, Amer's triumphant voice said in her ear, 'You mean you do want to but you don't think it's going to happen.' Admittedly he had been talking about marriage not love. But Leo flushed as violently as if he had been there in the car with them and reading her thoughts.

'Not me,' she said very loudly.

The Trustee of the el-Barbary charitable foundation was having a bad time. Normally Sheikh Amer was more approachable than the old Sheikh. But on this visit he was proving even more difficult than his autocratic father: elusive, pre-occupied and now downright irritable. He was tapping his gold fountain pen on his papers as if he could hardly bear to sit through the meeting a minute more.

'Several matters for Sheikh Amer's personal attention.'

Amer did not bother to disguise his impatience. 'Give the list to my assistant.'

The Trustee did not hear. 'Dinner at your college. Oh, I see you've already accepted that. Reception at the Science Museum to launch the second phase of the Antika Research Project. They have asked—'

Amer's face was thunderous. Hari intervened swiftly.

'Shall I deal with those?' he suggested in a soothing voice.

The Trustee handed them over, relieved. But he was a conscientious man.

'Antika have asked if His Excellency will contribute something to their book.'

Amer looked as if he were going to explode.

The Trustee began to gabble. 'Fund-raising. They're bringing out a collection of essays by celebrity sponsors. As His

Excellency is Chairman... They say all the other board members have written something...'

There was a dangerous pause.

Then, 'Get the details,' Amer told Hari curtly. He stood up. 'That concludes the meeting, gentlemen. I have an appointment now, but I hope to join you for lunch later. Hari will show you where to go.'

Hari marshalled them out.

Amer got up and moved restlessly round the room. When a tall, quiet man was shown in, he looked round. His visitor was shocked. There were deep new lines at the corner of the Sheikh's eyes and when he smiled you could see that it was an effort.

'Major McDonald.' He held out his hand. 'Good of you to come. I need your help.'

He explained succinctly.

'I've had the sharpest private detectives that money can buy digging into it for six months. The woman has disappeared,' he concluded.

'No,' said the Major with quiet confidence, 'they have just not looked for her in the right way. You're sure she's English?'

'Yes.'

'Then let me use my contacts. I'll find her for you.'

Amer went to the window and looked out. The city street looked like a mineral maze in the spring sunshine. He said to the pavement below, 'If you find her, you bring the information straight to me. You don't tell her. Or anyone else.'

The Major was surprised into indiscretion. 'Are things so explosive in Dalmun, then?'

Amer turned back and smiled. It was not a pleasant smile. 'It is not Dalmun which is explosive,' he said in a matter-of-fact voice. 'It's me. This one is *mine*.'

The weekend with the Hartleys did not turn out as Leo expected. She thought it was going to be a relaxed, family affair, mowing lawns and cleaning swimming pools. She could not have been more wrong.

There was a dinner party on Friday night, when she and Claire got down there; a lunch party—'Just close friends, darling'—on Saturday; a sailing club dance on Saturday evening to which the entire household and their guest were expected to turn up; and a drinks party for over a hundred before lunch on Sunday. In between whiles Simon's mother, a cut-glass blonde, took her on a guided tour of the family pile. It was crumbling and, in Leo's view, badly in need of being turned into a conference centre. Simon's baronet father walked her through several acres of formal garden, equally neglected.

And Simon. Well, she did not know what Simon was doing at all. Except that he kept getting her on her own and telling her how well he got on with her father.

By Sunday afternoon, Leo was feeling breathless, uneasy and her wardrobe had given out.

'Shouldn't we be going back to London?' she whispered to Claire.

Lady Hartley, whose hearing would have roused envy in a bat, intervened.

'Simon, darling. You haven't shown Leo the river. Why don't you go now? You might see a kingfisher.'

'Who are the Kingfishers?' said Leo nervously.

Simon stood up, laughing. 'It's all right. The feathered kind. No more socialising, I promise.'

'Thank God for that,' said Leo.

'Is it like this every weekend?' she asked as they walked up the hill behind the house.

Simon shook his head. 'Mum wanted to make sure you had a good time.'

'Is that why I feel like I've been heavily marketed to?' Leo mused. She saw Simon's expression and said remorsefully, 'Oh I'm so sorry. That was a stupid thing to say. Of course your mother wasn't marketing. What would she be selling, after all?'

But Simon was a gentleman.

'Me, I'm afraid,' he said quietly.

Leo was deprived of speech.

Simon took her hand again and held it in a steady clasp.

'I won't pretend any nonsense, Leo. I respect you too much for that. Anyway, you'd see through it. The family fortunes have pretty much hit rock bottom, you see. The only way out is an injection of capital from—well—'

'Me,' said Leo. She still felt bewildered. 'Do they want to sell? I mean, I can see this place has potential. But would your parents really like to see it as part of the Groom Hotel chain? Anyway, they'd be better talking to my father or the Head of UK Operations than me.'

Simon looked down at their clasped hands. His expression was rueful.

'It's not the house they want to sell.' And as Leo still stared at him, brows knit in confusion, he said roughly, 'They want me to ask you to marry me.'

'*What?*'

Simon dropped her hand. 'There's no need to sound so shocked. You must have realised.'

'I—' Leo felt a fool. What was it Amer had said? *You don't know how to play this game, do you?* Oh boy, was he right. 'I'm sorry,' she said quietly. 'I didn't know.'

Simon looked wretched. 'I thought at least your father would have hinted...'

'My father—?'

And then she saw, quite suddenly, what it was all about. Why Gordon Groom had brought Simon to Cairo; why her mother had asked about her feelings for him all those months ago; why ever since she got back she had been pushing files around her office trying to find the job that her father assured her was there.

Fool. Fool. *Double* fool. If you want a son and heir and all you have is an ugly duckling daughter, buy her an amenable husband and go for the next generation.

'There never was a career for me at Grooms, was there?'

said Leo. She was not talking to Simon. 'It was just to keep
me quiet until I got married.' She did not know which was
worse, the hurt or the humiliation.

Simon did not seem to notice. He nodded, relieved. 'Will
you?'

She wanted to scream. She wanted to cry. She wanted to
rage at the Heavens. She wanted to tell her father exactly
what she thought of him before stamping out of his house
and his nonjob.

But none of that was Simon's fault and Leo was fair
minded to a fault.

'No, I won't marry you,' she said quite gently.

Simon was taken aback. After all, thought Leo savagely,
he worked for Gordon Groom, too.

'I won't give up hope,' he assured her kindly.

And then she did scream.

'Well,' said Amer in quiet satisfaction, 'you said you'd do it
and you have. I'm impressed.'

Major McDonald shrugged. 'I put my team on it. The stat-
istician pointed out that Leonora is so unusual it doesn't even
get recorded in most profiles of first names. Add that bit of
information to someone who was able to hide her identity
from the start of her arrival in Cairo, and you've got a spy,
a criminal or an offspring of the seriously rich. Fortunately
for you, she is the latter.'

'Fortunate indeed,' agreed Amer affably.

He showed his teeth in a smile that made the Major wonder
what Leonora Groom had done. He liked and admired Amer
but, just for a moment, he felt almost sorry for the woman.

Amer flipped open the file.

'Leonora Groom,' he said. He rolled it round his mouth
like a fine wine. 'Leonora Groom.'

'There's only one picture,' the Major pointed out. 'At the
Antika opening. She seems to keep out of the photographers'
way, even at these charity receptions. It's almost as if she
wants to stay anonymous.'

'As you say,' Amer agreed suavely.

He was very angry. How dared she lie to him? She had strung him along like some negligible tourist.

A small voice reminded him that he had been less than candid with her, too. He had not even told her his full name, after all. He ignored it and closed the dossier decisively.

'Hari will settle your account. Goodbye and thank you.'

Hari handed over a substantial cheque and showed the Major out. He came back to Amer. He was surprised to find that he was bent over his desk writing fast and he did not like the look of his friend's expression at all.

'What are you going to do?' he said in trepidation.

Amer narrowed his eyes at the paper in front of him. He gave a soft laugh. It made Hari's blood run cold.

'Need you ask? Make her come to me, of course.'

Leo intended to have the whole thing out with her father as soon as she got back. Only she had forgotten that he was away on an extended trip trying to rescue his Far East operation. In his absence it almost seemed as if she had a real job after all.

So she stayed.

May came, sending long tendrils of engulfing wisteria all over the front of the Wimbledon house. In the morning Leo sniffed the heady scent in pure pleasure. But at night, in the dark, it recalled another night, when you could see the stars and the only scent was a man's skin and unfamiliar cologne. She would remember that cologne for ever.

'Don't think about him,' she told herself fiercely. 'Just—don't—*think*.'

But it was not easy with Simon calling regularly, pointing out that she liked him—didn't she?—and she wasn't committed to anybody else. He did not phrase that, Leo noted wryly, as a question. And anyway, she could hardly say that she was haunted by the shadow of a man whose body never touched hers.

In the effort of not thinking about that, Leo ripped through all the work she could find and looked around for more. This turn of events terrorised her secretary to such an extent that when a cardboard parcel arrived by courier, Joanne rushed it into her office as if it was a communication from Mars.

Leo considered it without interest. 'Looks like a souvenir programme of some sort,' she said indifferently.

'But *biked over*,' said Joanne, impressed.

Leo shrugged.

'Okay. Open up and see what it is.'

But Joanne was doomed to disappointment. 'It's just that book of essays the Antika Project were putting together. Mr Groom got one of the PR writers to do it for him.' She flicked through the index. 'Yes here it is. "Gordon Groom on how to ruin a hotel." It was funny.'

Leo was mildly interested. Her father was not noted for his sense of humour.

'That's what they asked for,' explained Joanne. 'Everyone was supposed to write a piece sending themselves up.' She ran her finger down the index. '"Food Poisonous Food" by the Chef of the Year. "Come With Me To The Casbah" by Sheikh Amer el-Barbary. "Heartthrobs Don't Get Measles" by Jeremy Derringer.' She looked up. 'What?'

'Run that by me again,' said Leo. She was very pale, suddenly.

'"Heartthrobs Don't Get Measles"', said Joanne obligingly. 'Do you know Jeremy Derringer then? Gosh, he's gorgeous.'

Leo did not answer. She put out a shaking hand for the book. Joanne gave it to her. Leo did not even notice when Joanne left the room.

Amer had enjoyed writing the article. He had started it in a white hot rage with Leo. How dared she challenge him like that when all the time she knew she was deceiving him about her identity? And then to run away, covering her tracks so totally that he had the devil's own job to find her! She knew he had intended to see her again. How dared she disappear, without so much as a word of regret? He was going to bring her back on her *knees*.

But then, as he wrote, Amer's fury began to dissipate in sheer amusement. He finished it at a tearing rate. Then he sent it off before he could have second thoughts.

Leo, of course, did not know that. But she did know Amer. As she read, she could hear his gleeful voice. That arrogant cynicism stretched a mocking arm off the printed page and tweaked her nose until tears started.

"Rudolf Valentino has much to answer for," Amer had written enjoyably. "He gave women what they wanted. Then said it was to be found in men of the desert. For those of us who carry this terrible responsibility, I suggest a few tips."

What followed was a precise outline of his strategy for their evening together. He had forgotten nothing. Not lifting her into the boat. Not her reluctant capitulation to the comfort of the cushions. Not putting his jacket round her shoulders. Leo shivered to remember it. That made her even more furious. Not—oh God, her heart beat in an agony of shame as she remembered—her mesmerised unsophistication.

'You really don't know how to play this game, do you?' he had said. And there it was in black and white.

"Never forget you are taking them on an exotic journey through their own fantasies."

'Oh *no,*' moaned Leo.

"Stay in charge. They will accept any rules you lay down, however lunatic. It is what they secretly want. Only they cannot bear to admit it."

Leo put the article down. 'I'll kill him,' she said aloud. For a moment she could almost believe she meant it.

She flung the book so hard across the room that its spine split. *Good,* thought Leo. She was shaking and very cold. She felt as if he had stripped her publicly.

How many women had he taken on his Nile fantasy? she thought savagely. How many had he looked at in that way until they started to shake with tension? While all the time he was laughing at them.

Leo hugged her arms round herself protectively. It was like the worst of her adolescence, all over again. The painfully acquired assurance counted for nothing. Suddenly she was awkward, clumsy, unsubtle and plain. No man would look at her, ever.

Except Simon. He might not be in love with her, but he liked her. He even respected her, for God's sake. And he was honest about it.

Leo picked up the phone.

Amer took breakfast in the conservatory of his Mayfair house. He basked in the warmth of sun filtering through glass, while he sipped orange juice and leafed through the morning papers. He was not, he assured himself, waiting for anything. Just because Leo would have had the booklet with his article in it four days ago was no reason to stretch his ears for the burr of the telephone.

Still, the Embassy had been briefed that Miss Groom was, exceptionally, to be given his private London number. And no one could say that the papers were gripping. Amer reached the 'Forthcoming Marriages' column without interest and was on the point of turning that page, too, when—

The crystal glass fell from his hand, scattering shards and orange juice all over the marble floor.

She could not have done it; she was not stupid. She *could* not.

But it was there. Irrefutably. "Leonora Jane, only daughter of Gordon Groom of the Wisteria House Wimbledon and Mrs Deborah Groom of Kensington, W8 to Mr Simon Hartley, eldest son of Sir Donald and Lady Hartley of Seren Place, Devon."

She had got herself engaged.

'I'll kill her,' yelled Amer.

CHAPTER FIVE

LEO rang her father in Singapore to tell him that she and Simon were engaged. Gordon Groom's reaction startled her.

'At last.'

'Excuse me?'

'It's taken you long enough. Still, he's a good lad and I'm pleased.'

Why did it sound like the approval he used to dole out when she came home with a good school report?

'Thank you for your good wishes,' said Leo drily.

'I'm going into a meeting. Tell Hartley I'll call him tomorrow eight o' clock UK time.' He rang off.

'Yes, I'm sure we'll be very happy,' Leo said to the buzzing phone. She flung it back onto its stand and attacked her In box as if it was a personal enemy.

Maybe her mother would react more normally, when they had their girls' lunch, she thought.

But, unlike Gordon, Deborah disapproved and made no bones about it.

'You can't fool me,' Deborah announced. She knocked back a gin and tonic as if it was medicine. 'This is your father's doing.'

Leo shook her head. 'Pops hasn't done anything. Simon asked me to marry him. I said yes. That's all. I did think about it first, Ma.'

Deborah looked at her with tragic eyes. She had just come from a whole morning at her favourite Bond Street beautician and her exquisite make-up enhanced the tragic vulnerability. Leo's feet felt like boats. Under the table, she shuffled them. Her mother took no notice.

'*Think,*' she said dramatically. 'If you're in love you don't

73

think. You just *fly*.' Her gloved hands made a large gesture similar to a plant bursting into flower.

It was all too reminiscent of childhood dance classes. Leo looked over her shoulder to check that no passing waiter had had to dodge Deborah's expressiveness.

'Come on, Ma. Keep the music and movement down.'

Deborah blinked the long silky lashes which were the only feature she had bequeathed to her daughter.

'You're laughing at me. You don't know how serious this is.'

'I take getting married very seriously,' Leo said stiffly.

Deborah ignored that. 'Have you been to bed with him yet?'

'Mother!'

'I thought not,' said Deborah, pleased with herself. 'Don't you think that's odd? If he is in love with you, I mean.'

'He's not in love with me,' Leo said quietly.

That stopped Deborah as nothing else would have done. 'Oh, Leo. Oh, darling.'

'Ma, you're barking up the wrong tree.' Leo leaned forward and spoke earnestly. 'It really was my decision. Simon doesn't love me and I don't love him. But we have a lot in common. It will work out.'

Deborah looked as if she was going to cry.

Leo thought desperately for something to reassure her. 'He tells me the truth.'

It did not have the effect she expected. Her mother sat bolt upright.

'Tells you the truth?'

'Yes.'

'The truth about what?'

It was unexpected. Leo floundered. 'Well who he is. What he feels. What he wants.'

Deborah put her head on one side. 'So who doesn't?'

Leo was scornful. 'Oh come on, Ma. You know more about men than I do. You know they play games. Tie you up in knots. And not one damn thing they tell you is true.'

She stopped. She realised that Deborah's eyes were uncomfortably shrewd.

'Are we talking about the man who told you to grow your hair?' her mother asked interestedly.

Leo could have thrown something. 'What do you mean?'

'You've cut your hair like a space helmet for years. Then suddenly it's on your shoulders. Looks good, too. So someone has been giving you style advice. Who is he?'

Leo tensed. 'No one. You're imagining it, Ma.'

She spoke more curtly than she meant to. Deborah's eyebrows flew up. Leo was never curt with her.

'He hurt you,' she said on a note of discovery.

'Nonsense.'

Deborah ignored that. 'Darling, we all get hurt sometimes. Men,' she said largely, 'don't *think*. That doesn't mean...'

But Leo was not listening. She gave a harsh laugh.

'Some of them think. Some of them think a whole lot. In fact, they have a tried and trusted plan of campaign ready for use on any woman they come across.'

Deborah stared. 'But—'

'*Any* woman,' Leo said with emphasis.

'Oh, darling,' said Deborah with compunction, 'you haven't fallen for a Don Juan? Not you?'

'I haven't fallen for anyone,' said Leo furiously. 'And I'm not going to.'

'Well, lucky old Simon,' said Deborah.

None of which sent Leo back to the office any happier. She was still fuming when she sat down and applied herself to her e-mail. Almost at once she found a name that added fuel to the fire.

Quickly she paged through the list of the day's callers. He had called again. And again. And—

She buzzed Joanne.

'I'm looking at my message list. Tell me about Sheikh el-Barbary. What did he want?'

Amer was in a cold rage.

'Are you telling me she won't take my call?' he demanded.

Hari shrugged. He was puzzled by this excitement over a woman he had never heard of.

'The secretary claims Miss Groom is not in the office.'

'I don't believe it.'

Hari started to shrug again. Then caught sight of Amer's steely expression and thought better of it.

'The switchboard operator said she has just announced her engagement. They have been swamped with calls of congratulation this morning, apparently,' he offered placatingly.

'I am not,' said Amer between his teeth, 'offering my congratulations. What the hell is she doing?'

'Out choosing the ring, I expect,' said Hari crisply.

He encountered a look that startled him.

'Who is this woman?' he demanded, shaken.

Amer picked up Major McDonald's file and flung it at him. Hari picked it up and started to leaf through it curiously. Amer paced the floor, his shoulders hunched.

Hari finished reading and looked up. 'Leonora Roberts? Your mystery lady in Cairo is the Groom heiress?'

'Quite,' snarled Amer.

'Well, she sure didn't behave like an heiress,' said Hari, astonished.

Amer stopped pacing. 'No, she didn't did she?' he said in an arrested voice. 'I wonder—' He made a decision. 'Call the woman again.'

'But she is out.'

'Not Leonora Groom,' said Amer impatiently. 'The secretary. I want to know if she has read the Antika Project's Celebrity Essays.'

Hari suddenly understood. 'You sent her that?' he gasped. 'Twenty Ways to Catch a Woman by the last of the Ladykillers? You must be out of your mind. She'll never speak to you again.'

Amer strode to the window. The cherry trees in the garden were coming to the end of their blossom. He stared at them unseeingly.

'She will,' he said in a low voice. 'If I have to kidnap her and lock her up to do it, I'll make her listen to me.'

Hari looked dubious but he made the call.

Amer rested his brow against the window-pane. His temples throbbed. He should never have let her get away that night in Cairo. She had been so nearly his. He was experienced enough to know that if he had just put out a hand and touched her she would have gone with him wherever he said. She was too unsophisticated to hide her feelings. Maybe even too inexperienced to recognise them. But Amer had recognised them all right. He could have done whatever he wanted with her that night.

But he had wanted— Well what had he wanted? He asked himself now, with bitter irony. Whatever it was, he had had six months to regret that he had not taken what was in his hands.

He was not, Amer promised himself, going to let that happen again. The next time he got his hands on Leonora Groom, she was not getting away until he got what he wanted. Whatever it was.

Hari put the phone down. 'She has read it,' he said in a voice of doom. 'Her secretary was quite sure of that. Because it was immediately after she left Miss Groom reading it that she called Mr Hartley. That was when they got engaged.'

There was a disbelieving silence. Then Amer swore.

He had dared to call her! Leo's first flare of rage turned into something more complicated. She was honest enough to admit that it was largely excitement.

What sort of person, am I? she thought, horrified. Engaged to one man, getting goose bumps when another man calls me!

She tried to talk to Simon. His office said he was visiting the Birmingham hotel.

'Oh,' said Leo disconcerted. She had expected to go on the Midlands trip. 'Oh well, I suppose it isn't urgent.'

But somehow it felt urgent. She moved about her office

restlessly. There were three applications in her In box but she just could not *concentrate*.

Joanne buzzed.

'The front hall rang up to say your car is ready when you are.' There was a faint question mark in her tone.

Leo chuckled. 'Conscience car. Simon knows he should have taken me to Birmingham, too.'

'I expect he thought you had other things to do.' To her surprise Joanne sounded uncomfortable. 'Shall I lock up for you?'

'I suppose so,' said Leo, dissatisfied. 'It's been a messy day. Maybe I'll do better if I take some work home.'

Fifteen minutes later she was running down the steps of the Groom building, a portfolio under one arm a substantial brief-case in the other and her handbag looped over one shoulder. She went straight to the parking space reserved for Board members. A uniformed man leaped out and opened the door for her.

'Hi,' said Leo, surprised. 'Darren got the day off?'

But the man just smiled and took the portfolio and brief-case from her. She sank into the seat and stretched her legs out. It was a shock. Her feet came nowhere near the back of the seat in front. Even her father did not demand this degree of luxury.

She became aware of a still presence beside her just as the chauffeur started the engine.

'Good evening, Leonora,' said a voice out of her dreams.

Out of her dreams. Out of her nightmares. Out of her sleepless nights. Leo went hot, cold, then deathly still.

The limousine eased silently through the gates and out into the rush hour traffic.

Leo said, 'What are you doing here?' Her frozen lips barely moved.

'Talking some sense into you before you do something neither of us will be able to put right,' said Amer with commendable honesty but a certain lack of tact.

'Let me out of this car.'

He gave a soft laugh. How she hated that laugh. It sounded gloating. It also made those goose bumps break out up and down her spine again.

'You don't mean that,' he said confidently.

Leo pulled herself together. 'You know I do. This is kidnapping,' she pointed out.

He waved that aside. 'There was no time for the courtesies. I needed to see you urgently.'

The car was gliding through the traffic at a fair speed. Leo discarded the thought of leaping out. So she did the next best thing. She crossed her legs, leaned back into the aromatic softness of leather and looked at Amer with all the mockery she could muster.

'Really?' she said politely. 'Six months, is it? Seven? Urgent indeed.'

Amer's mouth compressed. 'You covered your tracks well.'

Leo bit back a smug smile. 'I wasn't aware I had covered my tracks at all,' she said airily.

'False name. Phoney job. No forwarding address. No continuing friendships. My enquiries met stone wall after stone wall.'

'Enquiries?' Leo slewed round in her seat, smugness evaporating. 'Are you saying you put a private detective on to me?'

She was furious. But she felt oddly excited as well. So he had not just let her walk away without a thought. She had imagined Amer giving a philosophical shrug at the escape of one insignificant girl and turning to the next one.

Amer waved that aside as well. 'I wanted to find you,' he said as if that justified anything.

'Oh well, that's all right then,' said Leo affably. She was shaking with rage. And other things which she was not thinking about at the moment. 'Whatever the Sheikh wants he gets, right? Never mind what anyone else wants.'

He smiled. 'You've grown your hair.'

Leo was so angry she did not even blush. She drummed her clenched fists on her knees in frustration.

'It suits you. I knew it would.'

'Stop this car. Let me out at once.'

'Don't panic. I'm taking you home,' he said soothingly.

'I am not panicking,' said Leo between her teeth. 'And I don't want to go home. I'm supposed to go to a reception at the National Gallery.'

'You work too hard. Your secretary can apologise for you tomorrow.'

'Ah. The Sheikh wants again, huh?'

He laughed suddenly. 'Stop spitting at me, Leonora. What is one reception among so many? This is important. We have unfinished business and we both know it.'

'I'm engaged,' said Leo harshly.

She wished she had the ring on her finger to prove it. But she and Simon had not yet taken the time to choose one.

Amer smiled tolerantly. 'Yes, that's one of the things I want to talk about.'

Leo slewed round, her eyes wide with outrage. 'Excuse me?'

He leaned back in his corner and gave her that slow, sexy smile. Why had she only remembered that it set her heart pounding and not that it annoyed her to screaming point?

'It was very silly to get engaged just to spite me,' he said indulgently.

'*What?*'

'You weren't engaged before I hit town.'

'Coincidence,' said Leo curtly. Her heart was beating so hard she thought he must be able to hear it.

'Was it coincidence that you read my piece in that charity book and got engaged immediately afterwards?' he asked shrewdly.

'How did you know—?' Leo broke off. But it was too late. She bit her lip.

'A very understandable reaction,' Amer assured her kindly.

'I have read the thing again and I admit I went over the top in a couple of places. But—'

'Over the top?' Leo glared at him. 'Oh I wouldn't say that. I think you got it all pretty accurately. At least from what I remember. But you should check with your other victims.'

'Victims?' That startled him, genuinely.

'Targets then,' said Leo, showing her teeth. 'How does that sound?'

'Calculating,' Amer said slowly.

She gave him a wide, false smile. 'I couldn't have put it better myself.'

He said on a note of discovery, 'Was *that* why you got engaged then? Because you thought I was playing games with you?'

'Are you trying to tell me you weren't playing games?' Leo looked at him with ineffable scorn. 'That heavily stage-managed incident in Cairo was all leading to love, marriage and a lifetime's devotion, was it?'

Amer frowned. 'I don't know where it was leading,' he said shortly. 'You didn't give us time to find out.'

'But marriage was on the cards?' pressed Leo, mocking.

There was a pause. Then, 'No,' Amer admitted heavily.

'The truth at last,' Leo said with contempt. 'So face it and get out of my life.' She leaned forward and tapped the chauffeur on the shoulder. 'Trafalgar Square, the National Gallery Sainsbury wing. His Excellency made a mistake. I've got a reception to go to.'

The man looked in the driving mirror for instruction. Amer's expression was masklike. He nodded.

Leo had a tough week. Her father and Simon seemed to be talking to each other but they only left one message a piece on her answering machine. Which left far too much time to think about Amer el-Barbary.

Especially as he did not call her. Of course she would not have talked to him, if he had, Leo assured herself. She read his outrageous essay again to remind herself exactly why. She read it several times.

After Simon's message, an exclusive jeweller brought round a selection of engagement rings for her to try. Leo recognised the logo. It was a shop her father used regularly. Disturbed, she chose a ring almost at random.

If Amer had rung then, she would have talked to him. He did not. Just as well, Leo told herself.

Instead she had to give an interview to a magazine. Leo always shied away from personal publicity. But this time the journalist was a friend of Simon's and he had asked her to do it as a favour.

So Anne Marie Dance of *Finance Today* came to interview her. Only she did not behave like a friend of anyone. She went on the attack at once.

'How does it feel to work in your father's shadow all the time?'

It was not the first time she had been asked that one, though the woman's hostility was a shock.

After a moment she said in her driest tone, 'Educational.'

Anne Marie nodded, as if a worthy opponent had scored a point. But not won the game. She leaned forward.

'It won't happen you know.'

Leo said blankly, 'I'm sorry?'

'You won't take over Grooms. Has your father ever appointed a woman director? A senior manager, even? Why do you think he brought Simon Hartley on board?'

Leo gave her a tolerant smile. 'Come on, Ms Dance. You know the rules. Happy to talk about the business. My private life is off limits.'

The journalist raised an eyebrow. 'So what's private about your life?'

Leo stiffened.

At once the woman said, 'I'm sorry. I shouldn't have said that. Is it all right if I ask whether the el-Barbarys are going to take a stake in Grooms?'

For the first time in the interview, Leo lost her professional poker face and she knew it.

'What makes you say that?' she demanded, trying to recover.

Anne Marie Dance's smile was faintly malicious.

'Surely you know the el-Barbarys? Oil? Minerals? Race horses?' The journalist was impatient. 'Ever since the oil boom they've been buying up large chunks of western industry.'

Leo's brain worked swiftly. Amer was using the company to get at her. Or he was using her to get at the company; a nasty thought that. Alternatively he was not interested in the company at all but he had been asking about her and the journalist misinterpreted.

'What makes you think they are looking at Grooms?' Leo asked carefully.

But the journalist just laughed. 'You can't expect me to tell you that, Ms Groom. Got to protect my sources. Let's just say—they have been showing an interest.'

She snapped her notebook shut and got up to leave. Leo escorted her to the lift. As she held out her hand to say goodbye, the journalist looked down at it almost with compassion. Disconcerted, Leo looked down. And there it was, the characteristic ink stain, half-way down her middle finger. She stuffed her hand into her pocket but it was too late.

'Goodbye, Ms Groom. Good luck.' She almost sounded as if she meant it. It was disturbing.

Leo almost ran back to her office. Her secretary looked up surprised.

'No rush. The reception doesn't start until six. Plenty of time to get to the Science Museum.' She added in sudden concern, 'Have you hurt your hand?'

Reluctantly Leo brought it out of her pocket. She shrugged, mocking herself.

'No. It's just the ink stain on the right doesn't really go with the rose diamond on the left.'

'What you need,' said Joanne comfortably, 'is a shower. Thank God for a decent ladies' room.'

'I don't think this is a very good idea.' Hari was beginning to feel seriously alarmed. 'I mean what's she going to do? You know what women are. False pretences. Sexual harassment. They can get crazy.'

Amer shrugged.

'Think of the scandal,' moaned Hari. 'After all the trouble you took to set up a meeting with the disaffected tribes. It's a risk we don't need.'

Amer's mouth set. 'I must see her. I am going to see her.'

'I don't know what's happened to you. I've never seen you like this.'

The dark grey eyes were suddenly, startlingly, intense.

'Maybe you've never seen me a hundred per cent alive before.'

Hari gave up.

Leo took her toilet bag and cocktail dress and went along to change. A couple of women were already there, repairing their make-up and chatting about their love lives.

'Clever men are hell, aren't they?' one of them told the mirror. She arched a friendly eyebrow, including Leo in the conversation.

Leo smiled but her voice was resigned when she said 'Try me on corporate recognition. Better still, high season occupancy rates. I'm the bees' knees at that. Men—clever or not—are a closed book to me.'

The pretty painted face in the mirror looked almost pitying for a moment. 'Join the club.'

She's sorry for me, thought Leo. That makes the second woman this afternoon. What a complete disaster I must be. And they only have to look at me to see it. It was a shocking thought.

The others left and she went into the tiny shower room.

Leo slid out of her clothes and turned on the shower. She felt numb. Automatically she applied her favourite shower gel. It was her one extravagance, specially imported from Japan. It made her skin soft as silk under her fingers and perfumed her whole body with the faint but lingering scent of spring blossom. Slowly, slowly, she began to feel again.

What she felt was anger. And suddenly, blessedly, ready to fight back.

How dared her father treat her like a cipher? Stick her in a nonjob and then stop speaking to her altogether as soon as she got engaged to the man of his choice! How dared Simon send her a mail-order engagement ring?

Above all, how dared Amer el-Barbary virtually kidnap her in his blasted limousine and then leave her without a word for over a week?

By the time Leo was dressed in designer black, with her newly washed hair piled on top of her head, she was glittering with the hunger for battle.

She glared at herself in the mirror and said violently, '*Bloody* men.'

The stunned look had gone but she was still too pale. Leo shook herself. This would never do. She had just got engaged, for Heaven's sake. Until she took charge of her own life and dealt with the men who had sewn her up she had to look *radiant*.

She made an inventory of her attractions. There were not many of them. But at least you could not see her big feet in the waist-high mirror, Leo thought wryly. Otherwise there was her porcelain skin, her embarrassingly voluptuous figure and a very expensive dress. That was it.

It was why all these men thought they could push her around to fit in with their plans. If she had been attractive, they would have thought about what was good for her. What she wanted; *listened* to her. As it was—Leo ground her teeth.

It made a mess of her make-up. She had to wipe off her lipstick and start again. That did not do much for her mood, either.

'Now calm down,' she said to herself. 'You can do make-up.'

At Christmas Deborah had given her a voucher for a whole day's beauty treatment. Leo had bought most of the cosmetics the make-up artist pressed on her, out of sheer self-defence. Now, she thought with acute self-mockery, all she had to do was remember which colour went where.

She remembered. Ten minutes later she hardly recognised the face that looked back at her. Slumberous eyes, startlingly long lashes, provocative mouth... At least no one is going to feel sorry for me tonight, Leo thought with a flare of savage satisfaction.

And as for her dress—she considered it clinically. It was low-cut and very plain, designed to show off her creamy shoulders. Well that was all right but—Leo wriggled it down further to accentuate the effect. Only that deepened the décolletage. Oh well, thought Leo, valiant with fury, why not?

She threw a brilliant embroidered shawl over her dress and stalked down to the car. On the way she noticed her right hand. Despite the shower the shadow of the ink stain on the middle finger was still visible.

'Damn,' spat Leo.

She dabbed at her finger with a tissue. And felt the spring which controlled her temper tighten another notch.

It did not show when she arrived at the Museum. She stepped out as haughtily as a queen. Or so thought Hari, who had been left on watch for her.

'Whoops,' he said under his breath.

He had only seen Leo once before and she had changed beyond belief. But he knew the signs. This was not a woman in the mood for romantic abduction. This was a woman who was in a mood to kill.

He went to warn Amer.

Leo accepted a glass of champagne from one of the Foundation's officials and allowed herself to be guided through a rather dull display of the Foundation's recent achievements. They all looked taken aback at this dramatic new Leo. Even

Professor Lane stumbled in his monologue and one or two of the students looked as nervous as they were admiring.

Good, she thought savagely. She downed her first glass and took another one.

She circulated grimly, skirting an early sewing machine, and pointing out crisply to Antika's Project Director that his business plan needed to be completely rewritten. He was sweating faintly by the time she turned away to inspect a large steam train.

'Whew,' said the Project Director, wiping his brow.

He went to look for reinforcements.

Leo hid a smile. At least that was one man who would take her seriously from now on. Feeling better and better, she took a third glass of champagne from a passing waiter. And then, from behind the huge engine, came a voice she thought she recognised.

'Tell her,' it said urgently. 'Tell her *now.*'

Leo's brow creased. Someone from work? No. Yet someone she had talked to today. A business contact? No. Then, suddenly, she had it—the unfriendly journalist. That was who it was. What was her name?

A man's voice muttered a reply. Indistinguishable.

'You can't do it,' said the journalist. She sounded on the edge of hysteria. 'It's crazy. Your whole life.'

'Anne Marie, don't. Not here. *Please.*'

Anne Marie Dance. Of course. And the man sounded desperate. Leo was about to back away tactfully when she heard the thing that stopped her dead in her tracks.

'Simon, you can't *do* this.'

Simon?

Simon?

She put her untasted glass down on the priceless exhibit and walked quite deliberately round the steam engine. Simon Hartley was standing there, holding Anne Marie Dance at arm's length. Leo stopped dead, all her bright triumph draining out of her. At arm's length, yes. But what intimacy there was in their closeness. They had obviously been closer than this many many times.

Anne Marie saw her over Simon's shoulder. Her face changed. Simon turned round. When he saw Leo he looked blank, then horribly sick.

'Oh God,' he said.

Anne Marie Dance, on the other hand, seemed almost relieved. Quite suddenly Leo realised why there had been that inexplicable hostility in the interview this afternoon.

'So now you know,' she said.

She put a possessive hand on Simon's arm. After a moment his hand covered hers protectively. As if he had made that gesture a hundred times before.

Leo felt as if a knife had gone into her heart, straight and true. Not because she wanted Simon, but because no one was ever going to touch her with that instinctive protectiveness. She blinked hard.

'Leo, I'm so sorry,' he said wretchedly.

'I'm not,' said Anne Marie in a quick panting voice. 'It's time someone showed your father there are things he can't buy. Like a son-in-law.'

Simon dropped her hand as if it burned him.

'Stop it, Anne Marie,' he said, suddenly taking charge. 'Leo, we can't talk here.'

'Why not?' said Anne Marie loudly. She shouldered her way round him and stuck her face close to Leo's. 'Your father told Simon to propose to you. He said you wanted to marry and couldn't get a man of your own.'

Leo felt as if she were in a nightmare. All the lovely defiance had evaporated. She felt cold and alone. Anne Marie's hostility hurt. But at least it was better than the pity that had followed it last time.

She said in a voice like crashing icebergs, 'He was wrong.'

She tugged at the newly acquired rose diamond with clumsy fingers. Even though she had put it on so recently it was difficult to prize off.

'Not here,' implored Simon, looking round anxiously.

But they were out of sight of most other people in the gallery. Leo set her teeth and hauled. Her finger turned white, then red. But in the end the thing came off. She dropped it into his top pocket.

'Don't worry. I'll tell Gordon I changed my mind,' she told him, still in that frighteningly icy voice.

She knew she should be devastated by Simon's betrayal. No doubt she would be when she had time to think about it. But for the moment she still felt blessedly numb. The worst thing was the humiliation. And if she kept a hold on herself and got out fast, she could even handle that, Leo told herself.

'He won't sack you if he thinks it's my fault.'

Simon flinched. That was faintly satisfying. She gathered herself to leave them.

'I'll send a cancellation notice to the papers tomorrow.'

Simon flushed. Leo thought—how could I have imagined it would work? How could I have *trusted* him? He's as bad as Amer el-Barbary.

She said with absolute finality, 'Goodbye.'

Out of the shelter of the great locomotive. Leo felt suddenly exposed. She went through the galleries as fast as she could without actually appearing to be running. All she wanted to do now was get home.

She was so nearly out of the door when she heard her name called that she could have screamed.

'Leonora!'

She whirled round. Sheikh Amer el-Barbary strolled forward. A scream, she decided, did not begin to cover what she felt.

'Hello to the end of a perfect day,' she said.

He was heart-stoppingly handsome, with his golden tan that she remembered—and lazy eyes which she had tried so hard to forget. Tonight they looked almost silver. In the flesh he was incredibly sexy. How had she managed to get by last week without reacting to it? She looked at him with acute dislike.

'What do you want?'

Amer's eyebrows flew up at her abrupt tone.

'How many of those have you had?' he asked, nodding at the champagne.

Leo ignored the question. 'I have not come here to talk to you. Go away.'

She waved her glass to emphasis her point. Some of the wine spilled over his immaculate grey suit. She ignored that, too.

'I see,' he said gravely.

He took her by the arm and steered her to a corner of the room. Hari hovered. Amer waved him away. He went.

Leo's dislike of Sheikh Amer el-Barbary intensified. She did not attempt to disguise it.

'And you needn't think you can order me around, either,' she said pugnaciously. 'That little man may be paid to hit the ceiling when you say jump. I'm not.'

'Quite right,' said Amer hugely entertained. 'But I really do have something to discuss with you. Business,' he added, as her eyes flashed.

'What business?' demanded Leo, suspicious.

'Antika's research. I gather you don't like the application.'

Leo pulled herself together and told him succinctly exactly what was wrong with the application. Amer blinked.

'No wonder you frightened the poor guy to death,' he murmured. 'Now, how can I resolve your criticisms?'

'What has it got to do with you?' Leo said, bristling.

'We are co-funding it.' He was smoothness itself. 'Professor Lane has asked me to see what I can do.'

His voice was like a caress. The faint accent and overprecise English added to the illusion. Many women, thought Leo wisely, would have melted into a warm puddle at his feet when he stroked them with that voice. On the Nile, she had nearly done exactly that herself.

She glared. Amer gave her a wide smile that showed perfect teeth and an indentation in one cheek that many women would have found irresistible. Leo thanked God she was not many women. She took a gulp of champagne.

'I don't believe it,' she said.

He was amused. 'How do I convince you?'

Leo eyed him over the top of her champagne glass. She was shaking with temper and more than temper. Suddenly a crazy stratagem presented itself. It would make him mad but it was irresistible. Anyway, Leo wasn't going to resist, not in the mood she was in tonight.

She gave him a wide smile and said with profoundly phoney calm, 'Okay. You believe in Antika's research. I don't. So carry on. Pitch.'

He was taken aback. Leo saw it. She savoured it. It did not make up for the humiliations of the day, of course. but it helped. It helped.

The caressing note faltered. 'Excuse me?'

'Pitch,' she said. She clicked her fingers impatiently. 'Give me your line.'

It was insulting. Amer stiffened. She eyed him with mockery.

'You have got a line, haven't you?'

'I don't think—'

Leo interrupted. 'No line? Fine.' She turned away. 'I'll be going. If you'll call my car—'

Amer stepped swiftly in front of her.

'I'll think of a line,' he said rapidly. 'Just give me a second.'

A hint of a caress now, Leo thought with satisfaction. Quite suddenly the Sheikh seemed to have dropped out of seduction mode and was prepared to do business. She began to feel triumphant at last.

Vaingloriously she drained her glass. Amer eyed the empty flute uneasily.

'How many *have* you had?'

'Enough,' said Leo.

He laughed suddenly. 'You're not at all what I thought you were in Cairo, you know.'

Leo blinked. 'What?'

He made a graceful gesture. He had beautiful hands, she

saw. Like a musician. Or a dancer. Or—the thought flipped into her brain like an acrobat—a snake charmer.

'What?' she said again, challenging him.

'Jack Lane got you wrong, too. He said you were a nice, quiet lady.' He sounded rueful. 'Not a fire eater in traffic light silks.'

Leo hugged the maligned shawl round her. 'You want to do business, I'll do business,' she said stubbornly.

'Excellent. Then maybe we could have dinner,' he said, smooth as cream. 'Then I can take you through the proposal.'

'I've been through the proposal,' said Leo, standing her ground. 'It's tosh.'

He did not like that. His eyes lost some of their laziness. After a moment he said kindly, 'It's probably a little difficult for a nonspecialist to follow. I would be happy to talk you through—I'm sorry?'

'I said, garbage,' explained Leo.

His eyes flashed. 'It is a visionary project—'

'So it may be,' said Leo, interrupting. 'It's a damned sloppy presentation.' She took a step towards him and prodded him in the chest with one finger to emphasise her point. 'I may not be a scientist with half a dozen degrees but I know how to read a business plan. That one stinks.'

Amer looked down at her as if he could not believe his ears. Well, he probably could not. She was vaguely aware that he would not be used to women prodding him in the chest. At least not in anger.

I am probably the only person in the world who sees him for what he is, Leo thought, somewhat muzzily. A snake charmer who thinks he can get anything he wants by mesmerising people. She prodded him in the chest again.

'Facts,' she said. 'You want me to give these guys a sponsorship deal? Give me facts.'

Amer sighed. 'If they had any facts, the research would be over and they wouldn't need a grant.'

Leo frowned, thinking about it. To her annoyance, it

sounded reasonable. Even spitting mad, she was fair minded enough to admit it.

'Okay. Hypotherase—' It got lost somehow. Leo tried again. 'Hypathetho—'

'Hypothesise,' he suggested helpfully.

Leo nodded. She raised her hand. Quick as an arrow, Amer caught her prodding finger before she could spear him for the third time. He was laughing, not lazily at all.

'No, please, not again. I will tell them to do as you suggest.'

'Good,' said Leo.

She found he was still holding her hand. She looked down at it, frowning in bewilderment.

'So now can we talk about us please?' he murmured.

He turned her hand over, studying it. That damned ink stain was still there. Leo swore and tugged her hand away. Without success.

'What do you mean—us?' she said nastily.

A long finger traced the ink stain thoughtfully.

'There is still that unfinished business.'

He looked up, provocatively. The dark eyes were teasing. But they were also surprisingly intense. Leo blinked.

'Isn't there?' he said softly.

And then he raised her hand to his mouth. He did not kiss it but held it where he could savour the feel and scent of her skin. He closed his eyes in appreciation.

As if, thought Leo wrathfully, her hand was a good cigar. She wrenched it out of his hold. He laughed, as if she had delighted him.

There was a nasty pause while Leo reminded herself that she was being played by a master. She controlled herself. It was an effort. Not helped by the fact that Amer was waiting for her next move with patent amusement.

At last she drew a long, shaky breath.

'Probably for the best,' said that hatefully appreciative voice.

Leo glared. 'What is?'

'Postponing our fight. You can't get up a really good head of steam when you're liable to be interrupted at any moment.'

'Our—' She choked. 'I do not,' she said with precision, 'fight.'

'Yes that's what I heard.' He sounded puzzled.

'And you're the last person in the world I would fight with if I did,' she raged.

That seemed to puzzle him even more.

'I'm sure you underrate yourself,' he said kindly.

For a wild moment Leo thought she was going to hit him. No, she thought. I won't. If I lose control, who knows where it will end?

She gathered her shawl around her and drew herself up to her full height.

'Good night.'

Amer interposed his shoulder, blocking her path. He smiled down at her.

'Why don't I take you out to dinner?'

Leo folded her lips together tightly before she could scream or burst into tears. She whipped round him, making for the front steps. To her consternation he followed.

'Surely we can negotiate.'

Leo increased her pace.

'I never negotiate.'

Even that did not put him off. 'But I do,' he said softly.

They were at the entrance. Leo stopped dead. She turned, head high.

'Okay,' she said in a goaded under voice. 'You want a deal? I'll give you a deal.'

She knew what she was going to say before it came out. It was crazy. Her better self did not want to have anything to do with this dark coda to the nightmare of the evening. But her better self was on hold, waiting for a cup of cocoa and a good cry in front of a blazing fire.

Her worse self was tired of being pushed around. Her worse self looked at his man and heard him admit that he pursued her cynically, knowing that marriage was not on the cards. Her worse self wanted revenge on the whole male sex.

Leo heard her worse self say in a hard voice, 'Marry me and I'll authorise that damned grant.'

CHAPTER SIX

THERE was a terrible silence.

Why on earth did I say that? I must be mad.

Then Amer threw back his head and laughed aloud. Leo could not believe it. She was still reeling with shock at her own words. And he *laughed*. At that moment she hated him.

But, even so, she needed to withdraw her stupid remark. And fast.

She said with stiff apology, 'That was uncalled for. I'm sorry. I didn't mean…'

Amer ignored that. He said softly, 'Be careful what you wish for. You might get it.'

'W-wish for?' Leo was outraged. 'Are you implying I wish to marry you?'

Amer looked soulful. 'What else is a man to think when a lady pays him the compliment of asking him to marry her?'

Leo choked. 'I did not ask you to marry me.'

'That's what it sounded like to me,' Amer said imperturbably.

Leo stopped feeling even the slightest bit apologetic. She glared.

'I said I'd cut you a deal. That's different.'

He raised his eyebrows. 'I'd be interested to hear how you work that out. Let us have dinner and discuss it.'

'No,' said Leo sharply. 'Thank you,' she added with patent lack of gratitude.

Amer smiled. 'I never sign up to a deal until I have explored the implications.'

She shrugged. 'Fine. So no deal. I can live with that.' She turned away.

He caught her by the arm. Well no, that was not exactly

96

true. He hardly touched her. But Leo stopped dead as if she had walked into an invisible electric fence.

'And I never turn one down before I've done just that.'

Leo looked over her shoulder at him. Her heart was thundering so hard it was all she could do not to press her hand against her shaken rib cage. What was worse, she was almost certain he knew it. She clenched her hand into a tight, tight fist and kept it at her side.

Amer's remarkable eyes crinkled at the corners as he met hers. The sensuous mouth remained in a prim line but Leo was not deceived. It was an amused, secretive look and it made her blood run cold.

He is laughing at me, she thought.

She said, as haughtily as she knew how, 'My car?'

'Of course.' It was as smooth as cream.

Not taking his hand from her arm he escorted her out into the evening. It had been a hot day and the air was full of the stale heat of combustion engines and too many people. Leo shuddered.

'Sticky,' he agreed with her unspoken distaste. 'You will be glad of a cool drink.'

He must have made some sign, though Leo had not detected it. A long dark car drew up silently in front of them. Amer opened the passenger door.

Leo was not getting caught like that again.

'That's not my car.'

'Of course not.' Amer was shocked. 'When I take a lady out to dinner, I pick her up and see her home.'

'You are not,' said Leo between her teeth, 'taking me out to dinner.'

'I'm glad you feel like that,' Amer said mysteriously.

He shepherded her solicitously into the back seat. To her own fury, Leo found herself complying. He shut the door on her and slipped round to the off side. In the car his smile was very seductive. She recognised that it was designed to be.

'I so much prefer to eat at home.'

Unseduced, Leo narrowed her eyes at all that deceptive openness.

'I'm not cooking for you, either,' she announced.

He chuckled. 'A pleasure deferred.'

'No, it's not. I'm never going to—' Leo broke off, as the car did not turn west as she expected. Instead it slid into Hyde Park and turned right. 'Where are we going?'

Amer widened his eyes at her. 'Why home, of course. Just as you wanted.'

'I live that way,' said Leo, pointing firmly in the direction from which they had come.

He was bland. 'How interesting.'

Leo ground her teeth. 'All right. Whose home?'

'Mine,' he said coolly.

Leo could be cool, too. 'Interesting,' she drawled back at him. 'Would that be the home from home palace or the bachelor pad where anything goes?'

Amer looked amused. 'Which would you prefer?'

Leo resisted the temptation to hit him. Only because she thought it might make her burst into tears. She felt she'd had more fights tonight than she'd had in the whole of her life up to now. She'd not acquitted herself badly. But it had taken more out of her than she could afford if she was going to lock horns with Amer el-Barbary.

She leaned back in her seat with an angry little sigh. A policy of passive resistance, that was the answer. If he got no reaction out of her, Leo reasoned, he would soon get bored and let her go home.

So she managed not to react to the imposing Palladian house. It was no more than she expected after all. She nodded at the butler, managing to stay as impassive as the perfect servant himself. She even kept her cool in the marble entrance hall, though the original Canaletto made her blink a bit. But when Amer led her through the house and out the other side, her strategy tumbled into ruins.

She stopped stock-still, gasping. She was suddenly in the garden of Eden. It was surrounded by an old wall, its stones

almost hidden by lush falls of lilac wisteria. Old trees formed
a copse at the end of the garden. While a perfect lawn, the
grass golden in the late-evening sun, curved away under huge
azalea bushes. They were so brilliant with bloom that she
could hardly believe it—apricot and lemon and buttercup and
champagne; and then a blaze of fiery pink that made her eyes
hurt. And the scent! Her senses swam.

'I don't believe it,' Leo whispered.

Amer liked her awe. He smiled.

'Better than the bachelor pad?'

Leo was recalled to herself. She looked at him with dislike.

'It may be beautiful. That doesn't mean that I want to be
here.'

'You'd rather we went to the bachelor pad,' he interpreted.

He raised a hand. The silent butler materialised.

'Bring the car round.'

The butler inclined his head.

'No,' said Leo hastily. 'No, I don't want to go anywhere
else.' In case Amer misunderstood—or pretended to misunderstand—she added with emphasis, 'Until I go home that
is.'

Amer bit back a smile.

'Then we will have to drink out here. Unless you are
cold?' he added courteously.

Leo was uncomfortably conscious of a heat that had nothing to do with the summer evening.

'No,' she said with constraint.

'Then bring drinks please,' said Amer, every inch the concerned host. 'Dinner in an hour.'

The butler bowed and disappeared.

Leo attempted heavy irony. 'So I'm staying for dinner, am
I?'

'I said I would feed you,' Amer reminded her.

'I don't remember accepting.'

He laughed. 'Then do so now.'

And as she looked mulish, he strolled over to her and put

an arm round her shoulders, turning her to face the golden garden.

'Look at that,' he said lazily. 'You can't honestly say you want to leave all this and go back into the dirt of the city.'

For the second time since she had arrived, Leo's senses swam. He was too close. His arm was too heavy. If she turned her head just a fraction, she would rest her cheek against the grey-suited chest. She could smell the warm skin and the faint expensive fragrance of orange flowers and orris.

She remembered that smell. She had thought she would remember it for the rest of her life. Now, she thought with sudden insight, she was going to have to be seriously careful to make sure that was all she remembered from this encounter. The whole evening was turning into an elephant trap for a woman with big feet and minimal experience of seduction.

She gave herself a mental shake and said firmly, 'I can say I don't want to be kidnapped, however.'

For a moment the hand on her upper arm tightened almost unbearably. Not so lazy, now.

'Don't fight me, Leonora.'

She looked up at him indignantly, forgetting for a moment that he was too close.

'Are you threatening me?'

Amer looked down at her. Yes, much too close. The grey eyes were unreadable. But Leo's breath still caught in her throat. Then his lashes dropped and he was lazy again. He gave her shoulders a squeeze, laughing.

'Say thank-you prettily and stop arguing. Let us savour the twilight.'

Leo thought: Something's wrong with me. I want to do what he says. I must be out of my mind.

The butler came back, carrying an enormous embossed tray. He put it on a filigree ironwork table. Still stunned by her unwanted revelation, Leo watched him lift an ornate jug that might have been brass or might—if that were not ridiculous—have been gold. He poured a cloudy liquid into crystal goblets and put them on another tray before presenting them to Amer.

Amer took both and held one out to her. Leo looked at it, not moving. He was amused.

'Lemon, lime, honey and a hint of cinnamon,' he said as if she had voiced her suspicions. 'Maybe a dash of rosewater, though that's a professional secret. Try. If you hate it you can always have more champagne. Though personally, I suspect you're over your limit.'

Leo was so incensed that she grabbed the goblet and swallowed the brew as if it were medicine. She barely tasted it as it went down. She did not care.

'I hate it,' she said deliberately.

Just for a moment the impassive butler was less than impassive. An expression of distinct shock passed over his face, Leo saw. Presumably the Sheikh's usual guests did what he told them and said thank-you for it. Well, this guest was going to be different she thought vengefully.

Amer, of course, was unmoved. 'Then champagne it is.' Without turning his head, he said, 'See to it, Harrods.'

The man left silently.

'Harrods?' said Leo, temporarily diverted. 'Is that really his name?'

'In a way. I dare say you won't approve,' Amer said with wry amusement, 'but the name goes with the job.'

She stared.

'My mother,' he explained. 'When we first bought this house she said the only person she knew in London was the man who delivered her orders from Harrods. Eventually she persuaded him to come and work here. But she had always called him Harrods. So—' He shrugged.

Leo was appalled. 'You made the poor man give up his *name?*'

'I knew you would disapprove,' Amer sighed.

'I think it's barbaric. It's as if you have bought up his whole identity.' She shivered at the thought of such arrogance. 'You really do think you can do anything you want, don't you?'

Amer frowned. 'He could always have left. In fact, he has stayed with us for thirty years.'

But Leo was still chilled by this further evidence of tyranny.

'You set your own rules and everyone else has to obey, don't they?' she said hotly. 'You just think you're above the rest of us.'

Amer was thunderstruck. 'Above— What are you talking about?'

Leo snorted. 'Look at this evening. As I remember, I said I didn't want to have dinner with you several times. Did you take any notice?'

'It's good for you to have new experiences.'

'So you have a right to decide what's good for me now?' raged Leo.

Amer's eyes gleamed.

'More like a duty,' he said blandly.

Leo was utterly unprepared for that.

'What?'

'Well, you keep throwing out challenges.' He gave her his most winning smile. 'What sort of a man would I be if I didn't take them up?'

Leo was speechless.

Harrods returned with a frosted bottle and a crystal flute. Amer flicked his fingers. Harrods surrendered the bottle to him without comment. But as he withdrew Leo thought she detected wintry surprise.

Amer dealt expertly with the bottle and poured the wine. He gave her the glass and took up his own, toasting her.

'Your health.'

Leo was still reeling. She raised her glass but could not think of anything to say. Amer clinked his goblet against hers.

'Truce?'

Looking up, Leo found his eyes were smiling straight into

hers. It made her feel as if the world was suddenly very small and turning so fast that she might fall off. It was all she could do not to grab hold of him to steady herself.

'Come on, Leonora.' It was as smooth as silk and twice as seductive. 'What have you got to lose? Call a truce until sunset.'

She did not trust him an inch.

'What sort of truce?'

His eyes gleamed. 'You don't tear into me and I don't take your hair down.'

Leo choked.

'Truce,' he said firmly and held out his hand.

To her own amazement, Leo found herself giving him her own. This is crazy, she thought. I ought to insist on going home *now*.

But she did not. Instead she let him shake her hand. And then, of course, hold onto it. He ran his fingers over the back of her hand in a movement that was not quite a caress. It set her shivering as none of Simon's most ardent kisses had though.

She hauled her hand back and said the first thing that came into her head.

'Wh-what an interesting garden,' she said quickly. 'No one would think you were in the heart of London.' I sound like my mother, she thought in despair.

Amer frowned.

'Is it difficult to maintain?' gabbled Leo. She held her champagne flute in front of her like an amulet.

Amer's frown deepened. He let out an explosive sigh.

'God spare me from Englishwomen. Every time anyone gets near your feelings you start talking like the Queen.'

Leo decided not to hear that. She started to stroll round the garden, asking intelligent questions about the plants. Their scent was almost overwhelming but she was determined not to let it get to her. Just as she took her wineglass with her but did not drink any more. She needed all her wits about her and she knew it.

So did Amer. He went with her, answering her questions with a barbed politeness that told her he knew exactly what she was doing.

'Bog standard azalea,' he said indifferently as she stopped in front of a ten-foot bush of honey-scented gold.

'H-how interesting.'

He looked down at her ironically. Then a thought occurred to him and his mouth tilted.

'It is, actually. This was the plant that intoxicated Xenophon's soldiers on the way to Trebizond.' He gave her a slow, lazy smile that set her pulses thrumming and her teeth on edge. 'Do you rate your resistance higher or lower?'

Leo's resistance was fraying at the edges with every moment and she suspected he knew it. When he looked at her like that, there did not seem to be much resistance left at all. It was not fair.

He laughed softly. Oh he knew what he was doing all right.

Get a grip, Leo told herself feverishly, *Get a grip*.

'I thought we had a truce?' she managed.

'I haven't laid a hand on you,' he pointed out, all innocence.

She looked at him. He laughed and opened his hands. As if he were letting go of a leading rein, she thought indignantly.

'All right,' he said kindly. 'I won't tease you any more.'

'Thank you.'

'A least not until sunset,' he murmured mischievously.

Leo looked at the sky. It was beginning to darken.

'Perhaps we'd better eat soon.'

'Coward,' he taunted.

But he led the way back to the house and gave the order.

They ate in a small room on the first floor overlooking the garden. Leo hardly knew what the quiet servants put in front of her. She had no appetite and did no more than pick at it.

Amer was concerned.

'Sorry,' said Leo. She was enough her father's daughter to

feel guilty about wasting good food. 'It's been quite a day. I think I just ran out of steam.'

She fully expected him to say something sexy and provocative. But he did not.

Instead he said gravely, 'Because of your broken engagement?'

Leo nursed her left hand. Her ring finger was still slightly sore. She gave a brief, unhappy smile.

'Among other things.'

Amer looked at her thoughtfully.

'Is this where you tell me why you are so anxious to get married?'

Leo jumped. 'I'm not,' she denied hotly.

'That was not the impression you gave me earlier. When you offered me that deal,' he reminded her.

She blushed. 'Yes. Well. I was angry.'

'Evidently.' He paused. 'I am often angry. It has never occurred to me to marry in order to vent my spleen.'

That gave her pause. 'Put like that it doesn't sound very nice.'

'Or very sensible.' He took a peach out of the silver filigree dish and began to peel it casually. Concentrating on the task, he said, 'So answer my question. Why do you—' He corrected himself. 'Why did you think you wanted to marry?'

Leo looked at him. With the steep lids dropped, he was no longer a teasing duellist. Just someone who wanted to know something about her. Not about the business, or her father. Her.

She said abruptly, 'I never thought I'd marry. I've always been the wallflower. I've sort of got used to it. I was going to run the business. I worked hard—' Her voice became suspended.

Amer's brows twitched together in a brief, fierce frown. He must have snicked himself with the knife, she thought.

Not raising his eyes, he said, 'So why Simon Hartley?'

Leo shrugged. 'The Hartleys want to save their stately home. Simon's the eldest son.'

'That explains his side of it,' said Amer without expression. 'What about yours?'

Leo stared out into the garden. Twilight had swathed it in a soft grey that somehow made her want to cry.

'My father doesn't really want me to work in the business, it seems,' she said in a hard voice. 'I needn't have bothered to go to Cairo or anywhere else. He wants to start a dynasty. Work experience isn't much good for that.'

Amer's eyes lifted. He put the peach down and regarded her for a frowning moment.

'And an impoverished aristocrat is?' he drawled.

Leo did not look at him. If she kept her eyes fixed on the garden and very wide, the shaming tears might subside.

'Yes.'

'I see.'

No you don't, she thought. You don't see at all.

She said, 'You must think I'm a fool.'

There was a pause. She did not look at him.

'I think you're a coward,' Amer said coolly.

Leo gasped, her eyes flying to him in spite of herself. He was smiling but the grey eyes were nearly black and there was a pulse throbbing at his temple as if he was so angry he could barely contain himself.

'But not because you did what your father wanted,' he went on. 'I think you did what you wanted. And for all the wrong reasons.' He was not drawling any more.

Leo thought: He sounds furious. He must terrify people when he looks at them like that. Why am I not terrified?

And then her own anger took over.

'How dare you?'

The unamused smile widened. 'You asked,' he clipped.

'You don't know a thing about it.'

Amer was coldly furious.

'I know you didn't get engaged until you realised that I was in the country.'

Leo felt her colour rise. 'What has that got to do with it?' she snapped.

Quite suddenly Amer smiled. 'So you don't deny it.' He sounded pleased with himself.

Damn. She looked away.

'The timing was an unfortunate coincidence,' she said loftily.

He raised his eyebrows.

'It *was.*'

He shrugged. 'Will you tell me something?'

'Probably not,' said Leo, thoroughly disturbed.

'Were you ever in love with him?'

'Simon?' Leo was shocked. 'Of course I—'

He held up a hand. 'Don't lie to me, Leonora. Tell me nothing, if you don't want to. But don't tell me lies.'

Leo was silenced. The fight went out of her all of a sudden. She passed a hand over her eyes.

'I don't know,' she muttered.

'You don't know if you're going to tell me anything? Or you don't know if you loved him?' Amer pressed.

She glared at him. 'Stop interrogating me.'

He laughed. 'All right. Have some peach.' He speared a segment and offered it to her.

She took it. But the little gesture shook Leo. It was too intimate. It seemed to imply that they had eaten like this many times before. And—even more unsettling—would again.

He watched her eat the piece of fruit. His expression was unreadable. So why did she feel as if she had just conceded him a victory?

'I don't understand you,' she burst out.

Amer leaned back in his chair. His body was utterly relaxed. But the sleepy eyes were watchful.

'But I am a simple man.' He was drawling again.

'Huh.'

He laughed. 'I am,' he insisted. 'Simple pleasures. Simple wants.'

Leo surveyed the table eloquently: Venetian crystal, embossed silver, hand-painted china...

'It looks like it,' she said drily.

'Don't judge by appearances,' he chided.

'What else have I got to judge by?'

He considered her thoughtfully.

'You could try asking a few questions.'

'Questions? About what for Heaven's sake?'

Amer raised his eyes to the ceiling. 'Me, you contrary woman,' he said exasperated. 'Don't you want to know anything about me?'

Leo blinked. Was there the faintest undertone of hurt there? Or was it all outraged vanity because she had managed to resist him? After all, he did not know what a struggle she was having to keep to her resolve.

She said drily, 'I know all about you.'

He was pleased. 'You've been asking about me.'

'No, I haven't.'

'Then you don't know anything.'

She gave him her sweetest smile. 'Well, let's just say I know all I need to know. You spelled it out for me.'

He frowned, puzzled. '*I* did?'

Leo said malevolently, '"Come with me to the Casbah", remember?'

His contribution to the Antika Foundation's book! Amer's brow cleared, enlightened.

'Is that what made you sign up with Simon Hartley?' He needed to know for sure.

Leo ground her teeth. 'Will you get rid of the idea that you have any influence on my behaviour? You are nothing to me.'

She thought he would be annoyed. But he was amused. Not just pretending, really amused. Leo looked at him with the deepest suspicion. He laughed aloud.

'Prove it.'

For an outraged second Leo thought she really was going to hit him. She, who had never hit anyone in her life? She clenched her fists in her lap.

'I think it's time I was going,' she said in a suffocated voice.

His eyes danced. 'No coffee?'

'I—'

'Very wise,' he said kindly. 'If you think you can't handle it.'

Leo glared. 'I can handle anything you throw at me,' she announced.

Amer threw back his head and gave another of his deep-throated laughs. She watched, helpless.

'You,' he said when he regained control over his voice, 'are a delight. And a terrible temptation.'

Leo was shaken. No one had ever called her a temptation before. *I knew this dress was too low-cut,* she thought. It was her only coherent thought. The rest was a panicky whirl of half-formed suspicions and wholly impractical escape strategies.

She huddled her shawl round her incendiary décolletage and refused to meet his eyes.

'If I have coffee with you, will you call me a cab?'

'If you still want to go.'

Leo swallowed. 'Then let's have coffee now.'

Having made her bargain, she turned her eyes away dismissively and looked pointedly out of the window.

Amer summoned the butler.

'Coffee in the conservatory,' he told him. With one eye on Leo's averted face, he added in a lower voice, 'And then, I won't be needing you again tonight.'

It was not the first time the butler had received such instructions from Amer. His expression did not change.

'Certainly, Your Excellency. And do you wish to speak to Mr Farah?'

'No,' said Amer unequivocally. He stood up and held out a hand to Leo.

'Come and see some more plants you can interrogate me about.'

Ignoring the hand, she got up and followed him. I must

not bump into the furniture, she thought hazily. I could not bear it if I blundered into one of his priceless bits of art in my dash for the door. With today's luck, I'd probably break it.

The conservatory ran the entire length of the house and looked out onto the now twilit garden. Discreetly placed lights illuminated palms, vines and a column of jasmine, covered with fragrant star flowers. At one end a wall-mounted fountain played. Leo's lips parted in amazement.

'Yes, you like that, don't you?' Amer was wry. 'I'm beginning to think botany is the only thing that turns you on.'

Leo swung round indignantly—and bumped into the butler, bearing the coffee tray silently behind her.

The butler recovered his balance. Not so the tray he was carrying. China flew, and the coffeepot tipped its contents in a neat stream down the front of her dress.

Leo closed her eyes. 'Today's luck strikes again.'

Amer whisked the stained shawl away from her. 'See what can be done with that Harrods.'

The butler bore it off rapidly.

Amer was blotting the hot coffee with an impeccable white handkerchief. His hands were quite impersonal. Leo swallowed and opened her eyes hurriedly. She was disconcerted to find that she did not feel impersonal at all.

He stood back, dissatisfied. 'This is soaked. We'll have to do better than this.' A thought occurred to him. 'Come with me.'

He whisked her up two flights of stairs to an imposing set of double doors in shining mahogany. Leo was taken aback. But Amer flung open their magnificence as casually as if they led to a broom cupboard and ushered Leo inside.

It was not a broom cupboard, of course. It was a bedroom. The most sumptuous bedroom she had ever seen. Luxury like this was something that Leo, well-off and widely travelled though she was, had never even imagined.

Gulping, Leo looked round in disbelief. It was like a renaissance prince's salon. The room she was standing in was enormous. Carved pillars supported a domed ceiling that was clearly intended to represent the sky and was nearly as big. The wooden floor had been polished until it shone like wine. Great swathes of gold brocade framed tall windows. One entire wall was painted with a desert hunting scene. Against it stood a gilded couch upholstered in royal blue and scattered with gold cushions.

And the bed. Leo swallowed hard. She kept an eye on that bed. It looked dangerous. It was big and low and *rich;* ebony inlaid with intricate gold decoration; and it was covered with a shimmering cloth that she had very little doubt was woven gold.

She said the first thing that came into her head.

'*Simple* pleasures, my eye.'

Amer was shaken by a silent laugh. 'Design approved by my cousin the Minister for Culture, I'm sorry you don't approve of his taste.' He waved a hand at the couch. 'Take off that wet dress and sit down. I'll find you something to wear.'

He disappeared through a door behind a pillar.

Leo unzipped her dress and sank down onto the couch, holding the damp cloth modestly in front of her. A tubular cushion fell squashily to the floor, its ornate tassels flying wide. Gold thread unravelled. It pooled on the polished floor like tangled knitting.

She winced. Leo Groom, true to form, causing devastation wherever she set her clumsy feet. It was the last straw. Leo choked and began to cry.

Amer appeared at once, a robe of some sort over his arm. 'What's the matter?' he said, concerned.

Leo looked up. 'I've spoiled your cushion,' she said tragically.

She pointed at the puddle of gold braiding on the floor. It had hooked itself round the diamanté motif on her smart black shoe and before she got it off became ten times more tangled than before.

Amer was blank. He cast the robe from him and went down on one knee beside her. Very gently he put a fingertip to her eye. Sure enough, when he removed it there was a tear on the end of it.

'You cry over a *cushion?*' he said in disbelief.

'I always spoil things,' said Leo. She sniffed. 'I always have. I'm clumsy. I break things and fall over things and get coffee down my dress…' Her voice became suspended.

'I count your getting coffee on your dress as a bonus,' he said softly. 'Believe me.'

Leo turned drowned brown eyes to his. He smoothed the anxiety lines from her forehead with a gentle finger.

'Believe me,' he repeated, his voice suddenly husky.

With a little gesture of surrender Leo leaned forward and rested her head against his chest.

'I think this has been the worst day of my life,' she said, her voice muffled in the ivory silk of his shirt.

Amer stroked her hair. His hand was not entirely steady. Leo was unaware of it.

'No, it hasn't,' he said caressingly. 'You broke off an engagement you should never have got into. And you put me in my place. Can't be all bad.'

Leo gave a choke of startled laughter.

'Put you in your place?' she echoed drily. 'Oh sure.'

She looked up and met his eyes. They were warm, the grey of the soft twilight sky outside. Intent. And very close indeed.

Leo drew a shaky breath. There was that fugitive cologne again. Leo moistened her lips. The scent of it seemed to curl round her like smoke, like fog, awaking all her senses.

She said uncertainly, 'I—'

Suddenly it did not seem to matter that she was an emotional mess; or clumsy; or not wanted in the business. She was in his arms—well, almost in his arms—and it was Heaven.

Amer touched her cheek. 'Hush,' he said. 'Hush.'

This time she did notice that he was shaking. It was a gentle gesture. No force. No demand. It should have been kind and comforting, but the tremor in his fingers distracted her and it was neither.

For a long moment they looked at each other in silence. Leo thought hazily: I've been here before. This is how he made me feel that night. I want...I *want*...

Very, very gently, he prised the dress out of her unresisting fingers. Her lace-covered breasts started at the sudden chill. She heard him catch his breath.

'Beautiful,' he said reverently.

Leo turned her head away. Acute need warred with acute embarrassment. She vibrated with tension.

Taking his time, Amer stroked the lace aside and bent his head. Leo kept her head turned away. She held her breath. Very softly he brushed his lips across the nipple he had uncovered. She groaned.

'Truce over, I think,' he murmured. 'Don't you?'

Leo was beyond answering; beyond concentrating on anything but this incredible feeling.

'Time we were somewhere more comfortable.'

He was on his feet. Leo watched him, dazed. He twitched the corner of the gold coverlet. It rippled off the bed like a water snake.

'Scratchy,' explained Amer.

He slid his arms round her, lifting. She could feel his every tiny muscle movement in her fingers' ends.

He laid her down so gently. She hardly felt her silks and laces slide away until he replaced them with the warm sensuousness of his mouth. Leo could not believe it. He ran his open palm possessively over her naked hip and she shivered. Nothing had ever prepared her for this exquisite sensitivity. It was so piercing that it was almost like pain. But at the same time it was like being bathed in sunlight. She closed her eyes, drifting in delight.

'I'm glad you grew your hair.' It was a whisper.

Leo turned her head to look at him. He was drawing the pins out of her sophisticated hairstyle and fanning her hair out on his pillow. He ran his hands through it, watching absorbedly.

'I knew I would do this,' he murmured.

He shifted his gaze and smiled down at her, right into her eyes. Wonderingly she put up a hand to touch his mouth, his cheekbones, the corner of those silver eyes.

He stilled. For a moment his eyes were not silver any more, or gentle. And all vestige of amusement left his face. For a moment he looked as if he was in agony.

Leo was alarmed. 'What is it?'

But he did not answer. Or not with words. Instead he bent over her unhurriedly and his hands began to move. They smoothed and moulded and explored every inch of her body. Slowly. Then his mouth followed the same path down her pliant limbs with butterfly kisses.

Leo had never imagined such exquisite sensations. Soon she was writhing with pleasure and a wholly new hunger. Eyes tight shut, she reached for him.

He let her get rid of his jacket, even helped her with the buttons of his shirt so that she could feel the amazing sensation of her cool, quivering flesh against his warmth. But that was as far as he permitted.

'No,' he said, catching her clumsy, seeking hands.

Leo froze and her eyes flew open.

Amer saw her reaction. His eyes darkened. Suddenly he was unhurried no longer. He pushed her back, his mouth urgent at her breast, his hands shifting her as if he knew without words what her body required. His fingers circled, spiralled, drew her irresistibly into a dark vortex of response.

Leo cried out. Amer said something harsh she did not hear—or did not understand—and then his caress deepened urgently.

A rhythm she did not know she knew took hold of Leo. She arched and arched. Her heart raced. The strange, fierce sensation made her cry out, almost in fear.

Just for a moment she saw Amer's expression. It was total triumph.

And then she convulsed and the world spun out of control.

CHAPTER SEVEN

IT WAS Amer who stirred first. Leo was lying across his chest, breathing in the scent of him. She felt shattered by her own sensations. At the same time the dark pulse still throbbed, cavernously deep, waiting to reignite, waiting to meet its fellow.

Now, she thought. Now he will get rid of his clothes. Now he will lose himself, too. This time we will travel together.

She could hardly breathe as he fanned her hair about her bare shoulders.

It feels like silk, she thought. It amazed and delighted her. *My* hair feels like silk. What has he done to me? She turned her head, and quickly, shyly, kissed the warm golden chest where his heart beat so steadily.

But he did not respond. And he did not kiss her again.

He said, 'You'll get cold.'

'Mmm?'

He caressed the curve of her shoulder as if he owned it. As if he savoured the ownership. But not with passion.

'I can't have you catching cold.' His voice was full of lazy laughter. 'Think what it would do for my reputation.'

Leo's heart turned over. Hardly believing it, she thought: He has had enough of me already.

She was shaken to the core by the sensations of the last few minutes. She had never even imagined feelings like that existed, far less that she was capable of them. And now she lay in his arms, getting colder and colder, tasting rejection as she had never imagined that, either.

But she had started the evening fighting back and she was not going to fall into a decline now. With a courage she did not know she possessed, Leo raised her head and narrowed her eyes at him.

'For that matter, what would it do for your reputation to have it known that you seduce women by pouring coffee all over them?' she taunted.

'Would you call it seduction?' he murmured.

Leo winced inwardly. But she continued as if she had not heard. 'The least I was expecting was candlelight and a string quartet to serenade me.'

Amer looked at her curiously. 'I'll do better next time,' he promised.

He picked up her hand and carried it to his mouth. In spite of herself, Leo could feel her muscles uncurl in response. Her eyes grew slumberous. Amer smiled and turned her hand over so he could press a kiss into the palm. Every nerve ending in Leo quivered.

Surely now he would...

But he was swinging off the bed, refastening his shirt.

'Come along, my little sensualist. I'll give you candlelight and your serenade if you let me wrap you up in something warm first.'

He dropped a soft velour robe over her. It was the colour of tawny port and sported the inevitable gold facings. She huddled into it, grateful for not having to pretend any more that she did not mind him looking at her nakedness.

Something in her expression must have given her away. Amer's brows twitched together.

Quickly she flipped the gold braid with a disparaging finger. 'More design courtesy of the Minister of Culture?'

'Probably.'

Amer sat on the edge of the bed beside her. He put his hand against her cheek, savouring the warmth.

'I've never seen such skin.' He pulled the velour aside and kissed her shoulder. 'Pale as moonlight. We have poems about that, you know. Up to now I thought it was a poetic invention.'

He pulled her against his shoulder. At once, of course, he felt the rigidity in her body.

'What is it?' he said concerned.

She could not bear any more. Scrambling off the bed she dived for the bathroom door. She banged it behind her and leaned against it, letting the tears fall at last.

It was only a brief storm. She was careful to make no sound. And when it was over, she bathed her eyes and flushed face. To steady herself, she took stock of the bathroom.

It was on the same excessive lines as the master bedroom. It had marble floors and Greek columns. And a round sunken bath that was clearly designed for more than one person. Arched niches following the curved wall held statues and urns as well as a startling selection of expensive oils. Even the soap was sculptured.

Leo picked up a creamy bar and sniffed experimentally. There was a shadow on the pale bar. She rubbed at it and realised that it was ink transferred from her own finger.

'Leonora Groom, walking disaster,' she muttered. 'You may go to bed with princes but you still have the writing habits of a fourth former. How many times have you washed your hands since you acquired that stain? Ten? Fifteen? It must be ground in.'

She put the soap down hurriedly and a faint elusive scent wafted up to her. Amer's! She would know it anywhere. She backed away from the bath as if he were lying in it, laughing at her.

'Time to go back to walking disaster mode,' she told herself.

She went back into the bedroom and announced, 'I've got to go,' before her resolve wore off.

Amer was standing at the window, looking down into the garden. Just for a moment as he turned his head, she thought he looked strained. But at her words he raised his eyebrows in surprise.

'Run that past me again.'

The look of surprise was almost Leo's undoing.

Remember his own words, she told herself. He had been quite specific in that little piece of satire. Any opportunity for seduction should be pursued. With any woman. She had handed him the opportunity on a plate and he had not even bothered to seduce her. Would it have been better if he had?

Leo swallowed. 'I've got to go.'

She scrabbled for her clothes.

'Hey.'

He skirted the great tumbled bed and strolled over to her, stopping her search by the simple expedient of putting one hand round her wrist and holding it. In spite of herself, Leo shivered with lust. How could he do that, just by touching her arm? When he didn't even want her. It was *cruel*.

'What's the matter?'

He was smiling. He didn't think it was serious. Well, of course, for him it wasn't serious.

Or for her, either, Leo told herself feverishly. It was all over emotional nonsense at the end of a highly charged day. She would see that in the morning.

As long as she was alone in the morning, of course.

'I must get home. Things to do. Work,' said Leo.

The excuses floundered but the desperation was evident. Amer let go of her wrist and stood back, frowning.

'I thought we would spend the evening together.'

He encountered a look of such horror from Leo that he blinked.

'Evidently not,' he answered himself drily.

'I'm sorry,' said Leo, in disarray.

She grabbed her clothes and dived back into the bathroom. She was crying again.

She scrambled rapidly back into her dress. There was nothing she could do about her hair or—she winced at her reflection—the softly swollen mouth. There was no disguising the fact that she looked like a woman who had made love. At least she did until you got to her eyes.

They looked like a woman who had walked into a nightmare and could not find her way back.

Leo looked away. She tidied her dress, trying to reduce its plunge without much success.

'I am never,' she promised herself, 'going to wear this dress again.'

She ran her hands through the tangle of hair, trying not to remember how it had felt running through Amer's fingers. She could not put it up again—she had no idea what had happened to her hairpins and she was not going to go rummaging among tumbled bedclothes to find out—but at least she could make it lie flat to her head.

She thrust her feet into the sophisticated shoes and felt a measure of normality return. She picked up his robe, straightened her shoulders and went back to face Amer.

He had no smile for her.

'Are you all right?'

'Of course,' said Leo, not looking at him.

He put an arm round her shoulders. Just for a moment she felt protected. It was heavenly.

It was also an illusion. She twitched away from him and bolted for the stairs. Amer let her go without comment. But his frown deepened as he went after her.

Leo dived back to the salon where they had supper. The garden beyond the window was now completely dark. Someone had turned on the lights but they were dim and atmospheric. Breathy saxophone music whispered from hidden speakers. There was another tray of coffee—this time with a vacuum coffeepot—on the table.

Leo stopped dead in the doorway.

'A real Don Juan's box of tricks,' she said bitterly.

At her shoulder, Amer stopped, a look of comprehension flashing across his face. For a moment he was disturbed. Then he took a decision.

'Don Juan?' he murmured, ushering her into the room. 'Unfair. Have you forgotten we're going to be married?'

Leo recoiled as if she had burned herself.

'Nonsense.'

'Well, you asked me,' he reminded her evenly. 'Have some coffee and let's discuss it.'

She looked at him with hot eyes. 'There's nothing to discuss. And I don't want any coffee. I want to go home. Will you call me a cab?'

Amer was shocked. 'Of course not.'

Leo glared. 'You mean I'll have to make a break for it and pick one up in the street?'

He was silent for a moment. Then he said, 'Leonora, what's wrong?'

She shook her head, blinking away tears.

'Did I rush you? I thought if—'

But she stopped him with a gesture so despairing that he could not push her. He sighed.

'If you insist on going I will drive you. Of course. Only—' he gave her his most winning smile '—I hope you'll stay.'

The smile did not work. It was almost as if she did not see it. As if she would not allow herself to see it.

To Amer's deep disquiet, he found himself driving through the electronic gates of the Wimbledon mansion forty minutes later.

'Yours?' he said, genuinely disconcerted by the mansion confronting him.

Leo gave a sharp laugh. 'My father's. I have the extension.'

'Ah.'

It was no more than a sound but Leo detected patronising, even criticism.

'What?' she said, bristling. 'What?'

Amer did not answer. Or not directly.

'Are you allowed to ask me in?'

'It's quite self-contained,' Leo retorted. 'We don't police each other.'

He was noncommittal. 'Really.'

'Come in, if you don't believe me,' said Leo goaded.

He did not need a second invitation.

She switched on all the lights defiantly. No seducer's shadowy atmospherics here. He looked round, interested. Leo had not realised how untidy her sitting room was before. The desk, computer and television were islands among the flotsam—magazines, newspapers, open books, unanswered letters, theatre programmes, the dry cleaning she had dumped on the sofa two days ago...

'I see you live alone,' said Amer with quiet satisfaction.

'You knew that.'

'I thought Simon Hartley might have acquired residency rights.'

'No,' said Leo shortly.

'So I see.' He sounded inordinately pleased about it. 'What are you going to do about him?'

Back on her home territory Leo was feeling braver. She was also feeling appalled at her own conduct this evening.

'It's already done. Not that it's any of your business.'

'Of course it is. I can't have another man thinking he's engaged to my fiancé.'

She found she could not parry his teasing any more. She felt deathly tired suddenly.

'Oh go away,' said Leo, at the end of her tether.

'All right,' Amer said peacefully. He touched her cheek briefly. 'But don't forget you asked me to marry you.'

Leo ground her teeth. 'I'm not likely to forget that piece of insanity.'

'And I accepted.'

'Don't talk nonsense.'

His eyes sparkled but he shook his head reproachfully. 'You can't get out of it that way. You're mine now.'

'Get out,' Leo yelled.

He smiled deep into her eyes, kissed the air between them and went.

Leo did not sleep well. Well, that was not for the first time and, in the circumstances, not surprising. She had even expected it. What she had not expected was that work would not be the all-engrossing antidote that it usually was. Twice she found her concentration drifting away from the papers in front of her. And once she forgot a meeting altogether and had to be smuggled in late. The only time she came fully into the present was when her secretary buzzed to say that Mr el-Barbary was on the phone for her.

'I'm not taking his calls,' snapped Leo.

By the end of the day Leo's temper was on a hair trigger and her secretary was torn between panic and tears. When Gordon Groom stormed into the office, it was the last straw. He only ever came out of the Chief Executive's suite when there was a crisis but, Joanne thought she had never seen him in a rage like this.

'What the hell do you think you're playing at?' he shouted, steaming straight into Leo's room without even checking whether she was alone.

'Hello, Pops,' said Leo. 'You got back from Singapore quickly. Did Simon call for backup?'

She twirled her executive chair round a couple of times and grinned brazenly. 'I'm free.'

Gordon was white with temper. 'Simon rang me and I came at once. What is this nonsense all about?'

'I'm sure Simon told you. We decided to break our engagement.'

'But you've only just got the bloody ring.'

'That,' agreed Leo gravely, 'is true.'

'It's no laughing matter.' Gordon was furious.

Leo tilted her head on one side thoughtfully.

'Oh I don't know. I got away without ruining my life. That must be worth a mild titter. I could have married a man who thought it was part of his job description.'

Her father's face darkened. 'That's not funny.'

'I don't think so, either.' She stood up. Suddenly she let her own fury run out on its leash. It was a heady feeling. 'In fact I think the whole thing with Simon was seriously unfunny. And all because I let myself be manipulated by the two of you.'

He gobbled.

'Don't get me wrong,' said Leo in a light, hard voice. 'I don't blame you. I blame myself. I should have had the guts to make my own choices. From now on I'm going to.'

Gordon realised that, for the first time since she was a small child, he was probably not going to get his Leo to do what he wanted. Shock and affront made him lose what little command over himself he had left.

'You needn't think you can stay on here as my pensioner,' he raged. 'If you want to make your own choices, fine. And pay your own bills while you're at it.'

In the act of pushing back her chair, Leo stopped dead. She stared at him, breathing hard.

'Your *pensioner?*'

'You don't think you earn the damned great salary I pay you, do you?' said Gordon cruelly.

She was suddenly very pale.

'No,' she said very quietly. 'Any more than I earned the right to live in the Wimbledon house. I take it this is a notice to quit?'

'Oh for God's sake.' Gordon was scathing. 'Spare me the melodrama.' He strove for control. 'Look, can't we sit down and discuss this rationally?'

'There's nothing to discuss, Father.' Her voice was almost inaudible but quite composed. 'When it come to my marriage you don't get a vote.'

'Then—'

She flung up a hand. 'No more threats, please.'

To tell the truth, Gordon was shaken by what he seemed to have done. Leo had never turned on him like that before. He was temperamentally incapable of backing down but he did realise he had gone too far.

'We've both said things we'll be sorry for,' he said heavily. 'Grooms is the only future you've got, one way or another. Go home and think about it. We'll talk in the morning.'

Leo did not answer him. He gave an exasperated exclamation and stalked out.

She sank back into her chair, shaking.

What am I going to do, Leo thought. What in the wide world am I going to do?

It did not take long for Amer to deduce that Leo was not talking to him. No one could be *that* busy. He frowned. In spite of what she had said last night, in spite of his own careful strategy, he was not entirely surprised.

He looked unseeingly at the file that Major McDonald had left. What went wrong last night? He had thought he'd done well, in the circumstances.

He had seen at once that it was more than the champagne that had sent Leo into that raging temper. But the champagne had fired a recklessness which he did not need his investigator's report to tell him was out of character. And he had so nearly taken advantage of it.

'I should have done. Then she would really have a reason for not taking my calls,' Amer said savagely.

He did not quite know why he had not. He was not used to denying himself. And God knows she had been alluring, in her wide-eyed amazement at how he made her feel.

And yet... And yet...

There had been something heartbreakingly unguarded about her last night. When she touched his face she seemed so young; as if she had found herself in wonderland and could not believe what she was doing here.

Quite suddenly he had wanted to keep that look of wonder on her face. To give, for once, without taking. It had seemed like a way of taking care of her.

Now he shifted uneasily. He was not used to that protective urge, either. It was disconcerting. Oh yes, he had been right when he told Hari he would go to any lengths to make her listen to him. Though he had not realised himself then, quite how much he meant it.

He opened the file again. The notice of her engagement stared out at him. Amer frowned, furious again.

And then—he read it again. ''Daughter of blah, blah and Mrs Deborah Groom of Kensington.'' Unless he was much mistaken he had already met Mrs Deborah Groom of Kensington. And she had lied to him, too. So she owed him, didn't she?

He reached for a telephone directory.

The first thing, Leo knew, was to get out of her father's house. Even though the flat was theoretically self-contained, Gordon Groom still thought of it as his territory.

She rang her mother.

'Darling,' said Deborah. 'How lovely. Do you want to get together and talk weddings?'

Leo laughed so hard that she could barely speak. When she controlled herself enough to explain, her mother was unusually silent.

'So what are you going to do?'

'I thought I might come and stay?' Leo said tentatively.

Deborah was brisk. 'Out of the question. I'm off to Spain and the flat is being completely remodelled while I'm away. No power, no water. Uninhabitable. Sorry darling.'

But she did not, thought Leo shrewdly, sound sorry.

'Well, I could always stay with Claire…'

'When you're running away from her brother?' Deborah gave a shriek of shocked laughter. 'Leo, you're the *end*.'

'But—'

'What you need,' said her mother sapiently, 'is a nice foreign holiday. Get yourself a tan and let your hair down a bit. You'll come back a new woman.'

Leo knew it was exactly what her mother would do in similar circumstances. For the first time since Gordon had marched into her room, she smiled, albeit faintly.

'Thanks. But I'm not sure it would work for me.'

'Works for everyone, darling,' Deborah assured her

blithely. 'Especially if you can find a nice man to help you have fun.'

Unbidden, unwelcome, the thought of Amer, his face contorted with triumph, flashed across Leo's inner eye. She shuddered.

'I've had all the men I can handle in the last week,' she said unwarily.

Deborah chuckled. 'Oh well, there's your answer,' she said pleased. 'Have fun, darling.' She rang off.

Amer did not make the mistake of telephoning again. He established Leo's movements by means of various devious and highly expensive means. What he learned, caused him to suck his teeth and make a number of international phone calls.

And then he plotted his strategy.

Leo was throwing things into suitcases when the bell rang. For a moment she thought it was her father and almost did not answer. But a quick look at her watch reassured her. Even for a major domestic crisis, Gordon Groom would not be home before seven.

So she smoothed her hands down the side of her dusty jeans and went to open the door. For a moment she did not recognise the tall, casually dressed man in dark glasses.

'You're home early,' said Amer displeased.

He did not wait to be invited but, taking off his dark glasses, walked past her into the sitting room. At the sight that met his eyes, he halted, his brows rising at the chaos.

'I thought it could not get more untidy than when I first saw it,' he remarked. 'I see I was wrong.'

Leo was in no mood to provide the cabaret.

'Packing,' she said shortly. 'I'm moving out.'

He nodded approvingly. 'I'm flattered you took my words to heart.'

Leo was speechless.

'Living in your father's pocket,' he explained kindly. 'Not healthy. Believe me, I speak from experience.'

Leo did not want to hear about his experience. She said so.

Amer beamed, not a whit offended. 'I hear you've made it a clean break all round. Excellent.'

Leo was not given to self-pity. She would have said the last thing she wanted was sympathy from Amer or anyone else. But somehow this cheery acceptance that losing her home and her job in one day was somehow life enhancing was too much to bear. For a wild moment she nearly launched herself at him, screaming.

But one look at the gleam in his eyes made her realise that this was exactly what he hoped for. She drew on all her reserves of self-control and kept quiet. Still, she retired behind a small coffee table in case the temptation to hit him became too great to resist.

'How did you know that?' she said acidly. 'Have you been spying on me again?'

Amer smiled. This was clearly a question he had anticipated.

'Interested enquiries into your welfare,' he said smoothly. 'I wondered if your father would give you grief after your bid for freedom.'

Leo winced. 'Shrewd of you.'

He laughed but his expression was sympathetic. 'When it comes to overbearing fathers, mine wrote the book,' he said wryly. 'Listen to the voice of experience. What you need now is a cooling off period.'

'Why do you think I'm packing?' snapped Leo.

'Got anywhere to go?'

She hesitated.

'I thought not. That's why I'm here.'

Leo regarded him with deep suspicion. 'I don't understand.'

Amer offered her a blinding smile. 'I'm offering you sanctuary.'

Leo's suspicions crystallised. Her temper, simmering all day, seemed to shoot out of the top of her head.

'How dare you?' she yelled.

Amer blinked.

'I'm not moving in with you. Not if you were the last man on earth. And if you think a disaster in my private life will push me into your arms, you've got me very wrong.'

There was a very nasty silence. Amer had not moved. But all of a sudden he looked dangerous.

'You are insulting,' he said softly.

Leo quailed inwardly. But she was not going to admit it.

'And you're an opportunist,' she flung back at him.

'You are so wrong,' he said. 'Was I an opportunist last night?'

Leo paled.

'Let me assure you—' his voice was very soft but the grey eyes were like chips of flint '—you have no need to fear me. I have never wanted you less than I do at this moment.'

'*Oh.*' Leo was so angry that she was not even upset. Maybe later, she thought. Now she just wanted to hit him. 'How dare you?'

'The last thing any man wants is a woman who thinks she has no alternative,' Amer told her. His voice bit. 'What fun is there in a woman who has been pushed into your arms?'

'In that case—'

He swept on, ignoring her. 'A man,' he said very softly, 'does his own hunting.'

Leo felt the shock go through her as if she had walked into a block of ice. For a moment it left her quite numb. Her brain was working. But nothing else.

She shook her head. 'I don't believe you said that.'

'Believe it.'

Her body came back on line. She found it was shaking. Was she afraid of him? The idea was insupportable.

'I don't like threats,' she hissed.

'What threats?'

'You implied I was some sort of—prey.' Leo could not help herself. She shuddered.

'That's nonsense and you know it. Prey gets killed. That's not what I want to do to you at all.'

She was not going to ask him what he did want to do to her. She was *not*.

'And you know that, too. You ought to.' The caressing note was back. Was it calculated? She just did not know. All she knew was that it was too horribly reminiscent of last night.

Reluctant, ashamed, Leo met his eyes. She could see that he was remembering last night, too. And she had almost managed to blank it out of her memory. Yet suddenly it was there in the room with them: what she had said. What, Heaven help her, she had done.

Leo shut her eyes. 'Please go.'

'No,' said Amer unhelpfully. 'You're my promised wife. I have a responsibility.'

Leo opened her eyes and glared. 'Will you please,' she said intensely, 'stop calling me your promised wife You know perfectly well I didn't mean it.'

'But I did.'

She could have danced with rage. 'Well too bad. Because I'm not going to marry anybody, And—'

There was a long peal on the doorbell.

'Now what?' said Leo exasperated.

She trod round the coffee table and suitcases and went to answer it. To her amazement it was her father.

'Pops!'

'May I come in?'

Leo was blank. Gordon Groom never came to her bit of the house. If he wanted to see her he left a message at work. A couple of times he had called and asked her over to the main house on the spur of the moment. But turn up humbly on her doorstep like any ordinary visitor? Never. She could not believe it.

'Yes, if you—' She remembered Amer. 'Well—'

Gordon did not notice her reluctance. He shouldered past her, frowning with his own preoccupations.

'You were worked up earlier,' he said. 'Now you've had time to think rationally—'

He caught sight of Amer. At once his hackles rose. Leo saw it with a sinking heart.

'This isn't a good time, Pops,' she began. Her voice shook.

Gordon did not take any notice of her. He thrust his chin out pugnaciously.

'Who are you?' he demanded.

Amer looked at Leo. She seemed frozen. Gordon swung back on her.

'How long has he been here? Have you been seeing someone behind Simon's back? Is that why Simon dumped you?'

Leo said numbly, 'Simon didn't dump me.'

Gordon ignored that, too. He gave a crow of triumph. 'I knew there had to be more in it that you said. I just knew it. You *fool*.'

It was like all their other arguments, ever since she was a child. The loud, hectoring voice, the refusal to listen to her— Leo knew it so well. And she still did not know how to deal with it.

'I'll call him,' said Gordon, the fixer, pursuing his own train of thought. 'See if I can smooth things over. He's a good lad. He'll listen to reason.'

Leo could feel the familiar helplessness swelling up until it closed her throat. She felt suffocated.

She found an arm round her shoulders.

'You are right,' Amer said quietly. 'I am Leonora's lover.'

Leo flinched. Then, under the pressure of his fingers, stood perfectly still. She felt numb.

Gordon was diverted briefly from his plotting. He looked impatient.

'Not any more you're not.'

It was his turn to be ignored.

'And I am going to marry her.'

CHAPTER EIGHT

TWELVE hours later Leo was on a plane.

Amer, more businesslike than she had ever seen him, had simply taken charge. She had been swept off to spend the night in a quietly exclusive hotel. And then this morning Hari Farah had arrived with her passport, tickets and instructions to accompany her to Dalmun.

Leo had not slept and she was feeling spaced out. Although Hari was exquisitely polite she regarded him with suspicion.

'Where is Amer?'

'He has some matters to arrange. Nothing of significance. But long-standing arrangements will need to be changed,' said Hari smoothly, conveniently forgetting the acrimonious telephone call that had been in progress when he left the Mayfair house. The old Sheikh had not been at all pleased at his son's news and was saying so at length.

Leo was too proud to ask any more. Anyway, there was no point in asking Hari the most burning question in her mind.

Why had Amer left her alone last night? She would have resisted to the point of violence if Amer had assumed that because he had decided for some reason of his own that it amused him to rescue her from her predicament, he was entitled to make love to her, of course. But she was disconcerted that he had not even tried.

So she allowed herself to be swept off to the airport, still in a daze from her sleepless night. Amer had managed a brief, courteous phone call this morning. But that was all.

'What is he *doing?*' she said to herself as much as Hari.

Hari did not answer. He was too polite. He could have

131

said he wished he knew. In all the years he had known him he had never seen Amer like this.

He had even said so, during the dawn telephone calls.

'Why are you doing this?'

'I'm going to marry her,' Amer replied.

Hari was grim. 'Since when?'

'Since she asked me.'

'Since she—' Hari was lost for words.

'Well, to be honest since she dared me not to.'

'You're crazy,' said Hari finding words came to mind after all. 'And what's more so is she.'

'Oh no, she's got very cold feet now.'

'Cold feet? You mean she wants to back out and you won't let her?'

'That's not a very romantic way of putting it,' said Amer reproachfully.

'Romantic! You *are* crazy.' A thought occurred to Hari. 'You're not in love with her, are you?'

Amer hesitated. 'She asked me to marry her,' he said obstinately. 'She's not going to wriggle out of it.'

'She'll hate you,' said Hari with gloomy satisfaction.

'But she'll learn not to go asking men to marry her because she's lost her temper.'

Hari stared at Amer. 'You're not serious.'

Amer stared back, implacable.

'You *are* serious. You can't do this. Not just to teach the girl a lesson.'

'I can do whatever I want,' Amer said haughtily.

Hari despaired and said so. Amer was unmoved. Hari banged off to pack.

When he had gone, Amer's arrogant smile died. He was not going to admit it to Hari but he knew that what he was doing was irrational.

At first she had just infuriated him, throwing out her challenging proposal like that as if he were negligible, a *nothing* in her life. He had needed, really needed, as he told her last night, to show her he was a man who did his own hunting. And made sure that every one else knew that she was *his* and no one else's. Hell, he had even been jealous of her dictatorial old father.

But there was more to it than that. He wanted to treasure her, to make her feel safe; to make her feel *wonderful*. To make her look again as she had in his arms, bewildered by bliss. And he wanted it forever.

And if she didn't want it, too bad! He straightened his shoulders. She would in time. If it was the last thing he did, he would make her want him as he wanted her.

Leo, in Hari's charge after Amer's polite and passionless phone call, had given up thinking. She told herself she did not want passion from Amer. Of course she did not. But the lack of it made her feel lost and even more bereft than her departure from home and job.

She hid it, allowing Hari to usher her into the first-class cabin and to probe—discreetly—into her relationship with his boss. Since she did not know what it all meant herself she did not give much for his chances of enlightenment.

'I am just coming to Dalmun for a visit,' Leo announced. 'My mother thinks I need a holiday somewhere warm.'

She said it several times. It sounded increasingly hollow. Hari, however, was too polite to say so.

She was clearly exhausted. He let her snooze. Time enough to pass on some essential background information when she was more alert.

She woke when the cabin crew started to serve lunch.

'I took the liberty of ordering for you,' Hari told her. 'You were sleeping so peacefully. But if you do not like anything, they will be only too happy to fetch you something else.'

'I'm sure it will be fine,' muttered Leo.

Awake at last, she wondered what on earth she was getting herself into. What she doing on this plane? How could she have let Amer el-Barbary take charge of her life like that? If she needed an exotic holiday why had she not gone to the Seychelles or Barbados on her own?

Because, said a cynical little voice inside her, nobody goes to the Seychelles or Barbados on their own. And Amer el-Barbary had not stopped to ask her permission.

'I am sure you will find it interesting,' Hari said diplomatically. 'Er, what exactly has His Excellency told you about the country?'

His Excellency! Leo winced. Hari could not have said anything which made her realise how far away her world was from Amer's. Or how little she knew about him really.

'Nothing very much at all,' she muttered.

Hari hid his dismay and embarked on a rapid thumbnail sketch.

'It is very old. Dalmun City was on the frankincense road.'

Leo struggled to concentrate. It felt as if she were in the middle of a nightmare.

'The frankincense road?'

'It went along the edge of the desert,' Hari explained. 'In the monsoon season, traders sailed to India and even China. They brought back all sorts of things that people wanted in Europe. Silks, feathers, spices. The road developed to take exotic goods north to the markets.'

Silks, feathers and spices. Exotic indeed. And for all Amer's Italian suits and Impressionist paintings, that was his real heritage. And she knew nothing of it at all.

Just because he could set her senses on fire, it did not mean that they had anything like enough to bridge that centuries-deep gap of culture. Leo felt very cold.

Hari ploughed on conscientiously. 'At one time there were several cities strung out along the road where the merchants would stop and trade. Just ruins now, of course. That is where His Excellency got his interest in archaeology, of course.'

'Amer is interested in archaeology? I didn't know,' said Leo, chalking up another failure of communication.

Unaware, Hari smiled reminiscently. 'He has always been interested, since he was a child. It was the subject he studied at his English university. For a while he even threatened his father he would make it his profession.' He laughed. 'His father had not spoken to him for a year. But when he heard that, he summoned him to the Palace at once. But I'm sorry to bore you. His Excellency must have told you this already.'

The nightmare pressed closer. His Excellency, Leo was beginning to realise, had told her precisely nothing about himself.

'N-no.'

Hari thought hard thoughts about Amer. How on earth was this woman going to deal with the seething politics of Dalmun without some background? It was like sending a tourist into the desert without a compass.

He set himself to repair the omission as best he could in the remaining hours of the flight.

Which was how Leo learned that Amer was the Sheikh's only surviving son and expected to take up the reins of leadership eventually. His father was passionate and volatile, however, and Amer was no obedient cipher. So they lived in separate palaces, more often than not at odds with each other.

'His Majesty is very—traditional,' Hari said, choosing his words with care. 'He does not like things to change. The ministers know that progress cannot be halted and that His Excellency recognises this. So they consult him on policy— but informally, if you follow me. Everyone looks to Sheikh Amer to persuade his father to improve things. But, of course, in the end it is always His Majesty's decision.'

'It sounds appalling,' said Leo from the heart. 'Responsibility without power. The pits. Especially if he is fond of his father.'

Hari looked at her in quick surprise. Not many of Amer's friends had understood that. None of the girl-friends that he could remember had come anywhere near appreciating Amer's dilemma. He suddenly felt a lot more hopeful.

'You are so right,' he agreed with enthusiasm. He became less correct. And a good deal less discreet. 'It's a real tightrope. His father is unpredictable. For example, last year he confined Amer to house arrest for a while when he refused to marry again.'

Leo froze.

Hari did not notice. 'We were all afraid,' he went on. 'But then someone presented him with a wild caught saker falcon and he insisted that Amer went on a hunting trip with him to try it out. And when they came back, all their disagreements were forgotten. Amer was allowed to go to Egypt just as if they had never had a disagreement.' He shrugged helplessly.

'Was that when I met him?' Leo said hollowly. 'After he'd just come out of house arrest?'

'Yes.'

'And just because he did not want to marry again?'

Hari was rueful. 'You must understand that there is a lot of tribal unrest in Dalmun. Officially we do not admit it but in practice there are several tribes—particularly some of desert Bedouins—who are dissatisfied with the part they are allowed to play in government. Amer wants to deal with this by negotiation but his father thinks that another family alliance is all that is needed.'

'I don't understand.'

'Amer's first wife came from a powerful border family,' he explained. 'They used to make trouble regularly. But ever since the marriage they have sided with His Majesty. Even after she died—' He stopped. Leo had flinched. 'What is it?' he said in concern.

'I didn't know.' Her mouth felt stiff. The words sounded strange. 'How did she die? Was it recent?'

Hari was shocked. Damn it, what was Amer doing with this girl?

He said reassuringly, 'It was years ago. Amer was still at university.'

'What was she like?'

Hari shrugged. It was years since he had thought about the spoilt beauty that Amer had married.

'I didn't really know her. I was very young. She was very beautiful, very fashionable.'

Leo's heart sank like a stone.

'How did she die? Was she ill?'

'No, nothing like that. It was an accident. She was thrown from a horse. Somewhere in France I believe.'

'How terrible,' she whispered.

Hari was startled. Then uncomfortable. 'It was a long time ago,' he said again. 'I do not think Amer is still grieving. I've never heard him mention her.'

'But he did not marry again,' Leo said. 'If it was so long ago you would have expected him to fall in love again, wouldn't you?'

She could imagine all too vividly how the death of his young wife must have struck him to the core. She felt desolate at the thought.

Hari saw he had made a mistake and did not know how to retrieve it. He pushed a harassed hand through his hair.

'Oh, he has not been short of love,' he said unwisely. 'There was just no reason for him to marry.'

Leo gave him a stricken look. He could have kicked himself.

'Look,' he said desperately, 'don't get the wrong idea. In Dalmun marriage is a strategic thing. For everyone involved. It is all very practical. Don't start thinking of Amer as some tragic, grief-stricken hero. He isn't.'

Leo did not answer.

So why had Amer accepted her vainglorious challenge? Why had he pursued her? She had thought she had the answer. Pride! But in that case why, when he had defeated her in every way there was, why was he still insisting that they were engaged in spite of her denials?

Well, now she had the answer to that, too. He did not want to make one of those practical, strategic marriages. Probably he was still in love with his tragically dead wife. He wanted her as high-class camouflage, to keep his father at bay when he pressed him to marry again.

Leo flayed herself with the thought.

Oh, there were other elements, of course. Amer, she knew
by now, wanted to win any game he played. When she
slipped away from Cairo without leaving him a message he
must have felt for a moment that he had lost that game. He
would not have tolerated that, hence the private investigators.

And there was sex of course. Leo's experience might be
limited. But she realised that the sexual current between her
and Amer was powerful by any standards. He would not want
to leave that unexplored. She shivered, remembering.

Hari said that Amer had not been short of love. She believed him—if love was what you called it. Those lazy,
laughing kisses. The unhurried touch. Even that final glinting
triumph. They all spoke of a man who knew exactly what he
was doing. Skill like that, thought Leo wincing, only came
with practice.

She could feel the heat in her cheeks. Oh it was effective,
all right. It might not have much to do with love but a woman
could forget that in the intoxication of those moments in his
arms.

Her memories were too graphic. She banished them, resolutely. It was as well she did. Hari's confidences had become crucial.

'Everyone thought he would not marry again after all this
time. Your news will be a great joy to everyone.'

Leo gaped. Hari smiled reassuringly and, quite uncon-
sciously, added the final drop to her cup of despair.

'His Majesty will come round in time. You'll see.'

In London Amer was in his final and most important meeting.
It was not one his father knew anything about, although both
the Finance Ministry and the Department of Health had con-
tributed to the paper under discussion. There were four men
on the other side of the table.

'It is all very well,' said a dark, angry man. 'But why is
it taking so long?'

'You know why, Saeed,' said one of his companions patiently. 'This time it will be different.'

'Because Sheikh Amer will pretend that these things are needed for his excavation.' The man was contemptuous. 'Why is the truth not enough? Our people have poor water and no electricity. Dalmun is not a poor country. We have oil, minerals. And His Majesty buys racehorses and bits of foreign industry! It is an outrage.'

Privately Amer agreed with him. He was too loyal to his father to say so, however.

Instead he said soothingly, 'Well, as you see from the papers in front of you, the electricity infrastructure will start to be installed next month. After that we start to implement the water conservation project.'

Saeed was not soothed. He was the only man in the room in flowing traditional dress. It kept tangling round the legs of the hotel chairs, as he kicked his feet in frustration.

He said mutinously, 'We have been waiting too long. People have stopped believing Sheikh Amer's promises.'

There was a chorus of protest from the other three. Saeed seemed to take confidence from it. He stopped wrestling with his robes.

'I warn you,' he said directly to Amer. 'There will be action.'

Amer broke into the outcry.

'What sort of action?' he said softly.

Saeed's expression became shifty. He shrugged. 'They don't tell me. I am too far away. But there will be something.'

'Another kidnapping?' Amer said lightly. 'I'm told it's starting to be offered as an exciting option for adventurous tourists.' His eyes were watchful.

'It is no joke to people who get sick from bad water,' said Saeed hotly.

'And I am not laughing at them,' Amer said at once. 'But is it sensible to deal with modern problems by thirteenth-century strategies?'

Saeed looked at him with dislike. 'Maybe we should be more *focused*,' he said mockingly.

Amer stiffened.

But Saeed's colleagues shouted him down so loudly that Amer judged it diplomatic not to pursue the subject. He did not forget it, though. As soon as he came out of his meeting he called Dalmun with an urgent message.

And then he gave instructions to the crew of the private jet which had been on stand-by all day.

A car with screened windows met Leo at the airport. Hari assured her it was to protect them from the sun but Leo was not convinced. It felt as if she were being kept out of sight. Though, when it was Amer himself who insisted on her coming to his country, she could not imagine why. She said so.

'Not at all,' said Hari.

He was sweating silently. It was not the first time he had adapted the truth to suit Amer's purposes. But, under Leo's sceptical gaze, he found it amazingly difficult to sustain. The gorgeous Julie in Cannes had been a lot easier to deal with, he thought.

As instructed, he took her to Amer's palace in the foothills. 'You will be pleased with it,' he said pleadingly. 'Amer inherited it from his grandfather and he has kept it traditional. The sunken garden and the courtyard with the fountains are exactly as they have been for centuries. For the rest—well he put in electricity and some modern plumbing, that's all.'

It was dark by the time they reached the palace. Pushing aside the curtains, Leo saw great wooden gates open silently. They were set in pale walls that must be twenty feet high, she thought.

'It's a fortress,' she said, taken aback.

Just for a moment she thought she caught a glimpse of a mountain ridge against the starlit sky. But then they swept into the courtyard and there were too many people for her to concentrate on the landscape. They surrounded the car with greetings and offers of service.

In spite of the vocabulary Leo had picked up in Egypt, their Arabic was too rapid or too accented for her to follow. She turned to Hari. She had the feeling that all was not well. It made her feel helpless. She did not like it.

Hari assimilated the information fast and, although he hardly reacted at all, Leo was convinced that her suspicions were right.

'What is it?' she said in quick concern.

But he was smiling, saying it was nothing, a few administrative matters only. She would be tired after her journey. She would want to rest. A room had been prepared for her in the women's quarters. Fatima, who spoke English, would show her the way and fetch her a light supper if she required it.

Leo smiled at Fatima, who had gentle eyes and was looking excited by their arrival. But all her instincts told her that something was wrong.

She said sharply, 'Has there been a message from Amer?'

'Yes indeed,' said Hari. 'He will be here tomorrow afternoon.'

Relieved to be able to tell the truth, he beamed at Leo. She distrusted him deeply. But he was right in one thing at least. After her sleepless night, and the conflicting emotions of the last twenty-four hours, she was exhausted.

So she let Fatima conduct her to a cool, vaulted room. The leaded windows looked out onto a skyline of palm trees. Above them, the stars seemed to quiver with the intensity of their light. A new moon curved like a scimitar slash above the horizon.

She opened the window and leaned out. The scent of the night rolled in at once. The smell was of heat and herbs she did not know. Leo suddenly felt very small and alien. And alone. She shivered.

There was a touch on her arm. She looked round, startled.

Fatima was offering her a small porcelain cup of some golden liquid. It was steaming. Her eyes were kind.

'Sheikh Amer will be here tomorrow,' she said comfortingly.

For no reason that Leo could think of, she found her eyes filling with tears. She dashed them away angrily. Tiredness, she thought. That was all it was. The mere presence of Amer—or anybody else for that matter—was not enough to make her feel at home in an alien land. That took time and patience and study; and depended entirely on the effort she put into it herself. Amer was irrelevant.

But it would clearly have been a waste of time to tell this to Fatima. So she shrugged and let herself be shown the beauties of the suite which the Sheikh had ordered to be prepared for her. Apart from the bedroom, there was a bathroom that could rival any she had seen in the most luxurious hotels in the world, a sitting room furnished with exquisitely carved furniture and strewn with jewel-coloured cushions, and a small roof terrace. The terrace was triangular and at its apex there was a statue of a falcon with its beak open.

'When the wind blows, the falcon breathes,' Fatima explained poetically. 'There is a legend...'

But Leo's eyelids were drooping. Fatima was sympathetic. She made sure that Leo had everything she needed and left.

Leo wanted to think but she could not. She fell into a bed. And a sleep too deep for dreams.

In the morning, of course, it was different. She awoke with a start, her heart pounding. At first she did not know where she was and the leaded lights in the window looked like prison bars. But then she saw the doors open to the terrace, with full daylight streaming in, and she remembered. She sank back among the pillows with a gasp of relief.

It was quickly succeeded by all the doubts that had beset her yesterday. Where was she? With the curtains closed she had not really been able to detect much of the route they had taken from the palace. Hari had taken charge of everything, including her passport. The prison analogy did not seem so far-fetched after all.

She pulled on yesterday's clothes and went to look for

someone, anyone. She needed to assert that it was she—not Amer and certainly not Hari—who was in charge of her life.

She found them easily enough. Asserting herself was more difficult. For one thing, everyone denied knowledge of Hari's current whereabouts.

'Perhaps he has gone to the airport to meet the Sheikh,' Fatima suggested helpfully.

She was delighted to bring Leo food. She attended assiduously to her comfort. She showed her round the palace and its shaded gardens. And when Leo grew restive, she introduced her to a quiet scholarly man who laid out books and maps and the Sheikh's archaeological finds for her admiration until Leo thought she would scream.

'Look,' she said dangerously, 'I'm not interested in His Excellency's leisure activities.'

'I hope you don't mean that,' said a voice from the doorway. An amused voice. One, she now realised, that had whispered through her dreamless sleep.

She swung round and yelled at him, 'Don't you laugh at me. Don't you *dare* laugh at me.'

Her quiet companion folded maps and retreated rapidly.

'You've embarrassed Hussein,' said Amer reproachfully.

Leo was shaking. With fury she told herself.

'Never mind Hussein. Where is Hari? And what has he done with my passport?' she burst out.

Amer blinked.

'And welcome home to you, too,' he said drily. 'Yes thank you, the flight was quite pleasant.'

'I don't care what sort of flight you had,' shouted Leo, thoroughly upset. 'I want to get out of here.'

Amer sat down on the other side of ancient map table and folded his hands together into a pyramid. He regarded her thoughtfully. 'Why?'

'*Why?*' Leo glared. 'Isn't it obvious? Nobody likes being held a prisoner.'

Amer remained calm.

'And what has convinced you that you're a prisoner?'

She made a despairing gesture. 'I don't know where I am. Nobody will tell me anything. They just say to wait for you. And they took my passport away.' To her dismay, her voice choked on this last statement. She looked away.

'I see.' He sounded unforgivably calm. 'Do you want to run away so soon?'

Leo rummaged in her trouser pocket for a handkerchief and failed to find one. She sniffed as unobtrusively as she could.

'I want to be in control of my own affairs,' she said when she thought she had mastered her voice again.

There was a pause which she could not interpret.

'A modern woman,' he teased. 'My father will be shocked.'

Leo raised her head, arrested. 'Your father?'

'We are having dinner with him,' Amer told her gravely.

Leo's heart fluttered in her breast. 'A-are we?' she said, uncertain all of a sudden.

He gave her that terrible, tender, deceiving smile. 'Unless you'd rather take your passport and go, of course.'

Leo wanted to demand her passport and sweep out of the room immediately. At the same time, she wanted him to take her in his arms and tell her that he loved her—and that he wanted her never to leave his side. It was not *fair*.

Amer sensed her dilemma, it seemed. He stood up and strolled over to an intricately carved cabinet. He opened a small drawer and extracted a little booklet. It was, Leo saw with indignation, not even locked. Amer tossed the passport across to her.

'There you are, my darling. Your freedom, if you want it,' he said with irony.

Leo caught it out of the air, like a starving monkey fielding falling fruit. She clutched it to her breast protectively. Amer's irony deepened.

'So am I to order the car to take you to the airport?'

To her own complete astonishment Leo heard herself say, 'No.'

His eyes lifted; lit with a wicked light.

'Ah.'

'If your father is kind enough to ask me to dinner, it is only polite to go,' she said with dignity.

'Oh, absolutely,' he said, smooth as silk.

She was sure her colour rose. To disguise it, she looked at her watch in her most efficient manner. 'Of course, I shall need time to get ready. I'm not sure whether I've brought anything suitable to wear. I wasn't expecting to come to Dalmun when I packed.'

He smiled. 'I can advise you.'

Leo had a sudden vivid picture of him, inspecting the clothes that Fatima had unpacked for her this morning. Padding around in her bedroom, no doubt as if he owned it. Which of course he did. Her breathing quickened.

'I think I can manage to sort something out on my own, thanks.'

Amer's eyes danced. 'But you will need advice on local conventions of dress.'

'I'll ask Fatima,' Leo said firmly. She was sure her colour was hectic.

He laughed and flung up his hands in a gesture of surrender.

'I will tell her that you are to borrow anything you require.'

Leo recoiled. 'Borrow! From whom?'

Was he suggesting she wear his wife's clothes? Was this where he told her about his wife at last? Suddenly she did not want to hear about his love for another woman.

He eyed her speculatively. 'I have guests from time to time. We are out of town here. It is not always possible for them to buy what they need at a moment's notice. So we keep a few spare clothes for visitors to borrow if necessary.' He read her mind again. 'Men as well as women,' he added kindly.

This time there was no doubt. Leo flushed scarlet. She could feel it.

He laughed again, quite differently.

'You look agitated. You should rest.'

'On the contrary,' she said with as much dignity as she could muster. 'I slept too long.'

'Then you have not recovered from the journey yet,' he said imperturbably. 'As I have not myself. Let us rest together.'

There was a shattering silence, broken only by the thump of her heart. Leo thought: He didn't say that. He *can't* have said that. He can't think I'm here to fall into bed with him when he snaps his fingers.

But Hari had said, 'He wasn't short of love.' And she had already fallen into bed with him, hadn't she? It was no thanks to her that they were not already lovers in all the ways there were.

Amer held out his hand.

She said harshly, 'You can't be serious. That is such a cliché.'

He was not put out. 'I merely suggest what we both want. Where is the cliché in that?' The grey eyes were warm.

Leo closed her eyes against the allure. If she did not look at him, she would be able to stick to her resolve.

'It's feudal.'

'And are you so modern?'

His voice was a caress. It set little shivers of desire rippling through every nerve ending. Oh, she could close her eyes and maybe her ears but he was in her bloodstream now and her whole body ached to turn to him. It wasn't *fair*.

She said, 'I don't believe in casual sex.'

He said nothing. Cautiously Leo opened her eyes.

Amer had folded his arms and propped himself up negligently against the corner of the table. He did not try to touch her. But he looked as if he was happy to stay there and debate with her forever. Or until she gave in.

'What sort of sex do you believe in?' he said in an interested voice.

Leo was thrown off balance. As, no doubt, he had intended, though she did not realise that until too late. Mistakenly she tried to answer him.

'Oh, when two people know each other. When they—'

'We know each other,' he murmured.

She glared. 'When they have spent time together and know each other's faults and reached a rational decision—'

He was disbelieving. 'Rational?'

'Of course.'

He shook his head. 'You are even weirder than I thought. What has reason to do with love?'

'Love,' said Leo contemptuously.

'Oh don't modern women believe in love, either?'

'We'll leave my beliefs out of it.'

'Running away again,' he said softly.

Leo's temper surged. 'Are you trying to tell me that you brought me here because you *love* me?' she flashed.

Amer stretched lazily. But his eyes were watchful.

'Is it so impossible?'

'You made me a *prisoner*,' Leo pointed out. 'Not very loving, that.'

'But we are all prisoners when we love,' Amer said soulfully.

Leo sent him a look of acute dislike.

'Don't keep talking about love. It makes me sick. You brought me here because you can't bear to lose a game,' she flung at him. 'Any game, however trivial. And I was winning, wasn't I? Until I got emotional and handed it to you on a plate.'

For a moment he did not answer. Then he said slowly, 'You are a very untrusting woman.'

'I'm a realistic woman. What grounds have I got for trusting you?'

Amer was rather pale. He unfolded his length from the carved table and came towards her.

He said, not laughing at all, 'But I told you I would marry you.'

'And you did not tell me that you had been married before,' Leo flung back at him.

He stopped dead.

'Is it true?'

All of a sudden, his eyes were quite opaque.

'Yes.'

She shrugged, though her heart was screaming with pain. 'My case proved, don't you think?'

She walked out of the room. He did not try to stop her.

CHAPTER NINE

THE cupboards in the guest quarters yielded up an infinite range of clothes for Leo to choose from: long dark robes that would cover her from head to toe, brilliant silks that would cover as much or as little as she wished, cotton, linen, lawn, even gold-encrusted brocade.

'Minister of Culture strikes again, I take it,' Leo muttered.

She selected a simple robe with a long overjacket in peacock silk. Fatima nodded approval and fetched her a heavy gold collar, like elegant chain-mail, and several intricate bangles to go with it.

'No,' said Leo, revolted.

She was not wearing Amer's wife's jewellery for anything.

Fatima was agitated. She did not have enough English to make Leo understand and ran out of the room. Leo felt slightly ashamed but she could not bear the idea of putting the heavy thing against her skin.

The heavy doors to her room banged back. Amer strode in, looking irritated.

'*Now* what are you making a fuss about?' he said in tones of barely controlled exasperation.

'I may have to borrow clothes but I'm not wearing someone else's jewels.'

Amer flicked a bored glance over the gold collar.

'They're yours,' he said curtly.

'No they're not.' Leo was nearly dancing with rage.

'Of course they are.' He flicked back the lid of the jewellery box for her to see the name of the Paris jeweller. 'A gift for my future wife. Flown in today.'

Leo was utterly taken aback.

'You bought me a *necklace?*'

'Of course.' He shrugged, bored. 'It's a trifle. We will, of course, choose your betrothal gift together.'

Leo sat down rather suddenly.

'But—I can't accept—'

Even to her own ears, she sounded like a confused child.

'I advise you to swallow your pride.' He sounded irritated. 'My father is asking other women to dinner tonight, as a courtesy to you. You will find them heavily jewelled. You will feel very odd if you aren't.'

He did not sound, though, as if he cared very much. And he did not give her a kiss or a kind look to go with the ornaments. Leo felt chilled and angry and would have said so forcefully but Fatima came back.

Amer smiled at her gently. *He did not smile at me,* thought Leo desolate.

He said something to her which made Fatima bow her head and give a small well-behaved giggle. And then he strode out. He said not one word more to Leo.

Leo was tempted to scream, but she gave up the idea when she saw how relieved Fatima was that she had given in over the gold necklace. Fatima was, Leo realised, quite seriously flustered by the fact that Amer was taking Leo to dine with his father. She did not have enough English to explain why. Leo could think of plenty of reasons.

She flung them at Amer when they got into the long dark car without number plates.

'Tell me,' she said chattily, 'does your father usually meet your playmates?'

'Do not speak of yourself like that.'

It was a command. Leo glared. But she did not quite dare to challenge him.

Amer was looking more of a stranger than ever tonight. He wore a loose jacket, heavily embroidered in crimson and turquoise, over his white robe. And there was a wicked looking dagger, the size of a small sword, in his belt. But it was not just his clothes. His mouth was set in forbidding lines and his eyes were strained. He looked like a diplomat going to a negotiation that could end in war.

Was meeting his father always so fraught? Leo thought. Or was it her presence that gave him that wary look?

'Will your father put me under house arrest for daring to lay hands on his son and heir?' she said provocatively.

Amer sent her an unsmiling look. 'I see Hari has been talking.'

'Unlike you.'

His jaw tightened. 'Don't try to make me angry, Leonora. We will talk, I promise. But now is not the time.'

'Great,' she muttered.

But they were at tall iron gates which swung wide as soon as the car nosed onto the approach road. Beside her, she could feel Amer straighten as if he was bracing himself.

Leo felt a brief remorse. It was soon dispelled.

'My father will ask you about our relationship,' he said rapidly. 'I advise you to tell him nothing.'

'Would he punish you for kidnapping me?'

A muscle worked in his cheek. 'I did not,' he said evenly, 'kidnap you.'

'Will your father believe that?'

He swung round on her, his eyes cool. 'Tell him and see,' he invited.

Leo's eyes narrowed. 'Why?'

He gave a crack of unamused laughter. 'He won't blame me. He is more likely to put you under house arrest until you marry me.'

It was like being doused in cold water. Leo sank back, silenced.

His father was not as tall as Amer but the gold on his robes made him seem somehow bigger. He had a grizzled beard and fierce, suspicious eyes. He spoke to Leo in rusty French which was courteous rather than welcoming.

They ate out of doors in a cool courtyard. A heavy oaken table, set with gleaming glass and china, was placed under a curved canopy. Behind them, the walls of the palace were white stone, warm to the touch. In front of them, date palms rustled in the evening breeze. Their leaves made a sound like rain, vying with the delicate tinkling of fountains.

'An informal supper,' said Amer. 'My father thought you would find that easier.'

'Informal?'

The King sat in a heavy oak chair with carved arms and a high back. It was as near to a throne as damn it, thought Leo. And there were at least twenty other people at the table.

Amer gave a taut smile. 'Just close family.'

Even so, everyone she met seemed to be a Minister or a Minister's wife.

Leo found that she was swept off to the end of the table to eat with the women. One or two wore what were clearly Paris designs but most, like herself, wore long robes. And Amer was right. To a woman, traditionally dressed or not, they all wore magnificent jewellery. But they were friendly and surprisingly sympathetic.

'Amer is a law unto himself,' said a pretty cousin.

'Always was,' said an aunt by marriage. She was wearing a stunningly simple black cocktail dress and sapphires.

'And so impetuous,' sighed a middle-aged woman with laughing eyes. She wore a gold encrusted smoking jacket and earrings like Baccarat chandeliers.

'Are you related to the Minister of Culture by any chance?' murmured Leo, eyeing the gold lapels with fascination.

'My brother.'

'Ah.'

'*He* says that Amer is the only one who is holding Dalmun together,' confided the Minister's wife. 'His Majesty is so very traditional. It is a heavy burden for Amer, especially as he has been alone for so long.'

Leo was not deceived by the airy tone. She winced.

'He told you,' she said, resigned.

'Told? In Dalmun? You're joking. Just rumours that you are, er, close. And—' She broke off.

'And?'

The Minister's wife leaned forward confidentially. 'And Amer not being able to keep his eyes off you.'

Leo looked down the table. Amer was sitting on his father's right, immersed in conversation. He was frowning slightly, tearing at the flat bread with preoccupied fingers, not eating any of it. As if he felt her eyes on him, he looked up suddenly.

Leo caught her breath. For a moment it was as if there was just the two of them. The cheerful conversation faded into nothing. She just stared and stared.

Take me away. Come down the table and take me home and make love to me.

It was so strong a wish that she almost felt as if she had said it aloud. She saw his eyes grow intent. His hands cast the maltreated bread away impatiently. But then his father said something, put a hand on his arm, and the moment was broken.

Leo sank back in her chair with a little gasp. Her pulse was racing. And deep, deep inside she felt a hollow need stir.

Afterwards, when he helped her into the car, she could feel the heat of his hands. Sitting close together in the back of the car was a torment. She was conscious of him, taut muscles hot and hard, and knew that the chauffeur and Amer's public image made him as out of reach as the moon.

When they arrived Amer waved the car away. In the sudden silence of the well-lit entrance, he stood in front of her for a moment, as if undecided.

Leo thought, *he's going to kiss me.* But he did not. Instead he leaned forward until his cheek just touched her hair.

'I will come to you later.' His voice was a rough whisper. 'May I?'

'Yes,' breathed Leo.

But he did not. She waited for hours in the strange room, moving restlessly from table to balcony and back. The night wind was cold. But not as cold as the lonely bed.

He did not come and he sent no message.

*   *   *

'I don't believe this,' said Amer.

'Your father wants you back at the palace,' Hari repeated.
'A report has just come in. Brigands on the northern border.'

'Brigands!' Amer was scornful. 'More likely tribesmen
who want decent water and a telephone line for their village.'

'Your father wants to send in the Army...'

Amer swore.

'All right,' he said at last. 'I'll go. But if I'm not back in
an hour—' He broke off.

'Yes?'

'*Hell,*' said Amer.

In the end the apricot light of early dawn slid along the bal-
ustrade of the balcony before Leo huddled down on the sofa
and did what she could to sleep. That was where Fatima
found her. She had not even taken off last night's finery. The
chain-mail necklace had marked her skin.

'Typical,' said Leo, refusing to cry.

Fatima was concerned. Particularly when Leo took off
Sheikh Amer's gift and threw it so hard across the room that
a link broke. Even more so when Leo refused to wear any
more of the borrowed clothes.

'I shall buy something myself. The car can take me to the
market, can't it?'

Fatima was uneasy. She began to mutter, losing her command of English.

'Or am I a prisoner here after all?' demanded Leo, savagely triumphant.

Fatima bit her lip and consulted Hari. They both strove
strenuously to dissuade her.

'Sheikh Amer said you were to have whatever you ask
for,' Hari told Leo at last. It clearly troubled him. 'It would
be wiser not to go to the market today, though.'

'So I *am* a prisoner.'

He gave in, stipulating only that she took an escort. Leo
set off in triumph accompanied by the scholarly map reader.

He looked rather alarmed. Leo interpreted it as a sign that he did not know much about women's clothes.

'It's all right,' she told him. 'We'll be back before sundown.'

'You'll be back in two hours,' said Hari firmly.

Leo went very still. 'Is that how long you've got before Amer wakes up and finds out you've let me go?'

Exasperated, Hari said, 'Be careful. Dalmun is not Knightsbridge.'

But Leo waved a careless hand and he stepped back. The electric gates opened silently and the limousine swept through.

'I hope I've done the right thing,' said Hari aloud.

Three hours later, his heart in his mouth, he was knocking on the door to Amer's suite.

'Come in.'

Amer was at his desk. It was clear from the table strewn with paper behind him that he had been working, not resting. He looked up.

'Have you been to bed at all?' said Hari, shocked by his look of exhaustion.

Amer shook his head. 'What time is it?'

Hari told him. He was startled.

'So late? Then I must see—' He broke off.

But Hari was beyond pretending to be discreet.

'She's gone,' he said brutally.

Amer stared at him. His face was masklike. Hari could not bear it.

'Not of her own accord. Hussein came back with a message. Oh, I knew I should never have let her go.'

Amer went very still.

'Go? Where?'

'She insisted on going out,' said poor Hari. 'I tried to persuade her— But you told her she was free to do whatever she wanted. And this morning she was like a caged animal.'

Amer flinched. Hari did not notice.

'I insisted that Hussein went along to interpret. But he is not a man of action. Saeed's people have taken her. They sent Hussein back. They want your father to sign the order for the new electricity system at the Council Meeting tomorrow.'

Amer looked at him for a burning moment.

'They'll keep her until he does,' Hari finished miserably. 'I'm sorry, Amer. I know you warned us. But it never occurred to me they would really do it. They've only ever taken an ordinary tourist before.'

Amer said. 'Get my father on the telephone.'

Hari blanched. 'What are you going to do?'

'Tell him the truth,' said Amer harshly. 'I have protected him from it for too long. Let him know that some of his subjects will turn against him unless he gives them a reasonable standard of living.'

'Very well.' Hari did not relish the task but he was a brave man. 'Do you want me to call your uncle and summon the Council?'

'That is for my father to decide,' said Amer. 'It's his Council.'

'But—'

'They will have taken her into the desert. I'm going after her. Get the land cruiser ready.'

Hari was startled into an undiplomatic truth. 'But you have to go to the Council. They will never be able to persuade His Majesty without you. They need you.'

'Leonora needs me.'

Amer was already opening cupboards, his mind on his expedition.

Hari was exasperated. 'But you've said it yourself often enough—these guys are harmless. She's in no danger. They'll probably give her the time of her life.'

Amer said, 'Does Leonora know that?'

'Well maybe not to begin with,' he admitted. 'But she'll find out…'

'Or she might not. Saeed is different from the other desert Sheikhs. More ambitious. Definitely more unpredictable.'

'He would not hurt her,' said Hari positively. 'It would be stupid.'

Amer turned. He looked strained.

'My head agrees with you. My heart can't take the chance.'

His heart? *Amer's* heart? Hari stared in disbelief.

'But why?' he said incautiously.

The smile became savage.

'Because she's *mine*.'

Leo was afraid. She told herself that Amer would find her. She told herself to believe her captors when they assured her that she was their honoured guest. But it was difficult when they sounded so terrifyingly efficient.

As they got farther and farther from the capital and left the metalled road for a dust track, her heart sank. Even with the windows closed, the dust seemed to whirl chokingly round the interior of the cabin.

The tropic dark fell like a blanket. The pick-up stopped. The driver got out. After a few minutes he came back and gestured Leo to get out of the vehicle.

All her banked-down panic surged up into her throat. She could taste it. Were they going to abandon her here, in the middle of nowhere? Amer would never find her, then.

She controlled herself. Amer did what he set himself to do. Besides this was his country. And anyway, she just knew that he would find her. Of course he would find her.

Leo hugged that thought to her. It got her through the next few hours. And she really needed something to hold on to because her captors seemed as if they did not know what to do with her. She was transferred from vehicle to vehicle no fewer than four times and, judging from the limited Arabic she had picked up in Cairo, none of the men taking charge of her was glad of the responsibility. Leo began to feel like a potato that had just been pulled out of the fire: too hot to handle. And the later it got, the jumpier each successive group of men sounded.

Eventually the last truck pulled up at a group of tents. They were hunched shadows under the brilliant sky. Leo stumbled out. She was swaying with tiredness as much as emotion.

They took her into an enormous tent with all ceremony, fed her coffee and speeches which she could not understand, then took her to a smaller tent where she tried to sleep.

She dreamed that Amer's arms were round her. And woke up with tears on her cheeks.

All through the morning Leo heard comings and goings in the main tent. She tried to stay calm but it was not easy. She drank a little water but refused all food. Eventually an impatient man arrived bearing a circular dish of bread and fruit. Leo shook her head but he took no notice, pressing bread against her lips. Leo shut her eyes so she should not see his expression. It was menacing.

Oh, Amer, get me out of this, she called silently.

There was a commotion outside. The man flung the tray away and stamped out.

Leo sipped some water, shakily. He had gripped her arm in his attempt to make her eat and the place throbbed. There would be a bruise there, she thought.

Soon enough he was back and abandoning other attempts at communication, hauling her into the main tent. Leo fought down another sick surge of panic. She had to keep her head, she knew.

The main tent was full of men. They all had their backs to her, looking at an imposing figure in the entrance to the tent.

For all her determined courage, Leo's heart contracted. Was this a gathering of rebel clans?

The man in the bright mouth of the tent seemed very tall. He wore a flowing black robe and turban. It made him look like the angel of death. His face was in complete shadow but Leo could see the arrogance in the way he held himself.

Was he cruel, too? The others were clearly in awe of him.

No, thought Leo watching the way they bowed to him, not in awe. Make that terrified. She felt her mouth dry with a reflection of their terror.

He was unaware of her. He said something to the bowing reception committee. His voice was harsh. He took a step forward and the robe proved to be a loose coat, the open front heavy with gold embroidery. It flashed in the sun. Under it he wore some dark shirt with a huge plaited leather belt worked in gold stretching from waist to slim hips. And he had a huge dagger, its blade a wicked upcurve. The sheath looked like pure gold and its haft was set with jewels. It was magnificent and utterly barbarian.

Even though she could not see his face, Leo saw that this was a leader. She felt a flash of terror, pure and primitive. She must have made some sound. The man turned his fierce attention to the far side of the tent where she was standing.

He strode forward. She caught a glimpse of high boots. And the gold flashed dazzlingly. She was terrified. She shut her eyes.

The man took hold of her chin. 'Are you all right?' he said in clipped, furious English.

Disbelieving, Leo looked up. It was Amer. But not Amer as she had ever seen him before. There was no laughter in the grey eyes that swept over her and barely any recognition. Amer was a brisk stranger on important business. His whole manner said that she was a major nuisance.

Inwardly she cringed. Aloud she said sharply, 'I'm fine. No thanks to—'

'Stop right there,' he said softly. He sounded so angry he could barely speak. 'I'll handle this. Keep your mouth *shut*.'

Leo fumed. But all her survival instincts told her to comply. So she folded her lips together and glared.

Amer turned back to their hosts.

'I am grateful to you for finding her,' he said formally. She could understand his Arabic more easily. 'The lady is a treasured guest and new to our country.'

He was not just formal, Leo thought. He was glacial. The

other men shuffled uncomfortably. It was clear, even to Leo, that for the time being Sheikh Amer was willing to pretend that the girl had just stumbled into their camp. But if they did not hand her over he was quite prepared to take her by whatever means were necessary. The unspoken threat of force hung heavy in the air.

Leo was not proud of herself for the feeling. But she was glad of the strong body between her and the rest of the tent's occupants.

'One wonders how such an honoured guest managed to get lost in the desert,' said one of the younger men defiantly.

He attracted fulminating looks from his companions. Amer contented himself with inspecting the man in nerve-racking silence for a full minute.

'One does indeed,' he said softly.

His tone made even Leo's blood run cold.

There was a general hubbub of disclaimers. The man looked mutinous but others, older and more cautious, were delivering a confused and contradictory account of how she arrived at the camp. It was not clear whether they expected to be believed. Amer made little pretence at believing them, in any event.

Above the hum his voice could be heard announcing, 'As my future wife she is doubly precious.'

It sounded, thought Leo writhing, more like a declaration of war than love. Of course, he did not realise that she could understand him. She folded her lips together and promised herself that he would never know. Once they were out of this she would never refer to it again. Never.

But it had its desired effect. They did not exactly congratulate him. But they surrendered her into his custody with every evidence of relief. After more ceremonial coffee drinking and expressions of eternal fidelity on both sides, they were escorted to a massive four-wheel drive vehicle.

'Not a camel?' said Leo mockingly. 'It would go better with the outfit.'

It was the first time she had spoken. Amer turned a look

on her which, if they had detected it, would have caused their hosts to doubt that she was so precious in their Sheikh's eyes. A muscle worked at his jaw. He looked as if he could cheerfully have murdered her.

'Not a word,' he said between his teeth. 'Not one more word. Or you'll wish you had never been born.'

'What makes you think I don't already?' muttered Leo.

But he had turned away and was making their farewells.

He drove off, his face set. He handled the big land cruiser with an easy mastery which Leo somehow would not have expected. For so much of their acquaintance they had been driven by chauffeurs, she thought. This coolly competent driving in difficult terrain reminded her—if she needed to be reminded—how little she really knew Amer.

She said in a small voice, 'Where are we going?'

'My camp,' he said briefly.

He looked at a dial mounted in the dash. With a slight shock, Leo realised it was a compass, not a decorative addition to an expensive car but a real float mounted compass. She swallowed.

'Is the desert very dangerous?'

'If you don't know it. Or if you are careless.' He sent her an ironic look. 'Why? Were you thinking of setting out across the desert in your high heels if I didn't come to rescue you?'

Leo thought: I am going to cry. All that time in captivity and I didn't shed a tear and now, when I'm safe, I could bawl like a baby. It was because he was so angry with her, of course. And because, in part, he had cause.

And because he would not be that angry if he loved her.

She swallowed something jagged in her throat and said, 'I never thought you would come to rescue me.'

'Oh? You thought I would leave you to Saeed's mercy?' He sounded furious.

This was horrible. Floundering Leo said, 'I mean I never thought you would come yourself. I knew you would not just abandon me, of course. But...'

'You thought I would send someone else to do my dirty work,' he interpreted.

Not just furious. Savage.

Leo said nastily, so that she would not cry, 'Well you set detectives after me.'

He slammed on the brakes so hard that the big vehicle skidded. Leo cried out as she was flung violently against him. Amer turned and dragged her across the control dock into his arms.

The kiss was savage.

This was not the laughing stranger who had wooed her under the Nile stars. Nor the sophisticate who had driven her to such unexpected passion in London. No unhurried love-making now. No drifting of teasing hands. This was a man way past laughter or sophistication. A man driven to the very limit of his endurance.

Leo thought: He'll never forgive me.

And then she stopped thinking altogether as desire engulfed her.

Amer twisted, slamming her body into the upholstery. Leo arched to meet him, her mouth hungry. Her jaw ached with the force of his kiss. She did to care. She heard cloth rip and did not know if it was his clothing or hers. She did not care about that, either. His fingers found her breast and she cried out in a sort of agony.

Amer gave a groan. She felt his breath in her ravaged mouth. He was too frenzied to be gentle. So was Leo. As fierce as he, she writhed against him. She needed to be closer, closer...

And he drew away. Unbelievably he drew away. Leo moaned in protest.

'*No*,' he bit out.

Her hands scrabbled for him. He caught them and held them strongly, holding her away from him.

'No,' he said again.

Leo was panting. She breathed in the smell of him, as familiar to her now as her own.

'You can't stop now,' she said in a ragged whisper. 'Please.'

He looked at her as if he loathed her.

'I can.' It sounded like a curse. 'I will.'

His ribs rose and fell hugely, like a ship's pump. He held himself utterly still. But Leo could see the fine tremor in his hands and knew Amer was a lot closer to losing control than he wanted to be.

She thought: *I want him to lose control.* It shocked her into immobility.

She felt dazed. It was as if she had fallen into a volcano. All right, she was out now. But she did not quite know how. Or what had been changed in the fire. Just now, it felt like everything.

Shaken, she started to wrestle with the tangle he had made of her clothes.

Staring straight ahead at the desert beyond the windscreen, Amer said, 'I'm not going to apologise.' His lips barely moved.

Leo did not answer. A button was missing from her trousers and her bra was beyond repair. Leo pulled it off and stuffed the rags into her pocket.

Amer shifted.

'That has been building up for a long time.'

Leo still said nothing. But she felt the quick look he sent her like a brand on her skin.

'For you as well as me.'

Leo flinched. He swung round on her.

'All right. I wish it hadn't happened like that,' he said in a goaded voice. 'But it was only a kiss after all. We could have—'

Then he saw her face. He drew a sharp breath. Halted.

'Damn,' he said with concentrated fury.

It was like a physical blow. Leo was remotely surprised that it was possible to feel so much pain and go on breathing.

He must not see the pain, she thought. He *must* not.

'I won't tell if you won't,' she said, quite as if she didn't care.

Evidently Amer was not taken in by her cynical tone. He sighed.

'You will see things more clearly in time.'

As if, thought Leo furiously, she was a child and he was a sage who was never, ever, wrong.

'No doubt I will. When I'm back home in London,' she retorted. And added challengingly, 'Once I've had time to put all this behind me.'

His mouth tightened. But he did not answer her. Instead he put on his sunglasses, switched on the engine and put the land cruiser in gear. As if he could not be bothered to waste time arguing with her, Leo thought. She could have screamed with frustration.

All right, she thought. If he would not speak, she would not, either. She folded her arms across her chest and stared out of her window, pointedly ignoring him.

Amer took no notice. His attention was divided between the compass and the track which unwound before them. It appeared and disappeared under drifts of dust. To their right pale dunes undulated across the horizon like lazy animals on the point of lying down to snooze. To their left, the plain of stony sand stretched away until it fell off the edge of the world in a golden dust cloud. In spite of the air-conditioning in the vehicle, Leo could almost taste the heat outside.

The road, such as it was, petered out. Amer coasted gently to a stop.

'I'll need to let some air out of the tyres.'

He swung out of the vehicle. The desert air blasted in as if he had opened the door to a furnace. Leo gasped under the impact.

Amer looked back.

'There's a bottle of water in the dash,' he said, remote but kind. 'Drink. It will take some time to get to my camp.'

It did. It was not a great journey. In spite of the land cruiser's mighty springs, Leo thought she would be sick with the uneven motion. And, although the air conditioning worked well, the hazy glare beyond the windscreen made Leo feel as if she were being grilled by aliens.

Amer was unmoved. He drove with easy competence, his body rolling with the vehicle while Leo bumped miserably from side to side.

Leo forgot that she was not speaking to him. The vastness of the desert was intimidating. It made her feel like an ant on some giant's beach.

'It's so huge,' she whispered. 'And all the same. Without that compass we could be going round in circles, wouldn't we?'

Amer smiled. 'No. This is my desert. Compass or no compass, I could get you out if I had to.'

Leo shivered. But, oddly, she found she believed him. I would trust him with my life, she thought. It was a revelation.

I am in love.

It was not a welcome revelation. She stared blankly out the window, trying to think. How long had she been in love with him? Since the evening at his London home? Before that?

And, oh horrors, did Amer know? All right, she had only just realised it. But he was so sophisticated, so infinitely more experienced than she was. Maybe he had picked it up from the first.

Leo felt sick again. And this time it was nothing to do with the motion of the vehicle. She pressed a hand to her mouth to force back a groan.

Amer looked sideways at her. 'Are you all right?'

She sought desperately for an alibi.

'Reaction setting in, I expect.' How could she sound so normal? She impressed herself. And added truthfully, 'I wasn't admitting it but I was really scared back there.'

'You did very well. Many women on their own would have lost their head.'

He sounded like a schoolmaster giving her marks in class,

she thought, irritated. It made no difference. She was still in love with him.

'Thank you,' she said drily.

'I mean it,' he said. 'I fully expected to arrive to find you screaming the place down.'

She shrugged. 'What would have been the point? It would just have annoyed them and made things ten times worse.'

He made a small, exasperated noise. 'Are you always that cool in the face of danger?'

I wasn't cool in your arms. Leo shivered inwardly at the thought. That had been danger all right. Alone in the desert with him, she realised the truth at last: She had lost her dignity, her common sense and her heart all in one massive attack. She had not seen it coming. But it had happened. Even though she had not realised it until now.

'Depends on the danger,' she said with bitter self-mockery.

Amer, she thought, was a greater risk to her peace of mind than anything her embarrassed captors had done. The only thing she could do now was keep quiet and hope that he did not find out. It would be the final humiliation if he discovered how she felt.

So she did not speak again until they got to the camp.

The first thing she saw was a black shadow. It turned out to be an enormous tent. As they got closer she made out other tents and several vehicles. They all cast shadows so deep that it looked as if a cellar had been dug in the sand beside them. Only a thin, windblown tree was not supported by a black reflection on the sand.

There was nobody in sight. It looked desolate. Leo shivered.

'Is this an oasis?'

Amer drove round the tent and parked in its sheltering shadow.

'No. It is the site of one of my excavations. We camped here because it is central to the area where we were looking for you.'

Leo looked at the shimmering dust. It was better than looking at Amer. In the course of the drive, his black robe had fallen back. She could see the smooth golden chest where she had ripped his shirt away.

She swallowed hard and spoke entirely at random. 'Excavation? *Here?* What did you do? Shift sand from one place to another?'

Amer laughed. 'You cannot see it because your eyes have not accustomed themselves to the subtlety of the desert yet. But over there are the walls of mud brick houses. In all probability they date back to the iron age.'

Leo peered at the rise of sand. It was as smooth as an egg.

'I don't see any walls.'

'The sand drifts back so quickly,' said Amer. 'I assure you they are there. I will show you later.'

He got out of the land cruiser and came round to help her down. The moment Leo put her hand in his, she felt that incredible tingle, as if his very touch woke the sleeping tiger at her body's core.

She snatched her hand away.

'I can manage, thank you.'

His mouth tightened.

'As you wish.'

The heavy gold ornamentation on the front of his robe glinted so blindingly you could almost overlook the fact that it gaped at the shoulder where a seam had parted in their frenzy. The naked chest was golden as the sun and so close, so close.

Leo's unbidden thoughts made her head swim. Hurriedly she looked round at the other vehicles. It was only then that she took in the size of the encampment.

'Where is everyone else?'

'Inside in the cool.'

She said curiously, 'Do you always bring such a retinue when you come into the desert?'

She had not meant it to but it sounded faintly scornful. Amer raised his eyebrows.

'You think I should have set out after you alone? Would that have made me more heroic in your eyes?'

Leo flinched from his sarcasm.

'Don't be ridiculous,' she said brusquely. 'I was just wondering if royalty is required to travel in convoy. To make sure everyone knows how important you are.'

He turned his head and looked at her for a long silent moment. The sun glinted off his sunglasses, masking his expression. For some reason, Leo found her chin coming up in defiance of that silent inspection, though.

'It is not wise to go alone,' Amer said at last levelly. 'It is nothing to do with being royal. We carry short wave radio and extra fuel and water. And we look out for each other.' He paused. 'Not something you high-powered business executives know much about, I think.'

It stung. As it was meant to.

Leo turned away. The heat lay on her skin like a blanket. She made for the cool of the tent without another word.

'Leonora—'

But she pretended not to hear. She did not think she could take much more without flinging herself into his arms and begging him to love her. She shuddered at the thought and kept on walking.

He caught up with her. 'I think you may prefer to go to the tent that has been prepared for you.'

She whirled, glaring. 'Is a woman not allowed to sit with the men, then?'

For a moment he looked utterly taken aback. Then he started to laugh.

'Not at all. You would be very welcome, of course. But I thought you might prefer...'

He made a graceful gesture. Leo looked down at herself. She had forgotten that her garments had suffered, too, in their mutual frenzy. Now she saw her naked breasts gleaming palely under a shirt that seemed to have lost all its buttons. She gasped and clutched the edges of material across herself.

'Come along,' he said, odiously sympathetic. 'Fatima will find you something less air cooled to wear.'

Leo took hold of the ends of her torn shirt and knotted them savagely over her midriff. Then, head high, she followed him.

CHAPTER TEN

AMER almost flung Leo into the arms of Fatima. Their approach had brought her to the entrance flap of one of the smaller tents. Her eyes widened as she took in the full enormity of Leo's ragged state.

'Deal with it.' Amer said harshly in his own language.

Leo was stricken. She turned her face away so that he should not see and swept past him without a word.

Fatima sent him an alarmed look and whisked Leo inside with little coos of concern.

'Those villains. What have they done to you?'

Leo was confused. 'What?'

'And His Excellency.' Fatima was genuinely shocked. 'They attacked him?' She sounded as if she could not believe it.

'No—'

But Fatima was plucking at the torn trousers, shaking her head, and Leo realised what she was talking about. She blushed.

'We, er, there was a bit of an accident,' she said lamely.

Fatima was horrified. 'You are hurt?'

To the heart, thought Leo.

'No,' she said.

Fatima was not convinced.

'You shall rest,' she said firmly. 'And then we will heat water and you shall bathe before you dine with His Excellency.'

They had set his own tent out as efficiently as ever. Even though he had left in such a hurry, his staff had followed with the full complement of equipment. The camp was now

170

the luxury resting place that they prepared when he and his father went on hawking trips in the desert.

Amer unbuckled his dagger and sank wearily onto a divan.

What a damned thing to happen. He had thought he could show her that he respected her. That he needed her. She already knew how much he wanted her, God help them both. And then Saeed and his heroes had frightened her half to death and he, Amer, had shouted at her and all but lost control in the terrifying rush of relief in knowing her safe.

She was not a trusting woman. Would she ever trust him now?

Amer gave a mirthless laugh.

Fatima brought Leo a lemon sherbet. While Leo sipped at the sharp, foaming drink, Fatima slipped her out of her ragged clothes and helped her into a cotton robe.

Leo saw that the tent had been prepared with care. The ground was covered in rugs, one piled carelessly on the other, worked in indigo and turquoise and a brilliant cornflower blue that burned like the sun outside. On the top one there was a design of the tree of life picked out in blood-red and jet.

'That is a masterpiece,' she said, hesitating to walk on it.

Fatima smiled approvingly. 'It was Sheikh Amer who told us to bring it. He said your tent had to be full of beautiful things to distract you from ugliness.'

She magicked a director's chair from somewhere and disappeared.

Leo sank into the canvas seat and looked around. She shook her head disbelievingly. She had not believed the comfort of her captors' tent. But that was as nothing to the sheer luxury of this.

In addition to the amazing carpets, the main supports of the tent were decorated with gauzy hangings on which there was the distinct glint of gold motifs. A low divan was covered with midnight velvet and strewn with cushions in velvet and brocade and shot silk in all the peacock colours: jade and emerald and sea-green and navy. Again there was the glint of gold trimmings and tassels. Leo blinked at the gold but it looked blessedly comfortable.

'Just the thing for the Sultan's favourite,' she said ironically.

So why had Amer ordered this bower to be prepared for her? Did he expect to spend the night here? Her heart beat faster at the thought. And if he did, what was she going to do about it? Fall into his arms as she just had in the land cruiser? Or try to be sensible and guard her heart from another wounding power contest?

Guard her heart? Who was she trying to fool? What was the point of guarding something already utterly breached? Her heart was occupied territory now.

She submitted wearily to Fatima's ministrations. And fell into an exhausted sleep.

When she was awoke, the tent was almost in darkness. A small light burned steadily on a carved stool. Leo stretched slowly. Her dreams had been sensual in the extreme. She felt wonderful.

Fatima came in, her feet noiseless on the rich carpets.

'You are awake. Good. His Excellency said not to wake you.'

Leo frowned. 'Amer was here?'

Fatima's smile was bland.

'But *here*? Here in my tent?'

'He wanted to be sure that you had not taken any hurt from those villains. He watched over you while you slept.'

'Oh,' said Leo, shaken. 'I didn't know.'

But her body had known. And her dreams. She swallowed.

'His Excellency will dine with you,' Fatima informed her. 'So you will want to bathe, yes?'

Her tone implied *and make yourself beautiful for him.* The Sultan's favourite indeed, thought Leo, amused. But the idea was oddly exciting as well.

'Yes,' she agreed slowly. 'Yes, I will.'

Fatima helped Leo to her feet and led her tenderly through

the hangings. Leo was stunned. Set out for her pleasure was a hip bath of old-fashioned design. Steam and a delectable scent wafted up from it.

Two girls stood to one side. They carried pitchers half as big as they were and were trying hard to look solemn. Not very successfully.

Fatima frowned at them. She whipped away the loose robe in which Leo had slept and held her hand while she stepped gingerly into the bath. She gave her an enormous sponge that someone had dived into the depths of the Red Sea to bring back.

The girls looked agonized as they tried to control their excited giggles. At Fatima's command, they brought oils and shampoo and added warm water. It smelled of rose petals. She said so.

Fatima smiled. 'His Excellency's personal instruction,' she murmured.

Afterwards Fatima massaged Leo with scented oils until her muscles felt exquisitely toned. The girls stroked perfume into her wrists. Then they outlined her eyes with the finest possible trace of kohl and brushed her hair until it shone. They left it loose on her shoulders. Leo wondered if that was His Excellency's personal instruction as well. Finally they dressed her in silks so soft that her body hardly felt clothed.

Fatima gave her a mirror. Leo saw a woman she did not recognise: huge eyes, soft skin, vulnerable mouth. Too vulnerable? With sudden recklessness, Leo thought, *I'll take my chances.* She, who never trusted anyone! It was exhilarating.

Amer would not know her, she thought. Ah, but would he like her in this new guise? Leo gave a long sweet shiver of voluptuous anticipation. Over her shoulder Fatima smiled in complete female understanding.

'I will take you to Sheikh Amer,' she said.

Outside, the heat of the day had given place to a pleasant warmth. There was no breeze. On the other side of the camp Leo caught a glimpse of fires and heard cheerful voices.

Fatima skirted the main tent and took her to another, set a little away from the others.

'His Excellency's tent,' she explained.

For a moment Leo's courage almost deserted her. She hesitated, half wanting to turn back. But Fatima gave her a little push and disappeared.

Leo swallowed hard and went inside.

It was more austere than her tent but more magnificent. The divan was huge. There was an intricately carved desk, as well as chairs and several brass-bound trunks. The hangings and the rugs were sombre. But everywhere there was gold: trays, coffeepots, an oil lamp. Even Amer's curved dagger which lay discarded on the desk glinted with gold.

This is a dream, Leo thought. A deserted dream. She stopped hesitating and went, soft footed, to a gilt chair. She sat on the very edge of it, trying to be calm.

She was trying so hard that she did not hear Amer's step. He stood in the entrance for a moment, watching her bent head. He frowned.

'Are you all right?'

Leo jumped at the soft voice. She looked up quickly.

He seemed very tall. He was wearing black again, a loose coat in fine lawn, with a chased silver border, over a light robe. As he strode forward, she saw that he was wearing a deep belt of plaited leather decorated with beaten silver. He looked devastating.

'I'm f-fine.' But there was a catch in her voice.

'You don't sound very sure.'

Leo was briefly indignant. How could he expect her to be sure of anything? She was sitting here like a traditional plaything, bathed and scented for his pleasure. She did not feel like herself at all.

She almost said so. But the events of the day must have taken their toll. She could not face pointing out to Amer that she was cast as Harem Favourite and did not know the words because... Well, she just could not face it, that was all.

He was so distant, standing there. How could he be distant

after that crazy episode in the land cruiser? Was this the man who had flung himself upon her, shaking with passion?

Leo could not meet his eyes.

'I'm happy as a clam,' she said brusquely, her colour heightened.

Amer did not challenge her.

He said curtly, 'I said I wouldn't apologise. I was wrong. I'm sorry.'

Leo stared. Was he apologising for making her feel that he had wanted her? Really wanted her, without reservations? Or because he hadn't, in the end, wanted her enough. She felt as if he had hit her where she was most unguarded.

He added irritably, 'But you shouldn't have made me mad.'

Leo recovered. 'So it's my fault you attacked me?' she said, brutal in her hurt.

If he had really been sorry, she thought, he would have grovelled. He would have excused himself for being carried away by the strength of his feelings. He would have said he never meant to hurt her. He would have promised never to hurt her again. Never to take her to the very edge of Paradise and leave her there, abandoned.

He didn't. Instead he looked at her very levelly, not speaking. Leo felt her colour rise.

'What? What?' she said aggressively. 'I invited it? Is that what you mean? Well, is it?'

Oh where had all that lovely voluptuous expectation gone?

Amer said quietly, 'No more games, Leonora.'

'Games?' echoed Leo. She was outraged.

'Games.' He was sober. 'Be honest. We have both done our share of throwing down gauntlets. And I for one have enjoyed it. I admit it. But the time for all that is over.'

'Oh,' said Leo, disconcerted.

'When Saeed's group kidnapped you I felt—' He hesitated.

Leo held her breath.

'Responsible,' he finished.

The disappointment was so great that Leo could have wept.

She said in a hard voice, 'There's no need to feel responsible for me. If I hadn't chosen to go to the market against all advice, I would not have been kidnapped in the first place.'

Amer made an impatient gesture. 'That's not what I meant. I—'

They were interrupted by a courtly servant. Amer looked irritated. But he nodded.

'They have set a meal for us at the old excavations,' he said. 'I thought it would please you.'

Leo stood up obediently. Just for a moment Amer's face softened. He reached out and slid a hand under her hair. She could feel the warmth of his palm against her nape. It made her feel soft and shockingly vulnerable.

If only he loved me. The thought came out of nowhere. She bit her lip and retreated out of reach.

Amer's hand fell. His face lost all expression. He turned and led her out under the desert stars.

A rug had been set for them on the other side of the steps he had pointed out to her. They effectively screened them from the rest of the camp. Food was brought and placed on a wide cloth. They ate, though Leo had trouble swallowing even a mouthful. Eventually Amer waved the servants away.

Leo looked at the desert, stretching away to its meeting point with the stars. It was awe inspiring. In this sculpted wilderness the moon, she found, cast shadows. The stars blazed like a jeweller's tray of diamonds.

It made her feel tiny. She shivered.

Amer looked up. 'You are cold?'

'No.'

It was true. There was a breeze but it was warm, scented with strange desert grasses and wood smoke.

'You shivered.'

'Not from cold. This—' she gestured '—makes us seem very small, doesn't it? Just for a moment I felt really alone.'

'Alone? But I am here.'

In the dark Leo found the courage to say, 'But you haven't been very companionable.'

'Companionable!' He snorted contemptuously. 'What do you think I am, Leonora?' He sounded furious again.

She was confused. 'I don't understand.'

'Pets are companionable. Cats and little lap dogs are companionable. Like your Simon Hartley.'

'Simon?'

He smote one clenched hand into the other. 'Tell me now, Leonora. Were you really in love with that fool?'

Leo could not believe that he would ask. 'W-with Simon?' she said incredulously.

'When you broke off the engagement you said it was the worst day in your life,' he reminded her.

Leo had forgotten. She struggled to remember.

'Well, the *day* was. I had a mail-order ring and a journalist taking me to pieces. And that was before I found out that my engagement was a done deal between my father and an ambitious subordinate. How would you feel?'

Amer waited.

Leo cleared her throat. 'And then you were in town and I didn't understand you. I didn't know what you wanted.' She swallowed. 'I still don't.'

He made a disbelieving noise. 'Yet it is clear enough.'

'Not to me.'

'I want you,' he said in a matter-of-fact tone.

Leo sat utterly still. A little eddy of breeze lifted her hair from her lightly clad shoulders. She could not look at him.

She said sadly, 'Me? Or just not to lose the game?'

'What?' He was astounded.

Leo made a helpless gesture. '"Come with me to the Casbah",' she said.

'Oh not that again.' He made an impatient movement.

'No. Listen to me. It seemed to me that—' Heavens this was difficult '—that what happened between us was a sort of competitive game to you. I left Cairo and you couldn't find me. So I sort of won. And then—when I saw you in London—it seemed as if you had to get your own back.'

'What are you talking about?'

'The way you found out about me,' Leo said, trying to put the feeling into words. 'Picking me up in the limo when I wasn't expecting it. Carrying me off to dinner when I didn't want to go. It felt as if you were showing me you could do anything you liked with me.'

Which of course was true. But it *shouldn't* be true. And he certainly shouldn't be allowed to take advantage of it.

Amer let out an explosive breath. 'I told you. A man likes to do his own hunting.'

Leo shivered. 'Yes but I don't like feeling like quarry.'

He leaned forward suddenly, trying to make out her expression in the dark.

'Don't you?' Suddenly there was amusement in his voice.

Leo avoided his eyes and desperately looked for something to keep her hands busy. Or she would reach out to him. And that would be disastrous.

She took a peach she did not want. At once Amer took it from her and peeled it with a gold-handled knife. He had done that before, Leo remembered. She tried not to. His fingers were long and dextrous. Leo swallowed and avoided looking at his hands as well.

He said, 'What do you think has been happening here?'

That, thought Leo mutinously, is just not fair.

Aloud she said, 'I was stupid enough to challenge you at the Antika reception. You can't resist a challenge. Hence this nonsense about being engaged.'

'Nonsense?'

He passed her the neatly quartered peach. Leo looked at it and wondered how she was going to swallow a mouthful of it.

'Well, joke then,' she amended.

'In that case the joke has got a little out of hand, wouldn't you say?'

That hurt.

'Probably.' Leo replied. 'I'd better go home.'

'Running away again,' he said softly.

'I'm not running. I have a life to get on with.'

'Do you think I haven't?' he said on a flash of sudden anger. 'Dear Heaven, do you know how delicate the situation here is? How hard we have to work to keep it in equilibrium? Why the hell do you think I did not come to you on the one night you had eventually decided to accept me? I was with the Council, God help me, trying to stop my father starting a small war!'

Leo blinked at the suppressed fury in his tones. He banged his hand down on the cloth so hard that the little gold-stemmed goblets jumped. One fell over.

Leo forgot that it was dangerous to look him in the eye. Her head reared up, startled. Their eyes locked. Amer gave an odd laugh under his breath.

'This is getting us nowhere.'

He stood up and held out an imperious hand. 'Walk with me.'

Leo got to her feet. She knew it was not sensible. But she gave him her hand anyway. His fingers closed over hers. It seemed as if she felt his strength flow through her.

The warm desert night was heady, too heady. The vaulting sky was so bright and clear that it looked as if you could touch it. Leo staggered a little, feeling the world wheel.

Amer dropped her hand and put his arm round her. The world did not steady, but she leaned against him involuntarily. It made her feel safe and yet unsafe. As if he would protect her from every threat but himself. Who was the greatest threat of all.

Leo felt the chill of excitement touch her skin like the desert breeze.

He walked her purposefully towards a thin tree on the edge of the site.

'This was an iron age village,' he was saying. 'We think they brought water from the mountains by means of underground pipes. We have found the access shaft here, we think.

But we don't know which direction the water came from, yet.'

Against her, his shoulder felt like a rock. Warm rock.

'H-how interesting,' Leo managed to say.

'There was a time,' Amer said very deliberately, 'as I mentioned to you before, when I thought I would be an archaeologist. My father has the right to chose his heir and he and I did not see eye to eye at all. I thought he would choose one of my uncles. Very traditional, very unyielding. To be honest I would have been glad. But the last three years he has been wavering. Now he says he sees that reform is necessary and I am the one to do it.' He sighed. 'So my water pipes will be discovered by somebody else.'

He paused, as if he expected a reaction.

Bewildered, Leo said, 'Why are you telling me this?'

The arm around her was like iron.

'Because I want you to know me,' Amer said simply.

She levered herself away a little and stared up at him. The moonlight hid his expression. She gave a cynical nod.

'Oh, sure.'

He was startled. 'What do you mean?'

'If you wanted me to know you, could you have told me about your wife,' Leo said before she could stop herself.

'My wife!' He sounded thunderstruck.

'If there was anything more to this than a sexy game of pursuit, wouldn't you have told me that at least?' Leo said quietly.

There was a silence.

Then Amer said fiercely, 'My feelings for my wife were nothing like this. *Nothing.*'

Leo thought it was impossible to hurt so much and not cry out with it. She removed herself from his encircling arm. She could not bear him to touch her any more and not *care*.

She said, 'I want to go back.'

'Leonora—'

'I want to go back *now*.'

She fled.

He let her get as far as their picnic site before he caught her. His arms shackled her, though she struggled wildly.

'Let me go,' she panted. 'You don't want me. Not really. For a few days at most.'

'A few days?' Amer speared a look down into her face that she could almost believe would pierce the dark. 'A few *days?*'

He pulled her hard into his arms. Leo suddenly saw the point of light, loose silks. His head blotted out the moon.

It was no good. No matter what her head said, her heart was his. She gave herself up to the moment on a tornado of desire.

He lowered her to the rug. The sand shifted underneath, moulding itself round them. Leo gasped. His hands were strong and amazingly competent. She felt the silks flow away from her. To be replaced by his mouth.

But this was not like London. This was no languorous lovemaking, luring her slowly up the winding path of pleasure. This was urgent. Desperate almost. And this time he was not holding back.

'Touch me,' he commanded.

Leo hesitated. He groaned her name. She had never felt so unsure of herself. His flesh was so warm. Tentatively she moved her palms along his shoulder, down his spine. It felt awkward. His tension struck her to the heart.

It was no use. She could not pretend.

With harsh honesty, Leo said, 'I don't know how to do this.'

Amer raised his head at that. 'What?'

In the starlight his eyes burned into hers.

Leo had no deceptions left. 'No one has ever made me feel the way you do,' she muttered. 'I didn't know anyone could. I have no idea how to make you feel that good. I've always been useless with men.'

She felt as if her whole body was one huge blush of shame. Thank God for the dark. At least he would not see it.

See? No. But he could hear. And feel. He was very still

for an agonizing moment. Then he moved sharply, pinning her hands above her head in the sand.

'And you accused *me* of treating this like a game,' he said, outraged.

Leo was disconcerted. She pulled against the imprisoning hands. 'What? What are you doing?'

But he did not let her go. It was almost as if he did not hear her. She started to thresh wildly.

'You're not a toy,' he said furiously. 'That's why I went after you in the first place. You were completely yourself.'

Leo tried to kick herself free. It was an incredible mistake. His hand only tightened on her wrist. But the worst thing was that it brought her into contact with the whole length of his aroused body. She sobbed in longing.

'You don't have to make me feel good.' Amer shook her wrists to emphasise his point. 'You don't have to make me feel *anything*. You have to be here. That's all. Be here now.'

'Let me go,' said Leo breathlessly.

Her writhings had taken them off the rug into the sand.

'Feel,' he said. 'Just feel.'

You have to be here. Now.

His concentration was total. It was like fire. She cried out again and again as he swept through defence after defence to reach the heated core of her.

You have to be. Here. *Now.*

Leo lay stunned. Her unwinking eyes gazed dreamily at the stars, wheeling with majestic slowness beyond his head. He was heavy across her, his forehead damp in the crook of her shoulder. She touched his hair with tenderness. And absolute love.

It did not matter if he did not love her. It did not matter how short a time he might want her for. She loved him. And he had loved her in a way for that explosive moment.

Amer stirred.

'I never meant to do that,' he said. His voice was slurred but there was an unmistakable undertone of laughter. 'Well not yet anyway. You go to my head.'

He rolled away and sat up. Leo lay there in the starlight, unashamed of her nakedness, though she knew he was looking at her. She gazed up at him with love.

He brushed her hair back from her hot face. It was a possessive gesture.

'I hurt you, didn't I?'

'No.'

'I think I did.'

Leo stretched her arms above her head. She gave her limbs a shake all the way down to her pointing toes. She made a little purring sound.

'No,' she said, laughing in her turn. 'All in good working order. In fact, this is the best I've ever felt in my life.'

Amer bent and kissed her quickly. 'Me, too.'

'You?' She came up on one elbow, astonished. 'But—'

He said rapidly, 'I know I should have told you about Yasmin. Only it's painful. I've got out of the way of thinking about it.'

Leo leaned forward and put a hand to his cheek.

'Yasmin was your wife?'

For some reason it did not seem all that important, any more. She loved him. That was enough.

'Yes. We were too young, I suppose. And it was a political alliance. She had been spoilt by her father. I was too young to know how to deal with it. It made her cruel.' He looked into Leo's eyes suddenly. 'When she died she was tormenting a horse she had been told she should not ride. I couldn't mourn. I couldn't forgive myself for not mourning. It's a bad package, that.'

Leo pulled him forward until his head was against her breast.

'Oh my love.'

'I'm not proud of the way I've lived since then. I wish it had been different. That's why I held back that night in London. I wanted—it seemed a way of loving you.'

Leo's eyes were full of tears. She bent her head quickly to kiss his temple. Her lips trembled.

'I have never wanted any woman to have my children,' he said so quietly that she could barely hear him. 'Until now.'

Leo went very still. Amer raised his head.

'That's why no more games.' He stroked her hair. 'It's a lot of fun and sexy as hell. But I want more.'

She was utterly unprepared. 'I can't—I hadn't thought—I didn't know—' She swallowed. 'But you don't love me.'

'Don't I?'

'You haven't shown any signs of it.'

Amer gave a tender laugh. 'That's because you don't know what a saint I normally am. Hari tells me I've been unbearable. And doing crazy things, just for the chance of getting you into bed.'

'Oh,' said Leo, hopefully.

'My father could tell you, too,' Amer added thoughtfully. 'I said that unless he agreed to meet you I was going to take up an archaeological job in the UK.'

'*Oh.*'

'Marry me,' he said urgently.

Leo blinked, disconcerted.

'All right,' he said in a reasonable voice. 'Spend the night with me. We'll talk about the rest in the morning.'

Leo was startled into laughter. Amazed, joyous laughter.

'But I'm clumsy. And I bump into things. And I get ink on my fingers. What sort of wife will I make?'

'The only one I want.'

Amer kissed her throat. 'Are you going to spend the night with me or not, you difficult woman?'

Leo moved against him voluptuously, her eyes drifting shut.

'I'll take that as a yes,' said Amer amused. 'And what about marriage?'

Amused, yes. But he was shaking. He wanted her. He really wanted her!

Leo opened her eyes and gave him a long look of shameless triumph.

'Yes,' she said.

EPILOGUE

IT WAS, everyone agreed, a magnificent wedding. It went on for four days and included every ceremony that the bride's and groom's respective families could devise.

After the ceremonies came the feasting; after the feasting the entertainment. The Minister of Culture, in his element, hung the palace halls with cloth of gold for the occasion. The international photojournalists were in their element.

Leo went through it all without bumping into a thing. Every time she felt nervous she looked up. And Amer smiled at her as if he and she were the only people in the world.

Eventually she slipped away from the music and dancing and out into the courtyard where the fountains played. He followed her, as she knew he would.

'Tired?' The soft murmur was a caress.

'No.'

'So you would like to dance until dawn?' he teased.

'No.'

'So what am I to do with you, then?'

'Love me.'

His arms closed round her, hard as iron. 'Always.'

'Take me home, Amer.' Her voice was a thread of pure desire.

He took her back to his own palace then; to his private room, with its books and the mountains beyond. And shut the world out.

Leo gave a little delighted shiver and went into his arms in total trust.

'It seems too much. I can't believe it. Hold me, my love. Make me believe it.'

'Believe what?' he said, his voice husky with desire. 'That

I adore you? That when I am away from you, I can barely wait to return to you? That when I return, all I want is you in my arms?'

Leo was trembling. 'That I am the Sheikh's bride, after all.'

He picked her up and carried her to the bed.

And in the end, dazed with delight, humbled by love and completely overthrown by tender laughter, she said, 'I believe it. Oh boy, do I believe.'

SHEIKH DADDY

BARBARA MCMAHON

To Anne Canadeo,
you have expanded my horizons tremendously.
Thank you.

CHAPTER ONE

SHEIK ROEUK BIN SHALIK!

Megan stared in stunned fascination at the familiar face staring up at her from the glossy photograph she had just been handed. After all these years... Her heart jumped. She caught her breath. *It was Ben.* A flood of emotions swept through her, mostly bad—heartache, nostalgia for what might have been, the strong feeling of abandonment. But foremost was the anger that flowed surprisingly intense and hot and fresh. It had been ten long years ago, yet she felt it as if it had been yesterday. Damn him!

Today she would see him again. She traced her finger along the edge of his jaw, almost feeling his heat, as if he were real instead of an image in a glossy black-and-white photo. Wishing she could rake her nails on that flawless skin, aching to hurt him as much as he had once hurt her, anger roiled within as she clenched her jaw. After all this time, shouldn't the intensity have faded?

"You okay?" Jeff asked, perched on the edge of her desk.

Megan blinked and looked up, consciously relaxing her muscles. It was only a picture. "Sure. Tell me again about this assignment." Resolutely she kept her eyes on the face of the news journalist in front of her, though she longed to study the picture. Longed to see how the years had treated him.

"I knew you weren't listening. Paul was going to cover the event. He's been working on the prelims all week. But today his wife went into labor and Paul's determined to be at the birth. So we get the job. This sheik is meeting with the president at ten, on the lawn since no rain is forecast. It'll just be the usual goodwill-between-nations garbage. But the boss wants to carry some pictures. Any country willing to give the U.S. first crack at its oil reserves without going through the cartel gets a lot of positive press.'' Jeff shrugged. ''You take good pics, I'll try for some interview, or some new angle to appease the boss.''

Megan nodded, her eyes drawn irresistibly to the photograph. ''What do you know about him?'' she asked. She searched the image for signs of the man she'd once known, curiosity rampant. He'd disappeared from her life without a word. She hadn't even known if he was dead or alive. Somehow, she had come to think him dead these last few years. But the picture portrayed him in the best of health, virile masculinity personified. A feeling of betrayal blossomed. For years she'd wondered, worried, mourned. What had happened to him? She had been so in love. *They* had been so in love, or so she'd thought. They had even discussed marriage. Then he had packed his bags and vanished without a single word. What had changed? Why hadn't he at least told her goodbye?

''I don't know much about him beyond what I've told you. I have Paul's background file that I'll read on our way over. Bring a selection of lenses so we can do close-ups and distance shots. Knowing White House security, we won't be allowed too near his august presence. Plus, his own bodyguards probably won't want the press close.''

''I do know my business,'' she murmured absently. She ought to know it, she'd been doing it long enough.

The questions now were did she want to do this shoot? Dare she do this shoot? Could she calmly focus her camera on Sheik Roeuk bin Shalik when she would rather fling it in his face? Could she do her job and walk away without giving in to the urge to vent some of her seething anger?

"Yeah, yeah, I know. You're Mason's fair-haired child. Can't do anything wrong," Jeff said easily, referring to their boss.

Megan grinned at that remark and tossed the picture aside. Meeting Jeff's teasing glint, she wrinkled her nose at him. "You're a great one to talk. Who's up for a Pulitzer Prize?"

"So we're both his fair-haired children. Come on, traffic will be bad. We'll be lucky to get there before the event is over, much less before it starts."

"You drive," Megan said as she began to gather up her equipment. She could do this, she told herself. She was a professional. She would take two cameras, several lenses, a dozen rolls of film. Not that she planned to use all of them, but she liked to be prepared. She had tried hard over the last decade to anticipate every eventuality so she would never be caught as surprised and unprepared as she had been ten years ago.

"I want you to drive, I have to read the background," Jeff protested.

"I'll read it to you," she said, throwing her bag over her shoulder. She was used to the weight of the cameras. She felt comfortable and confident in her ability. She'd been in Washington long enough to acquire the coveted White House coverage for the paper. She knew some of the security guards personally, some of the current administration's staff. What she didn't know was how she would react when she saw Ben in person after all these years. She wanted to rant and rave and throw something. Instead, she would probably just take the pictures and leave. She tilted her chin in determination. She could live through this. She'd lived through far worse.

Roeuk bin Shalik accompanied the president out into the sunshine. The deep green lawn had been recently mowed, and the smell of fresh-cut grass lingered in the warm air. There was a slight tang of exhaust fumes from the traffic beyond the wrought iron fence encircling the grounds. The humid air carried the sultry fragrance of the flowers blooming so profusely. He savored the various aromas, so different from those in his homeland.

The distance to the barrage of microphones was short. Dignitaries and staff members from both nations followed. Several dozen were already waiting in front of the microphones in the chairs provided, or standing to the sides. Security was tight. Roeuk noticed both uniformed and nonuniformed personnel, but the openness of the setting pleased him. He liked America and was glad to be visiting again.

Roeuk was also satisfied with the just-concluded breakfast meeting. While primarily a rehash of the negotiations that had been conducted over the past few months, neither side had anticipated any major changes. His visit was one of goodwill and friendship...and financial gain for his own country.

But for Roeuk, the visit to the United States was something special. For the first time in ten years he was back in America. He planned to take a vacation after the treaty was signed, linger in the States while his ministers returned home. He was going to start in Berkeley. His plans beyond that depended on what he learned there. For ten years he'd thought about Megan O'Sullivan. He had tried to locate her in the months following his departure, only to find she'd disappeared. Depending on others to locate her had proved unsatisfactory. He knew why earlier investigations had proved worthless. This time he was going to see what he could discover for himself. No one would stop him.

A slight breeze blew his burnoose behind him. He adjusted the formal caftan and came to a halt beside the president before the mikes. He and the ministers that had accompanied him wore their desert garb proudly. It represented their land and gave the cameramen a good show, he thought cynically. Western attire would have suited him; it was more and more the norm in his country these days. But he bowed to custom and protocol. And the expectation of the American public.

The Washington Monument towered in the distance, gleaming white in the morning sun. From the White House lawn, Roeuk could see the crowds already queued up around the base of the obelisk. He would like to go up in it but doubted it would be possible this trip. Maybe he could slip back into town after his West Coast venture, return incognito.

As he had lived in Berkeley.

He had happy memories of his days at the California university. Not all of them centered around Megan, though most of them did. The old, almost-forgotten anger pricked. Megan. What had happened to her? Where had she disappeared to? What had she done with her life? Had she forgotten him?

His eyes drifted around the crowd as the president made his opening speech and introduction. Idly, Roeuk studied faces, wondering who he would meet at the functions being held over the next week in his honor and who were in attendance today because he wouldn't meet them later. Who was important to the future welfare of his country, and who was milking the event for personal gain?

The press was to the left of the seated dignitaries, behind a taut rope. Photographers snapped pictures. Men and women spoke softly into handheld recorders, or scribbled on—

Roeuk's gaze focused on a young woman hidden behind a camera. For a moment, he thought he recognized her. Was it only because he was in Megan's country? Only because he'd been thinking about her that he saw Megan in the tall, brown-haired woman?

The camera focused on his face. He could see the photographer's finger snapping exposure after exposure. The woman dropped the camera and for one blinding moment Roeuk's gaze locked with hers. Then she dropped her gaze to her camera as she coolly changed a lens.

It was Megan! Stunned, Roeuk stared at her. While he believed in fate and in the karma that guided everyone's lives, he had never expected to find her so easily. His first trip to the United States in a decade and he was at the same place as Megan. His lips tightened and his eyes narrowed. Was it possible? As soon as the ceremony was completed he would send Salid to bring her to him. Talk to her again as he had wanted to so many times over the last years. Discover why she'd disappeared ten years ago. Find out what she was doing now. Had she married another man? For a moment, anger and another strong emotion threatened to flare out of control. She was *his*.

"—present Sheik Roeuk bin Shalik," the president concluded with a warm smile as he turned to face Roeuk.

The smattering of applause recalled Roeuk to his reason for being there. For a split second he almost forgot his speech, almost forgot his country, the reason for his visit. He wanted to call across the open space and demand Megan leave the press section and come to him, to make sure she didn't disappear from his life a second time.

But thirty-four years of training held sway. Calmly, Roeuk stepped up to the microphone and began his speech, thanking the president for his invitation to visit in person, extolling the virtue of the proposed treaty. He gave the speech without referring to notes, without hesitation for a single word. His command of English was perfect, if a bit influenced by his British schooling. From the nods of his fellow countrymen and the pleased looks in the audience, he knew he was saying what everyone wanted to hear. But his mind was churning with thoughts of the young photographer only a dozen yards from him.

Megan.

He turned to offer his hand in friendship to the president, conscious of the constant click click as dozens of cameras recorded the event. Smiling formally, nodding, speaking clearly for all to hear, Roeuk wanted nothing but to talk to Megan. How long would this continue? How long before he could get her alone and find out where she'd been for the last ten years?

When he turned to look at her again, she was gone. For a long moment, he searched the press section, then turned his attention back to the president. There would be time enough later to find Megan. He now knew where to start looking. He needn't wait until his official visit ended. If it took his entire stay in Washington, he would find her.

Stupid, stupid, *stupid!* Megan berated herself as she banged her fist impatiently on the steering wheel. The last thing she needed was Jeff asking a thousand questions when he joined her. He would wonder why she'd dashed off so quickly, ask what she thought about the honored visitor, how her pictures had come out. The last thing she wanted was an inquisition. Her nerves were stretched too taut for that. She should have stayed in the press section until the other journalists were ready to leave. She should have mingled and exchanged small talk as she normally did. Of course that is what she should have done.

But she hadn't. She couldn't.

Not after Ben had recognized her. She shivered as she relived the moment his gaze had locked with hers. His dark eyes had been unfathomable. She had gleaned nothing from his expression, but the jolt of anger that had shaken her was stronger than ever. She couldn't chance a meeting. Not daring to trust herself, she had fled for the safety of the company car.

She longed to drive back to the office and turn the film in for processing and development. The sooner she got it out of her hands the better. The pictures she'd taken seemed to burn through the camera; she wanted to get rid of them. Though she would not be able to get rid of the pictures in her head as easily.

Ben Shalik. *Sheik Roeuk bin Shalik.* Damn him. She had thought she'd known him ten years ago, had thought they'd shared something special. God, she had never loved anyone as much as she'd loved him. Yet he had never even hinted at his true identity. A sheik, an Arabian prince! How ironic. She had thought him wildly romantic and endearing when they'd known each other in Berkeley. He had been so special, that dark man who spoke with such a charming accent, who delighted in the simplest of pleasures. Who had relished the rowdy sport of football with the same enjoyment he'd shown at the ballet and the symphony. What had he been doing, dabbling with the commoners? She had thought him just another college kid, only to discover he's Arabian royalty.

Taking a deep breath, Megan tried to calm her rioting senses, quell the intensity of her emotions. That was in the past. A decade ago. She was never again going to fall for some heart-stoppingly handsome man. She'd learned her lesson, hard as it had been. Just because his eyes looked like liquid ebony with starlight shot through was no reason to feel soft and mushy when he looked at her. She was a competent career woman, no longer some silly impressionable naive teenager.

Just because he still had that adorable dimple in his left cheek when he smiled was no reason for her knees to turn to jelly. He meant nothing to her. Less than nothing after his betrayal.

Just because her pulse was still pounding from being so near him was no reason to think she wasn't totally in charge of her emotions. She would get control. She had built a good life for herself…and her daughter, Norrie. She would not fall prey to mere sexual attraction again. She would not be drawn into any man's web, deluding herself that it was love.

Who was she trying to kid? She had been crazy in love with Ben. Loved everything about him, from his odd sense of humor to his enchantment with everything American. She had loved him long before she had shared her body in love. They had talked of marriage. He'd said it might not be easy, but they would work it out together. She had thought he loved her in return, that the difficulties had to do with their different cultures. In that he was correct, they were a world apart.

But then, she hadn't really known him at all, had she? She hadn't known he was a prince; she hadn't even known his full name. She hadn't known what happened to him when he'd vanished from her life so long ago. She felt betrayed anew. He had deliberately let her think he was an average foreign-exchange student.

"Where did you disappear to?" Jeff opened the door and climbed in. "Since you're sitting behind the wheel, I assume you're planning to drive back. Why did you leave so suddenly? We could have gotten a few more shots of His Royal Highness mingling with the hoi polloi."

"Right." Megan gunned the engine and shot out of the parking space. "I took plenty of pictures. The paper's only going to use one or two. I think the handshake came out great. Shows solidarity in our relationship with—"

"Stop it, O'Sullivan. What's the scoop?"

"Nothing. I got what I came for. The crowd was starting to get to me. Drop it, okay, Jeff?"

"Sure. Glad you're driving. I can read more of his background, since I still don't have a special angle to use." He reached for the folder in the middle of the seat and began reading the biographical information Paul had collected.

"This guy's been around. Schooling in England and the U.S. Set up foreign offices for some of their state-run businesses. Seems to prefer England and France to the other European countries, though he visits Switzerland a lot in the winter." He hummed tunelessly as he continued to read. "Sure likes the ladies. Was close to a couple of English ladies...ummm, Lady Susan Fair-

child, fancy...a French actress. Married a few years
back..."

Megan's hands gripped the wheel tightly as everything started to spin. He'd married? For a moment tears
threatened. She took a deep breath, swallowing the ache
in her throat. Why shouldn't he have married? Just because she never planned to permit anyone that close
again was no reason for him to abstain. Obviously the
promises he'd made to her had had no binding effect.
But then, she'd known that for years. Only, somehow,
she'd thought—

"Oh, wife died a couple of years later. No kids, apparently. He's got three brothers, all younger."

The portion of the background material Megan had
read on the ride to the White House had surrounded the
trade treaty that was being negotiated. She hadn't read
any of the personal stuff. Now she was glad. Could her
voice have remained normal? She was having trouble
driving. Thank God the office was just up ahead. She
couldn't wait to get to her desk and garner some semblance of privacy. Even though she shared a large room
with a dozen others, the shoulder-high partitions gave a
modicum of isolation.

It was over. She'd seen him and survived. The rest of
the day would be busy and tomorrow was Saturday,
nothing scheduled for her. Maybe she and Norrie could
go on a picnic in Rock Creek Park, or visit that video
store in Alexandria that specialized in old horror films.
For some unfathomable reason, Norrie loved old movies
of that type.

The important thing was that Megan would go on with
her life. A thread from the past had briefly touched her,
but nothing had changed. Life would continue as it had
for years. Megan took another deep breath and tuned out

Jeff's muttering, focusing on getting her emotions under control.

The brief cool spell from Thursday's rain ended by Friday afternoon. Saturday dawned hot and muggy. By midmorning Megan wished for the thousandth time that she had a place in the mountains. At least it would be cool there. The house was air-conditioned, but she had yard work to do and a dirty car to wash. Norrie had spent the night at her friend Stephanie's and wouldn't be home until later. Megan wanted to keep busy. She would finish her chores, then be free to spend the afternoon with her daughter. She needed to keep from thinking of yesterday's press conference and the unexpected eye contact with Ben. Had he really recognized her? Or had it been too long since he'd seen her? Had she been only one in a long line of women? From what Jeff had muttered, the sheik was used to escorting beautiful and prominent women in several countries. While not exactly a flamboyant playboy, he obviously would have no time for a quiet photojournalist he'd once known briefly a decade before.

Megan finished mowing the lawn and had put the mower away in her detached garage, when the sleek black stretch limousine purred to a stop in front of her house. She stood by the driveway, her heart sinking. Transfixed, she watched as the car stopped and a man climbed out of the front and reached back to open the rear door.

Oh, God.

Sheik Roeuk bin Shalik climbed out and stood on the sidewalk, surveying her house through dark glasses. She couldn't determine from his expression what he thought, but it no longer mattered. For one brief moment she toyed with the idea of dashing back into the garage and hiding.

But it was too late to run. He'd seen her. He strode confidently toward her. Megan couldn't move, she could only stand and hold her ground. She wondered where his robes were. He was dressed in a business suit as normal as any American businessman's. Except on him, it was a work of art. He was as tall as she remembered, as exciting. He'd already been a man when she'd known him, but he had acquired a deeper maturity. Her heartbeat increased.

Roeuk's eyes scanned Megan as he slowly walked across her lawn. She looked almost as young as when he'd last seen her, yet she had to be twenty-nine by now. God, she would be thirty on her next birthday. Hard to believe. Ten years gone, what had she done during those years?

He smiled as he let his gaze trail insolently down the length of her. She was wearing short white shorts, almost indecently skimpy. Attire like that would only be suited for the beach in his country. These were grass-stained and revealed a long length of tanned legs. They fit her like a second skin. For a moment he wished she would turn around so he could see how they hugged her bottom. The yellow tank top she wore enhanced the honey tone of her skin. Her light brown hair was much shorter than when he'd known her. Yet the mop of curls that danced around her face was enchanting.

His smile faded when he drew close enough to see the wary, unfriendly expression in her brown eyes.

"Hello, Megan," he said. He wished he'd changed out of the suit before stopping by, but he'd been too impatient to see her again. Now he felt warm, dressed

to the nines in this heat, and her revealing casual attire
didn't help his temperature.

"Do I bow or curtsy?" she asked. She stood tall, feet
braced, her chin tilted a bit pugnaciously, her eyes hos-
tile.

He smiled grimly. Some things hadn't changed; she
had always had a smart remark ready. He had an almost
overwhelming urge to lean over and kiss her, bend her
to his will until she was breathless and pliant. He wanted
her anxious to please him and be pleasured by him.
"Neither. A simple 'Hi, Ben, it's been a long time,'
would do."

"It has been a long time. If I had known you were
coming by, I would have read up on proper etiquette.
Or left home at first light."

"Megan."

She looked beyond him at the limousine. "Sorry I
don't have servants' quarters where your chauffeur and
bodyguard can wait." She looked him square in the face.
"How long are you staying?"

"If you'd care to invite me inside, I'd appreciate it.
It's hot out here, and I'm not exactly dressed for the
weather." His imperious tone grated on her nerves.

"It must be as hot in your country. The one you never
talked about. The one you never told me about when we
knew each other in Berkeley." She blinked, annoyed at
the prick of angry tears behind her lids. Her hands
clenched into fists as the outrage spread.

He cocked an eyebrow, his gaze never leaving hers.
"It is as hot in my country but not as humid. And I live
beside the Mediterranean. It's pleasant there. We often
have a breeze, which keeps the temperature comfortable." He glanced around the neighborhood. The houses
were built fairly close together, the yards nicely main-

tained. It was an older neighborhood, the trees mature
and lush. The shrubbery surrounding her house needed
a trim. The grass was freshly cut.

"Yes, well, I'm not quite dressed for such illustrious
company. And I'm sure my house would not—"

"Megan, shut up." He whipped off the sunglasses and
stared down into her astonished gaze. "It took all of
yesterday and part of today to locate you. Why didn't
you come to see me after the ceremonies yesterday? You
must have recognized me. I certainly recognized you the
instant I saw you."

"I never thought about it," she lied. "I'm surprised
you bothered to look me up. I thought you made it quite
clear ten years ago that our *friendship* was at an end."

"And you didn't hang around very long to find out,
did you? I thought you'd planned to pursue an education
at the university."

"Plans change all the time. You should know that as
well as the next man. Of course, I was the only one
planning a marriage, you were planning an escape."

"I can explain my part of what happened, but I've
often wondered at yours."

"There was no 'my part' in your leaving. And at least
you knew who I was. I don't even know what to call
you. Is it 'Your Highness'?"

Roeuk reached out to brush an errant curl from her
cheek, giving in to the impossibly strong urge to touch
her, however briefly. "You used to call me Ben." His
hand dropped to his side, his fingers still tingling with
heat from her satin-soft skin. "But you may call me
Roeuk now, if you wish."

Run! Megan fought the command her mind was sending. If she had an ounce of sense, she would run from
this man as far and as fast as she could. He'd hurt her

unbearably once. She didn't need the confusion and turmoil his presence brought. She shivered at his touch. The feel of his fingers on her cheek instantly evoked memories of his touch years ago.

His eyes were so dark and deep she felt she was drowning. He should have kept on the glasses. She had been safer with that slight barrier. Now she couldn't pull her gaze from his. She felt flushed with heat, and it wasn't from the sun. *Where have you been all this time,* she wanted to shout. *What have you done? Why did you betray me with lying words of love and then abandon me?*

Taking a deep breath, Megan caught the scent of his after-shave, deep and dark and mysterious, just like the man. Mixed with the fragrance of the fresh-cut grass it was earthy and entirely too enticing. Her anger deepened, some of it turned on herself for feeling anything beyond the fury of betrayal.

"Megan, ask me inside," he insisted.

She closed her eyes at the inevitable and nodded, turning to lead the way. She would agree to see him for a minute. Then he would be on his way. Tilting her head, she threw back her shoulders. He was a dignitary visiting her country. It no longer mattered that he was also the man who had broken her heart.

Megan stopped suddenly. *Norrie would be coming home soon.*

Roeuk reached his hand out to steady her, his lean fingers gripping her upper arm. She hardly noticed. She had to get their talk over with quickly. She couldn't have Norrie arrive while Roeuk was here. She had to get rid of him! The old anger she felt was instantly overshadowed by concern. She didn't want Roeuk to find out about Norrie.

CHAPTER TWO

"THIS REALLY ISN'T a good time," Megan said a bit desperately. She didn't want to go into the house. Didn't want him to stay another minute. Norrie could be home any second. Her glance flickered to the sidewalk, it was still clear.

"I'm only going to stay a few minutes. I finished one set of meetings this morning and will need to review my notes before getting ready for a reception tonight. But I wanted to see you first."

"Why?"

"Megan, move."

He continued up the walk to her front door, his hand like a hot band around her arm, teasing her, sending shimmering waves of longing and forgotten desire through her. Involuntarily, Megan brought her arm in close, so the back of his fingers brushed against her unconfined breast. Big mistake. Sparks ignited a flame deep in her belly. She pulled away, forcing him to release her. That way lay danger. He had walked out on her ten years ago. He was only here today because of a chance encounter on the White House lawn. If Paul's baby hadn't decided to be born yesterday, Roeuk would never have seen her, would not have felt whatever obligation or curiosity had driven him to show up today.

And she wouldn't be torn apart by her own emotions. She would resist wanting to find out every scrap of information about him; she needed to protect herself from becoming involved. How dare he show up as if he was a long-lost friend. She longed to yell at him for the past, yet despite everything, she felt a tug of familiar physical attraction. She would guard her heart wisely. He was here for a short time, and then gone forever, never forget that.

Megan opened the door and stood aside as he entered. Curious to see his reaction to her home, she studied him as he stepped into the living room and surveyed it. If he dared make some scathing comment—

"Nice. It reminds me of you. Your apartment in Berkeley was welcoming, too." He strode into the center of the room as if he owned the place. Blatantly masculine in his appraisal, he looked at her furnishings and the collections of pictures on the wall.

"Have a seat," Megan said reluctantly. Conscious of the minutes ticking by, she wanted to end the meeting as quickly as possible.

Roeuk sat on the sofa, watching her closely as she crossed to a nearby chair.

He had matured exceedingly well, she thought as she gazed hostilely at him, waiting to hear what he had to say. His hair was rich and glossy black, not a trace of silver showing. His skin was smooth and tanned, except for the lines near his eyes. Laughter or something else? she wondered. His shoulders seemed even broader than she remembered. But maybe it was the suit, it looked as if it had been designed specifically for him, which it probably had. He was a sheik, remember, well able to afford the best.

"You are looking well." His eyes traveled over her again, lingering on the soft swell of her breasts clearly defined by her damp cotton top, then moving slowly down her long tanned legs.

"What do you want?" she said curtly, longing to

snatch a coat from the closet to cover herself. She was disturbed by the tingling awareness that shimmered through her at his look. God, what if he touched her again? The skin on her arm was still blazing from the feel of his hand, his fingers.

She gazed at him, willing him to say his piece and leave. He looked totally out of place in her modest living room. He was better suited to elegant continental drawing rooms, or royal palaces or the endless expanse of Arabian deserts. Certainly not a small space like her home.

"I wanted to explain what happened ten years ago," he said. "I know my leaving was, shall we say, unexpected. Unforeseen. I tried to contact you later but you had moved and no one knew where." His tone was cool, almost impersonal.

"Oh? Yes, I moved. There were…I…moved." She swallowed. What could she say? It made no difference now. And at the time, she'd had no choice. After all, it was he who had walked away without a backward glance.

"Why did you try to reach me?" she asked finally to fill the silence that stretched between them. Slowly, Megan leaned back in the chair, unable to relax. She hadn't known he'd tried to reach her. If she had been able to stay longer in Berkeley, would things have turned out differently? Probably not. She wiped nervous palms against her shorts.

"To let you know where I was, of course."

"I see," she said politely. She wanted him gone. Couldn't he tell? His very presence reminded her of a time she wished to forget.

"Damn, I don't want some polite little response, Megan. Didn't you care that I had left so abruptly?"

"Of course I did." She held her breath for a moment, but the old anguish wouldn't be stilled. "I thought we were in love," she said, almost yelling with the old anger and hurt. "I thought we were going to be married and share our lives together. Instead, you disappeared without a word. Then I find out ten years later that you're not even the man I thought I knew—"

"Hey, Mom, did you see that cool car in the front? Is it a limo? Who—" Norrie paused in the archway to the living room when she spotted her mother and the stranger. The man rose and turned to face her. For an endless moment, time stood still.

Oh, God, not this, too. Megan couldn't bear it. She stared at her daughter, examining every feature, trying to see her as Roeuk would see her. Norrie was an average American girl, dark eyes, light brown hair, childish features. *Please, don't let him guess.*

Roeuk felt as if someone had kicked him in the gut. Megan had had a child! She was a very young image of her mother. Her short curly hair was light brown with sun-bleached highlights. Her eyes were unexpectedly dark, however, and wide-spaced. In every other regard this child was the spitting image of Megan. Roeuk stared at the little girl. Anger flared as the evidence of her lack of faithfulness stared back at him. He'd been a fool to think she would wait for him. Had their relationship been only a brief college fling? Had she turned to someone else the minute he'd disappeared? By the child's apparent age, she must have.

"The limo is mine," he said to the little girl. "Would you like to see it?" He wanted to have a few minutes to garner some control before continuing to talk with

Megan. The hot throb of rage that filled him needed to be calmed before he spoke to her again.

"Would I? That'd be great. Mom, have you seen it?" Norrie smiled and came into the room, dropping her sleeping bag and backpack on the floor and dancing over to her mother.

Megan reached out and ruffled her daughter's hair, smiling with difficulty. The last thing she wanted was this. Could she bluff her way through? "I've not seen that particular one, but I've ridden in one before. If it's all right with..." She couldn't even call him by name. "It's fine with me. But don't get it dirty."

"Oh, Mom, Stephie and I were swimming. I'm squeaky-clean." Norrie smiled at the stranger and dashed to the door. Pausing, she looked back. "Will the driver let me see it?"

"I'll make sure." His eyes narrowed on the child, Roeuk crossed the room and followed her outside.

Megan watched as the two left, a feeling of doom and imminent catastrophe claiming her. She sat as if paralyzed, mesmerized by the turn of fate she'd had no control over. Ben had to realize. The age was right. She wasn't married, did he know that? Oh, God, what would she do if he realized Norrie was his? More important what would *he* do?

She observed them through the front window for a little while then went into the kitchen and took three glasses from the cupboard. She wondered how long it took to examine a limousine. They'd been outside for ten minutes. She couldn't sit still any longer and decided to prepare some lemonade. How long was *he* staying? Nervously she hunted for a tray. Normally, she and Norrie each got their own drinks in the kitchen and carried them out if they were having them elsewhere. Today she would be a bit more formal. The circumstances seemed to call for it. Besides, it gave her something to do.

"How old is your daughter?" Roeuk was standing in the doorway, filling it. His expression was hard, remote. His eyes stared at her like black ice.

Megan turned to face him. She wasn't the one who had done anything wrong. He was the one who had left her without a word. "I beg your pardon?"

"Dammit, Megan, don't play games with me. How old is she? How long did you wait before finding another man?"

Megan blinked and looked away lest he guess how surprised she was at his supposition. He didn't know Norrie was his. She took a deep breath. "Actually, I don't believe that is any of your business," she said.

The words were scarcely out of her mouth before he crossed the room in two furious strides and grabbed her arms. Leaning over until his face almost touched hers, his dark eyes blazed down into hers. "As you so conveniently remembered in the other room, we were supposed to have been in love. I tried to contact you two weeks after leaving Berkeley, and you had already gone. Had you connected up with someone in that short a time?" He shook her once.

"Let me go! How dare you come into my life again and talk about what we had ten years ago! You're the one who lied about his identity, kept his background a secret. What kind of relationship did we have when you weren't even honest enough to tell me your own name? It was nothing but lies. From start to finish—"

"It was not lies. Not all of it. Allah, give me strength, you try a man's patience. I came today to explain but find that perhaps I needn't have bothered. Obviously you didn't miss me long enough to matter.'' He flung her away as if the sight of her disgusted him.

Megan leaned against the counter, her knees trembling so, she was afraid they wouldn't hold her. ''Oh, that's just great, try to make me look like the one who did wrong. What about you? I called and got no answer. I was so worried about you. I went to your apartment and begged the landlord to let me in. He knew we'd been close. How do you think I felt when I saw the empty apartment? Not one stitch of clothing remained. Not one book. Nothing. You had vanished without a trace and without a single word to me. Would it have hurt to drop me a postcard, or call to say you were leaving? I thought you were in trouble. After not hearing from you all these years, I thought that you were dead! I never even knew your full name or where you were from. I never knew you were a sheik!'' She hadn't meant to raise her voice. But the accusation was too much. The old anger bubbled up and spewed forth.

''Megan.''

''Don't start with me, Sheik Roeuk bin Shalik. You mean nothing to me now. Where have you been for the last ten years? Playing Rudolph Valentino, sheik of the desert?'' She shouldn't have said that. Couldn't she keep her mouth shut? Now he would think— Oh, she didn't care what he thought. She just wanted him to leave, give her a chance to regain some measure of control. To get her life back the way it was before Friday morning. She didn't like feeling so out of control.

He glared at her, his manner intimidating as he drew himself up to his full height, almost threatening. ''I came here today to tell you what happened in Berkeley, why I left so suddenly. I thought we could see each other while I was in the States, see—''

"See if we could take up where we left off while you're here? What did you expect me to be, your Washington paramour? No thanks, I'm busy."

His gaze locked with hers. "You are correct, you didn't know where to find me. And I couldn't find you. I tried."

"You left the end of May. I couldn't stay once school was out. You didn't try soon enough. A phone call, that's all it would have taken. Ben, you knew my number, you called it often enough. One lousy phone call. You said you loved me, you knew I loved you! One phone call, a note, *something*. After all we'd meant to each other, surely I deserved something better than what I got." She shut her mouth. All the anger and anguish of that long-ago time was threatening to overwhelm her. She took a deep breath, fighting for control. It was in the past. She had made something of her life as a single parent and she sure didn't need him barging in on her life at this late stage. Especially when his staying record was so poor.

"There were circumstances..." He glanced at his watch, frowning. "Never mind, it's more than I can go into right now. I'm already late. You'll get your wish. I have to leave. But we're not through, you and I. Tomorrow I haven't any engagements until a reception at seven. I can come by—"

"We have nothing to discuss. Just go." God, she couldn't deal with this again.

"I beg to differ. I want to talk to you about what happened ten years ago, and I want to hear about your daughter." His voice was hard, the look he gave her determined and implacable.

She shook her head, but he stepped closer, reaching for her shoulders. His hands were warm and hard. Despite their punishing grip, his touch sent sizzling tingles through her though she longed to deny it. She was still so blasted angry she thought she would explode.

"Yes, Megan, tomorrow we will talk."

"Not here, then. Not with Norrie around." Was there anything he could say to make any sense after all this time? Norrie was his child. Perhaps she owed it to him to at least tell him something about her. But that was as far as she was willing to go, she would not let him know Norrie was his. She and Norrie had their lives, and Ben obviously had his. A very different life than she'd ever envisioned for him over the years. She'd been a fool to waste one minute of worry on him. He had lied to her, made love to her, then abandoned her for the luxurious life of royalty, while she'd been so afraid he'd been in trouble.

His thumb traced the line of her collarbone. Megan reached to grab his wrists, tug his hands away from her. She couldn't think when he was touching her. He was too potent. His dark eyes too sexy for coherent thought, his warm skin too tempting. She needed space.

"Just what are you suggesting?" she said.

"That's part of what we'll need to discuss. Tomorrow?"

"Not here," she repeated, feeling uncertain.

"I'll send the limo for you tomorrow. We can talk at my hotel."

She shook her head. "I don't know." She didn't want to go there, on his own turf, so to speak. Yet she dare not risk Norrie's overhearing them.

A grim smile crossed his lips. "I do." It was another order, yet with his smile, the dimple deepened and Megan's heart fluttered. Her fingertips actually ached to touch his cheek, to feel his warmth, dip into that slight indentation. Her eyes drank him in. He was so gorgeous, more so now than ten years ago. He was a mature male, a splendid specimen of the breed and her heart thumped heavily behind her breast at the very sight of him. She longed to turn the clock back a decade. Longed for an endless moment to rediscover the openness and love she'd once known. Wished she did not know it had all been built on lies and deceit.

"I'll send the car at one, then we'll talk."

She hesitated, catching her bottom lip between her teeth, knowing the uncertainty she was experiencing must show in her expression, in her eyes. How could he guarantee this wasn't leading to further disaster?

He tipped her chin up with a long, tanned finger, and gazed down into her light brown eyes, his narrowed as he looked at her.

She swallowed hard, feeling his soft breath caress her cheeks, feeling his heat and strength through his finger. Could he read her mind? Could he feel the anger that still simmered just below the surface, see the hesitation in her gaze?

Slowly, he lowered his face until his lips brushed against hers. Once, twice, he skimmed across hers, then withdrew. "Tomorrow at one."

With that he was gone. Megan stared after him, listening to his quick stride down the hall, to the sound of the front door opening and closing. Then the silence.

Blood coursed through her veins, pounding in her ears, scorching every inch of her. She rubbed her tongue lightly across her lips, tasting him, feeling the imprint of his lips as clearly as if he were still present. Turning to the sink, she ran cold water, splashing it on her face, rubbing her lips to erase his touch. She was not some starry-eyed teenager. She was a grown woman, too smart and too scarred to ever fall victim to his charm again. She'd learned that lesson well.

The front door slammed. Norrie hurried into the kitchen, her face radiant with happiness.

"Oh, Mom, that limo was so cool! It was almost as big as my bedroom. And it had a TV and a refrigerator. Not big like ours, but a little one. And there was soda. Fahim, that's the driver, said I could have one, but I didn't want to spill it. The inside had carpet all over the floor. It was so cool."

Megan smiled at her daughter, her heart catching again at the sight of her. She'd lived with her baby for nine years, but somehow, after seeing Roeuk today, she realized anew what a treasure her daughter was.

Reaching out, she drew the little girl into a warm hug, hoping nothing would ever change for them. Afraid everything was changing.

"So you thought that was pretty cool, huh? What's really fun is to ride in one and imagine you're a princess or something and wave to the other cars on the road. Because of the tinted windows, no one can see in, so you can have a fine time pretending."

"Is that what you did when you rode in one?" Norrie asked, intrigued, grinning up at her mother.

"Once. I had a lift to the airport and I was all alone. The window was closed between me and the driver." Megan shook her head, how foolish she'd been, but it had been fun.

"I wish I were a princess and could ride in a limo every day."

As Norrie pulled away and reached for one of the glasses of lemonade, Megan was struck by the thought that her daughter probably would have been a princess if she and Ben had married. At least in his country. Had things been different, Norrie might have gotten her wish. Time to change the subject before Norrie got caught up in the fantasy…and before Megan began to doubt the wisdom of keeping Norrie's parentage a secret.

"I have a meeting tomorrow afternoon. Do you think you could go to Stephanie's? I'll call her mother to see if it's all right with her. If not, we can ask Mrs. Hanson to come over."

"Sure, that'd be cool. We can swim. I wish we had a pool. It's been so hot lately." Norrie pushed out a chair and sat down, turning her glass around and around before her on the table, her eyes on the condensation and the patterns she was drawing through it with her finger.

"You get to swim almost every day at Stephanie's. And I'm glad it's her father that's taking care of the pool and not me."

Norrie grinned and nodded. Drinking the last of the lemonade, she set the glass carefully back. Darting a curious look at her mother, she said carefully, "Mom, who was that man?"

Megan felt as if she'd been kicked. Collapsing on one of the wooden chairs opposite Norrie, she looked at her daughter. She had never expected this. She didn't have a clue what to say.

"Why do you ask?" she said, stalling for time. Afraid to say the wrong thing, praying for some inspiration, she ran through a dozen possible responses.

"Just wondered. He doesn't talk like us, and I never saw him at your office." Norrie met her gaze with open curiosity.

Megan cleared her throat. "He's just someone I knew a long time ago. He came to Washington on business and met with the president. I covered the event for the paper and he saw me. So he came to visit."

"Is he nice, Mom? He seems nice, letting me see the limo, and all. Or was that just to get rid of me?" Norrie wandered over beside her mother, leaning against her when Megan put her arm around her daughter's small waist.

"I'm sure he wanted you to see the limo, to enjoy it. He probably knows what a novelty having one in our neighborhood is."

"That limo was so cool," she repeated. "If he comes to visit again, maybe I can ride in it."

"Don't count on it, toots. He doesn't live in the U.S., you know."

Norrie nodded wisely. "That's why he had that funny accent."

"He hardly has an accent at all, just a charming British intonation." Charming and sexy as hell. Especially in the dark of midnight when whispering love words. Had she ever forgotten?

"Um, what's for dinner?" Norrie asked.

Megan gave Norrie a quick hug then swatted her lightly on the bottom, glad to change the subject. "We're having deluxe hamburgers on the grill, if you'll help me keep the marauding insects at bay." Feigning a lighthearted attitude she didn't feel in the slightest, Megan rose. There were hours yet until dinnertime, she still had the weeding to do in the yard. Once again, Roeuk's touch in her life had been brief. She needed to make sure she kept it in perspective.

She was not going to dwell on the past. She was firmly entrenched in the present and that's where she was staying. What she and Ben had shared had been a fleeting moment. She had her life and he had his, and they were vastly different.

She wasn't ready for the feelings that swamped her at

the sight of him that afternoon. She had always liked
being with him. Around him she felt more feminine, and
she had always liked that feeling, knowing it comple-
mented his own strong masculinity. He had been the
most exciting individual she'd ever known. And he was
far far from her realm. Sheik Roeuk bin Shalik.

The short drive to Roeuk's hotel was accomplished in
total silence. From the time the handsome Arab driver
had knocked on her door, until she walked into the opulent lobby of the Williams Hotel, Megan said not a
word. Once ensconced in the luxurious back seat of the
limo, she questioned her actions. She should have firmly
refused to see him again. Should have let yesterday end
things for all time.

She glanced out the tinted windows blindly. In times
past, Ben would have come for her, not sent a car. He'd
changed. Of course, he was not Ben. There had never
been a Ben. He was Roeuk.

Megan took a deep breath. Older and a lot wiser, she
would be able to deal with the situation, she told herself.
No matter how angry she remained, she would conduct
herself calmly and rationally at this meeting. Then bid
him a cool farewell. She hoped.

The chauffeur stopped before the portico of the hotel,
and the Arab who escorted her quickly opened the door
for her. Silently, he took her arm and guided her to the
elevator. In seconds they were in the elegant sitting room
of the suite occupied by Sheik Roeuk Bin Shalik.

"Ah, Megan." He stood near the windows as if he
had been studying the city of Washington. Today he
wore casual clothes, a green polo shirt and tan slacks.

Her eyes flicked over him, raised to meet his dark
gaze. Despite herself, her heart rate increased. He was

tanned, from the Mediterranean sun, no doubt, his body strong and lightly muscled. Holding on to her anger, she stayed near the door, refusing to let herself be charmed by him.

"I'm ready if you wish to tell me about your leaving Berkeley ten years ago." Long-dormant questions hovered on her lips. The mystery would finally be solved. Then what? Go on with life as she had made it over the last decade, what else?

"It's both simple and complex. Won't you sit down?"

She looked at the facing pair of brocade sofas, glanced warily back at him before slowly crossing to sit on the edge of one.

Roeuk sat opposite her, across the low Queen Anne table that stood between the sofas.

"My father suffered a major stroke. He had heard of our liaison and wanted to end it. To state it bluntly, he used his illness as the means to break us up. Two of the *sajine,* guards for the royal family, arrived late one afternoon. They were waiting at my apartment when I finished my last final exam. Their orders were to escort me home. I feared my father was dying."

"Was he?" That explained the abrupt departure. She still waited to hear why she had never heard from him again. He could have called from the airport, from his home when he arrived. She still wanted to know why he'd never told her who he was. Why he'd never shared something so basic with her, even after they had become lovers.

"No. He was partially paralyzed, had a mild case of aphasia, speech disorientation. He recovered. But he was very ill for many weeks. We all feared for his life."

"So you stayed to be with him." Megan understood family loyalty. Of course he would want to be with his father while the man was so ill.

"I was commanded to do so."

CHAPTER THREE

"COMMANDED?" she asked, surprised at the word.

"He was my father. I was commanded to stay to prepare to take over in the event he died. The stroke gave him the first sting of mortality. He desperately wanted me ready to assume control when he died. My first allegiance was to my father and my family."

"Of course. But you could have let me know! I had the police at your place, I was certain something awful had happened to you. You could have told me where you were, that you were all right. A letter, a cablegram, a call at four in the morning, something!" For a moment, Megan relived those frantic days. She had been so worried and so scared.

"I sent letters but—"

"I never got any. Maybe I had already left Berkeley before they arrived." She was restless, nervous. Rising, she paced to the window, staring blindly out over the view of Washington. She didn't see the marble buildings, the expanse of the Mall; she was seeing the past, that frightening time when she'd first realized she was pregnant, alone and pregnant. Remembering when she'd first accepted that Ben would not be coming back for her.

"No, you never got any. I believe they never left my country."

She spun around. "What?"

"My father had them intercepted. He knew I would try to contact you. He wanted to end it."

Megan stared at him, realistic enough to realize a
sheik might have a fling while studying abroad, but that
didn't mean he was going to bring the girl home to his
family. So even if he had remained in Berkeley, they
would never have married. His family would have forbidden it. How naive of her to assume that love would
be enough.

"Well, that's that, then. I'll be going." She turned
toward the door, hoping her shaky legs would carry her
across the room. She should never have agreed to see
him, she told herself again. Somehow, deep within her,
there had been a small bud of hope that something could
come of talking over what had happened. That bud died
with his words.

"No, do not leave yet, Megan. We still have much to
discuss."

She paused by the door and turned to face him. For
one awful moment, she was afraid she would blurt out
her fury that his family hadn't thought her good enough
for him and rail at him for turning aside his daughter so
easily. She bit her lips, he hadn't known about his
daughter. And that was how she meant to keep it.

"Come back and sit down," he ordered.

She shook her head. "Maybe in your country you can
order people around, but I've got news for you, buster.
This is the U.S.A., and we don't take orders from…from
sheiks!"

"Megan, come back and sit down and stop acting like
a child." His voice was hard, brooked no refusal.

Slowly, she returned to the brocade sofa, her eyes
glaring into his the entire way. "There is nothing more
to discuss," she said defiantly.

His lips softened into a smile. "But there is, *chérie*,
you need to tell me all you've been doing since I last

saw you. I've missed you, Megan. I have thought about you for years, wondered where you were, what you were doing. Did you ever marry?"

"Like you did?" she snapped. She had thought *they* would marry. Instead, Roeuk had married someone else. It shouldn't matter, not now, not after all this time. But the fact of the matter was, it did hurt. Intensely.

His face tightened. "My marriage occurred five years after I'd last seen you. At the time, I thought you had returned my letters and were no longer interested in me. The marriage was an arrangement that my father urged upon me. Don't throw that up into my face, Megan. It's obvious you wasted no time in finding someone to replace me in your bed."

She felt as if she'd been slapped. But of course he would think that, and she had to let him continue to think that if Norrie's identity was to be kept a secret.

"Did you love him?" he asked harshly.

"Who?"

"Norrie's father."

She shrugged, her eyes drifting to the left. "I thought I did."

"As much as you loved me?"

Meeting his gaze again, she shook her head. "What we had was nothing. Lies on your part and stupid teenage infatuation on mine." Ironic that he suspected she'd had another lover. She had never made love to any man but Roeuk. She hadn't even dated much over the past ten years.

"We talked of marriage," he reminded her.

"Talk is cheap. Where were you when the chips were down?"

"In what way were the chips down?" He went curiously still.

She moved restlessly, avoiding his eyes again. "Never mind. I need to get home."

"Not yet. I'll have Fahim take you back soon. Tell me what led to your job at the *Sentinel*."

"Why are you asking? Why do you want to know?"

"We are different than the two people who knew each other in Berkeley so long ago. I want to get to know you again. See who you are now."

"Why?" she repeated.

"When I return to Manasia, I want you to come with me," he said.

Fear licked through Megan. She couldn't believe what he'd said. "Why?" She was beginning to sound like a broken record, yet she could hardly think, much less articulate a full sentence.

"I want you. I wanted you ten years ago, and I want you today." He tossed off the statement as if he were commenting on the weather.

Her heart pounded in her chest, blood rushed through her veins, heating her body. She wanted to run, to hide, to disappear from his life and never be found again.

"What about your father? Has he changed his mind?"

"That doesn't matter anymore. He died a couple of years ago. I make my own decisions now."

Slowly she shook her head.

"Yes, Megan. There's time for us to get to know each other again."

"I won't go back with you."

"It's early yet."

He crushed his desire to insist. She was as skittish as a young colt. He was used to gentling horses. Could he apply the same technique to Megan? Accustomed to instant compliance when giving orders, he realized instinctively that this was different. Megan was not used to his ways. He would do better to bide his time and achieve his goal through other means than sheer strength of will. He had time. He would use it wisely. In the end, she would come with him. But for now, he would go slowly, gentle her into accepting him again.

"Spend the time I am in Washington with me. Let me get to know you as you are now. You are no longer the young college student I once knew. I am no longer the graduate student so intrigued with all things American." His tone mocked the young man he'd been.

"We're too different now. I can't imagine what we would have in common, what we could talk about. Even your name is different." Her eyes watched him warily.

"We never had trouble finding things to talk about before."

It was tempting, oh so tempting. But she would not be so foolish as to think they had a common meeting ground. He was foreign royalty; she was a working single parent and an unwed mother, to boot. Any time spent with a visiting sheik would surely give rise to speculation on who she was and why he was seeing her. She didn't want to be another in his long list of women. She couldn't begin to compete with Lady Susan Fairchild, or that actress in France. She dare not risk the gossip. She had her daughter to protect. And her own heart.

Shaking her head slowly, she responded to his offer, "I don't think it's a good idea."

He would bide his time, but if she thought she would rout him with a simple no, she really didn't know him. One lone woman would have no chance to withstand his assault. He smiled. It wouldn't be easy, but nothing worthwhile in life was ever easy. And after ten long years, he had found her. The rest would just take a little longer, the most difficult part had already been accomplished.

"Did you know I was planning to go to Berkeley after the meetings here?" he asked.

"No. Why?"

"To look for you."

"What?" She flicked him a startled glance.

"I didn't finish explaining about trying to find you. Actually, after the letters were returned, I tried to contact your father."

"I'm sure that got you nowhere," she said sarcastically.

"It appeared that he didn't want me to contact you any more than my father did. He didn't seem to like me. Is it because I was a foreigner here in America?"

She shook her head. Obviously her father had not told Roeuk why he didn't want anything to do with him. But Megan knew.

"Did you know my mother is French?" Roeuk asked.

"Let's face it, Ben, or Roeuk, or whatever I should call you, I know very little about you. And what I thought I knew from ten years ago apparently wasn't much."

"You can call me Ben or Roeuk. Even *chéri*, if you like."

"French for darling? I hardly think so." But the warmth that flushed through her at his words was sweet. For one long moment, she wished she dared call him darling. Wished that she could trust in him as she once had. Wished she could love him again with the soul-soaring intensity of her younger self. Would she ever find such love again? Would she ever dare to try?

"French is a beautiful language for love. I have always been glad for my mother's native tongue,'' he said with his hint of British accent.

"How many languages do you speak?''

"Four fluently. We are getting off the topic, are you deliberately trying to change it?''

"Because your mother is French, your father did not like your trying to contact me.'' She rubbed her fingertips across the silky brocade. She wished he was sitting beside her, instead of across from her. Then she wouldn't be so tempted to let her eyes feast on him. Maybe she could better garner her strength to withstand what was turning out to be an inquisition.

"My parents' marriage was not all that happy. A lot had to do with the cultural differences and the antipathy in the region for the French. My father was determined to make sure I did not repeat his mistake. So he did not wish for me to continue any contact with a foreign woman. He wanted me to marry one from my own country. He had picked out the bride for me, Sasela. She was the daughter of one of his ministers. ''

"How long had she been your chosen bride?'' Megan asked.

Roeuk stared at her with his dark eyes narrowed as if assessing just how she would react to his response. "Since we were teenagers.''

Megan nodded as the chill of the truth penetrated her being. "So even when you were in Berkeley you were betrothed to her.'' Her voice was flat, but at least she had hidden the pain his words provoked.

He shrugged. "There was an understanding between our fathers. Sasela and I had only seen each other a few times in our lives. Remember, I spent many years abroad in school.''

"I don't believe this. All the time you were making love to me, you were engaged to another woman?"

"No. You are distorting the situation. There was an understanding between our fathers, nothing between Sasela and I."

"Until you married."

"Five years later. You are in no position to judge. How long after I left did you take up with Norrie's father?"

Megan clamped her lips tightly to keep the truth from bursting out. Resentfully, she glared at him. "Can I go home now?"

"Stay for dinner."

"No."

"Stay for dinner," he insisted.

"I can't. You forget I have a daughter. I have to get home to Norrie."

"I can't forget that for a moment." The deep anger that swept through him was startling. He knew Megan had had every right to go on with her life after his father had forced him to return home. Yet the fact that she had, and so quickly, burned deep. The only saving grace was that Megan was alone again. He would not let history repeat itself. She would be his again. This time he would make sure of it.

"I'll send for your daughter. She can eat with us."

"No!" Megan didn't want them around each other. Roeuk was too astute to remain ignorant of the truth for long if he spent any time with Norrie.

He stared at her thoughtfully. "Why not?" Was there a reason she didn't want her daughter around him? Would the child speak of her father? Did Megan still have some sort of relationship with the man that she was trying to hide?

Megan felt the magnetism of the man from across the distance between the two sofas. He was probing too close for comfort. She wanted to escape.

Rising, she took a deep breath and calmly faced him. "I need to get home."

He rose, as well, standing close to her. She tipped her head back to see him and almost trembled at the sensations that flooded her. His dark eyes were as compelling as ever. His masculine scent sent tendrils of awareness shooting through her. She longed to step back, but didn't want to give a hint of her own vulnerability.

He reached out and captured one of her curls between his finger and thumb, brushing over it lightly, the satiny strands as soft as down. "Why did you cut your hair? I remember it as so soft, so shiny, so sensuous. I loved it when we kissed and I could gather its fullness in my hands. I always felt as if I held liquid silk in my palms. When we made love, I reveled in the feel of it against my bare skin. When you snuggled against me afterward, I would spread it across my chest and rub its softness against me."

She closed her eyes, almost melting in a puddle of hot honey. She remembered. Remembered the feel of his fingers smoothing her hair over his chest, threading through the tendrils and massaging her scalp. It had been a special time in the afterglow of love.

She broke away from the spell his hypnotic words caused. Thrusting away, she headed to the door, needing to put distance between them. He had the power to produce hot urgent need within her with just a look or a touch. After all that had gone on between them, that made her too vulnerable. She wanted nothing more from him. Taking a deep breath, she tried to get her senses into order.

Roeuk watched her. She wasn't indifferent to him. Why did she keep him at a distance? Foolish of her to try, he would have her.

"I cut it because it was too much trouble to keep wearing long." She would never tell him that she'd cut it off because of the longing that had almost overwhelmed her. That she remembered every touch he'd ever given her and had wanted to change things drastically enough to forget some of the torment of her life without him.

"I'm glad no other man enjoyed your long hair. I like knowing I was the only one to spread it across his chest," he said smugly.

"Why, you arrogant—" She broke off and whipped around to face him, hands on her hips. "It was my hair, I can have it whatever length I like. It's none of your business how many men I—"

His black eyes blazed down at her. He seemed to loom over her, threatening, intimidating.

"And how many men have you had over the years?" His voice was as smooth as cream, but the dark gleam in his eyes was pure danger.

She blinked, almost afraid of what she saw. She tilted her chin. She was not so easily intimidated. "Not many," she confessed. "Not nearly as many men as women you've had, if the reports my colleague Jeff read me are anything to go by."

His hands reached for her shoulders as his gaze held hers. "How many?" he demanded.

Her eyes dropped to his lips, drawn into a firm line as he waited for the answer. She shifted to look at the spot on his cheek where the dimple appeared when he smiled. She wanted to lie, wanted to pretend she had had dozens of lovers, that she was a swinging woman who hadn't lived the life of a woman scared to trust her own emotions, her own judgment. But she couldn't.

"None," she whispered, feeling his fingers tighten at the word.

"I'll call Fahim to take you home." He released her and stepped to the phone. In only moments she was on her way. Alone in the limo, she shivered as she recalled their conversation. Suddenly, she froze, her heart pounding. Oh, God, when he'd asked how many other men she'd slept with, she'd responded truthfully. Would he remember she was supposed to have slept with Norrie's father? Don't let him remember. Don't let him figure it out, she prayed urgently.

Roeuk watched from the window as she left, almost giving in to the urge to go with her. But he didn't want to see her home again. Didn't want to see the signs of her life without him. At one time, he had planned to face his family's disapproval and risk everything for her. He was glad now he had not. He would see her while he was in Washington, then take her to Manasia for a visit. Once he got her out of his system, he would go on as he had before. Maybe marry again. While his brothers all had children, he had none. It was time to establish a family.

Salid entered quietly. "Is there anything you wish, Excellency?"

Roeuk turned from the window. "Yes. The woman who was just here, Megan O'Sullivan, has a child. A little girl. Find out when she was born, where and who the father was. A copy of the birth certificate should provide all that. Then send a large bouquet of flowers to Megan. At her office, I think."

"Very good." Salid left as quietly as he had entered.

Roeuk frowned, annoyed at his obsession at learning more about the man that had fathered Norrie but determined to find out all he could. He wanted to know everything about Megan, all she'd done since he'd last seen her. She would find out he had means and methods to obtain anything he wanted. Even her.

It was after five when Megan opened the door to her house. She was tired. The events of the day had bombarded her nonstop. First, the worry about seeing Roeuk, then the confrontation with him. To top it off, the fear he would pick up on her confession that she'd never been with another man was making her almost frantic.

Switching on the lights, she headed for the phone. Time Norrie came home. Tomorrow she could invite Stephie over for dinner and maybe to spend the night. Megan wanted to give the Andersons a break from her daughter practically living at their house. But right now, she just wanted to see Norrie, be with her.

"Hi, Margie? It's Megan. I'm back, you can send the ragamuffin home. I appreciate your taking care of her."

"She's never any trouble. She and Stephie swam, then we rented some movies and they've been giggling together like maniacs. Sure you don't want us to keep her a little longer?"

"No, send her home. Thanks again. Maybe Stephie can come over for dinner tomorrow?"

"Sounds great. I'll let Sam know we can plan a dinner *à deux*."

Megan went to the door, impatient to see her daughter, to hold her safely against her. Talking with Roeuk had been harrowing. She was appalled she still felt some attraction toward him, especially after all she'd learned this afternoon. But there it was. Her best bet was to stay far from him. These feelings were probably just left over from when they were younger. He would be gone soon. And she would make sure she knew if he were ever returning to Washington so she could arrange to be absent.

The flowers arrived at the *Sentinel* office while Megan was out on assignment. But she learned about them the instant she stepped onto the floor.

"Megan, who are the flowers from?"

"Megan, you have a secret admirer?"

"Hey, love, who are you seeing that owns a florist shop?"

The comments followed her from the door to her desk. There sat the most beautiful bouquet she'd ever seen. The spring flowers were fresh and colorful. She recognized the daisies, roses and carnations. Some of the more exotic blossoms were unknown to her. But the arrangement was lovely. And lavish.

Her fellow journalists and copy editors crowded around, asking who the flowers were from, urging her to open the note that sat so prominently among the blooms.

She shrugged off her camera case and reached for the envelope, a feeling of dread starting. Glancing up, she spotted Jeff watching her. For one long second, she hoped the flowers were from him. It would be so much easier to deal with. But she had a strong feeling they weren't from Jeff.

Have dinner with me. Roeuk.

She schooled her features to remain calm. She couldn't give way to frustration and nerves in front of all her co-workers. Slipping the note back into the envelope, she tossed it carelessly on her desk. Pinning on a bright smile, she faced the group.

"Flowers from a friend."

"A close, rich friend," someone murmured.

"You act as if you've never seen flowers before," she protested.

"Not sent to you."

She nodded, acknowledging the fact. "They are pretty, aren't they?"

Obviously seeing they would get no more from her, the others began drifting back to their desks until only Jeff remained.

He crossed over and glanced at the small, white envelope, then looked at her with narrowed eyes.

"Something you want to tell your partner?" he asked softly.

She stepped away, irritated. "No. I told you, they're just from a friend. But Sheila's right, I've never had flowers sent to me before." For a moment, she allowed the pure happiness at the gesture to rush through her. Then practicality reared up. "But I'll have to make it clear he's not to do anything like this again. I don't want talk."

"Honey, you've got talk around this place for the next few days. Give in and tell a couple of friends as much as you dare. That will keep the rest from badgering you. By the way, I've got a lead on a story about a drug bust going down, want to ride along in case it pans out?"

"Sure." Tucking the card into her camera case, she took another look at the beautiful bouquet before heading out behind Jeff. She would have to speak to Roeuk about sending her flowers. Let him know she didn't want him to do that. It caused talk and that was the last thing she needed.

*   *   *

When Megan turned onto her street that evening, her heart dropped when she spotted the long limo parked in front of her house. Her nerves stretched taut, she hurried from her car to the house. How long had he been here?

She stopped in the archway to the living room. Mrs. Hanson, Norrie's baby-sitter, was chatting calmly with Roeuk. He rose when he heard Megan and watched her as she looked at him, at Mrs. Hanson, then looked around the room.

"I didn't know you were coming by," she said breathlessly.

"I invited you for dinner. I called your office and they said you'd received the flowers, so I assumed you'd also accepted the invitation," he said coolly.

She flushed. She had been in such a hurry to leave the office that afternoon, she'd neglected to call to refuse the dinner invitation.

"I'm sorry, I should have called. I can't go." Her heart was racing. Where was Norrie? Had she spent any time with Roeuk? What had Mrs. Hanson told him about her daughter?

Roeuk raised an eyebrow. "Indeed, and why not?"

"I..."

"If you need a sitter, my dear, I'd be happy to stay longer," Mrs. Hanson said genially.

"Or we could take Norrie with us." Roeuk watched Megan closely. The last time he'd suggested such a thing, she'd refused. What would she do this time?

"No! I mean, I'm sure the kind of places you're used to dining in wouldn't be suitable for a child. They get very restless, you know."

He remained silent while she spoke with her baby-sitter.

"I do have other plans for tonight, Mrs. Hanson, but thank you for offering to stay. Is Norrie home?"

"She and Stephanie are just finishing their homework, in Norrie's room." Mrs. Hanson began gathering her things. "If you don't need me, I'll go on home now. I didn't start anything for dinner, you didn't leave a note."

"No, I plan to take the girls out to dinner, and then maybe go shopping at the mall." Megan cast a glance at Roeuk. "Already made plans to go out. I should have called. I'm sorry."

He nodded. "Maybe tomorrow."

She stared at him. What could she say? She didn't want to see him again. She certainly didn't want him coming to her house where he would see Norrie. Yet she couldn't keep inventing previous engagements. She led a very quiet life. What could she come up with that would satisfy him? Wishing for some inspiration, she stared helplessly at him.

Roeuk's lips twitched. She looked absolutely floored. Hadn't she expected him to persevere? He wanted to take her out, and he would. If she had plans for tonight, which he suspected she did not, he would take her out tomorrow night. Maybe that would be even better. He had the reception to attend at the Department of State; he would like to have her attend with him.

"Tomorrow, then. At eight. You'll escort me to a reception, then we can have a late dinner."

CHAPTER FOUR

MEGAN STOOD perfectly still as Roeuk brushed the back of his fingers against her cheek in farewell, then departed. It had been so long since she'd felt the gentle touch of a man's hand. She shivered slightly at the chill in his tone. She should have had things lined up all week, until he went back to his country. She should have come up with some excuse for tomorrow night. Normally, she could think fast on her feet. Somehow, around Roeuk, her brain stalled. Now she would spend hours in his company. Thanks goodness she wouldn't be alone with him. They would attend the reception. She would decline a late dinner and insist on returning home. That would end it.

Still tingling from his touch, Megan stared out of her front window as the limo pulled away. She could scarcely breathe. Roeuk's touch shimmered through her. She wanted to give way to the longings that surged through her and throw herself into his arms, beg him to kiss her again, demand that he hold her and never let her go. But that would never happen. She was awash with old, almost forgotten, feelings. Heat seeped into every cell. Her heart banged heavily against her breasts. It had been ten years, surely she was over him by now.

For a moment, Megan let some of the happy memories of their time in Berkeley surface. For so long she'd pushed them away, feeling the anguish of knowing they were memories that would never be repeated. But she and Ben had had fun. They had laughed and shared in their delight in college and the freedom of youth. They had talked for hours on end, sharing ambitions, planning how best to save the world. Then, near the end of the spring semester, they had made love. Not often, maybe only three or four times. Not nearly enough to last a lifetime. But it had been wonderful, the most wonderful experience she'd ever had. She had felt loved, cherished, adored.

Which had made the pain of his disappearance all the sharper. For a while she'd touched heaven, only to have it all inexplicably disappear. Now she knew it would never have ended differently.

He would leave, just like last time; she expected it now. She would not trust her heart or emotions to him again. Nor dare to trust her own instincts. The knowledge that he'd lied about who he was and the fact that he'd had no intentions of ever going beyond an affair in Berkeley rocked Megan. She had thought she knew him. Yet she'd never suspected he was engaged. Obviously, her judgment in such matters was impaired. She felt too uncertain to trust her own judgment again. She never wanted to live through such hurt and anguish a second time.

Roeuk settled back in the limo as Fahim drove away from Megan's house. Salid turned to look back from the front seat as if to ask a question, but upon seeing Roeuk's face, he remained silent. Roeuk clenched his fists, displaying some of the anger that swept through him. Megan could have worked around the children's dinner. Her baby-sitter could have managed the two little girls, of that he was certain. He should have challenged her on the matter. He was striving for patience in dealing with her, but she pushed his limits. The older woman would have watched Megan's daughter. He and Megan could have dined quietly, talked of their lives, caught up on what each had done. Taken steps to know each other again.

If she thought he would be fobbed off so easily, she really didn't know him. He would make sure she learned her mistake. Starting tomorrow with the reception, Megan would know he would not be turned aside so easily in the future.

His fists unclenched as he thought of how soft and warm and feminine she was. Her skin had felt like silk when he'd brushed her cheek. He craved her now even more than when they'd been in Berkeley. The years had done nothing to reduce the strength of his feelings for her. She was in his blood and no matter what obstacles she threw in their way, he would have her again.

He had not had a choice ten years ago, but he did now. He wanted to know everything about her, good and bad. He wanted to know what she had done after he left; had she finished college somewhere else? He wanted to know how she liked her job, how she liked living in Washington. And if she still saw her daughter's father.

He closed his eyes and leaned back in the luxurious cushions. Her stormy eyes danced behind his lids. He smiled sardonically. She thought her anger would deter him. If she only knew how beautiful she was even mad, she wouldn't flare up so easily. The sparks ignited something deep within him. He wanted to capture that fiery emotion and channel it into something that would burn them both. He'd been denied her love for too long. He could not change the past, but he did have some control over his future. And Megan would definitely fit into that future.

And Norrie. For a moment he thought of the little girl.

She was bright and friendly and reminded him so much of his mother. His heart ached a little. Opening his eyes, he gazed unseeing out the window. Megan had been fortunate. He had never had children. It was not too late, of course. Would she want to have a baby with him? What would such a child be like? He already had some indication by looking at Norrie. Megan would raise all her children with love and happiness. And he would devote himself to his children and their mother.

For the remainder of the short journey to the hotel he imagined Megan pregnant with his child. Imagined how she would look and feel. Jealousy hit deep and hard. Would the sight of her pregnant with his child erase the images of her with another man? He hoped so. He didn't want to live with this aching pain forever.

This was ridiculous, Megan thought the next evening as she peered at herself in the full-length mirror. She'd been to dozens of receptions in Washington during the last few years. There was no reason to be so nervous.

She rubbed her damp palms across her skirt. Yanked her hands away. The dark blue dress was perfect. With a jeweled choker collar, she had no need for any other jewelry. The halter top flowed from the collar to her waist in front, exposing the long length of her spine in the back. The skirt flared and swirled around her thighs as she walked. Its short sassy length displayed her long legs to great advantage. The high heels would be fine with Roeuk; he was tall enough to enable her to wear them. He also had the ability to make her feel more feminine than anyone else in her life. She wondered if it was a technique mastered in the Arabian desert. Men were so virile and manly, and the women so cherished that they had to feel special when around them.

She sighed and studied herself once more. Her makeup was flawless; her hair as good as it got. It didn't help, butterflies danced in her stomach.

The doorbell rang.

Panic flared. She wasn't ready for this. God, she felt sick. Why had she agreed? Taking a deep breath, she exhaled slowly as she walked to the door and opened it.

"Hello, Megan." Roeuk stepped inside and closed the door behind him, his gaze assessing. Reaching out to draw her into his arms, his eyes widened slightly when he realized her dress was backless, but he covered his surprise, drawing her closer and leaning down to kiss her.

She pushed against his shoulder, shortening the embrace. "I'm ready." It was a lie. She would never be ready.

"Good." He glanced around. "Someone is watching Norrie?"

"She's at Mrs. Hanson's for the evening."

He held the door for her while she scooped up her evening bag and preceded him from the house. One of his aides held open the rear door to the limo and she slid in, reveling in the sensual feel of the crushed-velvet seat back against her bare skin.

"You're not going to get cold tonight, are you?" Roeuk asked as he sank into the seat beside her. "There's not much to that dress."

"It's too hot and muggy to get cold. And if this reception is like others I've attended, there will be so many people around, it'll be almost too warm."

"You look beautiful," Roeuk said as the car pulled away from the curb. He wanted to order the driver to take them back to his hotel instead of to the reception. She was as pretty tonight as he had ever seen her, and he didn't want to share her with anyone. He wanted to hide her away, keep her solely to himself. He wanted her smiles and laughter directed at him. Her thoughts and attention focused only on him, as she had so strongly focused on him when they had lived in Berkeley. In those days he had been the most important person in her life. He wanted that again.

"Thank you," she said in reply to his comment. She glanced over. "You look nice, too," she replied seriously. He would probably look good in anything. Or in nothing. Closing her eyes, she turned away, heat seeping into her cheeks. She remembered when they had both worn nothing. A deep longing rose, she crushed it ruthlessly.

"Do you know, American women are the only ones I know who compliment men on how they look?" he asked whimsically.

"Oh? And have you made a study on this?" she asked. He would have the perfect research technique, date as many women in as many countries as he could. Not many would turn him down. She eased a bit away from Roeuk. His comment reminded her how different their lives were. He was used to dating cosmopolitan women in the world's capital cities. She rarely dated. They had nothing in common. After tonight, she would refuse to see him again. If he even asked.

"Not a scientific study as we were taught to do in our business classes at Berkeley."

She smiled politely and turned to look out the window. The evening stretched endlessly. She should not have come. She was as out of place here as he would be at one of Norrie's school plays. She tried to enjoy the ride, enjoy the luxury. The limousine was a far cry from the old Volkswagen Roeuk had driven in Berkeley.

For a moment, she forgot her anger, forgot his lies and remembered only the fun they'd shared in that old car. Did he ever think about that time? Or had he moved on and not looked back?

The silence threatened to become awkward.

Roeuk broke the silence. "I'm glad you were able to find a sitter for Norrie. Being a single parent must be difficult. Don't you wish to share the burden with someone?"

She shrugged, afraid to answer. She didn't dare let him know how much she had longed for him the first few years of Norrie's life.

"I guess I'm surprised you never married," he said.

"As you did?" She swung around to face him, hurt and anger clashing.

His gaze met hers as he slowly nodded. "As I did. Should I explain about Sasela?"

"Why? We had no commitment between us. You were free—"

He shook his head once, sharply. "No, we had no commitment, but I thought we'd shared love. As I've said many times, I was unable to locate you after I left. It was important to my father for me to marry, to have children. I am the oldest son. I was almost thirty when I finally gave in to his pressure. Sasela looked a bit like you, and I thought she would be enough like you that I would find some measure of happiness with her."

Megan stared at him in astonishment. His wife had looked like her? He had married Sasela hoping she would be like *her?*

"And did you find that happiness?" she asked, unable to assimilate all he was telling her.

"Sasela was a loving woman, affectionate and sweet. She tried so hard." He stopped and looked away as if looking into the past. He shook his head. "She wasn't you, Megan."

"The background reports at the paper mentioned that she died," Megan said softly, suddenly wishing to offer some comfort, yet not knowing how.

"Yes, a boating accident in the Mediterranean."

"I'm sorry."

"Thank you, I was sorry, too. She was a nice woman."

"And your father didn't push to have you remarry?"

"No. I think he saw that I was not happy in my marriage and decided to let me find my own way in the future. It also helped that my brothers had each had a son by that time."

The limousine came to a stop at the guard box at the west gate of the White House. A uniformed security guard checked the driver, then permitted them to pass.

"Is this where the reception is being held?" Megan asked, taking in the sweep of the driveway. She hadn't even thought to ask where the event was taking place.

"No. But we are attending with the president and his wife."

"Good grief, Roeuk, you didn't tell me. I shouldn't be here."

"Why not, don't you like the president?"

"I like him fine, I mean I don't know him, but like what he stands for. I mean, I've taken pictures of different... Roeuk, *the president*."

Roeuk smiled and reached for her hand, squeezing it lightly. "He's my official host for this event. It's the last one your government is having for me. I have one more to go to that some oil companies are holding, then I'm finished with official meetings. After that, you and I can spend some time together."

She froze as the limousine drew to a stop. She didn't want to see him again, and she would tell him...later. For now, the president was heading for their limo.

The night took on a fairy-tale quality. Megan met the president and his wife, and found them friendly and easy to talk to. She studied the pomp and ceremony surrounding their arrival at the reception, her photographic eye assessing everything as if she were planning a shoot. The bright colors of the evening dresses were a sharp contrast to the dark hues of the men's tuxedos. Diamonds, rubies and sapphires glittered beneath the crystal chandeliers, throwing flashes of light and color through the ballroom.

Despite her protests, she found herself part of the receiving line, next to Roeuk. It was like a dream, or nightmare. As one person after another looked at her in speculation as they passed down the line, she longed more and more to slink off somewhere and regain some anonymity. But she kept smiling, shaking hands and responding politely to the friendly comments.

Cameras discreetly caught the line and Megan was hard-pressed not to rush over and snatch the cameras from the photographers' hands; she was used to being behind, rather than in front of the lenses. And she hated to think of the inevitable speculation in the papers surrounding her accompanying Roeuk.

At last they were allowed to mingle. Roeuk's hand came to her back, steering her to the first group he wished to speak with. His palm was hot. Its heat swept through her and lighted a blaze deep inside. She leaned slightly against it, not wanting him to remove it, knowing she was playing with fire. But for tonight, she'd throw caution to the winds. It was the last time she planned to see him. There was too much past between them to hope their relationship could go anywhere.

"That wasn't so bad, was it?" he asked, leaning closer so she could hear him above the noise.

Looking up, Megan found his face was mere inches from her own. She licked her lips. "Do you do this kind of thing often?" The scent of his after-shave teased her nostrils. The heat from his body seemed to envelop her.

Roeuk watched her tongue dart out, retreat. He wanted to kiss her. His eyes found hers and he saw she was aware of the desire that swept through him. "Only when making official state visits. This is my first in the United States." If she didn't look so vulnerable and confused, he would be better able to control his instincts. But he wanted to protect her, cherish her, make sure she never looked lost again. If not for international diplomacy, he would drag her off right now and kiss her until the fire in his blood cooled.

"Champagne, sir, madam?" A waiter stood before them offering a tray of long-stemmed glasses.

"Thank you." Roeuk took one, his hand still on Megan's back. Her skin was so warm, so soft. He never wanted to let go. Slowly his fingertips rubbed the silky texture.

"Yes, thanks." Megan took a glass and clutched it with both hands. She already felt as if she were floating. Under the circumstances, was drinking a glass of champagne wise? If Roeuk didn't stop rubbing her back, she was afraid she would make a fool of herself by throwing her body against his and demanding a kiss at the very least.

Twenty minutes later, Megan was amazed at her acting ability. She was able to talk at some acceptable level, carry on a coherent conversation while her whole being was focused on Roeuk and his warm caressing fingers, which constantly stroked her bare skin. And the worst part was, she didn't think he even realized what he was doing. He talked with the men and women who came up to him, the entire time his fingertips brushing back and forth. Yet she didn't have the strength to move away. This fantasy evening would end too soon. She wanted the memories to take with her, to have, to enjoy as the long years passed.

When the affair drew to a close, Megan and Roeuk again joined the president and first lady in a White House limousine. Too tired to question where Roeuk's driver was, Megan climbed in and sat quietly in the spacious seat.

"Where shall we drop you?" the president asked.

"The Williams Hotel. I'll see that Megan gets home," Roeuk responded before Megan could say anything. Wondering what the president must think about her, she almost opened her mouth to explain, when it occurred to her that would involve even more explanations than she wanted to give.

When they reached the hotel, she bid their hosts goodnight and entered the lobby with Roeuk. He headed for the elevator, but Megan balked.

"I have to get home," she said.

"I planned a late supper for us," he replied, turning back beside her.

"I can't stay." Refusing to meet his eyes, Megan looked around the lobby. "I can take a cab."

Roeuk captured her face in the palms of his hands and tipped it up to meet his gaze. "Stay," he insisted.

She shook her head. "I can't."

"Can't? Or won't?"

She paused for a heartbeat. "I don't want to stay. I went to the reception, now I want to go home."

He studied her for a long moment, then nodded once. Straightening, he released her. "Very well, Fahim can take you home."

"It's awfully late to wake someone up just to drive me home. I can catch a cab."

Roeuk shrugged. "That's Fahim's job. Come up to the suite while I call him. It won't be long."

Megan hesitated, then reluctantly nodded.

"Did you enjoy tonight at all?" Roeuk asked as the elevator door slid open. They were the only occupants when the door closed silently.

"Yes, thank you for inviting me," she said politely.

Roeuk reached out and drew her into his hard arms to kiss her. She pushed against him, but it was like pushing against a wall. Keeping her lips tightly together, Megan tried to resist, but the insidious heat began invading her limbs.

When the elevator stopped at his floor, he set her back, his hand on her bare shoulder.

"Don't do that again," she said, more furious with her own traitorous reaction than with Roeuk.

He smiled. "You liked my kisses once."

"That was then."

"And now?" he asked, brushing his thumb across her damp lower lip.

She refused to answer, clenching her jaw tightly, trying to ignore the heat that sizzled at his touch.

"Will you go with me to the symphony one night this week?"

Megan shook her head slowly.

"Megan, I want to spend time with you while I'm here."

"It can't go anywhere, Roeuk." Her heart was pounding from his kiss. Involuntarily, her gaze found his mouth.

"It can go where we want it to go."

"I'll have to see." She was afraid, plain afraid to get too close to him. She wasn't able to handle these things like other people. When she loved, it was deep and abiding. She couldn't handle falling for him again only to have him walk away when his visit to Washington was finished.

Not that she would let herself fall in love with him again. Nor was he asking for that. Just a date to the symphony.

He opened the door to his suite and ushered her inside.

"Would you care for a drink?" he asked.

"No. I need to get home." She held herself stiffly, away from the temptation of being near him.

"No need to rush. It is not that late, and your daughter is being cared for. Since you won't stay for dinner, stay for a drink."

"I have to work tomorrow. I need to get some sleep." She walked over to the window, staring out at the view of Washington at night. The dome of the Capitol shone bright under the spotlights that illuminated it.

"Do you like your job?" Roeuk asked, coming to stand beside her.

"Very much. I was lucky to find work that I like so well and that pays enough to live comfortably."

"You didn't finish your degree?"

"No. One day I'd like to go back to college, but I don't need a degree to do photography."

Roeuk reached out to touch her hair lightly, wound a small strand around his finger.

She felt his touch to her toes. Closing her eyes briefly against the longing that invaded her, she pulled away.

"Please, could you arrange for me to get home, or shall I call a cab?"

His expression grew harsh. "Why is it every time I talk to you, you pull away? Does my touch offend you?"

She shook her head. How ironic he thought he offended her. "Rather the opposite, if you must know," she said, stepping another foot away.

"Opposite?"

"I didn't mean to say that. I need to go."

"Will you dine with me tomorrow? We won't have the crowd as we did tonight."

"No. I can't."

"Always you can't."

"Try to understand, Roeuk. I work all day, the evenings are the only time I have to spend with Norrie. I want to spend time with her. She's growing up so fast."

"Then I'll take you both to dinner."

"No!" The refusal came fast.

Roeuk was silent, studying the nervous woman before him. Slowly, his eyes narrowed. "Is there a reason you don't wish me to see your daughter?"

Megan swallowed hard and shook her head. "She's just a little girl, I'm sure you would be bored being around her."

"I like children. I have three nephews who I love spending time with. Norrie is a bit older and a girl, but I'm sure I would not be bored if we all went to dinner."

She shook her head, fastening her gaze on the Capitol dome once more. She needed to get home. Make sure her little girl was all right.

"How old is Norrie, Megan?" Roeuk asked softly.

She turned and headed for the door in blind panic. "I have to leave now, Roeuk. It's late and I need to get home and into bed..." She reached for the door, only to find his hand pressing against the wood, holding it closed.

"Megan."

"Roeuk, please."

His hand moved to grasp her chin, force her face around to his. "I have Salid researching birth records. He will come up with Norrie's birth certificate. But you can tell me now, how old is Norrie?"

"You have no right to her birth certificate!"

"I want to know about her father. I want to know about the man you turned to after I left." He stared down at her for a long moment. "*None*. Didn't you say the other day that you had not had any men after me?"

She stared at him mesmerized, fear choking her throat, her heartbeat rapid, her breath shallow. Oh, God, not this. *Please.*

"How old is Norrie?" he demanded.

She couldn't speak, couldn't move. Fear held her frozen.

"How old, Megan?" His strong will wrapped itself around her and she was helpless to resist.

"Nine," she whispered past the block in her throat.

"She's mine, isn't she?" He released her chin to slide his hand around her neck, his thumb on the pulse point at the base of her throat. "Norrie is my daughter, isn't she? Isn't she? *Why didn't you tell me?*"

It was too much. The old hurt, bitterness at his betrayal, the anguish she'd lived through all rushed through her like a tsunami crashing against the shore. Angrily, the words burst forth.

"Just when should I have done that? A week after you walked out without a single word, when I found out I was pregnant? Or sometime in the months that followed? The years that followed? How was I to do that when I didn't know where you were? I didn't even know *who* you were. Norrie is *my* daughter. I've taken care of her for nine years. I can take care of her for the next nine. I'm going home.''

''Not yet you're not.'' His hand tightened slightly. ''The last thing I expected tonight was to find out I was a father. You can't just throw that out and then walk away from it like it was nothing. I want to get to know her. She is *my* daughter.''

''Not as far as I'm concerned. I have a daughter, you have a sheikdom. I wish us both joy in what we have.'' She tried to pull away, but his other hand came up to her shoulder and he held her before him.

''You are wrong, Megan, *we* have a daughter.''

Closing her eyes, she hesitated a long moment. The feel of his hand on her bare skin was intoxicating. Shimmering streams of awareness flowed through her, awakening desire that had long lain dormant. She couldn't cope with all the emotions that churned inside her—anger, fear, desire. She had to maintain control, fight for her daughter. Finally, she opened her eyes, glared at him. ''Let me make one thing clear to you, Roeuk bin Shalik, from the moment I discovered I was pregnant, until this moment, I have been alone. I carried my baby alone, and I delivered her alone. At night, after working all day, I walked the floor when she was sick until I was so exhausted I didn't know how I would make it through the next morning. But I did. *Alone*. For over ten years I've been alone. Now you waltz in and expect me to welcome you with open arms. To offer to share my daughter with you just because you show up? *I* have a daughter. Leave us alone!''

Bending over until his nose almost touched hers, he

glared back, his eyes flashing black fire. "And I have a lonely, empty life, Megan. I have no other children. In my family, children are joyfully received, cherished. I will love my daughter, care for her, cherish her. Do not judge the future by the past. I did not know of her existence. Now I do. It makes all the difference in the world. I will get to know my daughter, and she me. Make no mistake about that!"

Was the fact he had a child just a novelty that he wanted to explore with the same enthusiasm he had attended football games at Berkeley or shared pizza at La Val's? A novelty to enjoy then walk away from without once looking back? Or would he want more? Would he ask for visitation? Was he planning to discuss custody? Would he actually go that far?

"Don't do this," she whispered, afraid of the determination she saw in his expression.

"*Chérie,* the time to not do something is long past, ten years long past. We do not need to be enemies. We were once lovers. Can we not at least be friends now?"

Or more than friends? The attraction he'd felt for her from the first moment he'd met her was still strong. He hadn't lied when he'd told her he had never forgotten her. He had ached with wanting her for years. He had even tried to assuage that longing with marriage to Sasela. Not even that had eased the craving he experienced for this woman. He felt it still. One way or the other, she would be his. Maybe he would have to wait. Maybe he would have the biggest battle of his life with his Megan. But sooner or later, she would be his. As would his daughter.

"Tomorrow, I will see Norrie." Roeuk straightened and stepped back. Releasing his hold on Megan, he reached for her wrist, clamped it in his hand and led her to the sofa. She sank onto it, looking lost, alone, defeated.

Reaching for the phone, Roeuk never let his eyes drift from her as he spoke. "Salid? Tell Fahim to have the limo out front in ten minutes."

Megan shook her head, frantic for some way to prevent this. She didn't want him invading her life. She had been reasonably content. He would change everything. And she feared for her daughter. What did he mean to do about her?

Roeuk hung up and sat down beside her, hemming her in. "Is my name on the birth certificate?"

She dropped her gaze to her hands, surprised to see how tightly she had clenched them. Taking a shaky breath, she licked her dry lips. "The father is listed as Ben Shalik which is the name by which I knew you."

"That makes things easier."

"What things?"

"I don't have to prove that I'm her father."

CHAPTER FIVE

THE FLOWERS GREETED her when she arrived at her office at the *Sentinel* the next morning. They were still as fresh and vibrant as they'd been when delivered. Had it only been two days ago? For a long moment, Megan stared at them. So much had happened, she felt as if a century had passed. Sadly, she wished she were being courted in an old-fashioned way. Wished that the flowers had been bought with her happiness in mind. Instead, she felt almost besieged.

"No new flowers today," her friend Sheila said teasingly, as she stopped in the opening to Megan's cubicle.

One of the copy editors stopped by, grinning. "You should let us have those out here in the open, so everyone can enjoy them."

Megan was halfway tempted, maybe she could think of something else besides Roeuk if the flowers weren't a constant reminder. But putting them out in the general area would give rise to even more comment. Shaking her head, she grinned good-naturedly. "I'll keep them right here, thanks." She really wanted to toss them in the trash, but that would cause too much talk.

"All right, get back to work. This is not some coffee klatch." Jack Mason strode through the newsroom and headed for Megan's desk. The couple at her doorway parted for the editor-in-chief and Sheila drifted back to her desk.

"We were just admiring Megan's flowers," Margot,

71

a copy editor, said, standing her ground. "She got them the other day from a *friend*."

"Probably the same friend who took her to a party last night," Mason said, slamming down a competitor's newspaper. A picture of Megan standing beside Roeuk in the receiving line filled a good third of the page.

"Oh." She stared at the picture unable to think of anything to say. The last thing she'd wanted was publicity or notoriety. Now this! Damn!

"You could have at least clued us in so we could have had a similar picture," Mason growled.

"Wow, Megan, isn't he that oil sheik that's been in the news recently?" Margot asked, her eyes avidly studying the photo.

"He's an old friend," Megan mumbled, snatching the paper and folding it as if hiding the picture could hide the knowledge of it from the world.

Raising her head, Megan forced herself to make eye contact with her co-workers. "I knew him years ago and when he found out I was in Washington, he invited me to this reception to visit a little. That's all." She smiled and held her breath, praying that her explanation would satisfy them.

"Back to work." Waiting until Margot left, Mason faced Megan. "Let me know next time you plan to attend a function with the newsworthy sheik. We could use some of the pictures ourselves," he said, turning to head back to his office.

Jeff stepped into Megan's work area, a quick glance at Mason's back. Smiling slyly, he walked up to Megan and tilted her chin up, assessing her with narrowed eyes.

"Is there a story here, Megan?" he asked suspiciously.

She stepped away, irritated. "There's no story, Jeff."

"Funny, you didn't mention knowing him the other day when we covered the speeches at the White House."

"I didn't know he would recognize me. It was ages ago when I knew him. I was surprised when he invited me to the reception." She shrugged, not wanting to go into all that had happened last night. She was desperately trying to forget it. "You have to admit, I don't usually move in such exalted circles."

Jeff studied her for a moment, then nodded as if satisfied with her explanation. "Come on, then, mighty sidekick, I've got an assignment that cries out for good pictures," Jeff said. But while his tone was jovial, his eyes remained watchful.

Glad to fall into the routine of work, Megan flashed a relieved smile and followed Jeff to their next assignment. She wanted to fill every minute with activity so she didn't have time to think about Roeuk.

It was later than normal when Megan pulled into her driveway that evening. Fortunately, Mrs. Hanson wasn't a stickler about time. The elderly widow enjoyed Norrie's company and never seemed to mind accommodating herself to Megan's somewhat erratic schedule. She was like the grandmother Norrie would never know. Mrs. Hanson spent her holidays with them and they always remembered her on her birthday with a huge cake and a small gathering of neighbors.

"Hi, Megan," Elsie Hanson greeted her when she opened the front door. "Long day?"

"Hi. Long and tiring. I think I'll turn in early and catch up on some sleep." Last night's sleep had been fitful. Over and over again she'd replayed the scene where Roeuk confirmed he was Norrie's father. And the ominous words echoed, *I won't have to prove that I'm her father.* Megan scanned the living room. Except for Mrs. Hanson, gathering her book and purse, it was empty.

"I didn't start dinner. You didn't let me know this morning," Mrs. Hanson said.

"I know. I didn't know what I wanted this morning, so I thought we could just get a pizza or something. Norrie home?" Megan placed her bag on the table by the front door and glanced down the hall toward her daughter's room.

"No." Mrs. Hanson paused by the door. "She went for a ride with that distinguished man who was here the other evening. They should have been back by now. I didn't want to leave before you got home in case they returned." She went to the table and picked up a folded note. Smiling brightly, she offered it to Megan. "He left this. It was all right to let Norrie go with him, wasn't it?"

Trepidation splashed through Megan. Unable to say a word, she nodded, the note almost burning her fingers.

"Goodbye, my dear, see you both tomorrow," Mrs. Hanson said.

Megan watched the older woman leave, feeling slightly ill. Slowly she opened the note. *Don't worry, I have Norrie safe.* The scribble afterward had to be his name.

Don't worry? She was sick with worry. Her mind whirling, she gazed blindly around her living room. Why had Roeuk taken her daughter? Where had he taken her? Were they even now over the Atlantic on their way to the Arabian desert? Would she ever see her darling little girl again?

Oh, God, Megan was going to be sick. She was trying her best to keep things low-key and he was doing his best to upset everything. Walking to the sink in the kitchen, Megan ran the water until it was cool, then filled a glass. Roeuk had no business taking Norrie without her permission. She swallowed the water, slamming the glass back on the counter, trying to calm her rioting nerves, quell the nausea that plagued her, slow her rapid pulse. She would not let him take her daughter!

In less than fifteen minutes, Megan pulled up in front of the elegant old hotel where Roeuk and his entourage were staying. She left her car in the No Parking zone, ignoring the call of the doorman. Almost running, she hurried to the elevators.

Fear had changed to anger. When she got her hands on Sheik Roeuk bin Shalik, she was going to strangle him! And make damn sure he knew to stay away from her daughter in the future.

When she spotted the men in the hall, she knew she was on the right floor. Stepping into the hallway, she headed toward them. Determined to get through, no matter what, she faced them brazenly.

"Sorry, ma'am, these rooms are private." One of the guards stepped out to bar the way.

"My name is Megan O'Sullivan, and my daughter is here with the sheik," she began, ready to battle anyone who dared stand in her way.

"Of course, madam. I am sorry I did not recognize you. This way. We were expecting you." The man bowed slightly, then led the way to the suite's door. Opening it, he stood aside.

Upon entering the luxurious suite, Megan's eyes were instantly drawn to the tall man standing near the window. Dressed in formal attire, his jacket slung across the back of a nearby chair, Roeuk looked every inch the royal prince. The white shirt emphasized his rugged good looks. For a moment her breath caught at his masculine beauty. Before she could utter a word, however, Norrie sprang up from the sofa and hurried to her mother, a beaming smile on her face.

"Hi, Mom." She flung her arms around Megan.

Flicking an angry glance at Roeuk, Megan knelt beside Norrie and returned her hug. "Hi, pumpkin. You okay?" she asked softly.

"Sure."

Roeuk remained by the window, silently watching them, his expression unreadable.

Megan held her daughter, her eyes meeting Roeuk's. He stared back, wondering at the myriad expressions that chased across her face. Anger, certainly. He'd known she would not like his taking Norrie for a visit. But was there also a trace of fear? He frowned at that.

"Mom, today was rad. I thought I was only going for a ride in the limo. Mrs. Hanson said I could. It was so cool. We rode around, and I did just what you said, waved to all the people on the sidewalk and pretended I was a princess."

Roeuk's lips twitched slightly. That's what that waving had been all about; he'd wondered. Watching Megan, he also wondered if he would get the chance again to indulge Norrie in her fantasies. He stood a little straighter. Time Megan knew where he stood. He was Norrie's father, and he would get to know his little girl.

"Then we came here, and I wasn't sure we should stay. I didn't want Mrs. Hanson to worry. But Roeuk said she knew I was with him and wouldn't worry. So we had ice cream from room service. I wish we could live in a hotel. They bring you whatever you want." Norrie's excitement and happiness shone on her face.

Megan held on to her composure with iron will. She was furious with Roeuk. She'd been scared half out of her wits, and he'd been indulging Norrie.

"Time to go home, now, pumpkin," Megan said, rising to face Roeuk defiantly. Taking Norrie's hand firmly in hers, she glanced once toward the door. Would anyone try to stop them if they left?

Roeuk crossed the room.

"How dare you!" Megan said when he drew near.

He cocked an eyebrow in disbelief. "If you knew me better, you would know I dare anything I want. If you are referring to my inviting Norrie to spend the afternoon with me, you know perfectly well why I did so."

"You have no right to abduct her." Try as she might, the anger sounded in her voice. She wanted to rail at him for scaring her so, for daring to act as if spending the day with Norrie was the most natural thing in the world for him. It was not. It could not be. Megan dare not let it.

"Abduct? Surely that's a bit strong." His voice sharpened as he stopped so close to Megan she had to take a step back to meet his hard gaze. "I have every right to spend time with her." His threat was implicit.

She shivered and took another step back. "She's my daughter, and I say who she can see and when."

Norrie looked from her mother to Roeuk, puzzled.

"Perhaps you would care to be seated while we discuss this further?" Roeuk said politely, but the expression on his face was formidable.

"There's nothing further to discuss. We're leaving."

"Not just yet, you're not." He reached out and took her arm in a hard grasp. "It's past time to air the truth of this situation. You overreacted by storming in here."

"Overreacted?" She would show him overreacting.

Yanking her arm free, she stepped forward, her eyes blazing mad. "You had no right to take my daughter, and if you ever do such a thing again without my knowledge and permission, I'll—"

"Do not speak to me about rights. I have as many as you and if you need me to prove that to you I'm willing to do so."

"Mom." Norrie tugged on Megan's hand. "Mom, are we going?"

"In a minute."

Roeuk lifted Megan's chin with a hard finger. "It's time to tell her, *chérie*. Either we do so together, or I'll do it on my own. Which do you prefer?"

She hadn't wanted everything to blow up in her face, yet it looked as if it were about to. This was not how she wanted to tell Norrie about her father. Would he try to take Norrie away from her? She needed time, time to decide how best to tell her daughter.

"Aren't you on your way out?" Megan asked, stalling for time, her heart tripping with fear. She didn't want to be in this situation. She had had enough problems over the last ten years; she did not need this now.

"I'm expected at a small impromptu reception in a little while, but I certainly have time for this."

She pulled her chin away and looked around the room as if searching for an escape route. She'd been angry when he'd arrived. Now she was scared. She didn't want to talk with Roeuk. She just wanted to go home, close the door and shut out the world. Shut out the threat to her very existence.

"Not now."

"I want to spend time with her. When are you planning to tell her?"

"I certainly don't want to just blurt it out."

"There is no reason not to tell her the truth, Megan. Past time, I'd say."

"I'll tell her."

"When?"

"Soon."

"No, Megan, today. Now."

"Are you guys talking about me?" Norrie asked, trying to follow the conversation.

Roeuk's features softened as he smiled at Norrie. "Yes, sweetheart, we are. Your mother and I have something important to discuss with you." He glanced at his aide and made a motion with his head. In seconds the man left and only Megan, Roeuk and Norrie remained in the room.

Megan swallowed hard, her hand tightening involuntarily around Norrie's.

"Ow, Mom, you're squeezing me."

"Sorry, honey." It was an effort to relax her grip, an effort to breathe. Her heart was pounding loudly, and she couldn't look away from Roeuk's compelling gaze.

She had to say no. She dare not let him appropriate Norrie whenever he felt like it. What kind of relationship would he build with Norrie? Here today and gone tomorrow? Would Norrie become so fascinated by the glamour of her father that she would find her mother lacking? Would she grow dissatisfied with their life and wish to learn more about how her father lived? She already was enchanted with limousines and room service. Would she be hurt when he left at the end of his visit?

Roeuk slowly raised Megan's hand in his, holding it in a firm grip. Megan felt the connection spread from her hand throughout her entire body. Her knees grew weak when he brought her fingertips to his lips and gently kissed each one.

"Now, *chérie*. Today," he repeated.

Her eyes were caught in his gaze, snared almost; she wanted to look away yet was unable to.

"I'll have to think about it."

"There is nothing to think about. I can demand my rights, you know," he replied in a silky tone.

She yanked her fingers from his grasp. "No."

"I grow tired of your constantly telling me no. Come." It was time to end the charade. He was tired of the situation. He wanted to know his daughter and he wanted her to know her father. He drew Megan and Norrie to the sofa and waited while they sank down on the cushions. He took the chair across from them.

Megan licked her lips. Slowly she turned to face her little girl. "Norrie, honey," she said, reaching out to brush her hair back from her cheeks. "Remember when you were a little girl and I told you your daddy had gone away? That I didn't know what happened to him, but I thought maybe he died?"

Norrie nodded, her eyes firmly on her mother's face.

"Well, I didn't know for sure. I just thought so because he went away and never contacted me. But he didn't die."

Norrie looked to Roeuk and then back to Megan.

"In fact, he came here to Washington and found us and—"

"It's Roeuk, isn't it?" Norrie guessed.

"Yes, honey, Roeuk is your father. He didn't know where we were living. He didn't know you were born."

"If I had, I would have come to see you immediately. I'm thankful now that I found you and your mother," Roeuk said.

"So do I have to go live with him now?" Norrie asked.

"Of course not, you're still my little girl. You'll live with me," Megan replied quickly.

"You don't know me very well, Norrie, but I want us to spend more time together so we can get to know each other. I had a nice time this afternoon with you. I would like to spend more time with you while I'm here in Washington."

"I don't know," Megan warned.

"I will spend time with my daughter, Megan. Nothing you do or say can stop me. Because of the trade treaty and my country's huge reserves of oil, your government doesn't want to harm the relationship between our countries. Don't tempt me to use that power to exercise my rights."

One phone call would do it all, Megan knew. She rose impatiently and paced to the window. She hated this. She thought she had her life in control, now it was spinning madly and she was helpless to do anything about it.

Roeuk spoke softly to Norrie then crossed to stand close to Megan. He reached out to caress her shoulders, easing some of the tension. Megan felt the warmth of his breath move lightly over her cheek as he drew her closer to him.

Her legs weakened, heat deepened. She felt dizzy with wonder and delight at Roeuk's touch. "I—" She couldn't think.

"You what?" he coaxed.

"I thought you had taken her back to your country," she said in a rush.

He frowned and spun her around. "Kidnapped her, you mean?" Gone was the gentle tone in his voice.

Megan shivered and nodded.

"What a fine opinion you hold of me if you think I

am capable of such a despicable act. When I want some-thing, I tell people exactly what I want. I have no need to kidnap my own daughter. I can easily petition your courts to gain visitation rights, maybe even full cus-tody.''

She paled at his words. ''Last night, you made such a big thing out of wanting to get to know Norrie, that when I came home today and found her gone I just thought—''

''And you find that so hard to believe? I'm her father. If I had known about her before last night, I would have tried to know her earlier. Why am I the villain in this just because I wish to know my own child?''

''You're not a villain. It's just hard to believe you want to know a child. You do have a certain interna-tional reputation—'' She closed her eyes, tried again, ''I'm not used to sharing her, and I was afraid you would take her away. Face it, Roeuk, you have more money than I'll ever see. You are influential, powerful, ruth-less—''

''Ruthless enough to take a child from her mother without either's consent? Were you ever going to tell me about her? If I had not guessed, would you ever have told me?'' He released her and stepped back as if it displeased him to even touch her. Thrusting both his hands into his pockets, he turned to stare out of the win-dow, anger evident in every inch of his stance.

''You said it yourself earlier, I don't know you, Roeuk. In truth, I never did. The man I thought I knew doesn't exist. I can only judge things by what I know. Ten years ago, you disappeared without a word,'' she tried to explain.

''I told you what happened. If I want my daughter, I have no need to kidnap her.''

Megan nodded at the truth of that statement. Fear lapped at her senses. Was he planning to petition the courts? With the full force of the United States government behind him, he should have no trouble getting whatever he wanted. She watched him warily, afraid as she had never been before.

He glanced at her and felt the familiar tightening deep in his gut at the sight of her. She was so damned beautiful. He wanted her with a hunger more suitable to some randy teenager than a man in his mid-thirties. And he obviously wanted her more than she wanted him. Even the fact that she had concealed their daughter from him no longer mattered. As his eyes studied hers, he realized she was afraid.

"There's a certain truth in what you said earlier."

"Huh?" Megan was so confused and afraid, she didn't know what he was talking about.

"You don't know me now. Nor do I know you. So I propose we change that."

"Change it how?" she asked warily.

"We will get to know each other again, of course, what did you think I meant?"

"I don't know. How will we get to know each other?"

"By seeing each other while I'm in Washington."

"To what end?"

He made an impatient gesture. "I don't know. Does it have to be toward some end? Can't I just learn about you and Norrie, what you've done with your lives and give you the same opportunity to learn about mine? I will spend time with Norrie. I'm asking you to join us. You can refuse if you wish."

"No, I'll go along," she said quickly before he could rescind the offer.

"Afraid to leave Norrie alone with me?" His voice taunted.

Meeting his gaze squarely, she nodded. Looking into his eyes made her body tingle. Forgotten yearning blossomed. She wished she wasn't afraid to take what he offered, a limited friendship for the time he was in Washington. She didn't have time for wild fantasies about a romantic interlude with visiting royalty. She was surprised he wanted to spend any time with her. It was Norrie he was interested in seeing, he'd been very clear about that. And she couldn't let herself forget it.

"We had something special once," Roeuk reminded her.

"It was magic and the magic is gone," she replied, refusing to be swept away by memories. "I have to get home. I'm tired, Norrie's tired. It's getting late."

"Did you drive here or shall I have Fahim take you home?"

"I drove." God, she'd just left her car where she had stopped it. She hoped it was still there.

"I will come tomorrow night to take you both to dinner. Be ready at six."

Megan didn't want this. She wanted things to go back to how they'd been last week. Was it just a few days since her entire world had been turned upside down? She was trying to hold on to sanity, but Roeuk wasn't making things easy. She was trying to protect her little girl. Roeuk would be leaving soon. Norrie could be badly hurt. She herself could be hurt. Megan would do anything to protect her baby, for herself it was already a decade too late.

"Norrie's not used to eating in restaurants that have slow service. It would be better to eat at home," she said, reluctantly agreeing to his demands.

"All the better. We can talk and I can see where she lives, where you live."

"You've been to the house."

"But not been shown through it. And I will tell you about my house and how my rooms compare to yours," he said.

"All right, at six, then." Turning, Megan crossed the room to her daughter. "Ready, pumpkin? Time to go."

Norrie peeked at Roeuk. "Bye."

"Bye, Norrie. I will see you tomorrow."

By the time Roeuk was due to arrive the next evening, Megan's nerves were frazzled. She had debated what to prepare for dinner, knowing she was not the world's best cook. Also knowing Roeuk probably had dozens of chefs who prepared his meals, she couldn't begin to compete. Instead, she tried a different tactic. She ordered a large pizza, tossed a salad and made a sinfully rich dessert they could have with coffee.

She felt as nervous as a schoolgirl on her first date. It wasn't all due to his determination to know Norrie. Some of it was her own anticipation at seeing him again. She couldn't forget the circumstances of their separation, the unhappiness she'd found as a result. But despite that, she was intrigued by the man. He wore his cloak of authority and power easily, comfortably. She had seen traces of it in Berkeley, but never knew what it would lead to. She wanted to know more about him. To learn what he had done in the intervening years. She would find out without jeopardizing her heart a second time.

Megan was wiping down the counters in the kitchen, cleaning up from the preparation of the salad, when Norrie wandered in.

"He's here," she said, pausing at the doorway.

"He?" Megan asked.

"The limo is out front."

Megan glanced at her daughter. They had spoken very little last night on the ride home and Norrie had gone straight to bed. After school today, she had gone to play with Stephie. She'd only been home a few minutes. Neither had broached the subject of Roeuk. What must her daughter be thinking now? How must she be feeling, having discovered that Roeuk was her father? Should she have told Norrie once Roeuk had contacted her? No, she had hoped to keep it secret.

"Norrie, later you and I will talk about Roeuk, okay?"

Watching her mother from solemn eyes, Norrie nodded.

The house shrank when Roeuk's presence filled it. He seemed larger than life, Megan thought as she looked around her living room and tried to remember it without him in it. He was dressed casually in brown slacks and a dark blue shirt. Fleetingly, she wondered if he ever wore jeans as he had in college.

"I didn't cook tonight. I ordered a pizza. Have you had any since you've been here?" Megan asked when he moved into the room.

"Pizza sounds good. I haven't had it in a long time. Do you like pizza, Norrie?"

She nodded, staying near her mother, her eyes watching Roeuk with reluctant fascination.

"I just need to set the dining room table. The food should be here any minute."

"Do you normally eat in the dining room or are you doing so solely for my benefit?" he asked.

She met his eyes. "For special occasions."

"I'd rather eat where you normally eat."

They ate pizza and salad at the kitchen table. As the meal progressed, Megan gradually started to relax.

"Not as good as La Val's, or is memory playing tricks on me?" Roeuk asked as he tasted his first piece.

"No. I haven't found any other pizza as good as La Val's," Megan agreed. "I don't know, maybe it's just the memories. Maybe it wasn't all that good."

"We should go back some day and try it."

Her gaze dropped to her own piece. *We should go back some day,* as if they would be together in the future. Don't count on fairy tales, she reminded herself. And don't forget, Roeuk was a man she didn't really know.

"What's La Val's?" Norrie asked.

"A great pizza place in Berkeley that your mother and I often frequented," Roeuk answered easily. Not for him any of the awkwardness that surrounded the meal.

"*Frequented* is the right word. As I remember, some weeks we ate there three times," Megan said.

"I had never had such good pizza before. In fact, I don't believe I had eaten pizza before," he explained.

"Don't you have pizza where you live?" Norrie asked, obviously unable to imagine a place that didn't have a staple such as pizza.

He nodded. "We do now. But ten years ago we didn't. Coming to America was a very educational experience for me."

"Let's see, there was pizza and beer, football and—" Megan broke off, remembering how enthralled Roeuk had been in so many things she had taken for granted.

"Pom-pom girls," he supplied, wicked amusement gleaming.

"Is that why you liked football so much?" she asked in mock outrage.

He smiled, his eyes warm and penetrating. "No, but it was a good part of the experience."

"And what about the beer? I thought sheiks didn't drink."

"Only strict Muslims. You forget, my mother is French. Do you think I could get away without learning all there is about wine? But beer..." He shook his head, smiling down at Norrie. "Never drink beer with college kids. I was sick for two days afterward."

Norrie giggled, her gaze darting back and forth between her mother and father, clearly entranced with the exchange, the glimpse of their lives before she was born. She was growing more relaxed around Roeuk, Megan could see it.

"So tell us about all the other educational experiences you've had," Megan urged, longing to keep the conversation light. She didn't want to talk about what she dreaded most, Roeuk and Norrie.

"Let's see." Roeuk addressed Norrie, "You must understand, most of my previous schooling had been in Europe. I was not used to brash American slang, hot dogs, professors who wore blue jeans to class, a fountain named for a dog and the sassy free spirit of American girls. While educational, I enjoyed it, too." His eyes caught Megan's on the last, held.

Megan finished her pizza. She reached for the large soda bottle at the same time Roeuk did. His fingers covered hers. For a long moment, they were motionless, each looking at the other. Slowly, he drew his hand away.

"I'll pour yours." Was that breathless voice hers? Hoping her hand wouldn't tremble, she filled his tumbler, then her own. Setting the bottle down with a thunk, she reached for her glass, angry at herself for reacting so strongly to the touch of his fingertips.

Flustered, Megan didn't realize she was staring at him until he asked if he had spilled something.

"No. I was just thinking that eating in the kitchen is not something you probably do much of," she blurted out, hoping to divert any suspicions that her thoughts were on a different track.

Roeuk smiled. "Not at home. But sometimes I spend time in the desert, especially now that we've found the oil reserve. Then I stay in a Bedouin tent. Even with carpets on the sand, grit infiltrates everything. At least there is no sand here."

"You stay in a tent? Do you ride camels?" Norrie asked.

"Horses, purebred Arabians. Some of the Bedouins have camels, but I've never liked riding them."

"But you have?" she persisted, her eyes wide.

"Yes. But I prefer horses. Do you ride?"

Norrie shook her head.

"Time you learned," Roeuk said.

"Riding lessons cost money," Megan said without thinking. She didn't want Roeuk suggesting things she would have to follow through on. Money and time were tight. She had all she could do to allow Norrie to play in the school soccer league. She couldn't manage riding lessons. Facing him, she strengthened her resolve, even though she felt as if things were sliding out of her control.

CHAPTER SIX

ROEUK WAS NOT USED TO frustration. With Megan, it was becoming a way of life. For every step forward, he took two back. Megan had begun to relax. He knew the reminiscences of Berkeley had been responsible. Things between them had begun to improve, now she had re-erected her walls ten feet tall. Damn, how could he get close to her if she wouldn't let him? He smiled grimly. He'd thought finding her would be the difficult part. That had been amazingly simple, she'd just appeared. The hard part was convincing her to trust him enough to let him back into her life.

"I can pay for Norrie to learn to ride," he said easily.

Megan paused in reaching for her glass, her eyes met his. "No, thank you."

"I'd like to learn to ride a horse," Norrie said shyly.

"And so you shall." Roeuk held Megan's gaze, his own strong and sure.

"That's not for you to decide," Megan said tightly.

Roeuk cocked an eyebrow. "Are you suggesting that just because I don't live in Washington, I can have no place in Norrie's future?" he asked in a deceptively calm voice.

Megan looked at her daughter's avid gaze. "If you are finished, Norrie, you may go outside and ride your bike."

"I want to stay here and watch you two fight," Norrie said.

"We are not fighting," Megan said calmly, though

the anger that roiled inside her gave the lie to her words. She wanted to scream at Roeuk to leave them alone, to go back to his desert kingdom and let her and her daughter resume their lives as they'd been before his arrival last week.

Norrie looked doubtful.

"Your mother is correct, we are having a discussion, that's all. Adults can have strong discussions without fighting," Roeuk said. "There will be no fight."

Megan fumed silently. If he would just go, there would be no fight. But if he thought she would quietly acquiesce to all his demands, he was in for the battle of his life!

Norrie looked back and forth at her parents. "I guess I'll go see if Stephie can ride now."

"Stay out front where we can check on you," Megan said.

The silence grew in the kitchen when she left. Roeuk crossed his arms and leaned back in his chair, tipping it on its back legs, watching Megan with brooding eyes. She stared at the table, unsure how to begin. She had to make her point clearly and succinctly. Yet she hesitated.

"Come on." He pushed away suddenly and stood up, reaching for her hand.

"Where are we going?" Startled, she rose, her fingers tightening with his.

"Into the living room. It'll be more comfortable. I want to tell you about my father."

When they were seated on the sofa, Megan tugged on her hand, Roeuk tightened his grip and rested their linked hands on his thigh. He looked at her through lowered lashes. "My father married my mother despite opposition from his own father. If you remember your history, you'll remember that the French ruled my country for years. We were gaining our autonomy at the time my father and mother met, so you can imagine the strong anti-French feelings that abounded. Despite everything, all the objections of both families, my father married her. Theirs was not an easy nor happy marriage."

"Did your grandfather ever come around?" she asked, intrigued by what he was saying, though a bit puzzled as to why he was telling her all this.

"A bit, when I was born. And more and more so after each son. But my parents' marriage was never easy. When my father learned I was in love with an American, he did his best to persuade me that further involvement would be a mistake. While he'd loved my mother when they married, he lived with all the difficulties of such a marriage and he didn't want the same problems for me."

"So he intercepted your letters," Megan said. It explained why, even deathly ill, the old man had found the strength to interfere.

"That and more. As my father's health improved, I became more and more worried about you. I tried to call, but your number had been disconnected. I wrote, sent telegrams, all to no avail. Finally, I hired an investigation firm to locate you."

"When?"

"It was late summer by then. I wish I could explain how hectic things had been up to that point, with my father's illness, with the turmoil it brought. By then, I was frantic for news of you. You thought I'd disappeared without a trace, I felt the same about you. By that time, I'd had no word of you or from you for almost three months."

"I guess I had moved by the time you hired the investigators."

"They found your father," Roeuk said slowly.

She blinked. "He didn't know where I'd gone." He hadn't wanted to know where she was going, or how she was going to manage. He had washed his hands of her. The old pain was only a dull ache now. She had accepted that aspect of the situation years ago.

"I know. Nor did he tell my investigator that you were pregnant. If I'd known, I would have moved heaven and earth to find you."

"What did he say?"

"What he said and what I was told he said were two different things. My father intercepted the report by the investigation firm. I found the original report after my father died last year. What I was given ten years ago was a report stating that your father said you didn't want to be bothered."

"Oh, Roeuk." Megan's fingers tightened with his as she thought of how strongly his father had opposed their relationship. So strongly opposed, he had lied and manipulated things to get his own way. Would it have made a difference if the old man had known she was carrying Roeuk's child? That was something she would never know. And now it was too late. Too much had happened over the intervening years for her to recapture the trust and love of years ago. And it was obvious Roeuk didn't feel the same toward her. He'd married, tried to start a family. She sighed softly for the lost love she'd once thought held such a bright future.

"Thank you for telling me, it explains a lot," Megan said softly.

"I want you, Megan. Now that you know this, what more do you need to come to me?" he demanded.

Her temper flared at his arrogance. "Well, Your Royal Highness, this isn't your country where you can decree anything you *want*. I'm not one of your minions to bow and scrape every time you walk by.'' She tugged her hand harder, the brief feeling of nostalgia fleeing as he so arrogantly stated his wants. What of hers?

"Did I say I enjoyed sassy free-spirited American women? I lied. I want you agreeable to whatever I suggest," he said grimly.

She glared at him. "I'm sure you do. Think a minute, Roeuk. You are Arabian royalty and can get away with anything you want, practically. I, on the other hand, am a career woman, an unwed mother, to boot. I have to watch what I do, where I go, who I see. I have a daughter to protect." *And a once-shattered heart to shelter.*

"If I offer marriage, would that suit you?" His eyes narrowed as he watched her.

Her heart pounded in glorious happiness. *Marriage.* Just as they'd talked about so long ago. Then reality crashed down on her. He had said nothing of love or commitment or even simple caring. He wanted his daughter, and he seemed to want her. But on his terms. And if he couldn't get her on one set, he was willing to offer another, all to attain his end.

"I can't," she said.

"Why not? Don't you trust that I—" He stopped. He nodded. "You don't trust me, do you, *chérie?*"

She shook her head. "No. I don't trust you, nor do I trust my own instincts about us. I loved you so much. You'll never know how hard I took your disappearance. You've reappeared, but for how long? And how would your family greet your marriage to me? We both know your father didn't want it. How would the rest of your family feel today? What if there is another crisis? What if you have to leave again suddenly? Will I be left behind again, without a word for another ten years? Have you told me the truth this time? All the truth? Or will I find out again that you lied? I'm not willing to take the risk. I have to guard myself in this.''

''Megan, think, I know where you live now, and you won't be going anywhere. You know where I am, you could contact me if anything unexpected like that ever happened again. My father is dead. I run our country now, small as it is. There is no one to interfere. I kept my identity secret, there were no other lies. You know who I am now. Circumstances are not the same, never will be again. I understand your hesitancy. You must understand my determination.''

''You want your daughter.''

''Yes.''

''You can visit her whenever—''

''Not enough, Megan. I have missed the first nine years of her life. Time passes too swiftly to be satisfied with a day's visit here and there when I am able to come to the United States. I want to spend the next nine years with her.''

''You can't just take her away from me.'' Her deepest fear was just that.

''I don't need to do that. I want you to come, too. If you need time to reach that same conclusion, I'm willing to give it to you.''

''I don't—''

He shifted on the sofa, released her hand and drew her into his lap, his hard arms encircling her, holding her against his chest when she struggled to free herself.

''Yes, Megan, I will have my daughter and her mother, if you will only comply with my demands.'' His mouth lowered to hers.

Megan wanted to resist. She longed to be able to show him how little he meant to her. But her body betrayed her, responding instantly to the delight of his touch. Her lips opened to his and her tongue met his, mating with it. Shimmering waves of pleasure lapped at her senses. Her arms crept up around his neck and she threaded her fingers in his thick dark hair, reveling in the sexy feel of him as his kiss deepened. For a moment, she was nineteen again and so much in love.

Despite being afraid of letting her emotions rule, she felt momentarily wild and free and almost safe. It was only temporary. She should be stronger than this, should stop his attempts to seduce her into compliance. Yet she was helpless to resist.

His kisses seduced her into traitorous thoughts. Dare she risk enjoying their time together knowing she would have to let go when he left? Dare she risk her heart again knowing how it would all end? If not when he left Washington this time, when Norrie was grown?

Had she ever stopped loving this man?

He eased her back, his eyes glittering with suppressed emotion. Gently, his index finger traced her damp lips and he smiled triumphantly.

Megan flushed with shame at having responded so freely. She tried to pull away, but his hard arms held her firmly where he wanted her. She should have been stronger. Should have resisted!

"I must leave now. I will take you to the symphony on Friday. I'll come for you around seven."

She shook her head.

"Yes. We will spend some time getting to know each other again. For Norrie's sake, if nothing else. At seven on Friday."

Maybe she could find a way through this morass by then. She nodded. "All right, for Norrie's sake."

"I have one more function to attend this weekend, then my official visit will be over."

She held her breath. The piercing pain that shot through her was totally unexpected, she had known all along he wouldn't be here for long.

"After that, I will be on my own time," he added.

And what did that mean?

"So I'll see you Friday," she said brightly, pushing away, striving to hide the turmoil that raked her. The end of the week he'd be finished. There was nothing to keep him here beyond that except Norrie. What could she do to keep her daughter safe?

Megan watched him walk to the limo from her front porch, wanting a promise that things would be different than the last time, but knowing there were no guarantees in life. For a moment, she was almost willing to let go and take all the happiness he offered for however brief a time. But she knew the price of such happiness, and she didn't think she could pay it a second time.

Norrie rode up on her bike and stopped near the limo. "Are you coming to see me again?" she asked.

"I'll see you Friday night when I come to pick up your mother. We're going to the symphony." Roeuk paused by his daughter, taking in her shining eyes, her pretty golden-brown curls. She looked so much like her mother, his heart caught.

Norrie wrinkled her nose. "That's that slow music that Mom's always listening to on the radio."

Roeuk chuckled and nodded. "Yes, we both enjoy it. You might like it yourself, one day. Next weekend, we'll do something together. You decide where you'd like to go, or what you want to do."

"Okay." She waved shyly and turned to ride down the sidewalk to rejoin Stephanie.

"Don't hurt her," Megan said automatically. She

wasn't the only one involved now, Megan couldn't bear to have her baby hurt.

Roeuk turned toward the house, his eyes angry. ''It has never been my intention to hurt either one of you,'' he stated.

Roeuk slammed the car door behind him, motioning Fahim to drive. He normally didn't display his temper in that manner, but he knew he had a hard fight ahead of him. Megan was proving much more stubborn than he'd remembered her being. He wasn't averse to a strong woman, but he wanted her strength on his side, not opposed to him.

Now the only thing that mattered was convincing Megan that she belonged to him, with him. He would override any objection she brought up. She would find out that when he wanted something, he got it.

With a twist of pain, he realized how much he had missed of Norrie's life. He had missed seeing Megan pregnant with his child. Missed seeing her nursing their baby. Not knowing about Norrie, he'd missed so much. He would make up for it with any other children they had.

And he had to hold on to the thought that they would have more. He would convince Megan and get to know his daughter in the process.

Time would do it. But he didn't have much time. He had a couple more weeks he could spare to stay in the United States, but then he had to return home and begin work on the new treaty. Begin the projects the infusion of cash into his country would make possible. He didn't plan to return home alone, however. Before he left, he had to convince Megan to join him.

*   *   *

"That dress is pretty, Mom," Norrie said when Megan stepped into the living room Friday night.

The dress she'd chosen for tonight was a deep rose. The soft drape of the bodice plunged into a deep vee in front, modestly covering her figure, yet hinting at what lay beneath. The skirt flowed around her hips, brushing against her legs as she walked. The dress made her feel sinfully sexy just moving in it.

It also gave her a certain confidence she desperately needed around Roeuk.

Nervously, Megan went to answer the doorbell when it rang. Mrs. Hanson stood on the stoop, smiling cheerfully.

"My, don't you look nice, Megan. That dress is beautiful. Wherever did you get it?"

"Come in, Elsie. Margie Anderson helped pick it out. We went to the mall. I appreciate your watching Norrie tonight."

"I'm glad to do it. We were getting into that jigsaw puzzle this afternoon, this gives us a chance to finish it."

When the doorbell rang again, Megan knew it had to be Roeuk.

Norrie greeted him shyly, still obviously uncertain about his place in her life.

"Norrie, I brought you a present," Roeuk said when greetings had been exchanged.

"A present? What?" Norrie moved closer, clearly intrigued.

"Roeuk, you shouldn't have. We don't need presents," Megan protested.

He merely smiled at her and held out a small box to Norrie. She took it and opened it. Nestled inside on white cotton was a gold locket, with a small diamond in the center. Lifting the delicate chain, Norrie stared at it, her eyes wide with wonder.

"It's so pretty."

"It is the kind that holds pictures."

"Oh, Roeuk, it's lovely." Megan would never spoil her daughter's pleasure, but she worried he'd spent too much on a piece of jewelry her young daughter might not be ready for.

"And for you, Megan." He held out a long narrow box.

Megan stared at it for a long moment. "I don't need a present," she said, staring at it warily.

He reached for her hand, turned it palm up and placed the box in it.

"From me to you."

Megan swallowed and opened the lid. The shimmering light that struck her from the delicate bracelet was like living fire. Every spectrum of the rainbow reflected. It was beautiful. She loved it.

"Wow, Mom, those look like diamonds!" Norrie said, peering into the box.

"Oh, Roeuk, I can't take diamonds," Megan said, stricken.

He went still. "Why not?"

"I—it's too much. I can't accept." She offered the box back. He made no move to touch it.

"You accepted the flowers I sent to your work." His manner was chill.

"That's different." Her fingers began to tremble. She didn't want to drop the box, why wouldn't he take it?

"How?" he snapped, clearly angry she wouldn't take his gift.

"Well, for one thing, they didn't cost a small fortune." She felt defensive.

He hesitated a moment, his expression softening, then he smiled. Her eyes focused first on his dimple, then rose to meet his warm gaze.

Reaching out to brush a strand of hair back from her cheek, his voice gentled. "Indulge me, *chérie*. I wanted to buy you something that would remind you of me. I noticed you wore no jewelry the other night. Take the bracelet. It will go with anything."

Megan looked at the box, then opened it and studied the bracelet once more. Carefully, she took it out and wrapped it around her wrist. Offering it to Roeuk, she let him fasten it. It was beautiful. The delicate gold work a piece of art, the diamonds sparkled and shimmered as they caught the light.

"Thank you, I shall always cherish it," she said softly. Tears pricked behind her lids. Was this a bribe, or a farewell gift?

"Thank you for my locket. I can't wait to show Stephie," Norrie said, turning toward the door.

"Not tonight, but you can call her if you like," Megan said, hoping to come back down to earth. She could feel the weight of the bracelet like a band against her arm. Her skin still tingled from the brushes of Roeuk's fingers.

"Ah, Mom, I wouldn't be gone for long and it's still light outside," Norrie protested, still moving toward the door, a cautious eye on her mother.

"*Pardonnez-moi, ma petite choute,* but I do not find it appropriate that you argue with your mother when she has forbidden you something," Roeuk said sternly.

Norrie looked at him for a long moment, then at her mother. She moved toward Mrs. Hanson. "Sorry, Mom. I'll call her. Can she come over here if her mother lets her?"

"That's up to Mrs. Hanson. We're leaving now, give me a kiss goodbye."

Megan was surprised she didn't resent that Roeuk had stepped in. He was the child's father, granted, but Megan was used to dealing with Norrie herself. Yet she now knew he wouldn't spoil Norrie as she'd thought he might, to make up for the years apart. It was oddly unsettling.

Salid stood by the limousine when Roeuk and Megan emerged from her house. He opened the door, and calmly greeted Megan.

"Salid attends with us tonight," Roeuk explained when the door closed behind him. Salid sat in the front seat with Fahim. Both men wore the short *kalfiyeh*, the loose headscarfs held in place by decorative cords.

"As a bodyguard?" Megan guessed.

Roeuk shrugged. "It is customary for me to have him with me. He will enjoy the music, as well. What pictures did you take today?"

They discussed her work on the short drive to the Kennedy Center for the Performing Arts. Megan tried to relax, tried to tell herself it was just a date between old friends. But she felt as if she were sitting on the edge of a precipice the entire time.

The Kennedy Center was crowded when they arrived. Fahim easily maneuvered through the traffic, dropping them off close to the main doors.

The crowd inside was already moving to take their seats when Megan, Roeuk and Salid entered. Megan spotted a Southern senator just as he saw Roeuk. In only moments they were discussing the different aspects of the recently signed treaty. The senator's young wife shook her head at Megan.

"Always shoptalk. Don't you get tired of it?"

Megan smiled and gave a noncommittal shrug. She was fascinated by it, and much too new at this to be at all upset by it. She also knew she was living a fairy tale. When Roeuk's business was finished in Washington, he would return home and she would return to her life as a newspaper photographer. But for the moment, she decided to enjoy the fantasy for all it was worth.

"Sorry about that," Roeuk said softly as he took her arm to lead her to their seats. Nodding to two other acquaintances, he waited while Salid produced the tickets to the ushers at the door.

"Part of your job, I assume," Megan said.

"I certainly would do nothing to upset one of your senators, if that's what you mean."

"I think I meant always being available to people. Having to stop and talk even when you are taking an evening for yourself."

"I don't do much of this, so it is not a burden. Ah, are we ready Salid?"

"Yes, Excellency, this way, I believe."

As they made their way down the hall toward the box seats, Megan thought about all the burdens Roeuk carried on his broad shoulders. It was hard to remember he was no longer the carefree college student she'd once known. He had a tremendous amount of responsibility now. Did he consider her just another burden in his list of responsibilities? Would he have preferred not finding her again? She hoped he didn't think of her that way.

CHAPTER SEVEN

MEGAN SAT in the opulent box and looked around her with thinly veiled excitement. It had been years since she'd attended the symphony. She loved music of all kinds, but especially the classics. She was amazed at the number of people she recognized. Many were from pictures she'd seen in newspapers and magazines. Some were from shoots she herself had done. Washington's elite were gathered here tonight, and she was a part of it. She smiled at Roeuk, happy in his company, in the night, happy with everything at the moment.

Salid settled behind Roeuk, between the sheik and the door. His eyes never settled on anything, they were constantly moving, searching out any possible danger. Megan glanced at him for a moment, then looked thoughtfully at Roeuk, her smile fading.

"Is your life threatened in any way?" she asked softly.

Roeuk leaned forward slightly until his shoulder brushed against hers. His dark eyes looked deep into hers. "The only danger is what I experience around you," he said seductively.

She flushed with heat, her heart rate doubling. "I meant, because Salid is always with you."

Roeuk nodded. "It is more form than necessity. My life has never been threatened in the sense you mean. But members of the *sajine* always accompany the sheik. The tradition goes back generations. Does his presence bother you?"

She shook her head, unable to look away from the heat of his dark eyes. She wanted to plunge into their depth, learn everything there was to learn about him. She didn't want him to be in danger. Didn't want anything to threaten his well-being. Her heart didn't stop pounding. She wanted only the best for him, always had, despite all that had gone before them.

"If it did, I would send him away," Roeuk said, his hand covering hers as it rested in her lap. Lacing his fingers through hers, he drew their linked hands to his thigh, resting them against the hard muscles. Slowly, his thumb traced patterns against the soft skin of her wrist.

"Don't," Megan whispered. The desire that sprang up at his touch was instant and insistent. She wanted to be closer, wanted to feel his lips against hers again, wanted more than he could ever again offer her.

"*Chérie,* there is more that I want, but this very public place is not conducive to that. I will resign myself to holding your hand only, until later."

"L-later?" Megan could scarcely form a coherent thought. The tantalizing enticement his touch wrought was driving her steadily crazy.

"I have planned a midnight supper at my hotel. It will afford us the privacy a restaurant would not."

"I need to get home after this. I don't want to go to your hotel."

"Shh, we can discuss it after the symphony. They are preparing to begin," he said as the house lights slowly dimmed.

Between the diamond bracelet on her left wrist and Roeuk's hand holding her right one, Megan felt surrounded by him. His presence invaded her senses. Around him she felt desired, cherished almost. He could be charming, there was no denying that. But he could also be ruthless. She'd seen glimpses of it, and hadn't he admitted he would do whatever he had to in order to get his own way?

The music was beautiful. The acoustics perfect for the delightful enjoyment of the orchestra's rendition of the classical music. Megan gradually began to relax. Conscious every second of Roeuk beside her, holding her hand, she was still able to forget the turmoil that plagued her and give herself up to the beauty of the romantic composers the orchestra played.

At intermission, they wandered out to the grand foyer of the Kennedy Center. Several well-known men stopped to greet Roeuk.

Senators, White House staff, a general expanded their circle. Roeuk conversed easily with everyone. He was never at a loss for words, always charming and seemed to have the ability to remember everyone's name and position. Megan saw the curious glances at their linked hands, but no one questioned them. She spoke quietly to each as they were introduced, but left the conversation to Roeuk. These men were here to woo the visiting sheik who was so generous with his oil, not to talk to her. She didn't mind. She was fascinated by this side of the man she'd once loved so deeply.

Scanning the area, she was pleased to note there were no photographers present tonight. She did not need to fuel the gossip that the last picture had started. Listening with only half an ear to the conversations that swirled around, Megan tried to imagine being a part of this all the time, as Roeuk was. It was quite a different experience than the ones she was used to. She was enjoying herself, but only because of Roeuk.

"Not too bad, was it?" he asked her when they returned to their seats.

She smiled and shook her head. "It was fun. I've never met so many congressmen."

"I'm sure each one envied me, because you were with me."

"I'm sure they were wondering who I was, but were just too polite to ask," she returned dryly, charmed with his compliment in spite of herself.

He raised their linked hands and kissed the back of each of her fingers. "Come to the hotel for a late supper with me," he coaxed.

She hesitated, then nodded slowly. She didn't want the evening to end when the music was finished. She wanted to see him just a little longer. And he was right, it would be more private in his suite than in a crowded restaurant. At least they would not have a constant stream of people interrupting.

Though Megan feared she was flirting with danger to spend time alone with Roeuk, especially in such a romantic setting as the elegant sitting room of his suite at the Williams Hotel, she'd agreed to go for supper. That was all.

Roeuk smiled with satisfaction and settled back in his chair to enjoy the rest of the concert. He was pleased with the way the evening was going. Megan had fit in perfectly at his side. She had held her own with the men he'd spoken with, had not been shy or uncertain as Sasela had often been. Megan was a strong, confident woman. He liked that about her. Among other things, he thought as he slanted a glance in her direction.

She was gazing rapturously at the orchestra, her eyes sparkling in the dim light, a light smile curving her lips. Roeuk wanted to crush those lips beneath his, make her respond to him as she had the last time he kissed her. The years had treated her kindly, her complexion was fresh and young, untouched by time. Highlights in her hair caught the faint light and shone beneath it. He wanted to thread his fingers through those curls and relish their soft silky texture. He regretted the loss of the long hair he had so loved, but it was still very beautiful. He wanted to feel it against his skin again, brush it out and tangle his fingers in the silky waves.

Shifting slightly, he looked at the orchestra. He needed to keep his thoughts on the music and not on the woman beside him. He had time later that night to woo her, and he would. She would know for all time that she was his. He would brook no refusal tonight. Megan would be his again!

When they were in the limo, heading for the Williams Hotel, doubts began to plague Megan. She should have insisted on returning home. She didn't need any more time with him, after all. It only made things more difficult.

"Tell me about Manasia," she blurted out. If she could keep him talking, maybe some of the doubts would fade.

"What is it you wish to know?" he asked.

"What's it like? I've never been to that area of the world. Is it all desert? The Sahara? Or do you have oases?"

He chuckled softly. "It is a beautiful country. We have a variety of topography, from the sparkling white shores of the Mediterranean to the harsh dunes of the Sahara. There are a few oases scattered in the Sahara, made all the more beautiful for being surrounded by endless miles of golden sand."

"You said you live near the Mediterranean."

"Yes. My villa has an expanse of shore, soft white

sand and a gentle slope that goes out many yards into the water before shelving down enough for swimming. It is perfect for children. They can play in the shallows safely. Older children and adults can swim there, as well.''

"It sounds nice." Like heaven, she thought. As a child, she'd spent many hours at Balboa Beach in southern California. She missed it. Washington was too far inland to visit the beach often.

"My villa is large, with lots of glass to give the feeling of being outdoors. I like to be outside, and when it's not possible, I still want to feel like I am."

"What grows in your yard?" she asked, trying to envision his home. He'd seen hers, she wished she could see his.

"I have date palms that shade the patios. The fruit is used in my kitchen. For color there is bougainvillea, oleander and roses. My mother is always bringing me new rosebushes. They are her passion, and her own home is so overrun with them, she has to foist new strains on me."

She fell quiet at the mention of his mother. All the doubts returned.

"You will like my home, Megan," he said gently.

Her eyes flew to his in the erratic light from other cars. "Do you have pictures you could show me?" she asked.

"No. You will have to wait until we get there to see it."

"I'm not going there," she said hastily.

"You and Norrie will come," he returned easily, his tight jaw the only indication his mood was not as serene as his voice indicated.

The limo stopped before the portico of the Williams

Hotel. Salid opened the rear door, permitting Roeuk and Megan to climb out. She should have been firmer when she'd told him she had no intention of visiting him in his home. If he brought it up again, she would be.

When the elevator doors opened and revealed an empty car, Roeuk shook his head at Salid and entered alone with Megan. Pushing the button for his floor, Roeuk then turned to her, and cupped her face with his warm palms.

"Did you enjoy the symphony, *chérie?*" he asked, gazing down at her.

"Yes, it was wonderful." She couldn't look away. Looking into his dark eyes, she felt as if she'd plunged into a magical midnight. Even as he lowered his head, she couldn't move. Slowly, her lashes closed over her eyes and she parted her lips for his kiss.

Liquid heat poured through her. His touch provoked a storm of sensations. She could feel each finger press into her like a brand. The soft caressing strokes of his thumbs against her cheeks sparked shivers of excitement, while the magic of his kiss drove all coherent thought from her mind. For the moment, Megan could only exist to kiss and be kissed. Her only reality was his touch. Her only tie to earth was his mouth and his hands. She was floating, reveling in the long-forgotten delight of being kissed by Roeuk.

The ding of the elevator announced the floor. Silently, the doors parted. Time stood still. Then he pulled back, slowly, reluctantly. Gazing down at her damp lips, he brushed his thumb across them once. Megan trembled at the sensuous caress, not caring that her heart was in her eyes. Not caring for anything but being back in Roeuk's arms.

"Come, supper awaits." He released her, and guided

her to his suite, nodding in passing at the men who stood on duty by his door.

Megan avoided their eyes, knowing they must have witnessed the kiss when the elevator doors opened. For a moment she had felt so special, but seeing the guards reminded her of the notation in Paul's preliminary report. Roeuk was used to escorting beautiful women in London and Paris. The guards were probably used to seeing him bring women back to his suite at midnight. Suddenly, she was angry with herself, with him. She didn't want to be just another woman in his life. She would rather have had it all end ten years ago than be one in a long line.

"I need to get home," she said, stopping just inside the door.

He cocked an eyebrow. "Why now?"

"It's late. I'm not hungry. I need to get home," she repeated. She refused to meet his eyes. She knew her own limitations. She was too susceptible to his charm. When she was with him, she had a hard time remembering what had transpired between them the last ten years. Being with him felt so right, she was tempted to give in to the longing to throw caution to the winds and accept whatever he had in mind.

But her sense of self-protection flared. She had to guard her heart.

"Come, I have had the dinner prepared for us. Stay and enjoy it and then I'll take you home," Roeuk said as he crossed the room to the table set exquisitely beneath the large window that overlooked Washington. Tall tapers burned, illuminating the table and the immediate area. The rest of the room was shadowed, with only discreet lighting here and there to relieve the darkness. Soft music filtered through. The setting was romantic, seductive.

Slowly, Megan walked to the table, feeling as if she were in a dream. No one had ever set the stage for seduction for her before. The pristine white cloth that covered the table was set with china, silver and crystal. A low arrangement of roses sat in the center, their heady fragrance permeating the air, adding to the dreamlike atmosphere. She glanced at Roeuk, but he was busy uncorking the champagne that had been resting in a silver ice bucket.

The pop startled her and she jerked, feeling like an idiot. Wiping suddenly damp palms against her dress, she felt wrapped in silken bonds that wouldn't allow her to move. She felt special, worthy of such attention, thrilled that Roeuk had seen to such an exquisite dinner. No matter that he had probably done this a dozen times before, it had never happened to her and she was flattered. And fearful. What did he expect from her?

"To us, Megan." He handed her a flute of icy champagne and touched the edge of his glass to hers. Sipping the sparkling wine, his eyes never left hers.

Megan sipped. *To us?* There was no us. In truth, there never had been. Without honesty, relationships withered and died. But she had loved him. Had longed for an *us*. She looked away before Roeuk saw something in her eyes that she would not admit to, not even to herself.

Roeuk noticed the slight trembling of her fingers and a feeling of deep satisfaction pervaded. She was not as cool and immune to the attraction between them as she pretended. He smiled and reached for her glass, taking it from her fingers and putting it on the table.

Leaning over, he brushed his lips against hers, again. Pausing to lightly probe the dark warmth of her mouth, he could taste the champagne and the sweet taste that was her own.

"Sit and enjoy it, *chérie,*" he said, guiding her to a chair, seating her.

He sat opposite her and studied her as one of the waiters from the hotel entered and served them. She looked lovely. The candlelight enhanced her beauty. Her brown eyes were a mixture of shyness and uncertainty. For a moment, he thought he'd glimpsed something more, but wasn't sure. In fact, he wasn't sure about her at all. And that made him a bit edgy. He was used to being obeyed, instantly; she fought him every step of the way. He knew why. She felt betrayed. He should have done more to find her before it was too late. But he had thought he'd done all he could. If he had suspected his father's interference, he would have taken steps. But nothing could change the past. Now he had to find a way to bend her to his will. To realize he would get what he wanted, one way or the other. Suddenly, he thought about Norrie. He felt a warm glow near his heart whenever he thought about his daughter. He wanted to get to know her, have her know him. Love him.

How ironic that his father had never known about Norrie. He would have loved a granddaughter. His mother would be pleased, Roeuk knew. She had been surrounded by males all her married life. A granddaughter would be someone she would delight in and probably spoil to death. He smiled at the thought. His mother would love Norrie. And Megan.

"Tell me what you did after you left Berkeley," Roeuk said when the waiter left. He wanted to learn all he could about her life. See what had forged her into the woman she was today.

Glad for the opportunity to end the awkward silence,

Megan complied. She told him how she had first done free-lance photography to earn enough money to keep herself and the baby. Then as Norrie had grown older, how she had found work on one of the Los Angeles papers.

"Then I had a lucky break. I happened to be at the right place at the right time when L.A. erupted in riots a few years ago. My pictures were picked up by AP and UPI. That led to the offer from the *Sentinel,* and so I came to Washington. I've worked my way up from social events to hard news. And I get to cover the White House."

Roeuk studied her as she spoke. She loved her work, it was obvious. Her eyes shone, her voice was animated, and her expression was one of contented happiness. Confidence in her ability came through. Gone was the sassy college student he'd once known. In her place was a beautiful, successful woman. Strong and courageous, she still possessed more femininity than any other woman he knew. He wanted her more than ever.

"And you like Washington."

"Very much. I can't imagine living anywhere else."

"Except Manasia," he said smoothly.

She blinked. "I'm not going there."

"You haven't even seen the place. You can come for a visit. If you don't like it, we will have to see what other arrangements we can make."

"Roeuk, stop. You talk like it's a done deal. I'm not going anywhere with you. Especially to your home."

He filled her glass again, ignoring her protests. Once she was there, she would like it. Its beauty would appeal to the artistic side of her. And there was much she could do there. She would not regret leaving Washington. And he would bring her back to visit whenever he returned.

"Are you listening to me?" she asked sharply.

He smiled and shook his head. "I'm only hearing what I want tonight." She was even beautiful when she was angry. The color flying in her cheeks deepened, her eyes sparkled.

"Perhaps I can change your mind if I tell you more about my country," he said as she glared at him.

"I doubt it," Megan muttered.

"Listen and see," Roeuk said, smiling at her pout. He then began to speak about his homeland. Painting pictures in her mind of the high desert, the lonely stretches of land that swept the far horizons. The beauty in the lush temperate area near the Mediterranean, the lofty peaks of the distant mountains. He spoke of star-studded skies, like black velvet with a million sparkling diamonds, the air so clear a person felt as if he could touch them. He spoke of a warm and struggling people, anxious to enjoy the benefits of modern western life while clinging to traditions and customs.

And he spoke of his family. Of his mother, who would love to meet Norrie. Of his brothers and their families. Cousins for Norrie to play with when she visited, aunts and uncles with whom to share their culture and family life.

Megan listened, and despite her attempts to stay aloof, she was fascinated. She would love to see Manasia with Roeuk by her side. She could imagine the sweep of desert dunes, almost feel the clean dry air rushing by if they went riding on the purebred Arabian horses he mentioned. She would love to swim in the Mediterranean, see the roses his mother had planted, explore the souks and Casbahs of the old cities.

"Come with me, Megan," he urged.

She almost considered it. It would be a wonderful vacation. And she could see where he lived, how he lived. But reality intruded. She shook her head. "I can't. I have a job, there's Norrie."

"I can take care of you and Norrie. Quit your job, come with me."

"No!" Megan pushed back her chair and stood, panic threatening. Roeuk was too persuasive. She had to get away. "I will not be seduced to do what you want. This elaborate setting notwithstanding, I will not go to Manasia with you. I'm going home. And I'm staying there."

She turned toward the door but had taken only two steps before his hard hands caught her shoulders and spun her around to face him.

"You think I'm seducing you to fall in with my wishes? Maybe we are not too far apart, after all, *chérie,*" he said. "Stay the night."

She shook her head, her hands balled into fists. "No. I'm going home now. I can get a cab." She tilted her chin, meeting his gaze squarely, determination shining from hers.

He lowered his face and kissed her cheek.

"No!" she said hotly, turning away, afraid of the traitorous feelings that began to curl through her.

He ignored her and brushed his lips across her jaw.

Involuntarily, Megan arched her neck, offering him better access to her throat. Roeuk accepted her invitation, his mouth moving against the delicate skin, until his lips rested on the pulse at the base of her throat. He lifted his head only enough to find her mouth and capture it with his own.

He kissed her deep and hard, until her senses spun. Until Megan lost her rigid posture and stepped closer to his embrace. His hands moved to mold her against him, tracing shivers of delight as he caressed her from shoul-

ders to bottom. The soft silk permitted the heat of his
hands to scorch her skin, offering no protection to his
touch.

"Make no mistake, *chérie,* I want you and you will
find I always get what I want," Roeuk said against her
lips before he eased back. His dark eyes glittered down
at her. "Come, I will take you home."

Megan moved as if in a trance. Her blood sang in her
veins. Her heart pounded so loud, she was sure he could
hear it; the guards in the hall probably heard it. Her legs
felt shaky, uncertain. Slowly she moved to the door, feeling besieged by him. His touch was potent, his charm
more than she could resist. Yet she knew she had to.
The past had shown her what the future would hold. He
had never mentioned love. She knew without it, they had
nothing.

When the limousine pulled away from the hotel,
Roeuk flipped the switch that slid the connecting window closed. They were cocooned in a dark world of their
own. He pulled Megan into his lap and kissed her before
she could think of resisting. His hands were against her
throat, threading into her soft hair, moving over her arm,
over her hip, up to her breast. She caught her breath as
his palm gently rubbed against her, his touch penetrating
through the material as if it weren't there. She felt the
old familiar heat building, the desire for closeness war-
ring with the need for sanity.

When his hand moved to her thigh and began its way
up her silk-clad leg, she reached for his wrist. "No,"
she said, shaking her head, her lips hovering near his.
She couldn't let the madness take hold. She had to draw
the line. But she ached with longing. Would it always
hurt so?

He linked his fingers with hers, but kept their hands

against her thigh, brushing back and forth, as they both reveled in the sensations that rippled through them. Her lips kissed, clung, moved. Her tongue darted out, danced with his, invited back. Her breathing mingled with his. Her heart beat in unison with his.

When the limo stopped in front of her house, it was several minutes before either realized it. Gradually, awareness seeped into Megan's mind. She lifted her head, tried to see Roeuk's eyes, but it was too dark.

Roeuk set her beside him and flipped on a small light. "You look thoroughly kissed," he said with blatant satisfaction.

"I feel thoroughly kissed," she murmured, loath to leave, knowing she had to.

"I'll call in the morning," he said. "I told Norrie I would take her somewhere. I want you to come with us. You two decide what we can do and tell me when I call."

Numb, Megan nodded. Roeuk flipped off the light and lowered the connecting window. In only seconds Salid had the door open. He escorted Megan to her door, while Roeuk watched from the car.

Despite the lateness of the hour, Megan couldn't sleep. She prepared for bed, climbed in and lay wide awake. She was totally confused. She became more attracted to Roeuk every time she saw him. She liked listening to him talk of his country. Appreciated the strong man he'd become since she'd known him. She was flattered beyond belief at the attention he was paying her. And almost, almost she was tempted to give in to the demands he was making.

But she was afraid to trust her feelings. Roeuk talked of wanting her, but he'd said nothing about love. Nothing to give her enough confidence to let her heart rule her head. She'd done that once before and the results had been disastrous. She dared not risk it again. She was older now, wiser. It was time to let her head rule.

Very much afraid she was falling in love all over again, Megan tried to argue herself out of it. Roeuk wanted her, but had he wanted those women whose names Paul had in his preliminary report? Roeuk had married. That hurt most of all. She had refused all other men, and he had married another woman.

But above it all was Norrie. Was he trying to find an easy route to his daughter? Was that all his attentions to her were about, a conduit to Norrie? Megan rolled over and pulled a pillow over her head as if that would block out her thoughts. She couldn't stand it if he only wanted her because of Norrie. Not when she wanted him so much for himself.

CHAPTER EIGHT

MEGAN AWOKE THE NEXT MORNING to the faint drone of the television and the wonderful aroma of fresh coffee. Mrs. Hanson had stayed the night, as she did the few times Megan had to be out late. She had obviously prepared breakfast. Stretching, Megan rolled over on the bed, remembering the previous evening.

Some parts had been like a dream. The wonderful music at the Kennedy Center, meeting and talking with some of the nation's most distinguished men, the candlelit supper with the beauty of the Capitol visible from the table. It had been the most romantic evening she'd ever spent.

Roeuk's kisses had only added to the romance. Though she knew he'd wanted more, he had brought her home safe and sound. Did that mean he really didn't want her as strongly as he said? Or was he honoring her requests because he wanted to please her? She didn't have a clue. But for this morning at least, she would revel in the sweet memories of a most memorable evening.

Her door cracked open and Norrie peeked in. Smiling when she saw her mother awake, she bounded in and hopped up on the bed, snuggling down beside Megan.

"I didn't think you were ever going to wake up, Mom," she said. "Mrs. Hanson is going to fix pancakes as soon as you get up. I'm starving."

"Starving, huh? Poor waif child." Megan tickled her, delighting in her childish laughter.

"Did you have a good time last night?" Norrie asked a minute later, her eyes watchful.

Megan smiled at her daughter. "Yes. It was very nice." What an understatement. *Nice* was not the word to describe how she'd felt all evening. *Special, spectacular, magical,* those would all be better words.

Norrie wrinkled her nose. "All you did was sit and listen to slow music. They didn't even have a video, I bet," she said.

"No, no videos, but the music was lovely, and after the concert we went back to Roeuk's hotel and had a late supper. With chocolate mousse for dessert." With a pang, Megan realized her abrupt departure had meant she'd left before she'd had a chance to eat hers.

"Did you bring some home for me?" Norrie asked hopefully.

Megan chuckled and drew her closer. "No, pumpkin."

"How come you and my father don't live together like Stephie's parents?" Norrie asked.

Megan's heart lurched. She had been waiting for the right moment to sit down with Norrie and discuss the situation more fully with her. Somehow the perfect time just hadn't arrived. She should have been the one to bring up the situation and explain it to Norrie. Only, she wasn't sure how she would explain everything.

"For one thing, Roeuk lives far away from Washington. So we can't live together."

"But he lived in Berkeley when you did. You were talking about it at dinner the other night. If he lived in the United States then, why did he leave?"

"He had to go home because his father was very sick and needed him at home." Megan was not going to tell Norrie how Roeuk's father had kept him in Manasia, how he had done all in his considerable power to keep his son from the American woman he felt would be wrong for him.

"Why didn't you go with him?"

"I didn't know where he went. He left very suddenly, without telling anyone where he was going." The old anguish flared, though it had lost some of its potency. Maybe he had tried to find her, maybe it was fate that had kept them apart. Though she couldn't forgive the fact that he had kept the important parts of his identity a secret from her. She had shared everything of her life, and he had only told her bits and pieces of his. Nothing of major importance. Had she meant so little to him?

"And he didn't ever come back to see you?"

"Well, I had to move away from Berkeley to get a good job, so I wasn't there when Roeuk tried to find me. Remember our apartment in L.A. before we moved here?"

Norrie nodded and remained silent for a long time. Megan drew a deep breath.

"What should I call him?" Norrie asked.

"Who? Roeuk?"

Norrie nodded. "Stephie calls her father Daddy. Should I call him Daddy?"

Megan was at a loss. What *should* her daughter call her father? Closing her eyes, she wanted the whole situation gone. She didn't like being in this position. She didn't want Norrie and Roeuk to build a closeness that would exclude her. Didn't want her daughter to rely on him when he might disappear again any day.

"Mom?"

"I don't know what you should call him. Maybe you should ask him when you see him." Megan knew Roeuk was planning to see Norrie today. He could answer her questions. Somehow, she couldn't picture him as a daddy. Yet Father seemed so formal for Norrie.

"Okay," Norrie said. "Maybe he will want to be called Daddy. I think I like having a daddy. Will he come see us again?"

Megan nodded. "I think so. He's going to call this morning to see if you want to do something." Megan was thankful that the question of what to call Roeuk was uppermost in Norrie's mind, and not all the other convoluted facts of their dilemma. If only things were as simple for her.

"I know. He told me. I want to go to Air and Space."

"You always want to go to Air and Space."

"But I love it. And you like it, too, don't you, Mom?"

"Yes, but we were just there a couple of months ago."

"Yeah, but I bet *he* wasn't. Maybe he's never been there."

"We'll see. Now, how about those pancakes Mrs. Hanson is going to fix us?" Megan asked. "I think I'm starved, too."

Norrie giggled and flung herself from the bed and out the door. "I get the first batch," she called as she raced down the hall.

A typical Saturday morning, Megan thought as she left the bed more slowly than she did on weekdays. Well, not typical, maybe. It wasn't often she had someone else prepare breakfast. What a treat.

They had finished breakfast and were lingering around the table. Mrs. Hanson had questioned Megan extensively about her evening, enjoying hearing about the Kennedy Center, the music and the late-night supper. In turn, she and Norrie had let Megan know how difficult it had been to complete the jigsaw puzzle.

The phone rang. Megan instantly froze, her eyes on the wall phone.

"I'll get it." Norrie pushed back her chair and ran to the phone.

"Hello?... Yes... Yes...Mom said you would call..."

Megan's stomach tightened, and her nerves felt stretched to the breaking point. It was Roeuk.

"Air and Space...it's really cool. There are old airplanes and spaceships, real ones, and hot-air balloons." She listened for a moment and then turned to her mother.

"Mom, you're going with us, aren't you?"

Megan nodded far more calmly than she felt.

"Yes, she's going. What time do we have to be ready? Um, you know you don't have to wear a suit to Air and Space?"

Megan's lips twitched. She wondered what Roeuk thought of his daughter's kindly letting him know what would be suitable attire for the museum. She wished she could see his face right now.

"Okay, we'll be ready at ten." Norrie hung up as Megan glanced at the clock. It was already after nine. She stood, gathered the dishes and moved to the sink.

"I'll do those. Sounds like you and Norrie have to get ready to leave before long," Mrs. Hanson said as she, too, gathered dirty dishes.

"No, I have time to do them. After cooking that wonderful meal, the last thing you need to do is clean up. Relax, have another cup of coffee. We have plenty of time to get ready. Right, Norrie?"

Promptly at ten the limo pulled up in front of Megan's house. She opened the door to greet Roeuk, Norrie hanging back a little.

"Good morning," Roeuk said, leaning over to kiss Megan as if he had been doing it for years.

Too surprised to move, Megan felt his lips brush against hers. Lightly, affectionately, nothing earth-shattering, even though she felt the touch in every cell of her body. He straightened and looked at Norrie, his face softening into a smile. "And good morning to you, *petite.*"

"Hi." Norrie was shy, watching Roeuk warily.

"I thought to dismiss Fahim, if we can take your car. It will give us a bit of anonymity."

"Sure, that's fine." Megan licked her lips and nodded. What did the problems with finding a parking place have to do with anything? If he wanted her to drive, after that kiss, she would agree to almost anything. Driving was the least of it.

"Salid not coming?" Megan asked as she watched the limo drive away.

"I think I can manage on my own for one day," Roeuk said dryly.

"You were the one who told me he went with you everywhere, that it was his job to accompany the sheik."

"Ah, but today I'm going incognito. So I certainly don't want him around to give rise to questions."

Incognito, as he had lived in Berkeley. What other secrets was he still keeping from her? To him, it was a lark, a way to escape his normal life. To her, it had been a betrayal of all her feelings. She had shared everything, he had shared virtually nothing.

"Now, what has erected that wall?" Roeuk asked.

"What do you mean?"

"Every so often I feel you softening toward me, and then immediately you erect an impenetrable barrier. What caused this one?"

"I don't know what you mean. I'll just get my purse and we'll be ready to go. Oh, Norrie has a question for you." She felt as if she were throwing her daughter to the wolves, but she didn't want to pursue Roeuk's line of questioning. Today, she was going to do her best to keep the bitterness away from them. The past was over. It was up to her to make the most of the present.

"And what is that, *petite?*" Roeuk lowered himself until he was at eye level with Norrie.

He could see she was shy around him. He wanted to grab her and hug her and tell her she had nothing to fear from him, but knew enough about children to know that would be a totally wrong approach. He would likely scare her to death. He needed to woo her carefully until she was comfortable around him. He was already enchanted with his daughter, he would do nothing to harm their relationship.

"I didn't know what to call you. I asked Mom but she said I had to ask you," Norrie said, her eyes on the top button of his casual shirt.

"Ah, that is something we have to decide, isn't it? Let's see. I called my father Father. What do you think?"

"My friend Stephie calls her father Daddy," Norrie said, raising her eyes as far as his chin.

"That's very American," Roeuk commented, feeling a small clutch in his heart at the term.

"Norrie is American," Megan said, standing near them.

Roeuk met her eyes, was there a challenge there? He stood slowly, his gaze locked with hers. "Of course, but she is also Manasian. How nice to have dual citizenship."

"Norrie, run along to the bathroom. It'll be hours before we're home again," Megan said, longing to break eye contact, mesmerized by the compelling gaze locked with hers.

"But we haven't decided," she protested.

"I think Daddy would be fine," Roeuk said.

"Okay." She scampered down the hall.

The tension in the entryway rose as Roeuk took a step closer to Megan. "And do you approve of her calling me Daddy?"

"I don't seem to have much choice in the matter. You made sure of that," Megan said.

"You wanted me to lie and say I was not her father?"

"She never suspected. You pushed and pushed until I had no choice but to tell her."

"Yes, you are correct. And I would do it again. She is my daughter. You should have told me when you first saw me."

"Well, there are probably a lot of things I should have done in my life and haven't. This isn't the only one," she snapped.

He stepped closer, giving in to the almost compulsive urge to tangle his fingers in her silky hair. The warmth of her skin enveloped him as he drew her closer. Her eyes were wide and wary, her body resistant. But he wanted her and she had never been indifferent to his touch. Nothing had changed in that. From the first time he'd seen her so long ago, she had inflamed his senses. She still did.

Slowly, he lowered his mouth to cover hers. His lips coaxed, his tongue beguiled. Slowly, she gave in, relaxing in his embrace, responding to the heat of his kiss.

"I'm read—" Norrie stopped dead.

Roeuk lifted his head and smiled at the bemused expression on Megan's face. "Good. We are ready, as well. Shall I drive?"

"No. I know my way around Washington, and it's my car. I'll drive." Megan needed something to calm her. Maybe accompanying them on this outing wasn't the best idea. Maybe she was opening herself up to a load of heartache.

Or maybe she would enjoy herself. Gradually, the tension lessened as she drove toward the Mall. Once among the crowd in the museum, she would regain her equilibrium. She held on to that thought as she maneuvered through the Saturday traffic, conscious every second of Roeuk sitting only inches away from her.

They waited in line to clear the checkpoint, then entered the vast lobby of the National Air and Space Museum. Above them hung various airplanes of different sizes, configurations and colors.

"Which one flew across the ocean?" Norrie asked, her eyes gazing with rapture at the suspended planes.

"That one." Megan pointed out the Spirit of St. Louis.

"Isn't this cool, Daddy?" the little girl asked, moving to stand a bit nearer Roeuk.

Megan glanced at Roeuk to see how he was taking the quick adoption of Norrie calling him Daddy, but he was looking at his daughter.

"This is magnificent. This was an excellent choice."

"Have you been here before?" Norrie asked.

"No. This is my first visit to Washington, and I have been tied up in meetings for most of the time. I'm glad we came here today," he replied.

Someone bumped Megan and she moved to get out of their way. The Air and Space Museum was always crowded, but especially on weekends. She moved closer to Roeuk to insure she didn't get separated and he reached out and drew her hard up against him, his arm around her waist.

She glanced up at him from beneath her lashes, her heart pounding. Did he realize just touching her drove every prudent thought from her mind? She wanted to lean against him, pretend everything was the way she once thought it would be. Knowing she could not dislodge him without causing a scene, she relaxed enough to allow herself to enjoy his touch, imprinting the feel against her so she could bring forth the memories to cherish in the years to come.

They walked around the first floor, stopping to study different aircraft, reading the plaques that explained them. Several times people stopped suddenly in front of them, and they had to move around them. The noise level was steady as patrons exclaimed over spaceships and gliders, satellites and hot-air balloons.

Gradually, the butterflies in her stomach settled down and Megan was able to take in the different exhibits, even though Roeuk's touch kept her on the edge. Once when Norrie turned back to share her delight in an exhibit, Megan's breath caught. For this day at least, they were a family—mother, father, child. The bittersweet sensation that rushed through her startled her. If things had been different, this might be a normal activity for them. They would go places together, share in their enjoyment of the different things they saw, their delight in being together.

Roeuk was attentive to Norrie. He listened to her when she shared her interest in different exhibits, answered questions she raised, and kept an eye on her to make sure she didn't get lost in the crowd.

He never stopped touching Megan. When they paused

to read a plaque, he would rest his hands on her shoulders, lowering his head near hers, reading over her shoulder. He pulled her back against his chest as they studied the various exhibits. When they walked, his hand gently encircled her neck, slowly brushing the wispy hair that grew to collar-length. Or his hand was at her waist, on her hip. At one point, he rubbed his fingertips lightly against her, commenting that she was too thin, he could feel her bones.

Megan was on fire. It took all her concentration to keep from flinging herself against him and demanding that he make hot love to her. Only the hundreds of people around them, and their very alert daughter, kept the limits of her composure. She was burning up, and if he didn't stop touching her, she might not be responsible for her actions.

Yet she cherished every second. She had never thought to feel this away again, not after the barren existence she'd led the past decade. She wished every moment could last for eternity. Wished things would never change and that they could wander through the museum forever, Roeuk's hands on her.

"I'm hungry," Norrie said.

Megan glanced at her watch, it was after one.

"I guess you are, pumpkin, it's late."

"And where would you like to eat?" Roeuk asked.

"The post office," Norrie said instantly.

He was puzzled. "At the post office?" He looked at Megan.

She grinned. "Actually it's the *old* post office. It's been renovated for shops and restaurants and fast-food places. It is nice. Want to try it?"

"If Norrie wishes it. This day is for her."

Megan nodded and turned to find the entrance, a bit

of the excitement gone for her. This was all for Norrie.
Well, what had she expected? If she thought about it,
most of the contact between them had been for Norrie,
if not directly, then as a means to get to know more
about her.

As they approached the Old Post Office, Roeuk studied it. "It looks almost European," he commented as
they entered through one of the arched doorways.

"A bit, because of its Renaissance styling, I guess,"
Megan concurred.

Inside, the crowds weren't much smaller than at the
museum. They wandered down to the floor of the large
atrium, where small fast-food places lined the perimeter.
In the center of the atrium, tables and chairs were full
of tourists eating from the various food places. Spying
a couple just leaving, Megan dashed over to claim the
table. Roeuk held Norrie's hand as they followed.

"What would you like, they have everything!" Norrie
said, her face alight with pleasure.

Roeuk studied the various shops that lined the different floors, the different restaurants. "This reminds me a
bit of the souks. Though you have built upward here and
the souks are on level ground."

"Souks?" Norrie asked.

"Shops," Megan supplied. She took out her wallet
and drew out some bills. "You walk around and see
what you want. I want two tacos." She offered the bills
to Norrie, but Roeuk intercepted and closed Megan's
fingers around the money.

"Do not be insulting, *chérie,* I will take care of the
meal."

She hesitated, then nodded, putting away the money,
her hand tingling from his touch.

In a short time, they were oblivious to the crowd

around them as they ate their lunch with relish. Megan was amused to see Roeuk had chosen pizza.

"Comparing to La Val's?" she asked.

He nodded calmly. "I think I shall make it as scientific as possible. Maybe while I'm in America, I can test a dozen or more and render a decision."

She giggled, picturing the aloof sheik going from pizza parlor to pizza parlor sampling each to determine the best.

"Ice cream for dessert," Norrie said as she wiped a napkin across her mouth. "In waffle cones."

Roeuk raised an eyebrow at the demand and looked across the small table to Megan.

"I'll have chocolate," she said, smiling.

As Megan watched as the two threaded their way through the crowded floor, her smile faded as her heart rate increased. The tall dark man was holding her daughter's hand, leaning over slightly to hear what Norrie was saying. Megan's heart was touched. The entire day was special, like a moment out of time. Something she had never envisioned in all the years she had had Norrie. Megan continued to watch as they wound their way back. Roeuk held two cones in one hand, his other firmly wrapped around Norrie's, keeping her safe. He would be a wonderful father, Megan acknowledged. He would love his children, shower them with attention and yet make sure they received the proper discipline to grow into worthy adults.

Tears blurred her vision as she looked away, blinking furiously. She had wanted him to be the father of her children. Why had fate played such a cruel trick on her?

Roeuk handed Megan her cone, noticing the spiky lashes. "Did something happen?" he asked, concerned as he discerned the tears still shimmering in her eyes. Had something hurt her? Instantly, he scanned the area.

She shook her head, and delicately licked her cone, blinking a couple more times. She was embarrassed he had noticed her tears. "Maybe after we're finished eating, you would like to see some of the shops," she said quickly.

"Mom always brings me a present if she has to go away on a trip. Are you going to take your mom a present?" Norrie asked.

"I think that would be a good idea, Norrie. You can help me pick it out."

"What's she like? Your mom?" Norrie asked shyly.

Roeuk studied his daughter. His mother was her grandmother. He hadn't really thought about what finding Megan and Norrie would do to his family. He'd been so astounded at the fact that he was a father, he hadn't thought about how the rest of his family would react. They would be surprised, he knew that. But pleased, he thought. "I will call when I get back to your house and have her picture sent to you. She is a nice lady. Not too tall, still has very dark hair. She loves children. She has three grandsons, but you are her only granddaughter."

Norrie smiled at him, at her mother. "I never had a grandmother before."

"You also have three uncles, two aunts and three cousins. On my side, that is." He remembered Megan had said she was an only child. Were her parents still alive? They hadn't spent much time talking about their families. In Berkeley he had deliberately steered their conversations away from their personal lives, trying to keep his identity secret. Now he wished he had handled things differently. He should have told Megan. Would it have made a difference in the long run?

"You don't have grandparents on your mother's side?" Roeuk asked. She was an open forthright child. He felt strangely at ease talking with her. There was none of the awkwardness he'd anticipated trying to get to know her. Was this a normal father-daughter bond?

"My mother died before I went to college," Megan offered.

"But she has a grandfather, your father."

Norrie shook her head. "He doesn't love my mom anymore. He said he didn't want her anymore. Mom and I both don't have a dad. Oh!" She looked stricken as she stared up at Roeuk. "Now I guess I do have one."

"Yes, you do. I didn't know about you, Norrie, or I would have come for you before now." He could already feel the tendrils of love circling his heart for this adorable child. Some of it was because of her resemblance to her mother. Her voice and mannerisms mimicked Megan's. But Norrie was a person in her own right, and he was intrigued to discover all there was to find out about this child he'd created and not known about.

He would have come for her before. Megan stared at Roeuk. What had he meant by that remark?

CHAPTER NINE

WHEN THEY FINISHED their ice cream cones, they left the crowded atrium and wandered around the Old Post Office shops. From expensive artwork and glassware to funky souvenirs for tourists, the various stores in the renovated old building offered a bit of everything.

Roeuk bought a beautiful cut-glass vase for his mother. While Megan would have worried about getting it to her house safely, he apparently had no concerns about transporting it all the way back to Manasia. He instructed the salesclerk to wrap it carefully, then carried it with no more care than if it had been a wooden block.

Both Norrie and Roeuk were intrigued with the different children's stores. He bought her a hippopotamus in a tutu that caught her fancy. At another shop, he purchased a windup train that needed no tracks. When Norrie expressed interest in a doll at an antique boutique, Megan quickly intercepted.

"Run along and see if The Fudgerie is making fudge. Stay by the window so I can see you," Megan instructed. When Norrie was out of earshot, Megan turned to Roeuk.

"She doesn't need another doll, especially one she could ruin if she played with it. Don't spoil her."

"I do not think a couple of presents will spoil her. You've done a fine job raising our daughter, *chérie*."

Megan flushed, feeling the compliment warm her heart. It had been so difficult, she was touched he was pleased with what she'd done.

"So they actually make fudge before your eyes?" he asked as they turned together to follow Norrie.

"Yes, and it's a wonder. Come and watch. I'm always amazed they never let a drop spill off the marble slab they use."

"Daddy, come stand by me," Norrie called when she spotted her parents.

Megan followed slowly, unsure how she felt that Norrie was becoming more at ease with Roeuk.

Roeuk looked at Megan when she joined them. Her gaze was on Norrie, her expression difficult to read, but he knew it wasn't the same carefree happiness he'd seen earlier. She was erecting barriers again. His lips tightened and his eyes narrowed as he tried to determine why she was so unwilling to give them a chance.

Granted, she'd been through a lot all alone. But he had made it clear he wanted her again. Yet she continued to resist. If he had to fight her every inch of the way, one day she would acknowledge that she belonged to him. His daughter deserved a chance to have both parents raise her. He deserved the opportunity to know his daughter, contribute to her life.

He wanted to contribute to Megan's life, as well, to make up to some extent for the difficulties she'd faced for so long. She would live like a princess in Manasia. She would not have to work if she didn't wish. She could do whatever brought her pleasure.

And he was certain she'd love the country.

If she wanted to help him, it would be an asset. There was much to do to continue Manasia's economic progress, if she wanted to assist. And if not, she could simply be his refuge when the demands of running the country became too great.

He remembered the days of laughter and heated discussion they'd shared in Berkeley. The dark nights when they would walk and talk long after the shops had closed and most people were home. He'd cherished those times with Megan, feeling closer to her than anyone else in his life.

Over the last ten years, he'd missed those times the most. Could he ever recapture that warmth and acceptance? Could she find it in her to forgive him the deceptions of that time? Forgive him for not finding her when she had needed him so much? One way or another, she had to. He would not let her go a second time.

When the fudge-making was over, Roeuk bought a large box of the candy for Megan. "If I remember correctly, you like chocolate."

She laughed softly. "Love it, actually. Thank you."

He took her free hand and threaded his fingers with hers. "My pleasure. Isn't that what people do here, buy candy, flowers, jewelry?"

She blinked and looked at him sharply. "People do that for what?"

He smiled and rubbed his thumb over the back of her hand.

Courting. She caught her breath. He was courting her! He had tried demands; since they didn't work, he was now trying softer means. But for herself or for Norrie?

Megan was glad to drive when it was time go home. She needed something to take her mind off Roeuk and the knowledge that he was still pursuing her. She didn't know if she could permit it to continue. She still couldn't forget the bitterness she felt at his betrayal. Didn't know if she dared let herself trust him again. She didn't know much about him, despite the numerous conversations they'd had over the past few days.

She did know she was still attracted to him. She

longed for his kisses and caresses. She remembered when they had been as close as two people could ever be. Her spirit wanted that again. Her body yearned for that closeness. His touch brought her one step closer. His kisses filled her with bliss. If she dared reach out for the happiness that teased her, would she find it, or find it all an illusion, just like last time?

Norrie ran to the answering machine when they reached home. The blinking light indicated a message.

"It's Stephie, she wants to know if I can go swimming. Can I, Mom?" she called as Megan and Roeuk settled the various packages on the coffee table in the living room.

"Yes, be back for dinner."

"Cool."

Megan smiled as she heard Norrie call her friend, then run down the hall to change into her swimsuit.

"I'm dead after all that walking. And she seems to have as much energy as if she'd just gotten up," Megan said as she sank onto the sofa and eased her shoes off.

Roeuk sat beside her, leaning his head against the high back. "Me, too. I have thought for many years that energy is wasted on the young. My nephews never seem to run down."

"Tell me about them," Megan said, anxious to learn more about him, more about his life.

"Let's see," he closed his eyes. "Hamid is the oldest. He's my next brother's child. At five, he is inquisitive and into everything. His parents taught him how to swim at a young age since he was forever plunging into the sea without a bit of concern about the water."

For the next few minutes, Roeuk talked about his brothers and their wives, and the three nephews who obviously enjoyed his deep love.

"But you'll see when you get there how bright they are. Hamid even speaks English. Not as good as he will one day, but enough to communicate. Norrie will have no problems with communication."

"You're going too fast, Roeuk. We're not going to Manasia," Megan said, the bubble bursting.

He opened his eyes a slit and looked at her. "It's not too fast, *chérie*. I have a lot of years to make up. Yes, you are both going. One way or the other. I'm hoping you will go as my wife."

Wife! She held her breath, her gaze locking with his. Was he serious? He seriously wanted to marry her?

She dropped her gaze to her lap. One fingernail had broken and she worried the ragged edge while she tried desperately to think. Ten years ago she had thought they would marry. Had wanted it more than anything. Now, she wasn't sure.

Roeuk watched her, sensing the nervous energy that was building. He reached out and covered her restless fingers with his, feeling the delicate strength. He had hoped she would throw her arms around him and accept immediately. Cynically, he reflected he should have known better. She hadn't exactly thrown herself at him during the past few days. Instead, she looked for all the world as if she were thinking up a polite way to tell him to go to hell.

"I haven't asked you, so don't build walls and barriers. I will ask before I have to leave the country, however, so you think long and hard about it. I want you, Megan. And I want my daughter. Marriage would simplify things. But if you want to do things the hard way, I can manage that, as well."

"Well, that certainly is a romantic way to look at things." She flung off his hands and stood, pacing across the room. Pausing only a moment at the window, she turned and walked back toward the fireplace.

The phone rang and Roeuk could see the relief on her face. She went to answer. He could hear the conversation, it sounded as if she'd been invited somewhere. Briefly, jealousy touched him. He wanted to know her friends, make sure there was not another man. For years he had assumed she had gone on with her life, had married and started a family. Gradually, he had accepted that. But the reality that she hadn't now made it imperative that she not consider anyone but him.

He rose as she replaced the receiver.

"Who was that?"

She looked surprised that he would ask.

"The Andersons, Stephie's parents. They invited us to come swimming, too. But I said no."

Roeuk leaned against the hall wall, crossed his arms over his chest and studied her. Why was she still nervous? Was she thinking about his comment regarding marriage? Was she going to be difficult about it when the time came? He would ask her today, but knew she would refuse. Given time, she would come around.

"It's one thing to go around in crowds where no one knows us, but I don't want neighbors getting the wrong idea," she blurted out, watching him warily.

"Wrong idea?" His voice was silky.

He was at his most formidable when using that tone. Megan shivered and shrugged, trying to dispel the sense of impending doom.

"They'd want to know all about you and I don't need that now. You're leaving soon. There would be too much talk about Norrie. I want to protect her."

He pushed away from the wall and stalked over to her, reaching out to take her shoulders in a hard grasp.

Slowly, he pushed her back against the wall, his eyes blazing down into hers.

"In other words, you have no intention of marrying me. You have made up your mind that you want nothing to do with me. You don't want anyone to know that Norrie is my daughter, is that it?"

"That's it," she said, raising her face to his. "You say you want something more from me, but it's early days yet. I've had proof of your staying power, it is totally lacking. I'm not risking my daughter."

"You're not risking your *heart, chérie*. Your daughter is the camouflage you use to hide behind. It's not Norrie we are discussing, but you and me."

"Okay, then, you're right! I don't trust you."

"So what must I do to provide you with enough trust to at least think of a future together?"

"I don't know." She blinked back tears she would not let fall. She wanted to believe in him. But he had never said a word of love. She wanted to trust that he would never lie to her again, never leave her alone, but she didn't. What would convince her?

"Time, I guess," she said, biting down on her lower lip to keep it from trembling.

"Time." He sighed softly and leaned forward, his lips touching hers, coaxing a response. Easing his grip, he drew her to him, opening her mouth to deepen the kiss.

Doubts fled when he held her like this. Fears and uncertainty melted as the heat they generated burned up every doubt, everything but the fiery love that blossomed each time he touched her. She loved Roeuk. She had always loved him. She undoubtably always would love him. If only she was brave enough to trust that love.

Megan slowly encircled his neck, her fingers tangling in his thick hair as she reveled in the sensations that pulsed through her. When his tongue swept into her mouth, her knees gave way. Roeuk strengthened his hold on her to keep her from falling even as she leaned into his embrace. She wanted to be closer, closer. Feeling the pounding of his heart against her breasts, she wondered if he could feel hers racing. Still she longed to be closer. His heat scorched her body, his strong chest pressed hot and hard against her soft breasts. The strength of Roeuk's long legs held them both as she gave herself up to the raptures of her love.

The shrill ring of the phone shattered the moment. Breathing heavily, Megan pulled back, almost unaware of where she was. She knew where she had been, in heaven.

"Hello?" Was that breathless voice hers? What would the caller think?

"It's for you." She turned and offered the receiver to Roeuk.

The conversation was short, and in Arabic. When he hung up, he looked at Megan.

"There is trouble at my home. Salid has notified me that I am needed. The limo is on the way to pick me up. I have to go, *chérie,* sooner than I had planned."

"What kind of trouble?" She resented the intrusion of the outside world. For several glorious moments, they had been in a world of their own.

He crossed the hall and entered the living room, going to stand at the window to watch for the limo. "Not everyone in Manasia was as excited about the treaty as I was. There are factions that would like to keep the oil to ourselves, or align ourselves with the cartel. Now that the treaty is signed, there are protests in one of the larger cities. It is not serious at this point, but I want to find out all I can and see what I can do to ease matters before they become more serious."

"Will you have to return home?" Now that the time might be imminent, Megan was afraid. She had known this was coming, but she just wasn't ready for it.

"I need more information on the situation before I can determine how best to handle it."

Gone was the impatient lover of a few moments ago. In his place was a man of stature and power. Megan could almost see his mind working as he focused on the problem. He was already miles away from her, his attention on the important problems now facing him from his country. For now, she had been forgotten. Again.

The limo turned onto her street.

He was at the door before it stopped in front of her house.

"Let me know what happens," she said.

He looked at her and nodded. "I'll call you." With that he was gone.

She watched him get into the limo, watched as it drove away. For a long time she stood by the window, wondering what she was going to do.

Turning away, she spied the packages on the table. He had forgotten to take the vase for his mother. She crossed the room and picked up the parcel, holding it against her breasts for a long time. Then she smiled. If nothing else, this gave her a reason to call him later. Let him know she could bring it over to his suite. Maybe she would find out more about what was happening in Manasia. Would it be serious enough to require him to return home? Suddenly, she silently admitted she wanted him to stay. At least for a while longer.

Megan and Norrie slept in late the next morning. Fixing waffles for breakfast, Megan took her time, enjoying the rare time with just her daughter. They talked about the previous day. When Norrie mentioned wanting to visit Roeuk's home, Megan nodded thoughtfully. Maybe they would visit one day. Maybe.

"Can I go see if Stephie can go bike riding?" Norrie asked after she'd finished eating.

"Tidy your room first. I want to vacuum and don't want to have to pick up a lot stuff off your floor," Megan said.

"Aw, Mom."

"After that, you can go play."

Mumbling under her breath, Norrie stomped to her room. Megan smiled at the familiar ritual. Why was it children didn't like to keep things tidy? Megan tried to remember her own mother's admonitions to keep her room clean, but she pushed the thoughts away. She didn't like remembering her family; it hurt too much. She and Norrie were a family, it was enough.

Lingering over a second cup of coffee, Megan wondered if she had the energy to clean the entire house. Actually, what she really meant was, did she want to, or would she rather contact Roeuk about the package he'd left?

"I'm done," Norrie said rushing down the hall. "Now can I go to Stephie's?"

"Yes," Megan said, wishing she had some of that energy and enthusiasm.

Suddenly, the phone rang, and she answered it before the second ring.

"Megan?" It was Roeuk.

"Great minds must think alike, I was just thinking about you. I was going to call—"

"No doubt to discover further information on the situation in Manasia." His sharp tone crashed around her.

"Is it worse?" It must be for him to bring it up. Was he leaving? A clutch of dismay gripped her.

"I'll leave that for you to find out some other way. I'm mad as hell that you used our relationship as a stepping stone for your career!"

"What are you talking about?"

"Don't play innocent with me, Megan, I'm no longer in the mood. I'll call you later in the week to arrange time to see Norrie. I think you can understand why I won't be bothering you any longer with my company."

"Roeuk—"

He severed the connection.

Megan held the receiver for several long moments, unable to believe what had just happened. What was he talking about? She slammed down the receiver and hurried out to the front porch to pick up the newspaper. It must be something in the paper, why else would he have referred to her career? But what?

She snatched up the Sunday edition and stared in disbelief at the enlarged close-up of Roeuk she'd taken at the White House and the lead article. Anti-U.S. Demonstrations in Manasia Threaten Oil Treaty. The byline was Jeff's. Quickly she scanned the article. As usual, the headline made things sound worse than they were. Whirling, she ran inside and hurried to her room to dress. She read bits and pieces as she threw on a comfortable pair of old jeans, pulled a short-sleeved cotton shirt over her head. She brushed her hair, glad its short length required so little attention.

Stopping only long enough to call Margie Anderson and ask if she would watch Norrie, she ran to her car and headed for the *Sentinel* office.

*   *   *

There were always people in the newsroom. Twenty-four hours a day, seven days a week, men and women kept watch over news breaking all over the world. Today the crew was small. It was Sunday and only a skeleton staff was on duty.

Megan found the duty editor, Sam Peters.

"Hey, Megan, what are you doing here, this your weekend to work?" he asked jovially.

"No, it's not. I want to know about the story on the front page, the one on Manasia."

"What about it?" Sam asked, "Problem with it?"

"Is Jeff here?"

"No, not yet, anyway. He's watching that one, he'll be in later. What's the problem?"

"How did he find out?"

"Hell, how does he find out about anything? Probably came on the AP."

"Can I get a copy of the printout?"

"Megan, what bee is in your bonnet? Why would you want a copy—"

"Just know it's important to me, Sam. Can I find a copy?"

"Look on Jeff's desk. It'd take more trouble than it's worth to find the duplicate in yesterday's roll. He probably had it there for backup."

Megan crossed swiftly to Jeff's desk. It was a mess. Sighing, she began to gingerly shift papers, not wanting to disturb any order Jeff might have had. Though to her it looked like scrambled eggs.

"Looking for something?" Jeff asked.

"Hi. Yes, I am. The AP printout that gave the story about the protests in Manasia."

"Why? Read about it in today's paper," Jeff said smugly.

"I already did. More important, so did Roeuk. And he thinks I gave the tip."

Jeff shrugged. "So? It's news. You're a journalist."

"I'm a photographer. And it makes a difference. Do you have the AP copy?"

"Is the sheik upset?" he asked slyly.

"Jeff, do you have the copy?" She was almost screaming with frustration. In no mood for teasing, she rummaged through the paper piled on his desk.

"Hold on, I'll get it for you. Don't go messing up everything."

She looked in disbelief at the chaos. "How could you tell if I did?"

"Shut up. Here's the damn copy. I'm monitoring the entire situation. You'll see an update in tomorrow's paper."

"Fine with me. I just need to prove to someone that I wasn't the one to give the story."

"Hey, that's your job. You're supposed to report news tips to the paper."

"This is something entirely different. And you didn't need me for this one, you had AP. See you tomorrow."

Megan clutched the precious printout and headed to her car. She was going to prove to Mr. Arrogant Sheik that he was too quick to jump to conclusions. He needed to develop some trust in her if he ever wanted her to find trust in him.

She drove swiftly to the hotel where Roeuk was staying, fuming all the way. How dare he think she had only used him to further her career. If he didn't know her better, it was past time for him to learn. Gripping the wheel, she realized what she was thinking. Was it because she was giving thought to his pronouncement about wanting to marry her?

Was she seriously considering it? She loved him. She should just admit it and see where that led her. She had loved him endlessly all those years ago. Or loved who she thought he was. But the time they'd spent together during this visit had shown her he had changed only a little. Granted, he was arrogant and incredibly strong-willed, but then a lot of successful powerful men were. And some of that arrogance could be tempered. He still had the power to excite her more than any other human being she'd ever known. His determination to get to know his daughter was endearing. When he spoke of his family, it was with pride and affection.

When he spoke to her, it was with passion and longing. Could he fall in love with her one day? Would it be enough to have his commitment if he never did? Was he courting her only for Norrie, or did he care for her, as well?

When Megan reached the hotel, she was shocked at the crowd in the lobby. Slowly, she worked her way through the newspapermen and TV cameramen pressing in near the elevators. The talk buzzed about the sheik and the situation in Manasia. At each elevator door stood a guard holding back the eager reporters. Obviously, the hotel was protecting its guest.

Megan slid into the elevator banks, and reached for the Up button.

"Are you a guest here, madam?" the guard nearest her asked politely. "I'll need to see your key."

She shook her head. "I'm visiting someone here."

"Sorry, ma'am. No one is allowed up unless they are a guest. Maybe you could call your party and have them come down to vouch for you," he said.

She nodded and turned away. Right. She had a life-size picture of Sheik Roeuk bin Shalik coming down to face this crowd just to vouch for her. He thought she was the one who started it all. Damn.

She moved to the house phones and requested Roeuk's room. As she had expected, the hotel was not putting through calls. She hung up and glanced around. Could she find the stairs? Were they guarded, as well?

Just then, a cry caught her attention. Turning, Megan spied a harried-looking woman pushing a baby carriage while a little girl of about three was crying. A small boy of about five was pulling on the woman's hand, obviously anxious to get where they were going. The mother stopped and stooped down to comfort the little girl, admonishing the boy to be quiet. As quickly as she could, Megan crossed over to them.

"You look as if you could use a bit of help," Megan said, smiling sympathetically. "I'm just going up myself. If you're heading for your room, I'll push the stroller for you while you handle those two."

The woman hesitated, doubt in her expression at the stranger offering help.

Megan kept her smile and shrugged. "Just wanted to help."

"Thanks, I could use it." Straightening, the harried mother lifted the little girl in her arms and held on to the boy. The woman watched to make sure Megan was coming as they braved the crowd.

The mother had her key ready and the guards let them on the elevator with no trouble.

Success! Megan thought as the doors slid silently closed behind her. She pushed the carriage to their room, accepting the mother's thanks before returning to the elevator. In no time, she was on Roeuk's floor.

CHAPTER TEN

MEGAN STEPPED OFF the elevator and faced the two guards standing in front of the door down the hall. Slowly she walked toward them. She didn't recognize either one. Would they recognize her? And if so, would they let her in? Or had Roeuk told them to bar her admittance?

They moved as one unit to block her way.

"These rooms are occupied," one said in a heavily accented English.

"I'm Megan O'Sullivan, and I need to speak to the sheik."

As one they both shook their heads, moving closer still, crowding her back toward the elevator.

Megan darted to the left. The guard caught her arm and hauled her before him. The other guard took her other arm and together they marched her down the hall.

"Roeuk bin Shalik!" she yelled, tussling with the two strong men. She would not give up easily. "Let me go. *Roeuk!* It's Megan, I want to talk to you!"

One of the guards pushed the button for the elevator, both silently continued holding her as easily as if she were a child. Their grips were strong, she could not break free.

"Roeuk!" she screamed, struggling to pull away.

Just as she heard the ping announcing the arrival of the elevator car, the door to the suite opened.

"Roeuk, I need to talk to you," Megan called. She wouldn't leave without a fight. This was too important.

Salid stepped into the hall and closed the door behind him. He motioned the guards to hold her a moment.

"I am afraid that His Excellency is occupied at the moment. In any event, I don't believe he has anything to say to you."

"He doesn't need to say anything to me, dammit. I have plenty to say to him! I need to straighten out a few things." She was so angry, she felt as if she might explode. She yanked her arm. The guards' grip tightened.

It was obvious by Salid's slightly bemused expression that most people didn't confront the sheik as she threatened. But she didn't care. All she wanted was to explain to Roeuk what had happened, make him eat his words and admit he was wrong, that she had never betrayed his trust in any way.

"I will let him know that you came by," Salid began.

"Roeuk!" she called again. "It's not good enough to tell him I was here, I want to see him!" she said between gritted teeth.

"What is going on out here? Salid, I thought you could handle things." Roeuk stood in the doorway to the suite, glaring at the small group by the elevator.

"I want to talk to you," Megan called, pulling futilely against the captive hands. "Or wring your neck, I'm not sure which." At that, both guards became even more alert.

Even Salid looked alarmed.

Roeuk, however, chuckled. "Threats against my person is not the best way to get an audience with me." He studied her angry countenance for a long moment, then shrugged. "Very well, I will give you five minutes." He turned and walked back into the suite.

The guards released their hold but continued to watch her closely as they all moved down the hall. Salid indicated she should precede him into the sitting room, and he closed the door behind them.

"Do you need me?" he asked Roeuk softly, still watching Megan.

"No. Don't worry, she may talk tough, but she's not going to wring anyone's neck. Megan is against violence."

"I used to be," she muttered, crossing the room, pulling the AP printout from her purse.

Slapping the computer paper against his chest, she burst out, "Read that, Mr. Know-it-all Sheik. Then you can fall on your knees and beg my forgiveness for ever doubting me. Doubting, heck, you had me tried, convicted and condemned without even telling me what the issue was." She stormed over to the window, turned and stormed back.

"On my knees?" Roeuk murmured softly as he glanced at the AP report.

"Groveling, for all I care." She paused and glared at him, swiveling around to pace back to the window. "I'm so mad I could spit! I hadn't a clue what you were talking about on the phone. I hadn't read the paper. Norrie and I had just finished breakfast."

She whirled and faced him. "How dare you think I would abuse whatever relationship we have just to get a news story! Do you think so little of me as to believe I'd do something like that?"

"*Chérie*—"

"It never even occurred to me that the situation was newsworthy. I was more concerned about you and if you would have to return to Manasia early. I never thought to call it into the paper. And of course, Jeff thinks I'm nuts not to have thought of that."

"Jeff?" His attention sharpened.

She waved her hands dismissively, pacing back to stand before him. "He works at the paper, it's his story. The one he got from the AP."

Roeuk glanced again at the printout from Associated Press.

"You're a fine one to talk about trust," Megan said. "Where was trust when you saw the paper this morning? You didn't even *ask* me about the article, just yelled at me and hung up. I've never given you a moment to doubt me. I've never done anything to lead you to suspect...suspect..."

Her emotions were catching up with her. She could feel the tears threaten. After all this time, she couldn't cry, she just couldn't.

Turning away, she crossed to the window, fighting for control. "I never lied to you. You always knew who I was, what I was. You always knew how I felt about you. I was so trusting. I gave you all I had."

He came up behind her, his hands gentle on her shoulders. "Yes, I know, *chérie.*"

"So how could you think I would do this to you? You should have at least asked." The tears slid down her face. She bit her lower lip, desperately trying to stall them. A sob escaped.

"Ah, Megan, don't cry." He turned her around and wrapped his arms around her, holding her tightly as the dam burst and she gave way to the grief long bottled up. She cried as if her world had ended, as it had ten years ago. The shattering of all her hopes and dreams had been devastating. She had believed so strongly in their love, only to find it in pieces at her feet. She leaned into his strength and gave way to the emotions that swamped her, feeling safe and secure in his embrace. For the first time in a decade, feeling totally safe.

Roeuk murmured soft words into her hair as he held her through the weeping. His fingers soothed her back, rubbed her head, bunching and releasing her hair as he sought to ease her anguish.

Gradually, the tears subsided. She leaned exhausted against him, the fingers of her right hand covering her face, her eyes. She knew she must look a sight. Her eyes would be swollen, her nose was running, she sniffed.

"You went to the newspaper office to get the Associated Press report?" he asked.

She nodded against him, wishing the floor would open and swallow her. She was so embarrassed. How would she ever face him again?

"Why?"

"To prove to you that I hadn't given the story tip. I never even thought about doing such a thing."

"Why was it so important to tell me?" he asked softly, his hands moving over her back, from her hips to her shoulders, and down again.

"I didn't want you to believe I would betray you," she whispered.

"It would be no more than I deserve. I betrayed your trust in me years ago."

She shrugged against him, breathing in the scent of him. It was warm and spicy and very male. Her eyes closed, she imprinted the scent on her memory so she would always be able to remember. She wanted to stay like this forever, even as she knew she could not.

"Maybe, but I didn't want you to think that of me," she said sadly.

"And why was that so important, Megan? Why did you go to all this trouble to make sure I knew the truth?"

"I want you to trust me," she said softly, not fully

understanding why it was so important to her, only knowing it was.

He tilted her head back, cupping her damp cheeks with his palms, brushing away her covering hand. Lightly skimming his thumbs across her spiky lashes, he gazed down into her flushed face.

"I must look a mess," she said, giving another sniff. She couldn't look away. The passion that shone from his eyes was mesmerizing.

"I think you are the most beautiful woman in the world. I always have." Lowering his mouth to hers, he kissed her.

Megan was light-headed by the time Salid interrupted a few moments later.

"The president is on the phone, Excellency." He stood just inside the connecting door, displaying no surprise to find Megan in Roeuk's arms.

"Duty calls. Stay here." He reached for a clean handkerchief and wrapped her fingers around it. Quickly, he strode to the phone.

Megan turned to stare out the window, blowing her nose and mopping up the last of her tears. She listened idly to Roeuk explain that the situation had been handled in his country. A tempest in a teapot, he called it. She smiled, finding it odd that a desert sheik could so easily quote an English saying. Must have come from his having lived in England so long. She wondered how he'd liked that country. Wondered why he'd never visited the United States after leaving so long ago. There was still so much she didn't know about Roeuk.

"Now, where were we?" he asked, slipping an arm around her waist and hugging her close to his hard chest.

"If I ask about the protest, will you assume the worst?" she asked.

"Not now that you've cleared the matter up for me."

"It's really over?"

"Yes. Very noisy and a little damage to some property, but nothing earth-shattering. The treaty is in no way jeopardized."

"And you don't have to fly home immediately to settle things?"

"I'm scheduled for a week or two to visit in America. My last function ends tonight, thereafter I'm free. Would you have dinner with me tomorrow night? We will find a place that has dancing. Remember how much we loved to dance in Berkeley?"

She nodded. She had loved everything about that year, dancing with Roeuk had only been one facet.

"I will pick you up at seven."

"I'll have to see if I can get Mrs. Hanson."

"If not, bring Norrie here. I'll have someone watch her."

Megan nodded.

"Did you eat lunch?" he asked, glancing at her.

She shook her head.

"Then stay and eat here, and have a cup of hot tea."

She smiled. "I was just wondering about your years in England, and now you offer me tea."

"Ah, but we drink tea at home, as well. Hot and sweet and strong."

"I'd like something to eat. Then I have to get back. I left Norrie with the Andersons and don't want her there all day."

He had Salid order lunch for them. They sat together on the sofa waiting for the food. Roeuk linked their hands and rested them on his thigh as he discussed the demonstrations in Manasia. Their talk drifted to other topics. He told her about his schooling in England as they ate a light lunch. He told her about the reforms and plans he had for Manasia while they sipped hot sweet tea after they'd resumed their places on the sofa.

Megan revealed how she had reached his floor despite the safeguards the hotel had installed to prevent it. She related more incidents about Norrie, as a toddler in Los Angeles, and what changes moving to the capital had made in their lives. Roeuk rested his warm palm against her thigh, his fingers lightly rubbing the inside seam of her jeans.

Her nerve endings screamed for release as her body began to heat and throb for a more intimate touch. She'd felt at peace after her bout of tears. But that peace was now shattered as every part of her yearned for him. She could scarcely talk, her mind was so caught up in the feel of his hand on her leg. She could scarcely breathe for the tingling sensations that shivered through her body.

She rested her hand on his and he linked her fingers through his, holding both their hands against her tingling leg.

She remembered his fingers gliding over her skin so long ago, his mouth kissing every inch of her naked body. She reveled in the hot memory of the delights they'd found in each other's arms, the long sultry nights when they'd been caught up in a world of two, nothing else important but the love they had shared.

She wanted that again. She wanted him to move his hand up beneath her shirt and caress her bare skin. She wanted to feel his lips against her breasts, capturing her nipples and drawing them into the heated cavern of his mouth. She wanted him to disrobe them both and lie down with her in a big bed or on the sofa or on the floor and make passionate love to her as he had so long ago.

The spell broke when the room-service waiter returned to gather the dirty dishes. Roeuk casually removed his hand from her leg and the shimmering tension eased slightly. Megan glanced at her watch. It was after four.

"I've got to go." She stood up abruptly. For more than one reason, she had to leave. It was time to pick up Norrie, and time to examine exactly what was going on between her and Roeuk. The tears had helped erase much of the bitterness she felt over his long-ago betrayal. But was she ready to believe in him again? Ready to trust him with her heart? She had to think things through, away from him. His presence was too disturbing. She couldn't think around him, only feel. And her feelings led her right back to Roeuk, every time.

"Until tomorrow night, then," he said reluctantly.

"Oh, you left the present for your mother at my place yesterday. I can bring it by on my way to work tomorrow if you like," she offered.

He raised an eyebrow. "On your way? Isn't this off the direct route from your house to your office."

She shrugged, grinning engagingly. "Close enough."

"Then yes, bring it by. Would you eat breakfast here?"

She shook her head. "I'll eat with Norrie, then stop by around nine. I can only stay a moment, I'll have to get to work."

He nodded and kissed her.

He walked her to the door of the suite and kissed her again.

He walked her to the elevator and, ignoring the stares of his guard, kissed her again.

"I will not accompany you downstairs," he murmured, resting his forehead on hers.

"I should think not. Every reporter in Washington seems to be there. I'll see you in the morning."

He kissed her one last time. When the elevator arrived, he watched until the doors closed behind her. There was a wealth of satisfaction in knowing she had come to see him to make sure of his trust. Whether or not she admitted it, she wanted him to trust her. She was coming around. He had felt the difference after her tears. Megan was his, and he was beginning to think she knew it.

Smiling, he entered the suite. He had only the reception by the oil companies to attend, then his time was his own. He'd get her to take time off from work. He and Megan and Norrie would spend time together during the next two weeks. Begin to build their family as it should have been built ten years ago. His heart hardened against the memory of his father and the machinations the man had pulled to keep them apart. Roeuk always knew that he and Megan were destined to be together, no matter what. Finding her again after all this time, free and available, had demonstrated that.

Megan floated through the rest of the day. She let the love she felt blossom. She was happy. A few more days like today and she would let herself believe in Roeuk again, dare dream of a future together. She hoped he would wait to ask her to marry him until they'd spent more time together. Then she was confident she could give him the answer he wanted.

The concern that he wanted her solely for Norrie faded. He had been wonderful, listening to her tirade, believing in her again. Holding her when she'd cried. How she relished that cherishing.

His calling her beautiful had made her feel special.

Even with a blotchy face and no makeup, he'd called her beautiful. She glowed with the compliment, the warmth in her heart a wondrous thing.

Her love even allowed her to forgive the past. He had explained the arranged engagement and marriage to Sasela, really a plan of his father's. His father was dead now. He couldn't hurt them again. Roeuk had not told her everything in Berkeley, but he knew now that had been wrong. Hadn't he shared with her the problems with the demonstrations in Manasia? Hadn't he shared his hopes and plans for the future? She wanted to know so much more, and the days before he left would give them the time to discuss everything under the sun, as they had on their long nightly walks at Berkeley. Only, in those days, their discussions had been the idealistic plans of youth to save the world. Now they could discuss their own lives and the hopes and dreams each of them held.

She hoped to meld them together and find common goals and dreams. Dare she reach out for the future and grab it to make it hers? She had the confidence now to do so. Her love made her strong.

The next morning, Megan was on tenterhooks wanting to see Roeuk. She dressed early and was ready to leave for his hotel the moment Mrs. Hanson arrived. Kissing Norrie, Megan grabbed the box that held the crystal vase and dashed for the car. Traffic was surprisingly light for a Monday morning and she made good time arriving at the hotel a full half hour before Roeuk expected her.

She was humming as she entered the lobby and headed for the elevators. Yesterday's crowd was gone. The news hounds had moved on to something else. The demonstrations in Manasia had fizzled into nothing and the reporters were after fresh game.

When the elevator stopped on Roeuk's floor, Megan recognized one of the guards standing by the suite from yesterday. She eyed him warily. He nodded and held open the door to the suite for her.

Smiling more confidently, she entered.

There was no one in the room. Connecting doors opened from both sides, she hadn't a clue which one led to Roeuk's room. Or maybe he had an entirely different suite for sleeping. She hesitated only a moment, then moved into the room. She was early, she knew that. He would be here soon. Maybe one of the guards was letting him know she'd arrived.

She crossed to the coffee table and carefully set down the vase. She would have to make sure he told her how his mother liked it. Norrie would want to know, as well.

A small stack of newspapers was on the table. Megan smiled when she saw today's issue of the *Sentinel* on top. Had that been done deliberately? Picking up the paper, she scanned the front page. Jeff had done a small piece on the demonstrations on the lower right-hand corner. So much for the big exposé.

Her attention was caught by the large picture on the front page of the second newspaper. And the headlines in bold print: Another Treaty In The Works? The *Sentinel* dropped from her fingers as she focused on the other paper. The picture of Roeuk was good, clear and sharp, as was the image of the woman standing in the circle of his arm. Megan sat down on the sofa, her legs unable to hold her as a sick sensation began to spread from her stomach.

The headline read: Sheik Roeuk Bin Shalik And Lady Susan Fairchild Attend The Gala Ball Given In His

Honor By The Oil Companies. Megan reached out and picked up the paper, her eyes skimming the article.

Roeuk had been wined and dined and feted by the large oil companies in honor of the recent treaty. His escort for the evening was Lady Susan Fairchild from London. Dear God, he had flown his date in from London to attend the event.

She read further, numb to all feelings.

"Megan, my aide said you were here." Roeuk entered through the side door. He paused when she turned blank eyes toward him. Flicking a glance at the paper in her hand, a fleeting hint of anger crossed his face before he schooled it to haughty indifference.

Megan watched, wondering if he was as adept at schooling his features to reflect passion that probably wasn't there to begin with. She folded the paper and placed it carefully on the coffee table.

"A friend of long standing, the article says," she said quietly.

"Megan, it's not what you think. I had invited Susan to accompany me some time ago when I first learned about the dinner and found out she was planning to be in Washington. I've known her a number of years."

"So the article said." She was numb. She knew she needed to get out of here. Needed to get as far away from this man as she could before she was totally destroyed.

"It meant nothing, *chérie*. It had been arranged some time ago."

"Like your engagement when you came to Berkeley. It meant nothing. It had been arranged some time before." History repeating itself. "Yet you never thought to mention it to me? Not the engagement, not last night's date."

"No, I didn't. It wasn't important enough."

"Or I wasn't important enough. You could have canceled the date," she said, finally finding the strength to stand.

"It wasn't a date. Susan is someone I've known for a number of years."

"Like Sasela?"

Roeuk stared at her, frustration building. "No, not like Sasela."

"You know the funny thing?" Megan edged toward the door. Away from all she had built her hopes on since yesterday afternoon. "I thought we were drawing closer. I told myself we would never have the same kind of problem we had before. But I was wrong, wasn't I? Nothing has changed."

"Megan, it wasn't important," he repeated.

"You're wrong, Roeuk. To me, it is of utmost importance. I thought we were communicating and that we had a chance to build something. I wanted to be a part of all aspects of your life, but you only want me for one part. And I wonder if I really had any special part at all or if it was all for Norrie?"

She reached the door and faced him, her hand reaching behind her for the knob.

"You once said you would do what you had to in order to see Norrie," she said. "Call the president, get yourself a lawyer, because you're going to need the entire weight of the legal system behind you to get to see me or my daughter ever again. And I'll fight you every step of the way."

She opened the door and slammed it behind her. Holding herself together through sheer willpower, she walked to the elevator, oblivious to the guards who watched her warily. She ignored the passengers in the car when she stepped on, concentrating on breathing, on not shattering into a thousand pieces. She clenched her teeth, holding out against the pain that pierced her heart once again. She had begun to believe in Roeuk and in her love, now she was right back where she'd been ten years ago. She had no one to blame but herself, not that it made the pain any easier to bear.

Nothing had changed. Arrangements made were arrangements kept, and none of her business. What other arrangements had already been made that he refused to share with her? Would he have continued behaving the same way if she had married him?

Slow hot tears dripped down her cheeks. Her head held high, she walked across the lobby and out into the sunshine. Deathly cold and sick at heart, she didn't even notice the sweltering muggy day.

CHAPTER ELEVEN

THE PHONE on her desk rang. She pulled her gaze from the printed schedule she'd been studying and focused on the phone. She blinked as if coming awake after a long sleep. Sighing, she reached for the receiver before someone else answered it for her.

"O'Sullivan," she said listlessly.

"Megan—"

She slid the receiver silently back onto the phone base, glaring at it. Roeuk had nothing to say that she wanted to hear.

The phone rang again, shaking her out of her lethargy. She picked it up, heard his voice, then dropped the receiver back. Once the connection was broken, she pulled the receiver off the hook and laid it on her desk. Glancing out of her cubicle, she reassured herself no one was paying any attention.

She looked at the schedule again but couldn't concentrate. She needed to get away; she was doing no good here. Taking time to tidy her desk, she grabbed her purse. Just before she walked away, she replaced the receiver.

She could hear the ring as she crossed the floor toward Mason's office. Ten minutes later, she was in her car, the rest of the day hers alone.

She would not think about Roeuk, she vowed for the thousandth time since she'd seen that paper that morning. She would be grateful she had found out before she'd done something foolish, like agree to think about his proposal.

Driving aimlessly around Washington, she tried to keep her thoughts channeled in directions that did not lead to the sexy sheik she'd fallen in love with. She refused to admit that love had lain dormant for years, only to be revived just by seeing him again. Her life was fine the way it was. She and Norrie could manage the way they always had.

She drove into Georgetown, parking near the canal. Getting out, she wandered down by the water, walking along the towpath, trying to force the peace of the setting to soothe her battered nerves. The water flowed silently between the banks, dappled by the sunlight through the trees that flanked the canal. The path was wide and dry. Ahead of her was a jogger, a couple walking together holding hands, three teenagers laughing and jeering at one another. It was not crowded as it was on weekends. She was grateful for the lack of people, for the semblance of privacy.

Walking slowly, Megan tried to put things into perspective. She ached with hurt, anger licked at her belly, regret filled her heart. From the moment she'd learned how his father had interfered, she had begun to hope. She had listened to his explanation of why he hadn't told her who he was, and had tried to understand. Despite her need to be careful, Roeuk had slipped beneath her guard and invaded her heart. Yet he had made no concessions for her. He had made no declaration of love.

When she felt the prick of tears behind her eyelids, she turned and walked purposefully toward her car. She had cried enough for a lifetime. She would not shed another tear over the man. It was time to make plans to counter his certain claim to Norrie. She had work to do, no time for mourning a love that was never meant to be.

When Megan arrived home a short time later, the house was empty. Mrs. Hanson often took Norrie with her on errands, so Megan wasn't worried. She changed into shorts and a loose-fitting top. Walking toward the kitchen to get something to drink, she noticed the blinking light on the answering machine.

She pushed the rewind, then played the message.

"Megan, I want to talk to you. We need to clear up this situation now before you throw away every chance we had. I thought at first you were jealous of Susan. But I don't think it's that. The plans for that reception were made long before I saw you again. You said I should have told you about it, perhaps you were correct. I looked on it as strictly business and didn't think to burden you with business matters. You looked on it differently. Call me, *chérie,* don't do this to us. Don't throw away what might be the best of life for both of us."

The machine stopped.

Megan stared at it, her heart hammering in her breast. His voice ran through her like hot wine, feathering along her nerve endings, warming her, filling her with nameless longings. She pushed the rewind button, listened to his message again.

And again.

Don't throw away what might be the best of life for both of us. She frowned and played the message again. It sounded almost like Roeuk was pleading with her. She shook her head. The arrogant Arabian sheik pleading with her? Ha, what a laugh. Yet... She played it once more. His tone was cajoling, though traces of the familiar arrogance came through.

She spun around and headed for the kitchen. She

would not be seduced by his sexy voice into whatever trap he was now baiting. She knew when to cut her losses. Rubbing her aching chest absently, she poured herself a glass of lemonade. He would be gone soon. She could get life into perspective and continue.

And sooner or later, this ache in her heart would fade. It had before. It would again.

The nights were the worst. Alone, with only his thoughts, Roeuk thought of Megan constantly. He had tried to woo her slowly, knowing she wasn't ready for the instant response he'd felt when he'd seen her again. If they had done things his way, he would have installed her in his suite that very day. He would not have let her out of his sight for a moment. But he had tried to go slowly for her sake. The nights only gave him endless hours to see where he'd gone wrong.

And he thought of Norrie. She was so adorable. His heart swelled with love whenever he thought of her. He had already come to expect her in his life. He wanted to know what she was afraid of, and what her favorite activities were. He wanted to bring that enchanting smile to her face, the one that reminded him so much of Megan, yet was Norrie's own special trait. He wanted to feel her small arms around his neck, and hear her childish giggles. Did she know she could depend upon him in the future? He had to reach Megan, for his own sake and for Norrie's.

The days were not much better. His ministers had returned home. Even the guards had been dismissed. Only Salid and Fahim remained. Few people in Washington knew he had stayed behind. None knew why. Not that it seemed to be doing any good. Without the pressing business matters to fill his days, they were as empty as the nights.

Roeuk stood in the rotunda of the Capitol and looked around at the dozens of Americans viewing the structure. He was doing a little sight-seeing, ostensibly the reason he had stayed. He did enough each day to keep Salid and Fahim from questioning the reason for their remaining. But he was not enjoying the sights as he once thought to. Moving outside to stand on the steps of the marble building, he glanced down the Mall, toward the Washington Monument and Lincoln Memorial. To his left was the National Air and Space Museum. His eyes were drawn to it as his memory played back that day. That was how he should be seeing Washington, with Megan and Norrie, not alone with only his thoughts to keep him company.

Frowning, he started down the steps. Fahim awaited with the limo a block away. Might as well go back, he wasn't seeing anything here.

Megan. Damn her! Every time he called, she hung up without saying a word. He had gone to her house once, only to find it empty, her car gone. The message he had left on her answering machine had not elicited a response. Had she even listened to it? Or once she heard his voice, had she erased it?

And Norrie, did she wonder where he was, why he hadn't been back to see her? He toyed with the idea of following through on the threats he'd made when he'd first realized he had a daughter, to do whatever necessary to see her. But he wouldn't.

Not yet, anyway.

What he should do is put an end to Megan's foolishness. He could easily go and get her and Norrie and take them both to Manasia. Once at his home, they would be totally dependent upon him. He could keep her there until Megan agreed to listen to reason, to see that what they had was too precious to let go. He had the power to do that, but he would not. He wanted her to come to him willingly, because she wanted to be with him as much as he wanted to be with her. He needed her to choose to love him again. Choose to live with him.

Walking with renewed purpose, Roeuk reached the limo. He would consider the plan, it would give some meaning to the day. He was not giving up on Megan. Not after all this time. He wanted her more than anything he'd ever wanted. This time, he meant to have her.

"Is the heat getting to you like it is me?" Elsie Hanson asked Megan when she reached home that afternoon.

"It is muggy, isn't it?" Megan said listlessly. Her hair had curled wildly in the humidity that blanketed the city. Even the air-conditioning in her car couldn't keep up. Thankfully, her house was a cool oasis in the midst of the heat wave.

Oasis. Was everything going to remind her of Roeuk?

"You look pale, dear, is everything all right?" Elsie asked.

Megan summoned a smile and nodded. "I'm not sleeping too well at night. I'll be fine."

Elsie nodded as if confirming a suspicion and began gathering her things. "Norrie seems to be suffering the same complaint."

"What do you mean?" Megan asked. She knew her daughter was upset they hadn't heard from Roeuk, but she had thought Norrie would get over it quickly. It didn't look as if that was the case. Her heart ached for the pain Norrie must be experiencing.

"She's been listless and depressed. Stephie called several times before Norrie agreed to go over. Even then she didn't seem very enthusiastic."

"I'll talk with her," Megan said, wondering what she could say to make things better.

"I started the casserole, it should be ready in another half hour. You know, Megan, I'm very fond of both you and Norrie. If you ever need someone to talk to, I would be honored to be the one you turned to," Elsie said hesitantly, worry evident in her gaze.

Megan felt a rush of gratitude and love for her neighbor. Giving the older woman a hug, she smiled. "Thanks, Elsie, I know that. I love you, too. But this is something that talking about won't change. I'll be all right."

"Of course, my dear. I'll see you in the morning." Patting Megan's cheek gently, Elsie turned to leave.

"One of these days, I will be all right again," Megan said as she turned toward her bedroom, anxious to get out of her work clothes. "I will recover from this as I did last time." The thought didn't give her much comfort as she began to believe she had never fully recovered from Roeuk's leaving a decade ago. This time she would. She would go on dates, find a mate, build a life that was satisfying.

Satisfying? Who wanted satisfying after they had reached the heights with Roeuk?

"I *will* get over this!" she said through clenched teeth as she rubbed the ache in her chest again. One day, if she lived long enough.

That night, sleep proved as elusive as it had every night this week. Tonight, Megan's thoughts were on Norrie and her bewilderment that Roeuk hadn't called or come to see her. Megan hadn't liked telling her that she ought not plan to see him again. Norrie had demanded to know why. From the shy hesitant little girl that had first spent time with him, Norrie had developed love for him that was perfect. Now Megan felt worse than before, knowing she was keeping them apart.

But only until Roeuk contacted attorneys or pulled some strings somewhere to get visitation rights. She held her breath for a long moment. He wouldn't try for full custody, would he? He had said he wanted to see Norrie grow up, but surely occasional visits would be enough. He could not have her daughter!

The hum of the air conditioner did not soothe her as it often did when she awoke in the night. Turning her head, she saw it was after one in the morning. Too late to still be awake when she needed to get to work early tomorrow. Closing her eyes, she tried to relax.

The telephone shattered the silence.

"Not now," she groaned, snatching the receiver before it could ring a second time.

"Hello?"

"Megan, it's Paul."

"I'm not on call tonight, Paul. Todd is," she said, lying back against the pillow. Not that she wouldn't relish an assignment. If she was going to be awake, anyway, she might as well be doing something.

"I know. We're on our way to a call. But I thought you would want to know about this one. It's a hotel fire, at the Williams Hotel. Isn't that where your friend is staying?"

"Oh, my God!" Megan sat up, gripping the phone as fear poured through her.

"How bad?" she asked, throwing off the light sheet and standing.

"We're on our way, it's bad from what the reports

said, sounds like the whole building is going up. There are already reports of fatalities.''

Oh, God, Roeuk!

Megan hung up the phone, counted to three and snatched it up again, dialing Elsie.

It rang and rang. ''Answer, answer,'' Megan chanted as she waited impatiently. Taking a deep breath, she tried to calm her rioting senses. She wanted to scream. Answer the phone, Elsie, answer the—

''Hello?''

''Elsie, I need you. I have to go, can you come to be here for Norrie?'' She was almost frantic. *Roeuk, get out of the hotel safely. Oh God, don't let anything happen to him!*

''I'll be right there, Megan.''

Throwing on jeans and a loose top, Megan felt the seconds ticking by at an alarmingly rapid rate while she hunted for tennis shoes. She found one, dammit, but where was the other? There. She thrust her feet into them, grabbed her purse and ran to the living room. Throwing open the door, she was relieved to see Elsie hurrying across the street, wearing her nightgown with a robe thrown around her shoulders.

''What is it?'' she asked softly as she walked swiftly up the walk.

''Roeuk's hotel is on fire. I've got to get there. Thanks, Elsie, I don't know when I'll be home,'' Megan said, giving her neighbor a quick hug and running for her car. In only seconds, she was speeding toward downtown.

Even before she reached the hotel, she could see the flames. The bright yellow and orange light shed a surrealist glow over everything. The closer she got, the worse it became.

The streets surrounding the old hotel were blocked off. She parked her car where she found a spot and ran down the sidewalk. When she reached the police barrier, she paused, but only for a moment. Somehow, she had brought her camera. She tried for a shot of the building, but her hands were shaking too badly. Lowering the camera, she watched, sick at heart, fear deep and insidious. The top five floors appeared to be engulfed in flames. She felt the heat from where she was, still almost a block away. As she hesitated, she heard the sound of breaking glass as yet another window exploded from the intense heat.

She counted six large fire engines, their engines rumbling as they pumped water in arcs against the side of the burning building. She could scarcely breathe. The top five floors, she counted again. Roeuk had been on the second to the top floor.

Oh, God, please let him be all right. She slipped beneath the barrier and began running toward the building.

"Hey, you can't go there." A cop grabbed her arm.

She shrugged him off and flashed her press badge. "Press, I'm not going to get in anyone's way."

"No one goes in."

"I do." She jerked free and ran. Careful to stay out of the way, she worked her way closer to the building. Flashing red lights bathed her face. Ambulances were lined up near one of the entrances to the hotel. Even as she watched, paramedics brought out two people, hunched over and coughing. Another team brought out a body completely wrapped in yellow plastic.

Megan moved closer. The noise was awful, the crackling of the flames, the pumps on the engines, the yelling voices of the firefighters, the piercing wail of the siren as an ambulance pulled away.

Roeuk. Please be safe. What would she do if something had happened to him? How would she live her allotted days if he wasn't in the world with her? She loved him so much, and had thrown away their chance at happiness just as he'd said.

Oh, God, please keep Roeuk safe! she prayed, trying to see what was happening, to find someone who could tell her what she needed to know.

Fear such as she had never known captured every cell in her body. She had been so blind, would she ever have a chance to make it up? She loved him. Nothing else mattered. They could work things out. Different countries, different life-styles, different ideas of what was important and what was not, all could be worked out, if they only had the chance to do so.

"Is everyone out?" she asked the nearest fire fighter.

"Ask the captain." He nodded toward a man surrounded by the press.

Pushing her way through, Megan confronted the man just as he started to turn away. "Is everyone out?"

"No, we're still evacuating. I've given the most recent update. I'll keep you informed as we learn more."

"What about the next to the top floor? Did everyone on that floor get out all right?" Megan grabbed his arm.

He looked down at her. "I don't know where everyone is from, lady. The hotel staff tried to go room to room before the flames engulfed the floor. I don't know who got out and who didn't. Maybe the hotel manager will have names. Check with him." He turned away, directing another fire fighter to the heart of the blaze.

"Megan?" Paul asked, coming up beside her.

"Oh, Paul, thank you for calling me. This is awful. I

don't think I've ever seen anything so bad. Do you know if the sheik got out?''

He shook his head. ''I don't know. But I do know that there are still some people inside. The firemen are doing all they can to get them out. Come on over here. Todd's here.''

Megan couldn't look away from the hotel as Paul led her to the side, out of the way of the men fighting the conflagration. Her heart, her love, might still be inside that burning building. She couldn't believe that Roeuk might be dead, but no one seemed to know one way or the other.

How could she not have given him a chance to explain? How could she have consigned them to living life apart? Nothing mattered but that they be together. Now that she realized it, was it too late? Had this been fate's cruel joke, to have her understand the special bond between them only when it was too late?

No, Roeuk had to be alive. She would know if he was dead. She would be dead, too, if he was gone. She would have felt it inside. He had to be alive. *Please, God!*

A paramedic emerged from the entrance half carrying a large man. The man was coughing, tears flowed from his smoke-stung eyes. The paramedic slapped an oxygen mask over the man's face, trying to ease the discomfort of too much smoke. Megan recognized him. Pulling away from Paul, she ran over.

''Salid. Are you all right? Where is Roeuk?'' She grabbed his arm, alarmed at how awful he looked.

''This man needs a hospital. Move away, lady.'' The paramedic led Salid toward a waiting ambulance.

''Where is Roeuk?'' Megan asked again.

Salid shook his head, wiping futilely at the tears. ''I do not know. We were assisting in the evacuation. Then

I could not see him. The smoke was very dense. I should have stayed closer to him. He is my responsibility.'' He was racked by coughs.

"Is he all right?"

"I do not know." Salid climbed into the ambulance. Another injured man was placed inside and the door slammed shut. The screaming siren began as the ambulance dashed away to the hospital.

Megan's fear rose. He had to be all right, she repeated like a mantra. He had to be all right.

She moved out of the way as another fire engine pulled in close to the hotel. Shattered glass crunched beneath her feet. She scanned everyone's faces, looking for the beloved face she was so afraid she would never see again.

"I need a stretcher over here."

Her eyes swiveled at the call. She watched as two paramedics ran over with a collapsed stretcher. In only seconds they were pushing it toward the ambulance, one paramedic working on the injured man even as his partner pushed.

Megan intercepted it just before it reached the ambulance. Her heart dropped. Roeuk!

The oxygen mask over his face didn't hide his identity. The angry burn on one hand demonstrated clearly how close to the searing fire he'd been. Tears sparkled in her eyes. At least he was alive.

Loading Roeuk into the waiting ambulance, one of the paramedics made to close the door. Megan darted inside.

"Hey."

"He's my fiancé. I'm not letting him go to the hospital alone!'' she said, wedging herself around the other attendant and sitting on the floor in the front of the compartment, near Roeuk's head.

With a shrug, the man slammed the door and they were off.

"How is he?" she asked, her eyes never leaving Roeuk.

"Smoke inhalation, burns on his arm and chest, should be okay," the medic responded as he worked on his unconscious patient.

Megan reached out and touched Roeuk's shoulder, leaving her hand against him, needing the contact with his warmth to convince herself he was still alive. Time stood still. She didn't move, only willed whatever strength she could into Roeuk's body. *Fight the smoke, darling,* she prayed. *Fight the damage done to your skin. You'll be fine. You'll be fine.*

"If you'll wait over there, we'll call you," the nurse told Megan when Roeuk was wheeled into the emergency room of Washington General Hospital.

Megan wanted to stay with Roeuk, but it was clear they would not allow that. She went into the waiting room. Sitting was impossible. She walked to the wide windows, and looked out over the night sky. In the distance, the curious glow from the fire was clearly visible. She walked back to the corridor. No one was paying any attention to her. Would they remember she was still here?

Slowly pacing around the room, her thoughts tumbled over and over. She loved Roeuk. No matter what was between them, she had to tell him. She would take whatever he offered. She wanted to be a part of his life, no matter how small. She would not be able to live with herself if she didn't include him.

What was taking so long? Was he still in that cubicle, or had they already sent him up to a room? If someone didn't come in pretty soon and let her know, she was going into the heart of their precious emergency room and demand answers.

"Miss?" The nurse was at the door.

"Yes? How is he?" Megan hurried over.

"He'll be fine. We'll be taking him upstairs in a few minutes. Can you help me fill out the paperwork?"

"Yes. Then can I see him?" The relief was marvelous, washing through her, renewing her. He was safe. He would be fine. She was going to see him in only a minute.

"Once he's in his room."

"He'll want a private room," Megan said as she walked with the nurse to the admitting office.

"Can he afford that?" the nurse asked, pulling out the admitting forms.

Megan smiled. "Nurse, he could buy and sell this hospital four times over. He can surely afford a private room for a night or two. Do you also have another patient called Salid? Roeuk would want Salid to have a private room, as well."

"I'll check. Now I need particulars."

Megan provided everything she knew. When next of kin was asked, Megan named herself. "We're to be married," she explained, hoping it was still true. Hoping Roeuk had not changed his mind because of her behavior over the last week. He could be coldly arrogant, but she would make sure he listened to her, make sure he knew she had been wrong to storm out as she had, to refuse to pay attention to his explanations. He had to understand that tonight had changed her perception of everything. Life was too short and too precious not to grab any opportunity with both hands when it presented itself. She had a feeling that Roeuk would give her the chance she'd refused him. He could afford to be generous to her, if he still wanted her. And she could not afford to let him think she didn't want him. She would tell him she loved him, and let him make the final decision. But she would fight him to make sure the decision was the one they both wanted.

The nurse picked up the phone and made arrangements for Roeuk to be transferred to his room.

"You can see him for a little while. I'm not sure he will be awake."

"But he's going to be all right?" Megan needed reassurance.

"I understand he is. The smoke inhalation was severe, he's on oxygen. The burn turned out to be only second-degree, painful, but not life-threatening. Apparently, he's some kind of hero. He saved the lives of an elderly couple."

Riding up the elevator, Megan thought about Roeuk. How like him to risk his own life to save someone else's. He had probably thought himself invincible. At least tonight he had been. She smiled for the first time since receiving the phone call about the fire.

CHAPTER TWELVE

MEGAN PAUSED AT THE DOOR to Roeuk's room. The nurses had propped it open. She glanced over her shoulder, but no one was paying any attention so she slipped inside and eased the door shut. The muted noise from the hall was cut off. The room was dim, quiet, still.

Dawn was just beginning to lighten the horizon. The small light near the bed gave enough illumination that Megan could see Roeuk lying so still in the high hospital bed. He wore an oxygen tube beneath his nose. His left arm was on top of the sheet, wrapped in bandages clear to his shoulder. Even in sleep, he coughed.

She stood by the bed, her heart flooding with love. Thanking God that he had been spared, she feasted her gaze on his face, tracing each beloved feature, from his strong jaw and chin, to the chiseled cheekbones covered by the taut skin tanned by the desert sun. She wished she could see his dark eyes again. She always felt as if she were lost in a velvet midnight when he looked at her.

Gently, she reached for his right hand, holding it in both of hers, cradling it against her breasts.

His eyes opened and he stared straight into hers.

"How do you feel?" she asked softly.

He took a deep breath and coughed harshly, his face contorting with the effort.

"I have felt better, *chérie,* how long have you been here?" He moved his hand in hers until he could link with her fingers.

181

"As long as you have. I went to the hotel."

He tugged her hands until he brought them to his face, kissing each finger.

He still wanted her. She breathed a sigh of relief. "I love you," she said.

"I love you, I always have," he replied simply.

She blinked. "You said you wanted me. You never said you loved me."

"Not only do I want you, I need you, Megan."

"Oh, Roeuk, ask me to marry you. I was so stupid to become upset about your English friend. I should have let you explain. But I was so afraid of being left behind again, like last time."

"So you ran away, instead? I don't quite see the difference. We were still apart," he remarked.

She grinned. "Put that way, there was no difference. You're a hero, you know."

He made a dismissing gesture. "Is Salid all right?"

"He's here in the hospital somewhere. I told the admitting office to make sure he had a private room. If you like, I can go look for him when you kick me out. He was worried about you."

"Kick you out? I'm more inclined to drag you into this bed with me. You have changed a lot from the wide-eyed teenager I fell in love with ten years ago. Kicking you out is not in my plans."

"I was so afraid you…" She trailed off, tears threatening as the relief of knowing he was safe pushed down barriers. She took a deep breath.

"I am fine." He coughed again. "Or will be as soon as I get this smoke cleared away."

"Does your arm hurt?"

He glanced at it in surprise. "No. Did I get burned?

It's totally numb.'' He tried moving his fingers, but there was no feeling.

"Second-degree burns, I was told. Not life-threatening.'' She edged her hip onto the bed, her hand tightly wound around his. "Saving those people could have been, though,'' she said.

"They were old, scared, confused. I'm still reasonably young. I couldn't leave them behind.''

She nodded. Roeuk was a man she could trust to risk his life to do what was right, and to care for those less fortunate. How much more would he care for her and Norrie, people he loved?

He moved their linked hands behind her, using the leverage to tumble her against his chest.

"Your arm,'' she protested, trying to keep from touching it.

"I do not want you on my arm. I want your mouth against mine.'' He pressed her again and she complied, joyfully reaching for him.

The kiss was hot and deep. She could smell the smoke that still clung to him. Taste it in his mouth, and yet still taste the sweetness that was Roeuk.

He broke the kiss too early, having to cough again.

"Damn.''

She smiled, brushing the thick hair back from his forehead. "It'll pass. As soon as you can get checked out, we'll go back to my place. I'll take good care of you.''

"As soon as I get out, I want to take you and Norrie home with me. It's past time my family met you. We can be married as soon as we reach Manasia.''

"I don't have a passport.''

"What's the point of being friends with the president of the United States if he can't help us out with an instant passport or two?'' Roeuk said arrogantly.

Megan smiled. That sounded more like him. "Then there's Elsie Hanson. She's the closest thing to a mother I have. She would want to see me married."

"Fine, she can come to visit."

"And the Andersons, Norrie will miss Stephie so much." Megan began to realize what marrying Roeuk would fully entail. "And my work."

"I'll charter a plane, everyone you know can come over for the ceremony, stay a week and enjoy my country. You and I, however, will be on a honeymoon for two."

"I don't know. There is so much to be decided. Where we would live. Norrie's schooling. We don't speak your language. School would be difficult there. And I still have my job."

"We can work everything out. Trust me on this, sweetheart. We'll spend the summer in Manasia. Then we can return to the United States for Norrie's schooling. If I'm needed at home, I'll fly back. My brothers can take a bigger role. We can decide about your job while we spend the summer getting to know each other. Maybe you would like to change your focus from photojournalism to filming subjects for books. We don't have to decide to today. We have our whole lives."

Megan shook her head wonderingly, almost afraid to believe it.

Ben smiled, satisfied. "Yes, it's a perfect plan. Stephie can keep Norrie company while you and I spend some time together. I will take you out into the desert, we will be alone, you and me beneath the warm sun. We'll find a lush oasis and fill our days discovering all we can about each other. And at night we will make love until the bond is so strong, nothing will ever sever it in this life or the next."

Her heart lurched, but she gave him a sassy look. "All this is predicated on your asking me to marry you, of course."

The teasing lights died from his eyes. "Megan, I love you. I would be most honored if you would become my wife."

She swallowed, tears threatening again. "I love you, too. And it is I who would be honored. Yes, Roeuk, I would love to marry you."

He kissed her again, threading his fingers through her soft curls, relishing the weight of her against his chest as he deepened the kiss.

When his coughing again broke up their kiss, Megan lay snuggled against him, relishing the feel of his strong body beside hers. She had been so afraid she would never be this close to him again. She shuddered, remembering the fire.

"I've loved you for ten years," she said softly. "I tried to forget you, but I never did."

"And I loved you, *chérie*. For a number of reasons, but the primary one is that you complete me. Before I went to Berkeley, I was always known as the son of Sheik Abdul bin Shalik, wealthy sheik of Manasia. In England, I attended school with the sons of dukes and earls. In France, I attended the upper academy of the wealthy and privileged. Berkeley was a new experience for me. New, exciting, democratic and very very different. For the first time, I found people liked me for who I was, not who my father was. A woman loved me for myself, not my title or my money or my position. It was a heady experience. One I never forgot."

Megan listened to his sexy voice, giving in to the sweet sensations it brought, enjoying the shimmering waves of happiness that splashed through her. "I never thought of that from your angle. I guess that explains why you didn't tell me who you were. You would never have known if I loved your money or you yourself.''

"Maybe in your case I would have known. I missed you so much when my father had me return home, commanded me to stay. I left part of myself with you.''

"While I missed you most dreadfully, I did have Norrie. She's been my joy since the day she was born," Megan said. "You will love her.''

"I already do. I love you, and I love our daughter. If it pleases God, we will have many more children to love. But for the others, I want to be there to see you pregnant, share that experience with you. See our children nurse at your breast. Watch them grow up together. Grow old together, with you.''

"I wish—''

"*Chérie,* the past is behind us and gone and there is nothing we can do to change it. Let us look forward from this day. Our lives together begin this day. We will have no regrets, no guilt. We will start our lives with joy and love and build on that.''

"Yes, Roeuk. Yes.'' She kissed him briefly.

"Now, find the doctor and see how soon I can get out of here. Find out where Salid is. If I am to remain another day, I want Norrie brought here. I have missed her these last few days and need to see her. And I don't want her worrying that my injuries are more serious than they are. Seeing me will assure her I will be fine. And we will want to share our news with her.''

Megan sat up and stared at him.

"I can see you are going to be arrogant and try to dominate this relationship from the beginning. But you need to know I will only stand so much. I'm not one of your minions to order around. You are in my country, buster, and we don't jump to commands by mighty sheiks.''

He laughed. ''We will have a wonderful life, *chérie,* but it wouldn't hurt you to have some awe for your husband.''

She grinned and brushed his lips with hers again. ''You'll just have to settle for love.''

* * * * *

Modern Romance™
...seduction and
passion guaranteed

Tender Romance™
...love affairs that
last a lifetime

Sensual Romance™
...sassy, sexy and
seductive

Blaze
...sultry days and
steamy nights

Medical Romance™
...medical drama on
the pulse

Historical Romance™
...rich, vivid and
passionate

29 new titles every month.

*With all kinds of Romance for
every kind of mood...*

MILLS & BOON®

Makes any time special™

MAT4

MILLS & BOON
FOREIGN AFFAIRS
A captivating 12 book collection of sun-kissed seductions.
Enjoy romance around the world.
DON'T MISS BOOK 9
latin liaisons–
Red-hot husband material...
Available from 7th June
Available at most branches of WH Smith, Tesco, Martins, Borders, Eason, Sainsbury's and most good paperback bookshops.
FA/RTL/9

Treat yourself this Mother's Day to the ultimate indulgence

3 brand new romance novels and a box of chocolates

= only £7.99

Available from 15th February

Available from 15th March 2002

*Available at most branches of WH Smith,
Tesco, Martins, Borders, Eason, Sainsbury's
and most good paperback bookshops.*

0402/35/MB34

Starting Over

Another chance at love...
Found where least expected

PENNY JORDAN

Published 15th February

Available at most branches of WH Smith, Tesco, Martins, Borders, Eason, Sainsbury's and most good paperback bookshops.

SANDRA MARTON

raising the stakes

When passion is a gamble...

Available from 19th April 2002